ALSO BY RINA KENT

LEGACY OF GODS
God of Malice
God of Pain
God of Wrath
God of Ruin
God of Fury
God of War

BEAUTIFUL VENOM

RINA KENT

Bloom books

*To those who run in the dark, where beauty
and danger are two sides of the same coin*

Copyright © 2025 by Rina Kent
Cover and internal design © 2025 by Sourcebooks
Cover design © Opulent Designs
Cover images © GLYPHstock/Shutterstock, Eclectic Anthology/
Creative Market, AcantStudio/Depositphotos, Bertl123/Depositphotos,
CreatifyIDStudio/Depositphotos, DianaKovach/Depositphotos

Sourcebooks, Bloom Books, and the colophon are
registered trademarks of Sourcebooks.

All rights reserved. No part of this book may be reproduced in any form or by
any electronic or mechanical means including information storage and retrieval
systems—except in the case of brief quotations embodied in critical articles or
reviews—without permission in writing from its publisher, Sourcebooks.

No part of this book may be used or reproduced in any manner for the
purpose of training artificial intelligence technologies or systems.

The characters and events portrayed in this book are fictitious or
are used fictitiously. Any similarity to real persons, living or dead,
is purely coincidental and not intended by the author.

All brand names and product names used in this book are trademarks,
registered trademarks, or trade names of their respective holders.
Sourcebooks is not associated with any product or vendor in this book.

Published by Bloom Books, an imprint of Sourcebooks
P.O. Box 4410, Naperville, Illinois 60567–4410
(630) 961-3900
sourcebooks.com

Cataloging-in-Publication data is on file with the Library of Congress.

Printed and bound in the United States of America.
KP 10 9 8 7 6 5 4 3 2

Author Note

Hello reader friend,

Beautiful Venom marks the start of an exciting new side of the #Rinaverse and can be enjoyed as a complete standalone.

If you're new to my books, you might not know that I write darker stories that can be intense, unsettling, and even disturbing. My characters and their journeys defy societal norms and aren't meant for everyone.

Beautiful Venom contains themes of consensual non-con, dub-con, and primal play. It also includes on-page depictions of road accident-related trauma and violence. Please be mindful of your triggers before diving in.

For more things Rina Kent, visit rinakent.com

Playlist

The Girl Who Stole My Heart—Blue October
Little Girl Gone—CHINCHILLA
Rip Me Apart—Unlike Pluto
Black Dahlia—Hollywood Undead
Shadow—Livingston
Cake—Melanie Martinez
Sick Thoughts—Lou Bliss
Hell of a good time—Haiden Henderson
Bad Timing—Blindlove
Backbone—KALEO
I Can't Go on Without You—KALEO
Lilith—Halsey & SUGA
Vicious—Bohnes
Neon Gravestones—Twenty One Pilots
Game Of Survival—Ruelle
All That Pretty Love—Atom & Breathe
SINS—Red Leather
Feeling You—Harrison Storm
Fickle Game—Amber Run

You can find the complete playlist on Spotify.

CHAPTER 1
Dahlia

LIFE AS I KNOW IT HAS BEEN SHATTERED INTO TINY, unrecognizable pieces.

The silver lining? I have nothing to lose.

No one to go back to.

Nowhere to call home.

So nothing stops me from pursuing the bloody path I've carefully traced.

My fingers tremble against the smooth plastic of the stadium seat as I remain hidden. My muscles burn and my knees shake, creaking from the crouched position I've forced myself into for twenty minutes or more.

A blast of icy air envelops me, frosting the beads of sweat coating my temples and upper lip.

The thing is, I'm not supposed to be here.

And I don't mean in this position per se, but in the whole place.

I certainly wasn't supposed to set foot in Graystone Ridge or on the campus of Graystone University—also known as GU. Most importantly, I'm not supposed to be sneaking around in their notorious Vipers Arena, home to the school's prestigious Vipers hockey team that just won a spectacular game.

'Just' is metaphorical, because that game ended hours ago and everyone has evacuated the premises.

Except for me.

And the three players below.

Loud thuds fill my ears as the puck checks the boards. The swish of blades on the ice adds a symphony of undiluted violence.

I peek from between the dark blue chairs, holding my breath despite the magnitude of sounds echoing in the arena.

The seating inside Vipers Arena, which has a capacity of over ten thousand, rises steeply, giving a dizzying, vertigo-inducing view of the ice below. I can still hear the roar of the crowd from earlier as if it's a physical force, reverberating in my chest in a persistent thrum. The clapping and chanting that ricocheted off the walls, rising to a deafening crescendo, was dull compared to the sound of the three players' fast-paced late-night practice.

Or should I say meeting?

I catch a glimpse of 'VIPERS' printed on the boards across from me as the ice gleams under the harsh, blindingly bright lights, casting a bluish tint over the rink. The crisp, biting sound of skates slicing across the ice sends chills through me as I follow the players' cutthroat maneuvers.

I've watched the Vipers dominate the arena countless times during my research, so I can recognize who has the puck without even checking their number.

Some might call this an obsession, and maybe it is, but if it can get me closer to the team, I'll be a simp. Or a stan. Or whatever correct term means I'm an expert on this bunch of snakes.

I lower my baseball cap over my face, switch my weight

from one foot to the other, then rest my clammy forehead on a tiny spot between the two chairs.

The three of them are so fast, so vicious, and so ruthless in their play, they nearly blur together in a sea of sharp glides.

My eyes cross as I attempt to keep up. They're alternating and playing two against one, probably to improve their flawless attack synergy everyone was singing praises about earlier tonight.

The reason those three play well together is probably because, even after everyone went home, they took to the rink again.

I've heard rumors that they often have these late-night 'meetings' and had to confirm it myself. Which is why I went to the restroom, stayed there until the place was nearly deserted, then snuck back into the arena and hid behind the chairs in the corner close to the ice but out of the players' field of vision.

However, I had to be dead silent because this place echoes even the slightest noise.

The three of them come to a halt in the middle of the rink, clacking their sticks together before tossing them onto the ice.

"That was lousy defense." Number 71, Jude Callahan, is the first to remove his helmet and shakes his soaking-wet black hair before he tosses it back like a dog.

He's the tallest and bulkiest of the three, standing at a whopping 6'5", and is the definition of fucked up. Jude is the most feared right wing in the college league. The rival teams' offense thinks twice before getting into his zone, and the defensemen can't handle his sheer size and unhinged energy.

Jude has anger issues and chose hockey to beat people the hell up. Everyone knows it, and anyone who has any dreams of a hockey career has learned to stay out of his way.

Number 13, Preston Armstrong, throws his helmet at the back of Jude's head, his deep voice carrying in the empty arena with a note of sarcasm. "Chest slamming is not an offense strategy. You would've been penalized for that. As always. Don't be a liability."

Preston is often labeled as the league's prince, probably because of his gorgeously attractive face, always styled sandy-blond hair, and Caribbean-green eyes. Despite his sleek appearance and refined mannerisms, he's known to be the most vicious snake on and off the ice.

His appearance is just another tool he uses to achieve his goals. Whatever those are.

In spite of my extensive research on Preston, I'm still in the dark about his true personality, and I doubt his teammates have a clue what he's truly capable of.

Unlike Jude, a notorious mass of muscles who acts with no regard for anyone, Preston is calmer and more calculated yet exudes a somber undertone.

Still, if I had to choose, I'd go with the latter. I can handle mind games, but Jude's brand of unhinged violence is hard to stomach.

As if on cue, Jude slams his body against Preston's with so much power, they both crash into the boards with a loud thud.

I hold in a gasp when Jude sits on top of Preston as if he's a chair. "What was that, dick?"

Preston's head bumps against the boards, and despite his lack of a helmet, I hear the echoing thump in my chest.

They clutch each other by the collar and Jude attempts to pick Preston up, probably to throw him across the rink, Neanderthal style. Preston, while not as bulky or as tall as Jude, is still 6'3" and manages to maneuver Jude's brute force by flipping him and then smashing him against the ice before jamming an elbow to his throat.

13 wears a smile as he speaks close to 71's face. "I said you're a liability, *dick*. Learn to control your animal strength. It's okay to look like one, but acting the part is too much, don't you think?"

I take it back.

There's no way I can handle Preston. I can't tell if he'll release the huge guy underneath him or choke him to death while smiling.

I nearly lose my footing and give away my position as Jude's face goes from red to blue in a matter of seconds.

In a blur of motions, Jude kicks Preston and then they're rolling on the ice like a couple of polar bears.

Without head protection.

The third player, Number 19, removes his helmet with a sigh, revealing damp tousled dark-brown hair and a soft frown between his thick brows.

Jude and Preston's fight filters to the background as the view of the Vipers' captain and center grips my throat with invisible hands.

And the worst part? This isn't the first time he's stolen my attention.

For some reason, I've often found my eyes unconsciously flitting to Kane Davenport, and I can't figure out why.

Yes, he's handsome, probably the most beautiful out of the three of them. While Jude has angular features and Preston is more of the princely type, Kane's beauty is unnerving.

His sharp, chiseled jawline affords him a naturally commanding look. His usually neatly styled hair is now haphazard, and he runs his fingers through it, making his thick strands look casually polished.

At 6'4", he's also tall, but not as threatening as Jude. Kane's lean yet muscular build complements his role as a dominant player on the ice. His body is sculpted for both power and agility, and his controlled movements reflect his innate leadership. He carries himself with confidence, his posture always straight and composed, giving off an aura of quiet authority.

And yet…his blue eyes are so pale, so blank, they're akin to those of an arctic wolf instead of a human. They're piercing, cold, and unreadable. Despite his outward calm, there's a flicker of danger lurking just beneath the surface.

And yet he's the only safe option on the team.

Kane is a responsible captain, a powerful leader, and the one who calms his teammates when they slip out of control. He's also the only senior player with a normal-ish personality.

Well, as normal as these assholes can get.

He's still part of that fucked-up organization no normal person would choose of their own volition. I glance at the black obsidian ring on his right index finger that doesn't shine under the light. I can't see it clearly, but I know there's a compass rose branded on the top of it, a depiction of his family's symbol.

The ring is proof of his monstrous ties.

He skates to the other two and forcibly breaks up the fight by shoving his body between theirs. Preston instantly jumps up and skates in circles, his rhythm and provocative facial expression taunting without his having to say a word.

Jude fights against Kane's hold, and his strength and thirst for violence form an invisible halo around him, eliciting goosebumps on my skin.

"Enough." Kane pushes him, and while the movement looks relaxed, it actually isn't. There's no way he'd be able to shove away a bear-like man if that were the case.

That's the thing about Kane. He somehow manages to make things look effortless when they're far from it.

"Is that all you got, big man?" Preston tilts his head to the side and pouts at Jude, mimicking an innocent kid. "I'm disappointed."

Jude dashes toward him. "You fucking—"

Kane extends his hands, punching them both simultaneously in the stomach. "I said enough. Save the energy for the rink."

Jude snarls. "I'll pummel his pretty face to pieces so he stops talking shit."

"Ruining my face won't stop me from dragging your ass." Preston grins wide. "It'll just show your inferiority complex. That jealous of my looks, peasant?"

"Your looks?" It's Jude's turn to mock laugh. "Which looks? Sickly and disturbing?"

"Said no one ever. But hey, I can find you a good plastic surgeon. Also a neurosurgeon so he can fix your messed-up personality."

"Only if your personality will undergo the same surgery."

"Blasphemy. I have a wonderful personality. Yours, however, revolves around mommy issues." Preston pouts.

"I'm going to fucking bury you." Jude charges, and Kane uses his body to absorb the shock and still gets pushed back.

"Pres." Kane stares at him. The energy shifts without his having to say anything else.

Preston lifts his shoulder. "What? It's fun to mess with him. Besides, he needs to be drained so he can sleep. Like a kid."

"The fuck you just say?" Jude asks in a dark tone.

"See?" Preston lifts his hands as if he's proving a point.

"Save the trash talk for the game," Kane tells him.

"Hmm…let me consider it." Preston taps his chin. "I refuse."

Kane sighs as if he was expecting the reply. "Did you use that same antagonistic energy to get that player penalized?"

"I suppose. Told him that his mom is letting his coach fuck her in all her loose holes so that a mediocre player like him can be kept on the team."

Sick bastard.

"No wonder he nearly killed you and was penalized for five minutes. Twice," Kane says in an unnervingly calm tone. "You're effortlessly annoying."

Preston grins. "I know, right?"

"That's not a compliment."

"Did she?" Jude asks, seeming to have forgotten about his vow to kill Preston.

"Did she what?"

"Let the coach fuck her in all her holes for her son?" Jude asks in a cryptic tone, and Kane watches him closely as if looking for something, though I can't pinpoint what.

"Dunno. Probably? Who cares as long as the story served its purpose." Preston releases a sigh. "People are so easy to mess with, it's getting boring."

Jude removes his gloves and throws them at Preston's face.

The latter scrunches his nose. "Uncultured as always, Callahan."

My gaze zeroes in on the black ring on Jude's index finger. Similar to that of Kane's, though his is branded with his family's symbol—a caduceus wrapped in thorny vines. Preston has one as well. His has the symbol of a sun and a crescent moon.

They weren't wearing them during the game, probably

due to regulations. They must have them on now because they're practicing on their own.

Maybe they don't want to be seen without proof of their allegiance.

Or proof of their power in this place.

People think Graystone Ridge is a sprawling, affluent town nestled in the US's Northeast, where history and wealth blend seamlessly with modern ambition. The heart of the town's center offers a mix of upscale cafés, designer shops, and historical landmarks lining cobblestone streets.

People also believe Graystone University, which is perched on the edge of the town, is a prestigious institution known for producing both academic and athletic powerhouses. Its historical architecture has aged well, harmonizing with its surroundings. While it offers renowned programs in business, law, sciences, and sports medicine, its true pride lies in its hockey program, which has become a breeding ground for future NHL stars.

The student body is a blend of wealthy legacy people—like Kane, Jude, and Preston—and ambitious scholarship students, drawn to Graystone for its connections and prestige—like me.

What people don't know, however, is that beneath this shining exterior, the university hides a shadowy influence: Vencor. The secret society tied to its and the town's founding families. Power here is not just earned but manipulated and handed down through generations.

Every corner of this place whispers power for the elite families who shaped the town.

The Davenports, Callahans, Armstrongs, and Osborns live in a gated enclave called Ravenswood Hill on the outskirts, in the mist-filled forest that looms above the town.

Behind heavy iron gates, their secluded mansions reflect a legacy of influence and control over the town. The roads leading to Ravenswood Hill are lined with towering oaks and hidden security systems, creating an air of exclusivity and mystery.

The Hill has always been off-limits to outsiders, which is why I have to approach these three at college instead.

Or more like one.

Kane is my best bet. I don't think he's an idiot I can fool easily, but he's at least a pacifist. Over the past few weeks, I watched many of his games online and in person—call the stalking police—and have never seen him indulge in violence.

Not *once*.

That's kind of a miracle in a physical sport like hockey.

If anything, he's an expert at breaking up fights. His cool is never ruffled and his authoritativeness can be felt through the screen. Probably why he effortlessly snatched the captain's position.

I'd rather not get close to any of them, but I have to, so it has to be Kane.

"Anyone you'll invite this time?" Kane asks Jude as he skates to the bench area.

"No," the latter says without turning around.

"Sure about that?"

"Yes. Fuck off." And with that, Jude leaves the ice and heads to the tunnel, disappearing out of view.

A faint mechanical hum from the ice machines overpowers the silence as Kane looks at Preston for a few heavy seconds. "You?"

"Contemplating it."

"You're expected to vet and bring someone to the initiation, Pres."

"You didn't tell Jude that."

"It's better he doesn't. He'll just force someone off the street to accompany him, and we don't want to deal with that mess. You're different. Use your conviction skills. I mean manipulation skills."

"Last time I did that, she didn't want to drink my blood. Nearly killed her before she was kicked out." He frowns. "How could anyone refuse *my* blood?"

"Normal people?" Kane asks what I'm thinking. Seriously, maybe that guy is only in Vencor because he was born into a founding family.

He obviously doesn't belong there.

"How about you?" Preston asks with a raised brow.

"I'm all set. Worry about yourself."

All set? Does that mean he already has someone in mind?

I was supposed to worm my way into his life so that I'd be that someone.

Not too long ago, I applied to be an intern for the team's physician, which is still on hold. My classmate said it was impossible that they'd accept a girl for the position while gloating that he'd be the best person for the job.

If he's right, then my chances of getting closer to the team are slimmer than ever before. I could apply as an assistant to the administrative manager or even volunteer. However, those aren't guaranteed with a popular team like the Vipers.

"All set, huh?" Preston repeats with a knowing tone.

"Go home, Armstrong."

"Aye, aye, Captain." Preston mock salutes, a sadistic smile painting his lips before he skates away. "Time to drown Callahan in the showers."

As silence befalls the arena, Kane stands in the middle of the rink for a few seconds, then picks up the pucks they left lying around and stores them in the appropriate compartment.

My legs hurt from the strain, and I know if I don't leave soon, I'll fall over and give my position away.

I bite my lip and remain motionless.

I'll leave after Kane does.

There's no way I'd be able to sneak off while he's there.

Stop being a Goody Two-shoes and go already.

The sound of skates blends with the ice machines and I get distracted with massaging my legs, so I don't notice that Kane has skated to my side of the stands.

As I lift my gaze, he stops right opposite my hiding spot.

Cold seeps into my bones, and the air becomes so crisp that it hurts to breathe.

In the oppressive stillness, Kane's calm voice carries through the empty arena. "You can come out now."

I hide further, hoping—no, praying—that he's speaking to someone else who was brave—or foolish—enough to sneak into Vipers Arena late at night.

"I know you're there. I suggest you show yourself while it's only me. I can't promise the others will be as understanding."

CHAPTER 2
Dahlia

MY HEART BEATS SO HARD, IT NEARLY SPILLS THROUGH MY rib cage.

Sweat is now covering my hands as I tighten my grip on the chair. No amount of icy air could extinguish the fire that erupts at the bottom of my belly.

Kane's words echo in my chest instead of my head, and I stop breathing altogether.

Yes, I intended to 'meet' him officially. But not like this. I was working on multiple plans to make it natural and believable.

Catching me in one of my snooping sessions is neither of the above.

Maybe if I make a run for it, I'll be able to get out of here—

"Am I that scary? I promise I don't bite." The note of amusement in his tone breaks the flow of my thoughts.

God, why the hell does this man's deep, gravelly voice sound like it's out of my darkest, most delicious dreams?

He sounds relaxed. Inviting, even.

Maybe it's because of that, or the fact that my legs are done carrying me, but I choose to seize the opportunity. The probability of having another one-on-one encounter with *the* Kane Davenport is slim to none. He's always surrounded by people.

All the time.

Everywhere.

Anywhere.

He's the magnetic field people find themselves pulled toward.

I'm the people. People are me.

With a sharp exhale, I slowly stand. My knees burn and my legs feel numb. In a swift movement, I remove my baseball cap and pat my hair into submission until the long, wavy brown strands smoothly settle beneath my breasts.

My sister Violet told me first impressions matter the most, and I hate that I'm not dolled up for the meeting I've been planning for weeks. But I did put some makeup on earlier tonight and I'm wearing flattering jeans that mold to my curves and a beige top that contrasts nicely against my deep olive-toned skin.

Sure, I could look better, but I can also work with this.

This will either make or break my plan.

After sucking in a deep breath, I look down, and I'd almost forgotten how effortlessly gorgeous Kane is.

Almost.

He leans against the boards, arms crossed, stick hanging from his hand, looking both unsettling and nonchalant. The opposing impressions he gives off are jarring and force goosebumps to surface on my skin.

The dark-blue hockey gear adds a sense of foreboding to his already intimidating physique. Despite a few rows of seats separating us and my average height of 5'6", he still looks intimidatingly tall.

A slight smile touches his full lips. "There you are. That wasn't so hard, now, was it?"

"Hi."

Shit.

I don't sound weak. Ever. What on earth is wrong with me? *Calm down, for God's sake.*

"Hello." His smile remains the same, exuding politeness. It's even welcoming. "May I ask what you're doing here at this hour?"

"I stayed behind after the game."

"I could tell. Why?"

"I...I'm a fan!" I blurt the first thing that jumps into my head.

Why the hell didn't I think of that before? Actually, I did. Fleetingly. But I figured the Vipers already had too many fans throwing themselves at the team members at every opportunity. So that wouldn't have made me stand out from the crowd.

But now that we're alone, it might.

"I see." The two words are followed by intense eye contact that's strangely devoid of warmth. I'm being scrutinized, but there's no sense of connection.

The glacial pale color of his eyes is similar to sinking into the Arctic Ocean as layers of ice form on the surface at an alarming speed.

This must be what it feels like to be iced alive.

I shake the image from my head. This is Kane, not Preston, or God forbid, the wild card Jude. He's my best—and *only*—option.

"Yeah," I continue in a more confident tone. "I'm a new fan. I didn't know much about hockey before, but I'm learning more because of the team. Go Vipers!"

"I'm happy we could lure you into the game." His words sound calm. Like an undisturbed ocean.

Right.

That's the vibe Kane has always given. Deep, controlled, and reliable. An ocean in all its glory.

"You did me the greatest favor." I smile wide. I've always heard I have a beautiful smile and I don't mind using it to my advantage. Beggars can't be choosers, and I'm definitely a beggar in this situation.

"Who's your favorite player on the team?"

"You," I say with no hesitation.

"Are you sure you're not saying that just because I'm here? If Callahan shows up, you'll switch, won't you?"

"Callahan is too aggressive and violent in his play. I don't find that entertaining."

"Most hockey fans do."

"Not me. I prefer your tactical prowess and your seamless ability to lead both in offense and defense."

"I'm flattered. Thank you." His voice remains the same. Unaffected, cool. He certainly doesn't sound flattered, or maybe he's been praised so many times before that his responses have become mechanical.

"No, thank you for taking the time to talk to me. It's hard to run into you on campus, so this means so much to me."

Gag. I'm not used to praising strangers this extensively. I'm starting to cringe.

"Anything for a fan. If you want an autograph, all you have to do is come closer. I *truly* don't bite."

That's when I realize I'm still nestled behind the row of plastic seats, gripping one of them so tightly that my fingers hurt. I release it and slowly take the steps down.

The entire way, Kane's gaze is pinned on me.

It's not threatening per se, but it's intense, like when he's reading his opponents on the ice. That should feel like a compliment, but I've watched this man crush so many of his rivals, the attention shoots a wave of unease through me.

I stop in front of him, and he stands to his full height. I'm not sure whether the gesture is meant to intimidate me, but I might have underestimated how tall he actually is. Add the skates and he's downright towering over me.

Up close, his jaw is sharper, his skin smooth except for some stubble. And his eyes are paler, much colder. Slightly disturbing, even.

He carries himself effortlessly with complete and utter ease.

I'm actually envious. How can someone be so...self-confident? So self-sufficient?

"Can I take a rain check on the autograph?" I say to murder the invisible tension. "I don't have a pen or paper."

"How about a picture, then?"

"That would be amazing." I fumble in my back pocket and retrieve my phone, then click on the camera.

Due to the height difference, I can't get a good angle.

"May I?" he asks after watching me struggle for a few seconds.

I hand him the phone with an apologetic smile and lean closer so he can take the picture. A whiff of woodsmoke and the faintest trace of musk flood my senses.

The scent is so masculine, my head turns and heat creeps up my neck. I've always found men who smell nice attractive.

I forget to smile a few times as he snaps some successive pictures.

As he hands me the phone, I stare at his black ring for a beat too long and hope my inner disgust doesn't make an appearance on my face.

"Now, why don't you tell me the real reason you're here, Dahlia Thorne?"

My fingers pause on the phone as he clutches the other end. He doesn't release it when his eyes meet mine. His expression hasn't changed, but a dark undercurrent has overshadowed his polite manners.

"How do you know my name?" I whisper.

"You applied for an intern position on the medical team, no? The résumé had your picture and name on it."

"And you go through every application?"

"As the team captain, yes, I do. No one gets close to the Vipers without my knowledge." He pauses and lets my phone go. "Or approval."

I knew that. I *knew* it, which is why getting close to the others would have been fruitless, not to mention dangerous. No matter who I targeted, I would've gotten Kane's attention anyway, which is why I went for him from the beginning.

"How do you know I want to get close?" I ask, not bothering to deny his words. Kane is smart and trying to deflect would only backfire.

"Aside from applying to be part of the medical team, you've been asking around about administrative positions and trying to befriend those close to the team members."

He found out about all that? *How?*

I stare at his ring. Vencor. Of course, as a member, he knows this place inside out.

Maybe I underestimated just how intricately they're woven into the university's and the team's fabric.

"Have I made you suspicious of me?" I smile, deliberately making it appear awkward. Sheepish, even.

"I wouldn't call it suspicion. Curiosity is more accurate."

I swallow the saliva stuck in my throat. "What are you curious about?"

"Your motive."

"I can't be a fan?"

"You can. But your actions don't reflect your claim."

"How so?"

"First, you're not wearing any of our jerseys, and while that's normal for an occasional viewer, it's bizarre for a *fan*. Second, you said you only got into hockey recently, and yet you seem to know about my and Callahan's play style as if you've been studying it instead of watching the game for fun. Lastly, if you were a fan, you would've jumped at the opportunity of getting a picture with me, Armstrong, and Callahan, but you were dead set on hiding and eavesdropping, so that tells me you have an agenda. That agenda is less related to the team and has more to do with my ring, because you've stolen at least three peeks at it since the start of this conversation."

Damn, he's good.

He's so good, I'm speechless.

The way he delivered his analysis in tranquil, precise words is both impressive and nerve-racking. Just how far has he read into me?

And is it even safe to get entangled with him?

He's frighteningly perceptive and a master at recognizing and linking patterns. It's fascinating on the rink but lethal in real life.

Kane raises his hand, showcasing his index finger. "Do you know the meaning behind this ring?"

"Everyone in town does," I say in a small voice.

"Correct, but probably not as well as you do. In reality, only a few have deciphered the actual meaning."

"I don't know what you're talking about—"

"No. Don't play dumb. It insults both of our intelligence."

"What do you want me to say?" I whisper, feeling trapped between his claws without his even having to touch me.

"What does this ring mean, Dahlia?"

"I don't...know."

"We're done here." He spins around and starts skating away.

I panic, my breathing coming in a chopped rhythm, and I draw endless circles on my thumb with my index finger.

I know, I just know that if he leaves, he'll never give me the time of day again. He seemed disappointed by my reply. He was fully aware I was lying, and instead of calling me out, he just chose to put an end to the conversation.

"Wait! It means you're a Senior Vencor member."

He comes to a halt a small distance away and slowly turns around. His expression is its usual brand of calm and distant. "What other ranks exist?"

"Trial, Member, Senior, and Founder," I say slowly, revealing I'm more entrenched than anyone should be.

I've completely put my cards on the table now, and it's his decision whether to flip them over or let me play. I could've lied and denied it, but Kane proved he has zero tolerance for bullshit.

The low timbre of his voice fills the air. "And how did a college student such as myself get a very high Senior position?"

"Because you are..."

"I am?"

"Biologically related to a founding family."

"True and false. I went through the ranks like everyone else. I just started early."

Oh. I didn't know that. I thought he, Jude, and Preston had gotten access solely because of familial ties.

"How...early?" I ask.

"Early." He speaks the single word with enough command

to ward off any further questions. "Now, why don't you tell me the reason you're so well-versed in Vencor when you were born in Maine and grew up in New Jersey, Dahlia?"

I swallow hard. Even though that information is public and mentioned on my résumé, the fact that he remembers it so clearly is unsettling.

"You know I'm on a scholarship, right?" I start in a composed tone.

"Yes, and?"

"If you've done your research, then you must know I receive grants. I was born to a poor fisherman and seamstress in a little coastal town in Maine, but I don't remember much of that life, because my parents died when I was six. But I do recall that Mom fixed the same dress at least five or six times instead of getting me a new one. I remember never having enough food to quiet the hunger in my stomach. The situation didn't change when I was thrown into the system and moved from one abusive home to another. Kids like us don't get nice things. Some of us become druggies, others sell their bodies, and many die in freak accidents. Nobody cares about the nameless corpse by the side of the road. We're just statistics that feed the machine. The few who make it, like me, are still treated like outsiders and discriminated against, no matter how book-smart or street-smart we learn to become."

I pause, largely because of the lump that's obstructing my throat. I didn't mean to get personal, but I have a feeling anything less than the truth will not move Kane in the slightest. For that matter, he might look down on me if I lie—he was certainly ready to axe the conversation when I attempted it.

Although I've just laid my unglamorous life out in front

of him, he doesn't react. There's not even a tic in his monk-like expression. He doesn't appear to be calculating whether or not I'm telling the truth.

"And?" is all he says, prompting me for more, sliding ghostly hands through my brain as if he wants to pick it apart piece by piece.

"And I'm tired of being on the outside. For once, I want to be on the inside. I want to wake up in the morning and not worry about how to survive for one more day. I heard Vencor can help with that. That if I become a member, my future will be guaranteed, like it has been for countless politicians, businessmen, and even ex-presidents. I want to be part of the powerful instead of the weak."

"And you thought the best way to do that would be to get close to the hockey team, where three players are Seniors and a few others are Members, and have one of the Seniors invite you to the upcoming initiation."

Not a question, but I still say, "Yeah."

"You thought right. I'll make your wish come true."

My lips part.

Did Kane just agree to help me without my having to resort to all the diabolical plans I had prepared?

What?

Why?

Does he perhaps pity me?

Honestly, I don't care. I'll be the most pitiful puppy if that gets me in. I have no time to focus on my pride in situations like this.

"Really?" I ask, still not believing my ears.

"Yes. I already had someone else in mind for the initiation, but I'll take you instead."

A shiver goes through me when he says, 'I'll take you

instead.' Even though his tone doesn't change, there's a strange shift in his expression.

A smile curves his lips, and I stop and stare. Am I supposed to find him this gorgeous?

It soon disappears as his mechanical tone fills the air. "Fair warning. This is not your run-of-the-mill initiation or some hazing ceremony where you'll be asked to take silly dares. You will be tested. You'll be pushed to your limits. And you'll be asked to offer your body and soul at the altar of demented people. If you refuse, you're out and banished for life. If you don't prove to be willing to be used for Vencor, you'll be sabotaged until you escape the country or shoot yourself. And if you betray Vencor, no one will find your bones. Are you sure you still want to participate? Sometimes, being an outsider is much safer than being a blood-bound insider."

Another chill runs through me and I tighten my hands on my phone. I've heard a lot of rumors and I'm part of dark web forums that discuss theories and stories about what these people are capable of.

Kane's words said in a neutral newscaster voice shouldn't shake me, but they do.

If I'd heard this a year ago, I would've turned around and left, but now?

Now, I have nothing to lose. And if I must use my life to avenge my sister, so be it.

So I say in a resolved, dead voice, "I'm sure."

Kane watches me, neither surprised nor approving. "If you change your mind before you're accepted, say a word only the two of us know and I'll make it stop. No matter what it is. Let's go with...red."

I nod. "Why are you helping me?"

He taps my cheek with his index finger on which he's wearing the ring. The cold metal sends a chill through me, but that's nothing compared to the electrifying fire that spreads down my belly as his skin touches mine.

"I'm curious if you'll last and how far you'll go, my fake fan." His smile drops as he pats my cheek one final time. "Don't disappoint me."

CHAPTER 3
Dahlia

DON'T DISAPPOINT ME.

Don't disappoint me.

Don't. Disappoint. Me.

It's been a week since Kane spoke those words to me. He's said nothing since then, and for some reason, I can't get them out of my mind.

I've been trying to sneak into the arena to watch the Vipers practice, maybe catch Kane's attention and ask him about what steps will be taking place going forward. However, their security is no joke. They have a zero-tolerance policy for outsiders. Even if they're the team's biggest fans. Doesn't matter if they go to Graystone University.

If it weren't for the very real pictures in my phone, I'd think the whole conversation I had with Kane and the promise he made about taking me to the initiation was a figment of my imagination.

Sure, no one knows when and where Vencor's initiations take place since, according to rumors, they change them up to keep the mysterious factor going.

But Kane is in the inner circle. The Senior level is the highest rank attainable for all members except for Founders. I have no clue what type of trials they must go through or how many souls they have to sell to the Devil to get there, but I suspect their own soul isn't enough.

I frown at my picture with Kane on my phone. I posted it on social media the other day and tagged him, but all I got was a like. That's all. No DM or further acknowledgment of my existence.

Nothing.

I'm supposed to be studying, but I find myself staring at the selfie.

Again.

Kane's expression is calmer than a starless night and just as deep. I can't imagine him selling his soul, to be honest. He genuinely listens and lacks Preston's shadiness and Jude's brutality.

He can be relentless during a game if need be, but I've never seen Kane be aggressive. Whether on or off the ice.

I zoom in on his hand, where the ring shows. He's still a Vencor, a Senior Vencor. For some reason, I seem to gloss over that detail whenever I think about Kane.

Which I've done constantly since our last encounter.

Vencor or not, I don't believe he's the type who dishes out empty promises.

But why hasn't he gotten in contact since then? He's kind of untouchable on campus, so I can't exactly walk up to him like we're acquaintances. We study in completely different fields in buildings that are on opposite ends of campus anyway. Him, business. Me, pre-med. So it would be hard to pop in there and pretend it's a coincidence.

Besides, would that be a smart thing to do? Initiating a public meeting? The other time, he made sure his teammates were out of earshot before he talked to me. I assume he doesn't want our deal to be exposed.

"Kane Davenport. You ain't playing about your crush."

My head whips up. I was so focused and lost in my thoughts, I didn't notice Megan getting close to my desk.

I fumble to flip the phone over. "He's not my crush."

Megan is my roommate in GU's dorms and is here on a scholarship like me, so at least there's not much societal difference between us. But lucky for her, she comes from a happy family and I often see her at the local cafés with her parents or siblings.

I keep to myself and she keeps to herself. She did try to befriend me in the beginning since she's a real extrovert, but after she witnessed me studying like a dog to earn the grades needed for my scholarship, she kind of retreated and decided to spend more time with her friends in the social sciences department.

Megan is a redhead with dark skin and a striking fashion style. She's rocking a red, white, and green kimono-style dress with slits in the skirt and glimmering chains for straps for one of her nights out.

"Girl, you were staring at that man like he was a snack." Megan checks herself in the full-length mirror near the entrance of our room.

"I was not."

"Uh-huh." She takes a few selfies in the mirror.

Her side of the room is full of colorful clothes piled on the bed from when she was picking her outfit. Some purses have fallen on the floor, but her desk is spotless, all her social science books neatly displayed like they're actual treasures.

My side is minimalist at best with my med books and laptop. However, my bedside table is covered with haphazard college hockey magazines that I've been studying more seriously than my school projects.

My three pairs of white sneakers are lined up by my side of the closet, while Megan's are full of all types and colors of shoes.

"And here I was wondering about your recent obsession with hockey. Gotta say, you have expensive tastes. You couldn't go for a lower-grade peasant from the team?"

I spin in my chair to face her. The other difference between Megan and me is that she's been at GU since her freshman year. As for myself, I was studying in the neighboring town, Stantonville. I initially applied to GU and Stanton River College—or SRC—but my application was rejected for GU and I was accepted into SRC. Which was a bummer, but at least Violet was accepted into SRC, too, so we moved from New Jersey to Stantonville.

Imagine my surprise when I was offered a random scholarship to GU for my senior year this summer. To say I was over the moon would be an understatement. GU's medical program is one of a kind, which is why I wanted to enroll here in the first place. And to be offered that opportunity for my senior year felt unreal.

Violet seemed a bit apprehensive, but she still bought me a little cake and we had a blast celebrating that night.

I thought this would be my new beginning.

And it is, but now, I don't have Violet with me.

Megan is actually a local to Stantonville and could've gone to SRC, but she purposefully applied for a scholarship here because, in her words, "This place is the shit. Aside from their famous hockey program, SRC doesn't have much to offer."

The Stanton Wolves are the Vipers' biggest rival. Both teams are known to produce the best NHL players, and their 'Cold War' games are easily the highlight of the college league.

Despite Megan not being massively interested in hockey, she was brought up surrounded by these two legends, so she knows more than the rumors I've heard and what my technical research can produce.

"I didn't go for anyone," I say to keep up the conversation. "He was generous enough to let me take a fan selfie after the game."

She shifts her attention from the mirror and hikes a hand on her hip. "You'll sit there and tell me with a straight face that you don't want to be anything more than a fan?"

I spin my fountain pen between my fingers but remain silent.

"That's what I thought," she says with a gloating facial expression, then looks at the mirror again to pat her red curls. "Better not get your hopes up. He's top of the food chain, as in royalty, in this college, town, and world. People like you and me don't mess with people like them and get out unscathed. So lower the standards...unless you only want to fuck him? In that case, get in line. I'd let that man throw me around like I'm his puck. I heard from an acquaintance of an acquaintance that he has a huge dick to match the energy."

"Megan!"

"What? Gotta do my research before opening my legs. And I just did yours, too. You're welcome."

I laugh despite myself. "What else do you know aside from rumors about his dick size?"

"That's all I need." She side-eyes me. "That's all you need as well if you want to stay out of trouble."

"I just want to know my chances."

"You have none. Those people who live up the Hill only get into relationships with each other, marry each other, and produce little minions like themselves who'll repeat the cycle all over again. We're outsiders, D. Outsiders get no chances." She looks up. "Dear God, in the next life, I want to be reborn as a rich man. Amen. Hold on. With a huge dick also. Big amen to that. No pun intended."

"So outsiders get no chances, but fucking is okay?"

"Hell yeah. Fucking is harmless fun. Anything beyond that is not. If you want to be super realistic, you'll get a better chance fucking that manwhore Preston—who accepts all girls' advances—than Kane. Hell, Jude might be easier to fuck than Kane. It's hard to get that man excited about anything other than hockey. His hookups are few and far between. Either he's training to be a monk, or he has one hell of an NDA in place, because all the girls want a piece, but few have managed to get it, and those who did don't talk about it."

Fucking Kane is the last thing on my mind right now. Okay, not *really* the last. I'd be lying if I said I don't find him hot. Under different circumstances, I'd be open to some harmless fun like Megan, but with my situation, I need something deeper.

A lot deeper.

"Have you ever been to Ravenswood Hill?" I ask. "You know, to snoop and see how they live."

"Hell no. This pretty head." She motions at her face. "I want it kept on this pretty neck. Thank you very much."

"Is it that dangerous?"

"Fuck yeah. Listen. I know you're probably one of those students who loves the thrill of secret worlds, haunted houses, and enchanted forests, but this is not a horror movie. Those who've dared to go close to the Hill have disappeared without a trace. Don't become a statistic."

I already have. I have nothing else to lose.

But Megan is right. Going to the Hill just to snoop without any entry or escape plan in place is just asking for death.

That's why I thought the best way would be to achieve entry through the team.

Megan sprays a cloud of perfume before she leaves, attempting one final time to invite me to the latest 'sick' party. However, she gives up when I tell her I'm studying tonight.

At least, that's what I intend to do.

I find it hard to focus and barely finish reading a case study for ethics.

My phone lights up and I check it to look at the pictures Megan's sent of "what I missed."

The pen nestled between my fingers stills and drops on top of my textbook when I find a DM from @kane.davenport.

Kane: Are you free tonight?

My heart thunders so loudly, I can hear it in my ears as I type: *Hi! Yes.*

Then realize it sounds too desperate, so I delete it.

Dahlia: Why?
Kane: The initiation is tonight. In two hours.

Oh God.

That came sooner than I expected. I didn't think I'd get a save-the-date card or anything. But a two-hour notice?

I'm not even mentally prepared.

Kane: Will you be there?
Dahlia: Yes. Where?
Kane: I'll send you a location. Be there in an hour and a half.
Dahlia: Okay. Thank you.

I think the conversation has ended as he sees my text and doesn't reply, but then a single word appears on the screen and my heartbeat quickens.

Kane: Dahlia.
Me: Yes?
Kane: Red. Say that word now and this nightmare won't happen. If you don't, you won't have a chance afterward.

My eyes fly over what he's written again and again. Just like when he learned about my interest, he's offering me a way out.

But he doesn't know that when my mind is set on something, I won't stop until it's done.

Someone in Vencor was behind my sister's attack and subsequent coma. I lost my only family because of them, and I won't rest until they're six feet under. Hopefully, after they suffer.

So no. Even if I'm going to die, I won't take the out that Kane's offered.

I like that he's putting the option on the table, though.

Dahlia: I'll be there.

There's a long stretch of silence from his end before he sends one final text.

Kane: Dress comfortably. It's going to be the longest night of your life.

CHAPTER 4
Kane

THIS ISN'T THE FIRST, THE SECOND, OR EVEN THE HUNdredth time I've faced such a scene.

It won't be the last either.

But it never manages to penetrate me. Not the screams, the gurgling of blood, the stench of fear mingled with the absolute realization that they've fucked up.

And that it's the final time they'll ever fuck up.

"Listen…listen…please hear me out…" the vice-chancellor, Fred, begs on his knees, his belly bulging from between his shirt's ripped buttons, his ugly purple tie tight, turning his face red.

Jude, Preston, and I asked Fred to join us for a ride after school.

He smiled with delight, thinking we were presenting him with an opportunity. It's not every day that a mere vice-chancellor gets a private meeting with three Senior Vencor members who'll become de facto Founder members as soon as they graduate.

And Fred, like any Vencor member, knows that only we who are born into the four founding families are granted the Founder position. So we've always held monopoly on the power balance on campus, even if we're still just Senior members. A position Fred will never reach.

Because instead of the opportunity-filled meeting he expected, we drove him to a warehouse owned by my family, located so far out of town, no one would hear him scream.

My father's cronies are stationed outside, waiting for us to finish with our fun so they can clean up.

Though, truly, it's more fun for Jude and Preston than me. I'm only here to finish a 'decapitation' mission. Meaning, cut the head off a snake that's starting to consider biting its master.

Vencor's power, aside from strong business relations between the four founding families, is all about control. If there's an opportunity, not only do we seize it, but we also eliminate anyone who forms any type of obstacle.

It's a secret society that's highly dependent on its Founder members and their connections. But unlike any other society, it's not exactly a brotherhood, and internal fighting among the four founding families to snatch the upper hand is common.

Senior members, the highest position any outsider can reach, are more primed to take upper positions in society like senators, leaders of political parties, or controllers of military and financial complexes. Their job is to grow Vencor's connections and serve its goals. They usually have Members catering to them, doing their bidding, and keeping an eye on them in case they go awry.

It's not unheard of for a Member to become a Senior for disclosing the betrayal of a previous Senior he worked for.

Since it's impossible for anyone not born to a founding family to achieve a higher rank, Preston, Jude, and I are anomalies on campus. We hold power over the team, and everyone at Graystone University bows down to us.

Today's mission is one I handpicked for myself, so the

other two didn't need to join, but then again, Jude has developed a pesky addiction to killing, and Preston suffers from an incurable case of bloodlust.

As Senior members, we're actually the ones who assign those lower than us in rank with these types of missions, and our role is to supervise from the shadows, only intervening if things spiral.

But I've always liked being hands-on. I don't trust anyone else to finish the job as efficiently as I do.

"Hear what exactly?" I lean back in a metal chair across from Fred, leisurely wiping my gun with a cloth and making sure it's in his field of vision the whole time. "That you're dealing drugs on campus behind our backs?"

"It was only a one-time thing…please…I have a family," he begs, droplets of sweat gathering on his upper lip and oily nose.

"Then you should've thought of that family before you crossed us." I stand up. "No one crosses Vencor. You're only a little tool to be used. It's bad form when you start believing you have agency. We do the thinking, not you."

"I promise I'll never do it again if you give me another chance."

"Don't be naïve. There are no second chances. One mistake and you're out."

"Especially when you thought you could get away with it." Jude slides behind Fred, grabs his tie, and tugs him so far back, I'm surprised his neck doesn't snap.

"The audacity is sending me." Preston kneels in front of Freddie, rolling the handle of his knife between his fingers. "News flash. Nothing escapes us. You can hide, but you can't run."

"It's you can run, but you can't hide," Jude tells him.

"Well, I meant it the other way around." Preston presses the knife close to Fred's neck, and the man holds his breath. Whether it's due to Preston's knife or the way Jude is strangling him, I can't tell.

"That's not how it works. Don't be an idiot."

"Ha. The pan calling the kettle black."

"The pot calling the kettle black, not pan."

"Same fucking meaning." Preston throws his hands back, slashing Fred's throat in the process. Blood gushes out like a fountain, spraying both of them with red. Their faces, hair, clothes.

Everywhere.

It even splashes my jeans and shoes.

What a drag.

Fred's mouth is open, his eyes staring at nowhere as he bleeds out in seconds.

"Argh…look what the fuck you've done, Jude!" Preston rises to his full height. "I didn't have the chance to watch him die."

"Me? You're the one who killed him, motherfucker. We didn't even get to torture him."

Preston squares up to him. "It was because you were being a smart-ass trying to correct me."

"I wouldn't have to correct you if you were right, now, would I?"

"I'm always right. Not my fault a peasant like you can't recognize a superior being."

"More like a superior pain in the ass."

"The fuck you just call me?"

Jude steps closer. "Pain." He taps his shoulder. "In. The. Ass." He hits him upside the head. "That clear enough for you?"

Preston grabs him by the collar. "I'm so gonna drown you in Freddie's blood."

They're about to start wrestling while bickering as usual, so I sheath my gun in my belt and say, "Just so you know, if you start fighting, I'm not breaking it up. I'm not getting stained by that filthy blood any more than I already am."

"Oh yeah?" Preston grins, and the motion looks manic with rivulets of crimson cascading down his face. Then he releases Jude's collar, all aggression disappearing, and places a brotherly arm around his shoulders. "Big man, is it just me or does it seem like Kane is looking down on us?"

"No, you're right. He has that holier-than-thou thing going on. It's revolting."

"That's what I'm saying. I think we should do something about it."

"Don't you fucking dare—" Before I can manage to escape, they jump me.

Jude and especially Preston get the blood all over me. And while I try to throw them off, these two are actually the perfect fucking team and they overpower me.

They've always done this, since we were in boarding school. They'd be bickering and I try to break it up, so they gang up on me just because.

I only manage to shove them off of me after Fred's blood is covering me from head to toe.

Preston laughs and Jude watches with a satisfied expression as I walk out of the warehouse to talk to my father's men.

Fucking children.

Doesn't matter how Fred died. It only matters that he died and won't be betraying Vencor anymore.

The upper echelon, aka the Founders, will pick a

replacement for him soon enough. That is, if they haven't already.

My mission as the Vipers' captain is to make sure the campus is under control and fulfills its role as one of Vencor's multiple tentacles.

Since this town is obsessed with hockey to the point of considering it a religion, it makes sense to use the most popular team as our base, through which we keep an eye on Graystone University and even recruit those we deem worthy.

Though, the vetting process only allows us to invite high-ranking members of society.

Usually, that is.

Because as I slide into my car, I'm thinking about the exception to that rule.

The fake fan who claims she wanted to be offered a chance to be on the inside. A chance I'm granting not because I sympathize, but because I want to see her on her knees.

Literally.

Figuratively.

I hit the gas. Time to get to the highlight of my evening.

Here's to hoping she doesn't disappoint me. If she does, I might have to drive her to one of our warehouses.

And it'd be a shame to turn those bright hazel eyes red.

CHAPTER 5

Dahlia

MONTHS.

It's been months of constant, careful plotting, thorough calculating, and painstaking patience.

Months.

And today's finally the day.

I wipe my clammy hands on my jeans as I park my bike in a parking space and power walk through the dimly lit streets. I actually followed Kane's advice and came in my most relaxed outfit—a plain gray T-shirt and my comfiest sneakers that are slightly beat up.

If I said I wasn't scared, it'd be a flat-out lie.

I've only heard rumors about Vencor's initiations, and they all mention a grueling interrogation process, having to endure physical and mental tests, and being stripped bare of one's humanity.

But they all remain rumors.

No one but Vencor members know the truth.

Despite the slight tremor that invades my limbs and the heaviness in my steps, no amount of fear will deter me from bringing Violet justice.

Violet and I aren't blood-related, but we met in a foster home—one of the most abusive ones I lived in—and we bonded. She protected me when the man who was supposed to take care of us got too drunk on liquor and hit us or when his wife tried to get me addicted to meth.

Then one night, Violet took my hand and suggested we escape. We were homeless for a while, and she refused to take us to a shelter or anywhere else in the care system. Neither of us trusted it. I was maybe twelve at the time and she was thirteen.

For some reason, our previous foster parents, Martha and Gerald, didn't report us as runaways or missing right away, and Violet said she 'took care of it.' I'm not sure how she convinced them, but something told me it was because of the black eye she was sporting, and I wanted to go back and kill them.

But the last thing we wanted was to be found and shoved into another abusive foster home.

Thankfully, Violet looked older than her age, so she got a job at some shady restaurant and begged the owner lady to let me study in the storage room while she worked the evening shift.

She fed me, made sure I was keeping my grades up, and took me for late-night walks. She's my mom, my dad, my sister, and my savior.

She shielded me when she was in the cold. She fed me and stayed hungry herself.

She was the warm shelter kids like me don't get.

Until she was snatched away from me.

Because of Vencor.

They cut off my lifeline, and now, I have nothing left except the need for cold-blooded revenge.

The light dims further until only a few lit bulbs remain. They're so far apart and barely there that I have to rely on my phone's flashlight to see the path ahead.

I follow the directions Kane sent me, which becomes a challenge when the lights gradually disappear, especially when I start taking twists and turns down an uneven path.

Finally, I arrive at the old three-story building that's no longer in use. The entrance to the front door is hidden in plain sight, concealed behind an overgrown iron gate that's covered with chaotic ivy and large bushes.

The stone appears chipped in a few places, and the upper level looks as if it's about to fall apart, the ground floor creaking under the unstable weight.

Six men in black leather jackets and pants stand on either side of the entrance. All of them wear silver masks with subtle engraved talon and feather details that shine under the low orange light coming from the rusty lamps.

I slow to a halt, unsure whether or not I can go inside.

The door opens with a loud squeak in the silent night, and I startle.

"Can I go in?" I ask the statue-like men, but I get no reply.

The eerie quiet is deafening.

I clutch my phone tight as I creep toward the entrance, figuring they'll stop me if I'm not supposed to go inside. A strange feeling of disappointment hits me when I scan the masked faces and don't feel Kane's presence.

I look at their hands, but they're all gloved in brown leather, so I can't see if they're wearing black rings.

My steps are careful as I slide through the ajar beat-up wooden door. The lighting is slightly better inside, but it's still dim, almost candle-like. Stretched out in front of me is a medium-sized reception area that looks similar to an outdated hotel lobby, with stained carpet, a worn-out tall desk, and a dark-green sofa that's probably behind the smell of dust and mildew that's permeating the air.

I notice four doors, one in each corner, painted in different colors—red, black, gray, and white.

A shadow gets caught in my peripheral vision and I spin around, my sense of alert hiking.

A woman appears in front of me, wearing the same mask and gloves as the men outside. However, she's in a black dress and a tight brown leather corset.

She stretches out her hand in the direction of my phone that I've been gripping tightly. I take one last look at the notifications in the hope of finding a text from Kane.

When I see nothing, I reluctantly give her the phone. She places it on the desk and mechanically pats me down. I try to sniff her, but I only smell the generic leather. I can't even tell the true color of her eyes due to the poor lighting. I do catch a glimpse of a silver serpentine chain with a talon pendant hanging from her neck.

She removes my fitness watch and places it beside my phone, then takes a step back, her hands clasped in front of her.

"Am I free to go?" My voice is heightened in the silence, too loud for my own ears.

She says nothing, looking ahead as if she's a statue.

"I assume I can choose whichever door to go through?"

No reply.

All right, then.

I avoid the red and black doors for obvious reasons. The colors themselves are ominous. I also vote against white. It might seem safe on paper, but if it's a psychological trick and the colors are reversed, I don't want to end up facing the worst trial.

With a deep breath, I stride to the gray door and then stop.

I recall something about what Kane said. Only Senior members wear black rings. I assume black is associated with them. Silver, which is the equivalent of gray on this occasion, is probably associated with the woman and the men outside, like their masks. They're not Seniors if they're tasked with mundane things like supervision and security.

At the last second, I change direction to the black door. Maybe Kane is behind it, and while I'm not sure if he'd help, I'd at least see a familiar face.

When I turn the knob, a loud creak echoes in the air, making goosebumps erupt on my bare arms. I steal one last look behind me to find the woman staring at me. Unblinking. Completely statuesque.

I gulp and go inside.

A low light hangs from the ceiling showing long stairs. I start going down and when I look back, the door I came through is closed.

I go down for some time and when I arrive at the bottom, I find another metal door. I carefully open it and walk in.

Deep darkness envelops me as the door slowly shuts behind me. The low creak is followed by a soft *click* that thuds in my chest.

I can't see anything.

Not even my hands.

I reach behind me for the knob and touch something cold and flat. Like a small metal plate. I feel around, my short nails getting stuck in the cracks of the wood, but there's no way to open it.

A shattered exhale slips through my lips, and I remain completely still, barely sensing my own existence.

I'm stuck.

I don't like feeling stuck.

Not after I was trapped in the car with my dead parents for several hours before I was found.

I'd like to think I've gotten over my slight claustrophobia, but the more I look and see nothing, the tighter my chest squeezes.

Drip.

I startle, searching around like a caged animal.

Drip.

Water. It has to be water coming from somewhere.

Cold air bites into my skin and the pungent smell of moist earth, along with the faint stench of something rotten, lingers in my nostrils.

I stretch my arms out on either side of me and touch damp stone.

A tunnel?

A cave?

Carefully, I take one step forward, then follow with another while still touching the stone. The silence is oppressive, only broken by the occasional drip of water ringing in the darkness. Each footstep is loud, almost as if the walls are echoing them.

Once I'm sure the ground is safe, I walk faster. My clothes cling uncomfortably to my skin and my heart beats loudly. So loudly, I can only hear the thumping in my ears.

Someone once said it isn't darkness that's scary, it's what lurks inside it.

So despite the complete annihilation of my vision, I still squint and blink and struggle to make out something, anything around me.

I'm not sure how long I walk, but it's long enough that I feel the strain and my throat turns dry. But maybe that's because of how hyperaware I am. As if I'm waiting for one of those horror-ride skeletons to jump out at me.

Though I could handle that or any other horror-esque scenarios. Fictional jump scares don't faze me. Not when I spent my childhood surrounded by actual monsters.

I walk farther, still feeling the walls, my heartbeat finally dropping to a relatively normal rhythm.

My trial is probably at the end of the tunnel. The sooner I get there, the better.

"Dahlia?"

I still, my breathing deepening, and a shocking shiver slashes through me.

M-Mom?

I haven't heard that voice since I was six. It's been over fifteen years. After my parents' deaths, I hopped from one home to another, meeting one foster 'mom' after the other until they all blended together, but I could never forget Mama's voice.

The softness, the affection, and the slight exhaustion from spending late nights sewing dresses.

No one has ever loved me like Mama.

"Dahlia, honey?" She speaks again in the darkness, like an angel.

I bite my lower lip to keep from calling out to her and telling her how much I miss her.

This is a trial. They're trying to mess with me.

A strong light shines in front of me and I squint, then close my eyes. An orange film forms behind my eyelids as my sight gradually adjusts.

The sound of giggles reaches me, and I slowly open my eyes again. There's a light before me, projected into a wall, that shows an old video of my toddler years. I look close to one year old.

My chubby little hands grab onto a leather sofa covered

with a colorful quilt, my brown curls chaotic and lighter than they are now.

"Come on, honey. Come to Mama."

My vision blurs when the camera shifts to Mom, who's sitting on her knees. It's been such a long time, I almost forgot what she looked like. After the accident, the bank foreclosed on the house, then auctioned most everything in it and threw away the rest or sent it to an old distant aunt who refused to take me in. I didn't even get a picture of my parents.

The only image I have of them is in my head.

After so many years, it's gotten distorted and changed, but as I watch the video, I can finally see my mama again.

I look so much like her, though her skin was a bit tanner, her hair lighter, her eyes brown, while mine are hazel.

She was a beautiful woman, but what I recall the most about her is the stunning smile that never left her lips, no matter how hard things got.

"Come, baby. One more step," she encourages, both her hands stretched out.

Little me finally takes the leap. I reach toward her and walk like a drunken man. "Mama…Mama…"

"Yes!" She squeals as I take a few steps and fall into her embrace. Mom hugs me tight, stands up, then whirls me in the air as I giggle uncontrollably. She stares at the camera, tears of joy forming a sheen in her eyes. "Did you see that, hon? Dahl's first steps."

"I did." Dad's voice sounds deeper than I recall. The video zooms in, slightly shaky, as he approaches us. The last still is a blurry image of Dad with his arm around Mom and me, his face unclear.

My hand reaches out of its own accord as a tear slides down my face. I've never seen this video. I wasn't even aware it existed. I don't know what I want to do. Touch the screen? Touch them?

Hug their image?

The still flickers on the screen and then a darker video appears. Road surveillance footage. My lips part as I see a grainy image of a car flipped beside a cliff. An older blue Toyota.

Dad's car.

My ears buzz when the video quickly rewinds, and I watch as a truck comes from the opposite direction, the bright headlights and the loud horn nearly splitting my skull open. Our car swerves and I drop to my knees on the cold, hard ground, slamming both palms to my ears to keep from hearing the crash.

But the sound penetrates my hands and explodes in my ears so loudly, I scream.

In a fraction of a second, I'm transported to fifteen years ago.

"Daddy, look, I made my doll a dress," I gloat, bouncing up and down in the back seat. "Hey, look, look…"

"Your daddy is driving, Dahl." Mom looks back and strokes my hair. "Don't distract him, okay?"

"But I wanna show my doll." I pout, then shove my doll against the back of his seat. "Daddy, look."

"Stop it, Dahl," Mom scolds harshly.

My lips tremble and I start to cry, hugging my doll tightly to my chest.

"Don't cry, baby." Dad glances at me. "Your doll looks beautiful."

"Really?" I sniffle between tears.

"Yes, but not more beautiful than you—"

"John!!!" Mom screams as blinding white light flashes through the car and a loud crash echoes in the air.

The last thing I see is a red mist and vacant, lifeless eyes.

I'm hugging myself on the damp ground, my sweaty fingers shaking, my face full of tears as I watch the video on the screen on a loop.

"Why did you kill us, Dahlia?" Mom's sad voice asks. "Why?"

"I didn't mean to… I…I… Mom…I didn't know."

"You disappointed me, Dahl," Dad's voice speaks so close to my ear, I shiver all over.

"Dad…" I whisper and turn around, but there's no one there.

All of my surroundings are filled with projection over projection of the accident. In front of me, behind me, on the walls, on the floor.

My nightmare is repeated in grotesque, vivid detail. Every time the crash echoes in the air, I scream. Every time, I smell the burning rubber on the road and taste the tangy, metallic blood of my parents.

My doll is bent, stained with my own blood. The beautiful tulle dress I made is torn and smudged with red.

I hug my knees to my chest, hide my face in them, and slam my eyes shut to ward off the gruesome images.

But I still can't block out the haunting sounds from my darkest nightmare.

The crash. The screams. The sirens.

The distorted medics' voices.

Make it stop.

Someone make it stop!

Please.

No one does.

My whole life, I've learned that if I want something done, I have to do it myself.

Knights in shining armor don't exist outside of fiction.

Luck has never been on my side and never will be.

The psychological torture repeats in a cycle of despair that erodes my sanity. I stop feeling my limbs as the shadows of the past stretch and contort, turning into new cruel whispers each time the scene replays.

You killed your parents. Why are you alive?

You should've died, not them.

If you weren't a spoiled brat, none of this would've happened.

You're the reason they're gone. Why do you feel sorry for yourself? You're not the victim here. Stop the main character energy.

Murderer...

Murderer.

Murderer!

"No!" I scream, jumping up into a standing position, wiping at the snot and tears covering my face. Adrenaline burns in my veins as I stare at the scene, unblinking, my hands fisted, my legs shoulder width apart. It hurts, but I don't look away. It hurts, but I watch it again from start to finish.

My parents are gone, but Violet isn't—at least, not completely.

Violet needs me.

And if I have to go through this torture for her, so be it.

When the video comes to an end, I ready myself for another round, another visual and auditory assault, but the projections disappear completely.

A small flickering wall lamp switches on.

I'm indeed in a tunnel. Through my teary vision, I make out a blinking camera light in the ceiling and stare at whoever is watching as I wipe my eyes with the backs of my hands.

You won't break me.

No one will.

"Congratulations, Dahlia," a man says, his suave voice filling the tunnel. "You've passed the mental test, but there's still the physical test left. Correction. It's both mental and physical. Since this is a trial, if you say the safe word you agreed to with the Senior member who invited you, everything stops. You'll be escorted out and banished from campus and town. As long as you stay quiet after that, you get to keep your life. If you don't… I'll leave that to your imagination."

I gulp, searching my surroundings. I already told Kane I wouldn't say the word, and that won't change now.

Nothing is worse than reliving my worst nightmare.

A door opens somewhere to the right, and I squint, but I can't see its exact location in the shadows.

A tall silhouette walks toward me—a man, judging by his build and height. He's dressed in a black T-shirt, jeans, and army boots. His hands are covered with black leather gloves and his face is hidden by a black mask that resembles a plague doctor. However, this one has sharp, unsettling serpentine and talon details swirling in the contours like a curse.

He stands there, his height eating up the small space as he stares me down. His chilling gaze seeps through my clothes and strikes my skin.

I look to either side of me, searching for an escape. He remains motionless, as if waiting for my next move.

The tunnel extends as far as my eyes can see. No ending in sight.

But maybe that's the point.

My limbs are still shaking from the assault of the video, but I gather my strength, turn around, and run.

I don't even make it two steps before my legs are grabbed.

The ground shifts and I fall with a thud, my knee hitting the dirt floor so hard, I feel it in my bones.

A large weight lands on top of me, pushing me down and forcing every breath out of my lungs.

I squirm and buck against him. I don't know what's come over me or if I should even be fighting.

It's a survival instinct. Innate and unconscious.

Deep down, I know I can't beat someone this much larger than me, but that won't stop me from trying.

A gloved hand wraps around my throat, lifting and twisting my face up until I'm looking at the gruesome mask.

"Red. Say it or submit."

My eyes widen.

Kane.

It's Kane's voice.

CHAPTER 6
Dahlia

MY HEART STILLS AND MY FINGERS FREEZE AS A TREMOR grips me.

I claw at the slick damp ground beneath me as Kane's front covers my entire back, his weight oppressive, his body an unyielding slab of muscle, like being squashed by a wall.

A faint mixture of cedarwood and citrus lingers in the stale air and seeps into my flaring nostrils.

I should feel some form of relief that he finally showed up tonight, but I don't.

Far from it.

My muscles lock and dread twists my insides.

A creepy tension squeezes my throat, and my breaths come in short, frantic gasps.

The air thickens and a gloomy cloud envelops him with a shroud of darkness.

This isn't the Kane I thought I knew. His presence doesn't soothe—it suffocates.

He's not the Vipers' agreeable captain or the 'philanthropist' who so generously offered to help me.

No. This is Kane Davenport. Vencor's Senior member.

I've often found it hard to correlate Vencor's destructive

nature with his personality, but right now, I can see the shadows he came from.

His voice is different—deeper, lower, and entirely alien.

He turns my face at an angle, and the shadows flicker on his mask, dousing him with a menacing edge. His grip turns my body into a prisoner beneath him, a crushing hold that paralyzes more than my limbs.

"Kane?" I whisper, a slight tremble seeping in.

"Shh…" His gloved finger glides across my cheek, slow, deliberate, before tracing my lower lip. "Don't say my name."

Goosebumps spread like wildfire, my skin tightening under the icy graze of his touch. The truth slams into me.

He's changed. Colder. Impersonal.

Terrifying.

The Kane I knew of never truly existed. Only this calm, calculated predator. His stillness is a façade, his serenity is laced with menace, wrapping around my throat.

The mask strips away his kindness, revealing the monster underneath.

"I warned you." His words drop like stones into the dark, each one heavier than the last. Then, in a flash, he lifts off me, flipping me over so violently, my vision swims.

I yelp as my back hits the ground and he settles between my legs.

Our eyes meet beneath the shadowy light. His look is as dark as the night with a slight glimmer, an unfamiliar gaze.

His gloved finger strokes my face again, and although the motion is gentle, it feels as cold as ice. Then he slides his finger down, over my pulse point and to my collarbone.

Kane rips my shirt and bra open down the middle, and my breasts bounce free, my nipples instantly hardening at the chill.

I don't have time to adjust as he drags my jeans down in one vicious movement. They stop at my knees, then he pulls them all the way off, throwing my sneakers aside in the process.

I lie beneath him in my ripped shirt and bra and plain black undies, my skin heating and a sense of humiliation rotting in my stomach.

The surprise slowly subsides, and rage gathers at the base of my stomach. I push at his chest and slam my legs shut. "What the hell are you doing?"

Kane isn't fazed by my fight as he leisurely unbuckles his pants. The clink of the belt opening reverberates around me like a curse, and a shudder goes through me.

Because his impassive eyes remain on me, studying me like a predator.

Too bad for him, I'm no one's prey.

I start to get up, but he presses me back on the ground.

Violet said I have the strongest survival instinct and an impressive sixth sense. I've always somehow known when danger is coming and that's helped me escape it in time, and I really should've listened to those instincts before I stepped foot into the building.

Everything inside me is screaming for me to remove myself from this situation.

I kick and claw at Kane, trying to hit him anywhere possible.

He doesn't allow me one inch.

Whenever I try to sit up, he shoves me down. Clawing, kicking, and even biting don't seem to faze him. Not even when I pull on his hair the hardest I can.

He covers my face with a palm and pushes me back, all the while he lowers his pants and boxers to reveal a huge half-erect dick.

My fight subsides for a second as I stare, dumbfounded.

Listen, I'm no virgin, but I've never seen a dick that big when not hard. Not even in porn.

Megan's acquaintance of an acquaintance was downplaying this so fucking badly.

That *thing* is not going inside me. No way in hell.

I find it difficult to get wet as it is and need to mentally prepare myself. I'd definitely also need to physically prep myself before he were to even touch me.

Kane must take my bewilderment as my being too tired to fight, and he bunches his fingers in my underwear, lifting my waist with them.

The fabric stretches, then tears under his ruthless grip, and the tatters cling to my waist. Cold air covers my pussy and I scream, "Stop!"

He doesn't.

Kane grasps my pelvis and drags me closer across the hard ground until my ass burns.

"Wait…" I murmur quietly at first, then scream, "I said, 'Stop!'"

I lift my upper body and slap him across the mask.

My palm burns from the plastic, but he does stop.

I think I see a glimmer in his eyes as he remains still. So still, the only sound in the air is my ragged breathing and the occasional drip of water in the dark.

Drip.

Drip…

Slap!

My hand flies to my burning cheek.

Did Kane just…backhand me?

I stare at him, bewildered, my face stinging and my head spinning.

"Next time you want to try something, think hard about whether you want to be on the receiving end," he delivers in a detached tone. "And remember, I'm much stronger and will not hold back."

This…sick bastard.

With a roar, I jump up and pull on his hair with both hands, my fingers yanking the strands until I feel some of it shedding into my palms.

I'm suddenly jerked back when he grasps my ponytail in his fist and pulls me back so hard, I think my neck will snap. My hands fall from his head, and I stare up at him as he incrementally applies pressure as if intending to tear my hair from my skull.

A scream rips out of me as I sink my nails into his arm.

And he just stares down at me, expressionless. "Let's try again. You do something, you receive it ten times worse. Got it?"

The pain in my skull nearly causes me to black out, and I kick blindly, my lower half flailing around to free myself from his merciless grip.

A groan spills from him and I realize I just kicked—or kneed—his dick.

My movements go still, and I shake my head. "No, wait! I didn't mean to—"

My words end with a shriek when he slaps my pussy. Hard. So hard, I see stars, and tears sting my eyelids.

I wish it stopped there. I wish it was only the pain and repulsion that came with the hit.

To my utter horror, my pussy tightens and my insides liquefy.

No, no, no…

What the hell?

"Are you done testing my patience?" Kane pushes me, using my hair until I'm lying back on the ground, then he parts my legs with one forceful movement.

God. Fuck.

I know I said I'd do anything, and honestly, I would've slept with Kane under different circumstances, but this guy is insane.

Who knows if he'll hurt me beyond repair?

He pulls the tatters of my underwear back to expose my pussy, then grabs my hips and drags me toward his dick.

"Wait…hold on…" I latch onto his arm, my hand trembling despite my attempts to suppress my weakness. "Please!"

"What?" He peels my fingers off his arm and slams my hand above my head on the hard ground.

"I don't want this. Will you stop?"

"Your words and begging do not affect me. Here's how it will go. I'm going to use you, Dahlia. I'll abuse and humiliate you until you scream and cry and beg me to stop. Your cunt will be my dick's punching bag, and if I'm not satisfied, I'll move to your ass and fuck you raw until you bleed. So unless you're ready to put all your holes at my disposal, say 'red'. That's the only word that will stop me."

My ragged breathing slows down.

This is my test.

I need to let him fuck me to be accepted, or I can just say the safe word and he'll let me go.

I'll be completely removed from the college and town and lose my one chance to find who's behind Violet's attack.

Compared to all the sacrifices she made for me, this is nothing.

With a new resolve, I say in a clear voice, "Can you use a condom?"

"I'm going to ram my cock into your cunt raw. A condom would get in the way."

With a shaky breath, I cover my eyes with my free arm and say in a resigned tone, "Do whatever you want."

I think I can feel his hand tightening around my wrist the slightest bit, but maybe that's just my head's way of making myself believe that a part of him cares.

That part of him can see how fucked up this is and maybe do it gently, unlike the way he promised.

But I should've known better.

Kane shoves my legs apart farther and thrusts inside me in one go.

My back arches off the ground as pain explodes inside me, and I let out a scream.

It hurts.

God. It *hurts*.

He's so big and I'm barely wet from when he slapped my pussy. Not to mention, my muscles are so tense, I feel like my back will snap.

My lips tremble and I squeeze my eyes shut as tears gather in my lids.

Red.

The word is red.

I sink my teeth into my lower lip to stop the single syllable from spilling out.

Pain is okay.

I've handled countless types of pain throughout my life. This is nothing.

This is just a nuisance that will be over soon.

His controlled breathing fills my ears, sharp and timed with his thrusts.

Inhale. *Thrust.*

Exhale. *Out.*

Inhale. *Thrust.*

Exhale. *Out.*

I decide to focus on the rhythm, waiting and praying for the ordeal to be over. He'll finish soon enough. All men do.

"Relax." His words sound like he's bored. "The more you stiffen, the longer this gets. Remember." He slaps the side of my ass. "I'll switch holes if this one doesn't satisfy me."

His words only manage to tighten my muscles further.

I've never had anal sex. If he does it without prep using that dick of his, I'll probably die.

Okay, let's be smart about this. Breathing deeply, I try to relax.

It's just another fuck, Dahlia. You were never really satisfied by them anyway.

Inhale.

Exhale.

It'll be over soon.

It doesn't help when he rams into me hard, driving into me with force like he hates me.

He's not fast or unhinged.

Kane fucks like he speaks. Deliberate and controlled. Like he's performing a task on today's agenda.

I'm the task.

The task is me.

He woke up today and chose me as the target of his entertainment.

"I can tell you're not enjoying it, and I can assure you I'm not either. You're still so uptight, you're about to cut my dick off." I can almost see the frown in his brow. Like, how dare I have sex on the damn ground and not accept him with open arms?

"Maybe if you were gentle, I'd be more wet and make it worth your time," I say before I can stop myself.

He stills deep inside me, his hard cock pulsing with tension.

"The fuck you just say?" He snatches my arm from my face and imprisons it with my other one above my head. "Look me in the eye and say it again."

You know what? I'm already in this position. What's the worst he can do?

Fuck you in the ass, Dahlia. Do you really want to provoke him, knowing how unpredictable the asshole is?

I bite my lower lip.

"Cat got your tongue?" His eyes darken, looking unhinged under the shadowy light.

"It's nothing."

"No. It was something. Along the lines of being gentle. Like this?" He slides out and thrusts in deep but slow.

Tingles dance at the base of my belly.

"Or this?" He releases my wrists and circles my clit in expert pleasuring movements while fucking me at a measured pace.

My pussy tightens and I feel every inch as I swallow him with each thrust. I accommodate him until I can barely register the size. My body relaxes despite the dirt floor beneath me, and my hips roll and meet his movements.

I even hear myself moaning the deeper he goes. I grab on to his arm and stroke his skin through the clothes.

For some reason, I've always needed to touch during sex. I guess I require a physical connection of sorts to eradicate the sense of vulnerability.

I need it more than ever now, and I wish he were naked.

Sweat covers my skin and I feel the buildup churning in my stomach.

"This gentle is okay for you?" he asks as his fingers tap, circle, and pinch my clit.

"Mmm, yes, that's good."

I don't think I'll come that hard, but at least I'm wet, so his thrusts don't hurt anymore. In fact, the way he stretches me with each move is exhilarating. I've only ever had lackluster orgasms whether alone or with others, and that's fine.

My sex drive has never been that high anyway.

"You seem to be under the misconception that your pleasure matters. I have news for you." Kane wraps a gloved hand around my throat and thrusts brutally. "It doesn't."

I shriek as he hits somewhere sensual inside me. He picks up his rhythm and goes deeper and harder, slamming against that spot over and over.

My back scrapes against the ground and I think he'll choke me to death as he fucks me.

"This is about *my* pleasure." *Thrust*. "*My* satisfaction." *Thrust*. "You're only here to receive." *Thrust*. "Your body was made to be used and marked however I fucking want." *Thrust*. "This is my cumhole, understood?"

I grab onto his arm with both hands, my nails sinking into the material as he plows into me. The mask makes him look like a demon in the night.

A madman set on destruction.

His rhythm leaves me breathless, and I don't have the clarity to think about anything except for that spot he keeps hitting.

"Your cunt is strangling my cock." He rolls his hips and thrusts again. "Can't wait for my cum to fill this hole? Such a greedy little whore."

My lips open in an O. My body is being violated in the most obscene ways possible and his words are so humiliating, but I can't seem to think past the hurricane building at the base of my stomach.

The whirlwind is severe and relentless.

I don't think I could stop it if I wanted to.

I've never felt anything equally uncomfortable, intense, and pleasurable at the same time.

"Wait…wait…" I choke out, but instead of slowing down, he pounds me, his cock nearly tearing me apart.

And in the middle of that pain, I think I'll die.

I'll die as he fucks me.

But the wave that hits me is a cloud of blinding pleasure. As his groin slaps against mine, liquid splashes out of me and I stare in horror as it drenches his jeans and the ground around us.

I don't get to focus on how I squirted for the first time in my life as my head rolls back. The orgasm sweeps through me in electric waves that swallow me whole. My legs shake and I lose control of my limbs.

I think I black out for a fraction of a second.

When I'm spat back into reality, Kane fucks me deeper, and I think the orgasm will never end.

But then he pulls out and releases my throat.

I think it's finally over and blink rapidly, but then he wraps a strong hand around my waist and flips me onto my stomach.

My knees throb as they meet the ground and he forces me on my elbows and pulls my ass up in the air. "This isn't working, let's try something different."

I try to look back, but he sinks his hand in my hair, shoving my face into the dirt floor, filling my nostrils with the dewy earth smell.

Slap!

A groan rips from me as his gloved palm meets my ass cheek. The sting rattles me to the bones, but before I can think, he spanks me again, this time on both cheeks.

I scream, but it's partially muffled by the ground and my sobs.

My eyes sting, and I realize tears are streaming down to the earth.

It hurts.

It hurts like a mother.

But somehow, the pleasure remains; if anything it burns hotter. And that terrifies the hell out of me.

"Stop!" I cry out, digging my fingers into the dirt. "Stop it…stop…"

"Mmm, that's it." He slaps my ass harder, as if I'm his punching bag. "Break for me."

"Please…" I sob as the pain intensifies coupled with blinding pleasure.

"More. Show me what you look like when you shatter to pieces like a dirty slut."

My skin feels like it's been doused with fire, so when he sinks his fingers into my battered ass cheek, I scream, but it's barely audible. All my strength seems to have disappeared except for the constant throb to come.

His cock forces its way inside me again, and I shriek.

My walls clamp around his size and I feel like he's going to break me. "This is more like it. Your tight cunt is strangling me so well. Mmm. More."

I reach a weak hand behind me, blindly tapping at his thigh, his jeans, anywhere I can reach. "No…no…stop it…please…"

I don't know if I'm begging him to stop because it hurts or because I'm scared by how much I'm turned on by this.

But a breath of relief escapes me when he doesn't listen.

Kane thrusts inside me with blinding power, going deeper than I thought would ever be possible.

"Look at your cunt dripping wet. You're such a natural at taking cock." He slaps my ass and I sob, tasting my snot and tears.

But no matter how much I wail and cry, he just goes on and on, impaling me with his cock.

Slapping my ass until pleasure and pain mix and become one and the same.

I think I'll shatter to pieces like he said or even faint or actually die.

As I cry a mumbled sob on the ground, it hits me that he said he'll only stop if I say 'red'.

It's at the tip of my tongue, but I don't say it.

I don't know why I can't.

I don't even *want* to.

His grip tightens on my hair as he rams into me, his groin slapping against my sore, battered ass, his rhythm intensifying, fucking me deeper, harder.

"You look so defiant, but you turn into a dirty little whore when you're being fucked." *Slap.* "You're dripping all over the place. What a fucking mess."

My insides liquefy, pain throbbing everywhere, but Kane doesn't finish.

Or slow down.

He's using me as a fuck doll, taking out his aggression and dirty sexual deviation on me.

And I'm still not putting a stop to it.

I think he'll never come as he drives into me with renewed intensity.

I think I'm really not going to survive this. Even if my juices are trailing down my thighs.

I've never felt this type of uncomfortable pleasure before, so deeply entwined with pain. So intense and foreign.

Oh God.

Blinding pleasure tightens inside me, and I close my eyes, ready for the orgasm.

But before it can hit, Kane pulls out.

What…no… The least he can do is let me come.

My pussy pulses and tightens in protest as his dark voice echoes in the air. "As I said, this isn't about you, slut. You came enough for one night."

The world spins as he flips me over again. I sob when my burning ass meets the ground.

I feel a shadow above me and my eyes widen when he straddles my head, knees on either side of my temple, looking down at me through the gruesome mask.

The fabric of his jeans is scratchy against my heated, stinging cheeks. Kane holds his hard cock with a stiff hand, the veins bulging on the back. "Open that fucking mouth."

I blink, still disoriented, all my strength gone. I'm so drained, sore, and full of sexual frustration, I'm surprised I haven't already passed out.

When I don't comply, he grabs a fistful of my hair, pulling my head up violently and slapping my mouth with the underside of his dick. And then he comes all over my face, his cum forming a sticky film on my eyes, nose, cheeks, mouth.

Everywhere.

His gaze remains on me as he messes up my face and I can only see a blurry version of him. "What a dirty, *dirty* little whore."

I taste him on my tongue as our eyes meet.

His are so detached, I wonder if there's any warmth

inside him. If he hadn't painted my face with cum, I'd suspect he was a robot who didn't enjoy what just happened.

"You could've been a better slut," he says in a tone as detached as his eyes as he stands up and tucks himself in. "If you can walk, go through the door to your left."

As he strides through said door, I stare overhead at the blinking red light in horror.

I completely forgot there was a camera.

Some sick perverts were watching me getting humiliated this entire time.

CHAPTER 7
Dahlia

KANE HAS DISAPPEARED.

And with that, the camera stops blinking red.

Soon after he left, he returned and threw a coat at my head—black leather with brass buttons like the ones the guards were wearing outside.

Then he vanished into the dark without looking twice in my direction, as if I'd disgusted him.

After he fucked me.

After he used me for his pleasure.

That thought is more humiliating than the fact that I had the roughest sex of my life on camera. And I came so hard, I squirted.

I need therapy. If only I could afford it.

My movements are stiff and automatic as I swipe my torn shirt over my face, the touch of it scraping against my skin like sandpaper. I find the cleanest shred and drag it between my legs.

The bruises he left on my pelvis and ass throb, radiating heat. Sharp, stinging pain lances through me with every small shift. The feeling of him inside me is raw, alive, like my body has been ripped open and filled with tiny, invisible shards of him.

My strained muscles protest as I pull my jeans up, slide into my shoes, then put on the huge coat and fasten the belt around my waist.

It smells like Kane. Woodsy and mysterious.

Enchanting at first, but a devil up close.

Serves me right for trying to humanize him in the beginning despite knowing exactly the type of organization he belongs to.

I thought he was the greenest flag in this godforsaken organization, but apparently, I was color-blind.

From now on, Kane, like every single fucking person in Vencor, is my enemy.

"Congratulations, Miss Thorne," a suave voice echoes overhead. "You proved both mental and physical resilience and, therefore, deserve to be a Trial Vencor member. From now on, you're expected to perform any mission the Senior member responsible for you dishes your way. Refusal will get you banished. Three consecutive failures to perform tasks will get you banished and stripped of any privileges. Your fate is bound to the Senior member who brought you in. If they discard you, you're out. Disclosure of Vencor's secrets or what takes place at the initiation or meetings will cost you your life. You will now undergo the acceptance ceremony."

On cue, a door opens to my left, and I hesitate for a second before I head in. I do my best to walk normally, but it's impossible. Painful soreness explodes between my legs with every movement and it's a struggle to breathe properly, let alone walk.

The room's walls are made of irregular stones, and the ceiling is shaped like a dome, adorned with a gruesome image of a vicious fight between a black snake and a large crow.

The vast space isn't as dark as the tunnel, but it's not bright either. Five people stand in a circle in the middle, holding lit torches with leather-gloved hands.

They're wearing long oversized black cloaks, so I can't tell their gender. Their faces are covered by masks just like Kane's. The serpentine and talon details look monstrous under the dancing fire.

The thought of these perverts watching Kane fuck me to within an inch of my life makes me physically sick.

My hands shake and I consider turning around and running as far away as possible.

But I don't.

Not after what I endured to get here.

Two cloaked Members ease back, allowing an opening in the circle. I take that as my cue to step in.

As soon as I'm inside, a suffocating presence materializes behind me. One—or a few—cloaked people glare at me through the tiny eyeholes of their masks, but I still turn to face whoever's hot on my heels.

A tall shadow towers over me, holding a silver cup with carved serpents coiling around it in his left gloved hand. The right hand, however, is naked, with veins protruding on the back, showcasing the black ring on his index finger.

Kane.

I don't know what it says about me to be able to recognize him from just his hand despite the fact that he's fully cloaked and masked.

He must've followed me in from outside, because the circle that closes around us still has five Members.

The throbbing between my thighs intensifies, and I'm not sure whether it's due to disgust for what he made me go through or something entirely different.

Kane places his right hand on top of my head. It's rough, big, and makes my heart beat faster.

Just when I think he'll probably crush my skull, he pushes me down firmly. "Kneel."

The single word is nonnegotiable, and I bend my knees, slowly dropping into position—not that I can refuse.

I just hope this isn't another exhibitionist sexual act. I don't think I can do it in front of so many people. Hell, I still feel nauseous knowing that these people watched my unraveling through the camera.

"Repeat after me." Kane's voice sounds so cold, my blood freezes. "I pledge my soul to the shadows."

My forefinger traces a small circle on my thumb, and I gulp the ball in my throat as I speak in a low but steady voice. "I pledge my soul to the shadows."

Kane's fingers dig into my scalp and I think he'll smash my head into pieces after all, but he releases me and outstretches his big palm in front of me. "Hand."

I offer him my left hand and he pulls out a black dagger from the back of his jeans and cuts my index finger. The sting is small, but blood pours out and Kane drips it into the cup.

Then he cuts his own index finger and I watch with bated breath as our blood mixes together as if it's a satanic ritual.

Kane dips his cut index finger into the cup, swirls it around, then uses the blood to draw what I think is a serpent symbol on my forehead.

Once he's done, he lets the cup fall to the floor, its loud clink echoing in the silence. I stare up at him, and although I can only see dark holes through the mask, they're glinting.

Shining.

I don't think I've ever seen his eyes so...thrilled? Is that the right word?

One of the men surrounding us speaks, his scratchy voice filling the space. "Now, pass her to the others so they can come in her mouth."

My skin prickles and my eyes widen.

I've been so focused on Kane's miniature movements, I somehow blacked out the other Members surrounding us.

My gaze searches his, but only for a second. A foolish one.

Because the truth hits me like a knife to the ribs. Kane isn't on my side.

No one in this room is.

Will I be able to lower myself that far? Even if it's for Violet, I don't think I can do it.

Kane doesn't react to the man's words. Instead, he reaches into his cloak and produces a silver mask—similar to the guards' ones—and straps it around my face.

He grabs my hand and pulls me up to a standing position so that I'm facing him. His chest grazes mine for a brief second, hot and hard, like a wall.

"Not interested," he says in his usual emotionless tone, but I think I detect tension beneath it.

"Then use her mouth in front of us," another one of the cloaked men around us says in a mischievous tone.

Is that…Preston?

"Still not interested. She fails to turn me on."

Ouch.

His words pierce me like a dagger. That's definitely not what a girl likes to hear after she's been practically used by a man.

But at least I don't have to go through any more humiliating acts.

"You sure about that?" someone else asks in a feminine voice.

"Yes. If you want to see my dick, just say it." Kane sounds bored, as if he can't wait to get the fuck out of here.

When no one else protests, he produces a necklace from his cloak—the same talon necklace I saw the girl wearing.

My face squashes against his muscular chest as he fastens it around my neck. As the chain clicks in place, he whispers in my ear so only I can hear him, "You really should've run away while you had the chance. Welcome to hell, Dahlia."

CHAPTER 8
Dahlia

AFTER WHAT I WENT THROUGH, I SHOULD'VE BURIED MY face under the covers and hid there the rest of the night.

And I tried that.

Thankfully, when I got back at one in the morning, Megan wasn't home yet. It's not unusual for her to spend the night with her friends or just stay out partying.

I had a shower in which I scrubbed my skin until it turned red, then slipped under the duvet on my stomach because my ass burns with every move. Whenever I close my eyes, images of my parents' accident and the rough, merciless sex invade my head.

Shame and disgust prickle my skin with renewed intensity, so I jump back into the shower. Under the scalding hot water, I rub my skin with enough force that new bruises join the existing sex bruises.

How the hell did I come by being used like that? By that demon?

Am I sick?

Part of me wants to hate it to its core, consider it assault even if I agreed to it. That part, probably some form of defense mechanism, whispers that I wasn't given a choice. That I only did it because I couldn't say no.

But I could have.

Kane gave me every chance to say that godforsaken 'red,' but I refused.

My head hurts long after I leave the shower wrapped in a towel.

I lie on my stomach on the bed and grab my phone that was returned to me on my way out of that damned building.

Instagram is open. Specifically, my last DM exchange with Kane, when I expected him to meet me by the entrance. And even though I didn't think he'd help me, I also didn't think he'd use me in that sense.

Though it's useless to feel wronged or attempt to feel victimized. Not when I was offered a way out countless times but still went with it anyway.

I click on his profile and narrow my eyes at the caption.

Vipers' Center & Captain.

More like a two-faced devil.

I studied Kane's Instagram page like an essay during my stalking stage, but now, I look at it through a different lens. It's hockey-themed and full of shots from games and practice as well as pictures with teammates, the coach, some professors, and fans.

There are others at fundraising events with the university's top brass and the Vipers' donors. The big names in town. His family, the Callahans, the Armstrongs, and the Osborns.

But those are few and far between, as if he doesn't want his background to be the main focus.

He looks perfectly cordial in all of them. No signs that suggest he's faking it or building an image.

His smiles give off a genuine, charming vibe, like he'd be great fun to talk to.

It isn't until now that I realize those smiles never reach his icy eyes. Not really.

They look beautiful because of the color, but that doesn't mean they smile with the rest of his face.

Maybe it's because I already met the other side of him, but the veil has been lifted and I realize that the random, sometimes uncoordinated pictures are just a game he plays so well.

Like the perfect disguise he hides behind.

And now that my fate is tied to his in Vencor, I need to figure him out. Somehow.

I need to get closer.

Any way possible.

I go back to our conversations.

Dahlia: Better test for that STD I gave you tonight 😏

What? That should get his attention.

I guess my only consolation about the whole fucking raw part is that Kane and his teammates tested negative on their latest medical tests. I know because I accessed their reports behind my professor's back.

My heart jumps when his reply comes immediately.

Kane: Very funny.
Dahlia: I wasn't joking.
Kane: You must be, because your cunt felt like it hadn't swallowed a dick in a long time. Almost like a virgin.

My cheeks heat, but I double down.

Dahlia: And you fuck a lot of virgins?
Kane: No. Not a fan.

Dahlia: Thank God. No virgin should suffer your vicious way of having sex.
Kane: Was it also suffering when you squirted all over my dick?

I rub my thighs together but type the entire opposite.

Dahlia: Uh-huh. Worst sex of my life.
Kane: Doubt it. You were swallowing my cock so deep. Almost as if you couldn't get enough.
Dahlia: No, I wasn't. Anyway, I'm just telling you. Chlamydia is nasty.
Kane: I'll take your word for it.
Dahlia: You'll suffer like a motherfucker.
Kane: Go to sleep, Dahlia.

I try to think of other insults, but I'm too agitated, so I throw the phone on the bed.

The necklace shines under the light and I grab the silver talon between my fingers, staring at the hideous serpentine chain.

Doesn't matter. The discomfort and shame will fade away. The most important thing is that I'm in.

Sooner or later, I'll be able to identify Vi's attacker.

Violet.

The urge to see her beats beneath my skin like a ticking time bomb.

I change into jeans and a T-shirt, then throw on a sweater before I head out of the dorm. I ride my bike to town.

Graystone General Hospital is huge and renowned for having large departments that benefit from the founding families' extensive funding.

It's also the prime beneficiary of Graystone Hope Foundation, which finances countless expensive surgeries throughout the year. It's the foundation that offered me the scholarship at GU and is paying for Violet's medical expenses and her stay in the hospital.

Forty-five days ago, my sister was driven by a black van with a fake plate to the hospital in Stantonville, where we used to live. A man whose face was entirely hidden dropped her on a gurney and sped away in the van before he could be identified. My sister was unconscious and had a wound at the back of her head and multiple less serious injuries all over her body. They transferred her to Graystone General Hospital because it's bigger and has a trauma center.

Since then, she's been in a coma for a month and a half. I've seen the bills she's incurred during her stay. Bills I wouldn't be able to afford even if I sold myself for parts on the black market.

So I'm thankful beyond words to the foundation. I don't even mind taking pictures with them and accepting charity money. I don't care if it's the rich people's way to avoid taxes. At least they're paying for the tube that's literally keeping my only lifeline breathing.

I lost my parents, but I'll never lose Vi. Not even if I have to offer my soul to the Devil.

I take the elevator to the fifth floor, where they keep comatose patients.

I greet the night shift nurses. They've seen me practically daily since Vi was admitted. The head nurse, Mrs. Hales, a plump blond with rosy cheeks, smiles at me and then frowns.

"Dahlia, honey. You look pale. Have you forgotten to eat again?"

"I'm fine. How's Violet?"

"Worry about yourself first." She rummages through the desk and then produces a protein bar. "Eat this before you faint."

"Thanks." I accept the bar sheepishly because she's right. I've been surviving on the tuna sandwich I had for lunch yesterday.

Violet shares a room with a young man who has dark olive skin and thick eyebrows. His name is Mario, and he had an accident shortly after Violet was attacked. They were both in the ICU for a bit, and now, they still share a space because the hospital couldn't move either of them to single rooms due to a lack of capacity.

I don't mind since they have a curtain separating them, so their privacy is respected when the nurses tend to them.

Mario, however, doesn't get any visitors. At least, I haven't seen anyone come to visit him for the duration of the time I've been here. Though I do find baskets of fruit on the table beside his bed sometimes, and Mrs. Hales often tells me to eat them since they'll rot and be thrown out.

Since Mario must feel lonely, I talk to him sometimes as well, mostly about the day's news or random anecdotes. I don't want to imagine what Vi would feel like if I stopped visiting her.

Putting on my most cheerful smile, I push the door open. "Vi! I'm so excited to have full-range access to the lab as an upperclassman—"

My words halt at the view of a tall shadow standing by Violet's bed. He's smothered by the dark, and a hoodie covers his head and face.

I barely get a glimpse of him and scream.

He sprints to the window, forces it open, and jumps out.

I dash toward Violet as footsteps rush in from the hallway.

Thankfully, she's still sleeping peacefully, and the machine by the side of her bed beeps in a slightly high but mostly regular rhythm. I still grab her pale hand and check her pulse just in case.

"What's going on?" A nurse peeks in, her cheeks red.

"Someone…was in this room." I motion at the window. "They jumped out the window."

"Impossible. They'd die from this height."

"It's true."

The nurse looks at me as if I'm out of my mind, then goes over and looks outside. "There's nothing."

"I know what I saw. Please check the security footage."

Her frown deepens as she slams the window shut and walks out.

My heart thumps loudly even as I feel my sister's steady beat beneath my fingers.

I throw a glance at Mario and release a breath when I find he's also peacefully sleeping.

Just to be sure, I leave Vi's side and peer out the window. All I see are cars speeding down the road below.

But I couldn't have been mistaken.

Someone was here and if I hadn't come in time, who knows what they would've done to Vi.

My blood turns cold.

Wait.

It couldn't have been whoever hurt her coming to finish what he started, right?

I rush back to my sister's side.

She'd look like an angel while sleeping if it weren't for her sickly white skin that's paler than the sheets. Her hair, which used to be a shiny strawberry blond, is now dull and lifeless as it frames her petite face.

Violet has always been a beauty whom everyone stopped and stared at. Flirted with. Tried to take advantage of.

Her now closed eyes are actually a deep denim blue, her facial features are petite and perfectly harmonized. She even has a dusting of freckles on her nose.

She often dressed like a hobo, never putting on makeup and even wearing thick-framed nonprescription glasses so as not to be noticed. I can't say that helped, because she often suffered malicious male gazes.

The thought that one of them could've done something to her just now forms a knot in my heart.

Ever since I became an adult, I've made it my mission to protect her just like she protected me when we were young. For some reason, men are not as attracted to me as they are to her. I mean, I get looks, but they're not like the ones she gets. As if she's blood and they're vampires who want to suck her dry. As soon as they see me, and usually, some of my pepper spray, Tasers, or the landlord's guns that I clean as a side gig, they fuck off.

But I couldn't protect her this time.

This time, one of them got to her first.

I hug her, my head pressing against her chest as tears blur my eyes. "You said you'd never leave me alone, Vi. You...promised."

The words constrict my throat and I tremble all over. Like the day she ushered me out of bed and helped me put my shoes on. She was also shaking as we hid by the corner. She was thirteen. I was twelve.

"Do you trust me?" Violet once asked me in the darkness of the room where we shared a bunk bed.

I nodded.

Living in the system since I was six, I learned not to trust anyone, but Violet is different. Some kids hate it when they have a foster sibling. They despise having less food to go around and sleeping in bunk beds.

They can get malicious and even violent.

Not Violet.

Ever since I arrived at this house in the New Jersey suburbs a year ago, she's shared her food and her hiding nook in the closet.

When I got here, Violet had been with Martha and Gerald, our foster parents, who only use the system for extra income, for six months.

Violet has often said we need to get out of here.

One night, Martha called her a whore who was trying to seduce her husband. I called Martha a bitch and her husband a creep because he was the one looking at Violet while licking his lips when she was wearing plain cotton pajamas. Vi never dresses in a revealing way. Like never.

She's been growing breasts and hips and getting curvier over the past year, and that creep Gerald can't take his sleazy eyes off of her.

Another day, Martha beat me up for talking back until she busted my lip open. Violet apologized on my behalf, promising I wouldn't do it again.

Vi apologizes a lot. She also stands with her head bowed, listening to Martha calling her an ugly whore just like her slut of a mother and telling her she should be thankful that they took her in or she would've died on the side of the road like her drug addict mama.

Violet always swallows the knife with its blood and buries her wounds deep. She never complains or causes trouble and prefers to suffer in silence. It wasn't until recently that I found out Gerald touches her inappropriately, letting his hands wander and linger where they shouldn't.

To avoid conflict, she chooses to remain silent instead of speaking up, but she always speaks up when it comes to me. She always tries to rectify the situation and shield me under her wings.

She always says I need to be careful with my spicy mouth, but I'm nowhere near as patient as she is and get easily wound up. I'd rather be beaten up and spend nights without any food and thrown in the attic than let Martha and Gerald get away with their shit.

Which is why Martha beat me the hell up earlier tonight. I clawed at her face, and when Gerald pretended to break up the fight, I kicked him in the nuts.

He punched me so hard, I lost consciousness. When I came to, I found myself locked in the attic.

It's a dark, airless box, and the only light is the white streetlamp's shadow slipping through a narrow, dust-coated window high on the wall. The wooden beams above are splintered and warped, cobwebs clinging to them like silent witnesses to the hours I've spent here.

The stale smell of mildew and trapped heat sticks to my skin as I pull my knees to my chest and rest my head on them. I stare at the light dusting of snow falling and landing on the windowsill.

Right. It's going to be Christmas soon. I hate the holiday season.

Ever since my parents died and I became an orphan, it feels like a needle stabbing an old wound, undoing the stitches and making me remember what I lost.

The floorboards creak under a hesitant step. I perk up as a key jiggles in the lock and then the door opens.

Violet.

She always steals the keys when they're asleep and brings

me a sandwich. Usually, she'll hug me and tell me to stop rebelling so I won't get hurt again.

This time is different.

She's dressed in leggings and a coat, with a duffle bag slung over her shoulder. But that's not what makes me jump up and run to her.

It's the black bruise around her left eye. Big, ugly, and so swollen, she can barely open it.

"Vi, what happened? That looks bad."

She strokes my face. "You have a blue bruise, too."

"I'm gonna kill them."

She smiles and it's the widest, most genuine smile I've ever seen on her face. "Want to get out of here, Dahl? Just you and me?"

It's been some time since we both wanted to get the hell out. Tonight is as good as any.

I nod, inspecting her face.

The bruise looks worse up close, and there's a small cut on her lower lip. "Who did this? It was that asshole Gerald, wasn't it?"

"Forget it. I'm fine." She caresses my cheek, and I wince at the sting of pain. "Your face looks worse, by the way."

We both burst out laughing and we have to cover each other's mouths so as not to be discovered.

As we sneak out of that horrible place where yet another couple is using the foster care system to act like God to helpless children, we're still laughing.

Hysterically.

For both Violet and me, this is the first time in a long time, maybe ever, that we finally feel free.

Alive.

Like we can do whatever we want without creepy foster

parents breathing down our necks, using us as a venting outlet for their unremarkable lives.

We stop by a bridge to catch our breaths.

The snow trickles down, covering our shoulders and shoes. But I still spin around under the lamppost and scream into the silent night, "We're free!"

Violet grabs my shoulders, looking as if she has a halo under the dim light and the falling snow. "Dahlia?"

"Yeah?"

"From now on, we're each other's only family."

"You'll never leave me alone?"

She hugs me and whispers the word that gives me new hope, "Never."

Sitting up, I stare at Violet's face and hold her hand between my trembling ones. "You said we were each other's only family. How could you leave me? Why didn't you tell me about the man who was threatening to kill you instead of writing about it in your journal?"

Actually, I might have an idea as to why.

Violet has been soft-spoken and sort of a people pleaser ever since I met her. She never raises her voice and finds it hard to say no to anyone who's in authority or who yells at her. However, she's always been a mama bear when it comes to me, quickly transforming into a vicious protective girl if anyone hurts me or says anything negative about me.

I don't doubt that she wanted to protect me from the man whose identity she probably uncovered. She'd rather die than have me implicated.

The joke's on her because I'd do the same.

She gave up a lot for me, and it's my turn to pay her back.

Vi used to say kids like us were always meant to be at the

bottom of the food chain, a fringe of the system, a cog in the machine. Our lives, suffering, and trauma don't matter.

No one cares.

But that's where she's wrong.

She matters more to me than the entire world.

I want to tell her that I'm close. That I've infiltrated the organization where that scum is. I'll find him, and, mark my words, I'll make him pay even if it's the last thing I do.

But I don't.

In fact, I've never spoken to her about my plans so as not to agitate her. I only share good news and tell her I miss her.

The nurse from earlier pushes the door open, the frown still etched on her face.

"Did you find anything on the footage?" I ask, my blood pumping.

"That's the thing. The cameras in the hallway and elevator have somehow been disabled."

CHAPTER 9
Kane

"CALLAHAN!"

The coach's voice grinds the scrimmage to a halt.

As usual, Jude has just flattened Price against the boards and skated away with the puck as if it's perfectly normal.

Coach Slater is a veteran of the game, born and bred in the town and a proud product of Graystone University's unmatched hockey program.

He's tall, lean, balding, and has a beer belly. Although he's strict, his understanding of team harmony and execution style is top-notch. He's known for pushing players beyond the limits they think exist.

Not Jude, though.

That motherfucker has no limits.

Instead of helping Price up, Jude glares at him for daring to interrupt his flow.

Coach stares at him from the bench, his skin turning red. "I told you not to touch my fucking players, Callahan. Save the destructive energy for the other teams."

Jude lifts his shoulder in pure disdain. "I thought this was a scrimmage and we were supposed to play as if it's a real game."

"Did you miss the part about minimizing the risk of injury?"

"Minimizing is not eliminating."

"Off the ice. Number 71, five-minute major for boarding."

"Come on, that was hardly a two-minute penalty," Jude argues with a murderous face.

"Off my rink. Now."

Jude makes a face as he skates to the penalty box.

Great. Now I have to make do with ten players. Sometimes, Jude is just the most unreliable human I've ever come across.

When his brain functions, he performs miracles. When he allows his impulses to take over, he's no different than an untamable wild horse.

I stare at him as he sits down, resembling a trapped animal. He's been strange lately. And by strange, I mean he's a hassle to maintain.

Even my impeccable containment skills have been falling short.

Something that hasn't happened in all the time I've known him.

Which is our entire lives.

"Ready to be buried beneath ice, Davenport?" Preston, the captain and center of Team B, asks before the face-off in their offensive zone. "Your team is useless without a right winger."

I keep my eyes on the puck.

Preston might be the master of pushing buttons, but that's only because he makes it his mission to exploit his opponents' weaknesses. He's an expert at studying human nature and singling out the exact words that will ruffle the other person's feathers. He's gotten checked and thrown around more times than I can count, but he often comes out of it grinning in that slightly provocative manner, while Jude goes ballistic and starts a fight.

It's been our dynamic from the time we were shipped off to boarding school. Someone picked on Preston because he was scrawny and weak-looking, and Jude dismantled them. Sometimes, while bringing me along.

I preferred making their lives hell without lifting a finger, though.

As we grew up, Preston lost the childhood weakness, but not the antagonistic behavior.

It became ten times worse.

Too bad for him, though. I have no weaknesses he can exploit, so his methods have never worked on me. His words are merely white noise.

I steal the puck for my team and tie the score. The coach shouts instructions at Preston's defense, sounding like he wants to strangle them.

Despite my best attempts to minimize the damage, Team B's power play allows them an advantage I can't shake off. By the time Jude comes back, we barely manage to hold on to the tie.

He body-checks like a motherfucker and nearly gets another penalty for the reckless play.

We end up winning, but the coach lectures us about being responsible on the ice before he lets us go shower.

"I have an idea for taking care of the Callahan problem," Preston whispers to me after I step out of the shower, a towel wrapped around my middle, and head to the locker side.

Preston has already finished showering, changed into jeans, a white shirt, and a Vipers jacket, and is currently styling his golden hair back with a comb. Every strand is perfectly in place.

I open my locker and drop my towel, then pull on my boxer briefs and sweatpants. "We can't break his legs."

"Aw, but that will save us from his shenanigans."

"It's a no." Still not looking at him, I rummage through my duffle bag for a hoodie, then pull it over my head.

Preston parks his back against the locker next to mine, his stare turning icy, and his light mood shifts so fast, it's as if it were never there. He's the textbook definition of ASPD. He's been diagnosed with sociopathy, bipolar disorder, and a basketful of other mental issues. He's rumored to have killed his mother. A fact no one but himself can confirm or deny.

Preston has the reputation of Prince Charming. A heartthrob with golden hair and bright-green eyes. He loves girls and fucks anything in a skirt who's willing to choke on his cock.

But Preston, like all of us, is an expert at maintaining an image. He may even be the best at it. Because behind the heartthrob princeling personality hides a monster who loves to watch others suffer. While he rarely indulges in violence, he gets off on the sight of blood and the view of eyes going empty.

Whenever we've had missions to eliminate potential Vencor enemies, I've taken them out with a silencer. Jude usually beats them to death, which is messy and unnecessary. Preston, however, makes sure to stretch it out for as long as possible. With his knife.

He also really despises those who ruin his plans and aspirations and becomes a fucking lunatic when things don't go his way. He's not impulsive like Jude, but he's deadly.

I can sense the subtle change in his tone even as he smiles. "I will not have that piece of fucking shit sabotage my game against the Stanton Wolves, so if you won't do something about it, I will."

"Our game."

"What?"

"It's not your game against the Wolves. It's *our* game. And you can dream on about winning without Callahan. He's known as the strongest right wing in the league for a reason."

"You talking about me?" Jude strolls out of the showers with no towel, his scars and multiple striking tattoos on full display.

He's never cared about what people think of him or the looks he gets from other team members. He just wears his bloody past like a badge.

That's the difference between Jude and me. He displays everything that's happened to him. I don't.

"Armstrong suggested breaking your legs so you won't ruin our upcoming games, especially the one against the Wolves." I slam the locker shut. Time for my usual morning run before my first class starts.

"I'll knock your teeth out." Jude squares up to Preston.

The latter laughs and pats his shoulder. "Kidding. Just kidding, big guy."

"Better be. Touch me and you'll end up in a freak accident."

"Oh yeah?" Preston grins wide. "Want to bet your next game on it?"

"No betting." I stare at Jude. "Either you fix whatever is fucking with your head or I'll make sure you're benched for as many games as it takes."

He glares at me, his jaw ticking, but I walk out before he has the chance to reply.

I might have grown up with those two, but that doesn't mean there aren't skirmishes all the time.

Especially between Jude and Preston. One minute, they're protecting each other. The next, they want to kill one another.

Since our families are the founders of the town, our clans have often been at each other's throats to become dominant.

We've been taught not to trust each other and that the possibility of war is a matter of when, not if. We might be equals right now, but who knows what will transpire in the future?

Who knows whether we'll be at each other's throat in a struggle for the top?

Though it's impossible for us to seriously hurt each other, not after the pact we made after we were thrown into that nightmarish boarding school.

It's the three of us against the world, not the other way around.

But that's not my concern now.

My priority is to win. Keep the team in one piece and control the fucking liability that is Jude and the ticking time bomb in the form of Preston.

I trust he's smart enough to stay out of trouble, but for some reason, I feel like he'll fuck up big at some point.

So I have to clean up after them. As usual.

I've always been rational, calm, dependable Kane. Nothing can rattle my cage or shake my foundation.

My father made sure of that.

Now, I'm just a weapon at his and the organization's disposal. Or, at least, that's what he believes.

For the time being.

Preston catches up to me, knocking his shoulder against mine from behind, then lowers his head to whisper, "How about we poison him?"

"No."

"Only temporarily."

"No."

"Hear me out. You know that new drug his family is developing? He'd make the perfect testing subject."

"No."

"Fine. Then let's kidnap him and ditch him on an island."

"No."

"Lock him up?"

"He'll just smash the place and escape."

"That's true. Hmm. How about…" He abandons the thought and nudges me with an elbow.

I lift my head and pause, my left index finger twitching against my thigh.

Leaning against the wall by the entrance of the arena in tiny shorts and an oversized hoodie is the thorn in my fucking side.

The rock in my goddamn shoe.

"Well, hello again." Preston slides to her side, his charming grin on display. "Dallas, was it?"

"Dahlia," she answers, her attention remaining square on my face.

Dahlia Thorne is of average height with naturally tan skin and hazel eyes that look more brownish yellow than green in the dim light. Her brown hair is tied in a ponytail, highlighting her high cheekbones and round face.

The shorts stretch and cling to her skin, showcasing her curves.

Curves I haven't been able to erase from my mind since the night I marked and claimed her three days ago.

Since then, she's been showing up at my morning practices like a fucking parasite.

Always there.

Same time.

Same determined expression.

After the mental and physical torture, I thought she'd be broken a little, jaded a bit. Better yet, I believed she'd throw in the towel and run away. I would've even made an exception and allowed her to get away.

But no, she's been wearing that expression like a badge. And she's been randomly texting me.

And now what?

Hello?

Don't tell me you tested positive for an STD? I hate to say it, but I kinda told you so.

That was a joke. I didn't give you anything.

Um, so you kinda need some lessons in communication.

OMG. Thanks for the box of chocolates after the brutal fucking. Oh wait, you didn't send one. And they say romance is dead.

This whole thing is anticlimactic. What happens after getting in? Are there, like, any secret meetings I should be aware of?

All righty then. Guess I'll continue marveling at your spectacular communication skills.

I ignored all her blabbering, but that didn't stop her from appearing in person.

Like an incurable migraine.

"Dallas. Dahlia. Both have a *D*." Preston grins. "Speaking of dick, Kane's is not that impressive. Want a better experience? I have a full-enjoyment-guaranteed policy."

"I'll think about it," she says with a fake-ass smile, her attention still on me.

"Think fast. Limited spots available."

"Maybe one day."

"You won't regret it. Easily five out of five."

"I won't bet money on it."

"Ouch. You hit me where I give a fuck." He places a hand on his chest and feigns pain. "Now, I have to defend my dick's untouchable honor. How about tonight?"

I calmly walk between the two and jog away from the arena in the direction of a hill.

"Wait!" Her voice reaches me before I feel her frantic footsteps following me.

I pick up speed until the trees start to blur in my peripheral vision.

"Kane!" she screams, sounding out of breath. "Slow down, damn it."

I turn around and run backward. She's struggling to keep up, her limbs shaking and her face redder than the fall leaves scattered on the ground.

"Why should I?"

She heaves but doesn't stop. "Because I woke up this early to talk to you?"

"Not my problem."

"I thought I was since I'm under your care and all that."

"Supervision."

"What?"

"Under my supervision, not care."

She slows to a halt and bends, hands on her knees, but when she sees I'm still running backward on the hill, she groans and picks up speed.

"Okay, so what do I do under your supervision?"

"Nothing. Disappearing would be a good start."

"What the hell do you mean by nothing? Aren't you the one who's supposed to teach me the workings of Vencor?"

I stop abruptly and she collides with me, her head bumping into my chest.

"Ow." She releases a moan of pain, her ragged breathing filling the quiet forest.

Her soft curves mold to my hard muscles, and I get a flashback of her cunt stretching to accommodate me, tightening and milking my cock—

No.

I don't think with my dick. *Ever.* I don't even use my dick to settle scores the way Preston does or to relieve aggression like Jude.

It's only a weapon used to exert power. Nothing more.

And yet I say, "If you're dying for another taste of my cock, all you have to do is drop to your knees."

She jerks back, putting distance between us, but not before her spicy jasmine perfume fills my nostrils. Like a damn fucking poison.

I've been pricked by countless venomous snakes as part of my training, but none of them left a strong aftertaste like her scent.

She crosses her arms, the hoodie stretching against her breasts. "No, thanks. I'd rather not go through the ordeal of fucking you ever again."

My index finger twitches, but I let my lips pull into a smile. "Do you often squirt when overcoming ordeals, Dahlia?"

Her lips push forward and a fire erupts in her eyes, darkening like a reckoning. It's impressive that her feelings are written all over her face, but that's normal. I suppose.

"I was faking it. You know, to pass the test."

"You can fake an orgasm, yes, but you can't fake a squirt or the way your cunt swallowed my cock, strangling and milking me. Admit it, you were disappointed I didn't fill up your hole with my cum, weren't you?"

The longer I speak, the redder her cheeks turn and the more I want to push her, see her reaction.

See how far I can edge her to the brink.

And this isn't like me. At *all*.

I couldn't give two fucks about people's emotions. If anything, I use them through those illogical, untrained, and destructive feelings.

"You…you…" She points a finger at me.

"Yes?"

"You're a freaking machine."

"Is that supposed to be an insult?"

A delicate frown appears between her brows. "Are you really a robot? Should we do a captcha verification?"

"A captcha what?"

"Oh my God. You are!"

Her voice.

It's feminine, but not soft, and she doesn't speak in the cooing, fake-as-fuck tone some of the girls use so I'll fuck them.

She's in your face. Or mine, to be more accurate.

Everything just spills out of her as if it's a goddamn fountain.

And I'm starting to despise how freely she can act—the first thing I noticed about her is becoming a vexation.

"Go back to school and stop following me. It's giving desperate."

I turn around, about to resume my run, but, of course,

the fucking nuisance who's been shredding my peace jumps in front of me.

"Wait!"

"Change your mind? I'll let you suck my dick after the next game if I'm in the mood."

"No, thanks." She swallows, fighting against a blush or rage, I can't tell. "I just want to know what's expected of me. What's the point of being a Vencor member if I'm kept in the dark?"

"You'll be contacted if something is needed of you. Not the other way around."

She pauses and I can see the wheels in her brain working in overdrive. I like how she thinks before she talks. The time between thinking and speaking could be elongated, but it's a good trait.

It's also how I knew she was plotting to infiltrate Vencor. I'm not entirely sure why, but that's why I put on the whole fucking show to have her initiated.

Best way to watch a potential hazard?

Keep it under your thumb.

Squash it if it wiggles around.

Now, I didn't need to fuck her, but it's still a power bargaining chip and she didn't use her safe word, so it's game on.

Everything is a game.

She tucks a few flyaways behind her ear and I follow the motion. How her lean fingers outstretch. Her nails aren't painted and are cut short, but they somehow look elegantly neat.

Then she speaks again, trying—and failing—to sound detached. "How about meetings and stuff?"

"Stuff?"

"You know. Whatever happens in said meetings."

"Whatever happens in said meetings is not for Trial members. Unless you get invited by a Senior."

"Invite me, then."

I step close to her, erasing the distance between us.

My chest expands with her scent again, and I resist the urge to pluck the goddamn wildflower in her and crush it to pieces.

There was a time when I liked beautiful things. Now, I want them all ruined.

Trampled upon.

Reduced to dust.

Dahlia glances up, her plump lips parting, the bottom one slightly fuller than the upper one. As I look down at her, a choppy breath spills out of her slightly parted mouth and I notice a mole on the corner of her lip, tiny and barely there.

And now I'm staring at her lip.

I rip my gaze to her eyes, slightly wide. Expectant, even. "What will I get in return?"

"What do you want?" Her low whisper sends an electric shot down to my dick.

Jesus fucking Christ.

Despite my better judgement, I grab her chin with my thumb and forefinger, tilting her head back so that I'm invading those eyes. Preston has always said mine are unsettling, and I can tell she feels it as I stare her down for several long beats.

"If I say your body and soul, would you offer them?"

Her lips part again, the perfect opening if I want to thrust my cock down her throat, then decorate her face with my cum.

Again.

"Do I have a choice?" Her murmur is haunting, somewhat lifeless.

And I hate the gradual disappearance of her fire.

How she slowly withdraws into her shell.

"You always have a choice, Dahlia. The word is 'red'. It offers you a way out of everything except for Vencor. That one, once you're in, you only leave in a casket or if I deem you unworthy."

"If…" She swallows thickly, her eyes searching mine despite the subtle fear lurking beneath the light yellow. "If I offer myself, will you protect me?"

"No."

She flinches, her body turning stiff, and I should probably release her.

I don't do that, though.

Even as her heat mingles with mine, sending the wrong signals to my cock.

"Why not?" she asks.

"I don't get emotionally attached to the people I fuck."

"I don't either. So it's a win-win."

"Liar. You've been trying to play it down and pretend that what happened that day is normal, but here's the thing. You're acting tough. I know you're uncomfortable. Your jaw is clenched, your body's tight, and you're usually dressed in a way that doesn't draw attention to your body. You're terrified that I'll fuck you and use you again. The idea makes you tremble. And that trembling turns me on." I rotate her pale face in my fingers. "Your fight and suffering turn me on. It makes me *hard*. So, Dahlia, disappear from my sight before I break you."

I feel the exact moment that her survival instinct kicks in.

The moment I release her, she steps back, the leaves crunching beneath her sneakers. She stumbles, her wide eyes never leaving my face before she turns around and runs back the way she came.

Dahlia is smart enough to sense danger. At least, now she is.

She should've seen it before she decided to approach the organization.

Or me.

Because even though I just let her go, it's only temporary so that I can keep myself under control.

It's only a matter of time before I trap her again.

CHAPTER 10
Dahlia

THE DETECTIVE IN CHARGE OF VI'S CASE AGREED TO assign an officer to watch over her hospital room.

After I saw someone on the verge of hurting her—or worse, finishing the murder attempt—Detective Collins found clear evidence of tampering with the hospital's security system.

Someone disabled the hallway and elevator cameras for that specific time on purpose.

Detective Collins suspects that this was a seasoned hacker's work.

Unlike the DNA samples the police managed to gather from underneath Violet's nails, this time, no evidence was left behind.

That unidentified DNA sample is the only clue I have about the attacker.

Detective Collins said that there's a strong likelihood that the attack happened after an altercation. In the initial blood test, there was propofol in her blood, so she probably fought before she was sedated.

And that makes the case more complex and elusive.

In fact, the Stanton Hospital surveillance camera that showed the man in the van dropping off Vi didn't capture his face. It was covered by his hoodie when he laid her on the gurney and then jumped back into the van. We only assume he's a man, judging by his tall height and broad build.

There's a possibility he's the attacker, but he did save her by bringing her to the hospital, so that possibility is small. That man is still probably the only witness to what happened.

I asked the police to look into medical professionals or those with access to hospital drugs, because it struck me as weird that whoever sedated Vi went for an anesthetic agent instead of opioids or something more widespread in the market. However, Detective Collins made it clear that I had no place getting involved in the investigation.

Which is why I started my own revenge journey after seeing Violet's journal. In that journal, I found a few entries where she mentioned someone following her.

In one particular entry, she mentioned a black ring on his index finger with unintelligible symbols she couldn't see from far away.

Then she wrote 'them,' which made me think it's a group.

But the clear evidence that made me go after the Vipers were these words:

I saw him today. The man who's been following me. On the local channel in the bar where I work. I never watch sports or pay attention to what's on TV, but I did today, and he was there on the screen, in his hockey gear, glaring at the camera. Apparently, he plays for the Vipers, a college hockey team from the neighboring rich town.

But even with the clues Vi's journal gave me, my revenge isn't going well.

After Kane terrified the hell out of me in that forest three days ago, I've stayed away.

For some reason, I thought he would fuck me and then kill me, and no one would be the wiser.

So I've redirected my attention to Violet.

Every day, after I finish school and my part-time job at a local grocery store, I go to spend the night by her side.

I take my laptop and study most of the night while watching over her. It's been almost a week since that potential attack, and I've been surviving on three hours of sleep and nasty energy drinks.

Tonight, however, I have to trust the officer to keep her safe.

Because I'm going to a party.

"I can't believe you're finally living a little!" Megan hugs me to her side as we saunter up to Drayton's house in the town center.

Gavin Drayton is the Vipers' goalie and one of the insiders. He's also a Vencor member, judging from the serpent necklace I've caught a glimpse of a few times.

Following the team's away-game win, he's throwing an open-house party for the campus students and townspeople. And while Drayton is part of the system, considering his dad is the town's mayor, he's a small fish.

The actual powerful families hold the town and beyond in the palms of their hands, and they're usually more detached from the townspeople.

The Davenports are pioneers in a centuries-old trade business, and they handle an extensive imports and exports network.

The Armstrongs control energy production and resource management from oil to various alternative sources.

The Callahans own the largest pharmaceutical company in the country and other massive medical complexes, including the town's hospital.

The Osborns are the aces of real estate, construction, and urban development.

They're benefitting from each other while maintaining a monopoly in their respective fields.

"Thanks for letting me join and for lending me this," I tell Megan and tug on the tight little black dress.

The stretchy fabric clings to me like a second skin and barely covers my ass. The strapless design shows more cleavage than what I'm usually comfortable with.

But then again, I don't have party dresses, so I'm thankful to Megan. She even lent me a golden purse and spent about an hour doing my smoky eye makeup that highlights their hazel color and my bold red lipstick.

"Anytime. You look hot as fuck." She narrows her eyes at my white sneakers. "Would look hotter with heels, though. Too bad we don't wear the same shoe size."

Thank God. It'd be embarrassing since I don't know how to walk in heels.

The Draytons' house stands proudly in the heart of the town center. A massive colonial-style home that exudes old-money charm with its white columns, dark-green shutters, and perfectly manicured lawn.

As Megan and I step inside, the lively energy envelops my senses.

The walls are adorned with framed certificates, degrees, and old photos showcasing the Draytons' family history. The soft glow from crystal chandeliers overhead reflects off the polished hardwood floors, their surface so shiny, I can almost see my reflection.

The scent of freshly cut grass mixes with the smoky aroma of barbecue from the food stations set up on the lawn and visible through the large French doors. Laughter and chatter rise from the crowd of townsfolk and university students, creating a hum of excitement. The air is thick with the smell of expensive perfume, beer, and grilled meat, making my stomach churn as we navigate through clusters of people.

Bass-heavy music pumps through the speakers, vibrating the wooden floors, the subtle rhythm beating under my sneakers. The faint clink of champagne glasses being toasted echoes from a nearby gathering of local politicians and the university's elite, mingling in small groups.

Megan snatches two glasses from a well-groomed waiter and winks at him before she offers me one. "I fucking love rich people's parties."

I accept the flute of champagne but don't drink it. Since the creep who rented his attic room to Violet and I tried to drug us with his 'homemade' wine, I never consume anything that's not sealed.

My gaze flits over the crowd, trying to locate the hockey players. I see Drayton with his dad and the Vipers' management crew, but the rest don't appear to be nearby.

"Nice dress," a tall, slender girl tells Megan as she sashays to us with two other stunningly beautiful girls.

Her blond locks cover her shoulders, and her sparkling silver dress catches the gleam of the chandeliers.

"Thanks." Megan smiles, but it's tight.

"I hope you didn't pay much for it at the thrift shop. I donated it to charity last year." Blondie motions at me. "That one, too. I wore them better, but it's nice to see they found a new home."

Megan's face twists as if she ate something foul and she tries to pull on my hand, but I remain in place and plaster a smile. "Thanks for your charity. You're such a good person."

Her smile stiffens and nearly falls before she forces a

wider one. Her friends, however, don't hide their shock, their eyes throwing daggers in my direction.

"Please keep donating so we can wear nice things," I add with a blinding smile.

"What's your shoe size? I'll send you heels so you can dress appropriately."

"Thanks, but I can't handle heels. Heard they hurt and I'm not a fan of pain."

Megan squeezes my arm, and I think that's her cue for me to cut it out.

"Funny." The blond leans over and whispers in my ear, "Because you let Kane use you like a worthless rug. You looked like you were in pain, but maybe that's a whore's kink?"

My hand trembles around the flute of champagne and I stare at her with wide eyes.

She was there? I look at her again, but she's not wearing the ring or the necklace. Is she part of Vencor? How…?

It's her turn to smile as she pats my hair and murmurs, "You're a worthless, penniless piece of trash, but I'm willing to consider you charity. That's all you'll ever be. Don't look up. Don't covet what's not yours. Stay away from what's mine before I squash you beneath my diamond heels."

And then she walks away in a cloud of flowery perfume, followed by her two minions.

"Bitch," Megan mutters under her breath.

"Who is she?"

"Isabella Drayton. Gavin's twin sister. She comes from old money and thinks she has a monopoly over the team players, especially Kane. She's a snotty princess, so just forget about her."

But I can't.

Not after I know she watched the initiation video.

Just…how many people watched that damn video?

My skin prickles as I sense eyes observing me, and I can almost hear whispers of recognition and judgment lingering in the corners of the room. The air ignites with subtle oppression and heats the blood in my veins.

I should stop thinking about that video and the man attached to it. This isn't about me. It's about Violet's justice.

Soft fingers stroke my arm as Megan smiles at me. "You handled her well. Why are you so pale, D?"

"I'm fine." I force a smile.

"Is it because of the dress?" She stares down. "I told you I get them from everywhere…"

"No, I'm really thankful you even lent it to me. Don't ever be ashamed of not having money, especially because of her words. You're kind and stylish as hell, even more than she is. Besides, you're a better person than she'll ever be, Meg."

She grins and gives me a quick hug.

Sometimes, she reminds me of Vi. Vi's a bit more in touch with her emotions, although Megan does love hooking up, unlike my sister, who I think is scared of it. Probably because of all the creeps.

Megan meets some of her friends and I stand with them for a while until I spot some hockey players going outside.

So I use a trip to the bathroom as an excuse and head out.

Fairy lights twinkle against the deepening twilight, casting a warm, festive glow over the gathering crowd. The sound of laughter and chatter mixes with the steady hum of the nearby fountain, adding a sense of surreal detachment from the underlying tensions this town reeks of.

I subtly watch every single person while pretending to marvel at the garden.

That's when I spot Ryder Price, the Vipers' defenseman, walking away from the buffet table. I catch a glimpse of his black serpent necklace, which means he's a Vencor member.

I feign studying the food and I grab the fork he used to eat some cake and even licked clean before he left it on the plate. Then I hunch down, making a show of tying my shoelaces. After I ensure no one is paying attention, I cover up with a table's drape, retrieve the DNA kit I bought, and take a swab of the fork, seal it in a bag, and shove it in my purse.

I let the fork drop to the grass and stand up.

One down.

I shadow the other players, spying their necklaces. Though the only Senior members on the Vipers are the trio, Kane, Jude, and Preston. And while I spotted Preston with a girl on his lap and Jude with his coach, I haven't seen Kane.

Which is a blessing, really.

For some reason, I can't focus when he's around. And after our last encounter, a chill runs through me at the mere thought of him.

I manage to collect Declan Novak's DNA sample after he sneaks off to smoke and then throws down his half-finished cigarette when a teammate calls him.

Declan Novak, Ryder Price, and…that's about it. I haven't seen the other players who have necklaces. And I definitely don't want to risk it with Jude and Preston. Yet.

Hold on.

I'm in Gavin Drayton's house. Sneaking into his room is the easiest way to collect his sample. Maybe I can even get my hands on his sister's?

If she could see that video, she's probably part of Vencor.

After a once-over of the crowd, I go back inside and upstairs.

Though it's not as busy as downstairs, there are quite a few people in the lounge, which makes it easier to blend in.

The music's volume goes down, and the chatter is more prominent, bustling and mixing in a fake social cloud. I wonder if anyone is listening to what the other person is saying or if they just talk over each other.

Since I'm not sure where Gavin's and Isabella's rooms are, I pretend to study the ugly paintings on the walls. Though maybe they're ugly because I'm uneducated and can only see chaotic lines in unmatching colors.

Now and again, I open a door or peek through an ajar one to see what's going on.

Sex. Making out. Screams of "Fuck off!"

Yikes.

The things I traumatize myself with for justice.

I wander off down a quieter hallway, needing to bleach my mind of all the scenes I just witnessed.

I hear a few unintelligible voices.

My heartbeat picks up, and after I make sure the hall is empty, I tiptoe to the room where the noise is coming from.

"...is a loose end that needs tying up."

My eyes widen. That's Isabella's voice. No one else sounds as haughty as she does.

"You're letting it get under your skin. That's unlike you."

My heart thunders behind my rib cage and I flatten myself against the wall, wishing I could somehow disappear.

Kane.

That was definitely Kane.

I draw circles on my thumb, hoping, praying that my heart rate will slow the hell down.

"That's where you're wrong. This is exactly like her. She's jealous, vicious, and resembles a snake better than her necklace."

Preston.

When did he get here? I swear he was about to fuck that girl who was rubbing herself all over him less than fifteen minutes ago.

"I'm not asking for permission. I'll go against the Osborns and Serena if needed." Isabella again.

"Be reasonable," a third masculine voice says. I want to say it's Gavin, but I'm not sure.

"That's like asking a shark not to bite." There's vague amusement in Preston's voice.

"Izzy's right." A girl's voice. "Let us do this our way."

"Truly, I don't mind. The crazier the better. Just give me time to prepare my popcorn," Preston says. "Davenport?"

Though I'm not sure what the hell they're talking about, I'm certain it's about Vencor, and I find myself leaning closer with bated breath to hear Kane's reply.

I suspected it before, but now I'm positive he has some leadership role. Not only as the head of the Vipers, but also their little group.

He's the right path to follow, if only I weren't so terrified of him.

A strong hand lands on top of my head. "What do you think you're doing?"

I slowly look back and my gaze clashes with Jude's glacial one. His eyes are so dark, there's barely any light in them. He's so tall and wide, he dwarfs the hallway and sends a shiver down my spine.

It might be because Jude was always the scariest—before I was introduced to Kane's true colors—but I feel like he might actually crush my skull between his fingers just to spill my brains out.

He sure glares at me as if he wants to put me six feet under.

"I was looking for the ladies' room," I say as calmly as possible, proud of how confident I sound, considering the circumstances.

His upper lip lifts in either a snarl or a look of disgust—I'm not sure which—but he pushes the door open and shoves me inside.

I lose my footing and land on my knees on the decorative Persian carpet, but I manage to keep my purse on my shoulder.

"Found this one eavesdropping outside." Jude strolls across the room and I instantly feel several pairs of eyes zeroing in on me.

Glaring.

Narrowing.

I raise my head and, sure enough, Kane is sitting on a large brown sofa, his arm stretched across the back. He's dressed in a black jacket, pleated slacks, and sneakers. Only the white shirt offers a break from the dark-lord aura.

Isabella sits beside him, her arm draped in his, and her malicious eyes nearly drill a hole in my face. Her two friends stand behind her like dutiful guards, while Preston sits on the edge of the sofa. Gavin is lounging in a chair and Jude goes to stand by his side.

Seven pairs of eyes.

They all watch me closely. The room's dim lighting casts a shadow of threatening intent on their features.

My skin tightens, heat erupting between my heart and rib cage.

All of a sudden, I'm transported to the initiation night

when I was surrounded by five cloaked Members. The same Members who probably saw the sex I had with the man sitting in the middle.

"What the fuck are you doing here?" Isabella's friend, the one with silver highlights, asks.

I start to get up, trying and failing not to tremble. "I was looking for the restroom. It was a mistake—"

Before I can stand, Gavin jumps up and pushes me back down so hard, I gasp.

He shoves his shoe against my back, flattening me against the green-patterned beige carpet. "Haven't you heard? There are some mistakes you pay for with your life."

My lips part, but I don't dare make a sound. Not even when I feel the sole of his shoe digging a hole in my back where the edge of my dress meets my skin. Or when my breasts hurt from being squashed into the floor.

I look up at Kane, and I don't know why.

He's never been on my side, and he's made that clear countless times.

If anything, I should fear him the most.

There's an icy calculating look as he looks down at me, as if I'm a bug he's considering whether or not to squash.

"Now." Preston smiles, but it's dripping with malice. "Don't go scaring Dalton. I still haven't fucked her yet."

"How about you do it here and now?" Isabella says with a viper-like grin as she strokes Kane's arm. "Wouldn't be her first time whoring around for the world to see."

"I'm happy to join in," Gavin says in a deep voice. "I wonder what made her so appetizing that Davenport refused to share."

My eyes sting and I feel like anything I say will be a choked sob, so I bite my lip and remain silent.

It's not like they'll listen to my protests. I have to save my energy to be able to fight and escape.

Kane rises, forcing Isabella to get her claws off of him.

He doesn't look at me as he calmly but decisively places a hand on Gavin's shoulder and pushes him away.

I inhale large gulps of air and stumble to a standing position, hugging my purse close to my chest.

But before I can make another move, Gavin grabs my arm and smiles. "Come on, Kane. You got to use the bitch. Time to share."

My arm hurts from his forceful touch, and the more I pull away, the harder he squeezes. I think he'll break it, but then his hand disappears.

Kane snatches Gavin's arm and twists it against his back as he stands behind him. With the height difference, he towers over him as he speaks low, close to his face. "What I use is mine and mine alone. I don't share my toys. Are we clear?"

"Fuck! Let go. You'll break my arm."

"After that, it's your dick's turn."

"Davenport." Preston slides to his side. "He's our goalie."

"Our goalie would know his fucking place, now, wouldn't he?"

His words are calm. So calm, they're chilling.

Isabella's face twists in an ugly expression as she rushes to her brother. "Kane, let him go! Why are you hurting Gav for this bitch? She's not even—"

"Shut your mouth, Isabella." His words are deep and final.

Forget Isabella, even I flinch, hoping to find a hole I can crawl into.

"Out," he orders, throwing Gavin at Preston. "All of you out. *Now*."

Isabella's friends run out of there as if their asses are on fire. Gavin, Jude, and Preston are next.

Isabella is the one who lingers behind, her face red and her breathing choppy.

He merely looks at her with his signature composed expression that could crumble mountains. "Waiting for an escort?"

"You can't be serious!" She points a finger in my direction. "She's an outsider. This bitch is a fucking *outsider*!"

"Call her a bitch again and I'll cut out your tongue."

I flinch. Again. As if I've been hit by lightning.

Isabella trembles all over, her legs barely holding her upright, but she stomps out of the room after stabbing me with one final glare.

Everyone, and I mean every single one who left, looked at Kane as if he were an alien before they exited.

The room is charged despite their absence. Hell, it's even more stifling than when they were all here.

My survival instinct kicks in and I slowly inch toward the door. The sooner I get out of here, the better.

I didn't sign up for dealing with this side of Kane tonight. No matter what this side is.

The moment I open the door, a hand slams it shut from behind and an oppressive warmth covers my back as Kane's deep voice fills my ears. "Where do you think you're going?"

CHAPTER 11
Dahlia

MY NAILS DIG INTO THE STRAP OF MY BAG.

My teeth sink into my bottom lip.

And I draw countless circles on my thumb in an attempt to properly breathe.

In.

Out.

You know how to breathe. Remember how to breathe.

But no amount of comfort movements dispels the tension sinking in my stomach.

"I'm just leaving." I speak clearly, though my voice is low. "Didn't you ask everyone to get out?"

"Not you."

My heart jumps, and I really, really hate my body's reaction to his words.

No. To his voice.

Rough, deep, and so close, I feel the vibration of his chest against my back.

He doesn't even yell, but it's commanding nonetheless. He has this impressively monotone volume that never rises or drops. But maybe that's why it's terrifying.

I've witnessed exactly what Kane is capable of, so his calm, agreeable image is now disturbing instead of intriguing.

Since his arm is above my head on the door, blocking my exit, I figure escaping isn't an option. After one last circle on my thumb, I spin around.

He's close.

Too close. His chest hovers near mine.

So close, I can breathe alcohol and mint off his lips.

This close, I can see the dark rings that circle his frosty-blue eyes.

So inhumanly close, I'm trapped by the warmth his body emanates, like a gateway to hell.

So unsettlingly close, my legs squeeze together out of a strange need to protect myself.

And the most infuriating part is that I can't read his expression.

Or lack thereof.

Like a blank board, his face is neutral and his eyes are muted, almost as if he's bored with the entire ordeal.

I wonder if he has this same expression while fucking.

No.

Why the hell am I thinking about Kane and sex?

I lift my chin. "What do you want?"

"What do *you* want?" There's a flare in his nostrils, a hardening in his tone that turns authoritative and firm.

"Me? You're the one who imprisoned me here."

"You're the one who keeps appearing in front of me. Again and again. Despite my clear warnings. So tell me, Dahlia, do you lack survival instinct, or do you have a twisted kink about dying young?"

"I didn't mean to appear in front of you tonight."

"Is that why you chose to attend a victory celebration party for *my* team? Or why you were snooping around business that doesn't concern you?"

"It's not that I wanted to be here. I was invited by a friend."

"An invitation you should've refused." He kills the distance between us and his chest grazes my breasts that suddenly grow heavy. "But you've never been good at refusing invitations, have you? You seem to always land yourself in a clusterfuck by just existing."

"Don't insult me." I don't know how my words come out coherent when I'm drowning in his scent. When his mere touch is sending me into flight mode.

But I'm standing.

Here.

Facing him.

As foolish as that sounds.

I've just never been good with people belittling me. It's often gotten me into more shit than I can afford, but I refuse to be trifled with.

Kane peers down at me, a mocking glint appearing in his eyes. "Or what? You'll offer your services to someone else?"

I raise my hand and slap him.

My palm stings and I immediately know I fucked up.

So when he lifts his hand, I close my eyes, waiting for the slap. I almost forgot he said that if I hurt him, he'll hurt me as well. Without holding back.

I brace myself for the hit, but what comes is the soft drop of his fingers on my chin. I slowly blink my eyes open and my lips part.

Kane's clutching my jaw like he did in the forest. His thumb and index finger are stretching across the skin, squeezing just enough to keep me immobile.

He's studying my face with utter fascination, as if he's never seen me before.

As if I'm a foreign being he's attempting to figure out.

"Why did you slap me?" he asks, his fingers stroking my cheek in what seems like a doting gesture, but is actually locking my muscles.

"Because you disrespected me," I whisper, holding on to my silly pride.

"Do you slap everyone who insults you?"

"If I can reach them, yes."

"You didn't slap Gavin and Isabella when they called you a bitch."

"I didn't get the chance since you kicked them out."

"Would you slap them if I called them in again?"

I purse my lips.

"You wouldn't," he announces as if it's a given. "Do you know why?"

"Because Gavin is stronger than me and can kill me?"

"I can kill you, too, but that didn't stop you. Want to know what I think is the true reason behind your actions?"

"No."

"I'll tell you anyway. Their words didn't get under your skin. Mine do." He swipes his thumb over my bottom lip, back and forth, back and forth like a curse. "Interesting."

"That's not true." His thumb grazes my lips and teeth, and he watches the motion.

I'm more taken aback by how my words sound like a lie to my own ears.

Kane's eyes remain on my mouth, watching with intense attention, as if he's in the midst of solving a math problem.

My lips tremble despite my attempts to remain calm.

"Don't." His voice deepens, forcing goosebumps to erupt on my skin.

"Don't what?"

"Don't tempt me."

"I'm not doing anything."

"You're shaking."

"Shaking?"

"I told you, didn't I? Your fear turns me on."

He thrusts his leg between mine, forcing me to part my previously locked thighs. My eyes widen at the feel of his very thick, very hard cock, hot and heavy against my naked flesh.

Memories of being fucked by this very same cock makes me shudder. It doesn't matter how long ago it happened. My body resurrects at the thought.

The other night, after he warned me off in that forest, I had a dream about him fucking me against a tree and woke up with my hand buried in my wet folds. I took a cold shower right after and promised to find another path and not get close to Kane again.

He's dangerous.

And not because of what he's capable of, but because of my reaction to him.

Because instead of being scared of him and the satanic organization he belongs to, all I keep thinking about is the blinding pleasure I felt in his ruthless arms.

Yes, fear still exists, but it's definitely not the only emotion I have toward this man.

I clench my stomach and my thighs, trying to harden my resolve and not be affected.

A deep, rough noise leaves his throat.

"Stop moving. Unless you're going to open your mouth and let me fuck your throat until I decorate these red lips with my cum."

My pussy pulses and the body-tingling sensation I had after that dream rushes back to the surface.

"You're sick," I whisper, though the words could also be directed at myself.

"I'm well aware. Which is why I warned you. Over and over again." He maneuvers his leg so that I'm sitting on his thigh. My dress bunches up to my waist, revealing my black panties.

Then he moves until his dick presses against my underwear, provoking deep pressure. I resist a moan. God, that feels so good.

"And *again*." He rolls his hips and thrusts again.

Even though clothes separate us, my pussy clenches, demanding to be filled. I've never been sexually frustrated, but I think that's exactly what's happening right now.

"But you don't do well with warnings, do you? You're a little rebellious wildflower that thinks it can survive anywhere. But guess what?"

He drives his hips forward, harder, rubbing his clothed cock against my starved pussy as he holds my face with both hands, forcing my eyes to remain on his.

It's a different invasion from the one below. He might be dry humping me, but his icy eyes…those are fucking my soul.

"I'm your winter, Dahlia. No flower can survive winter. Not even wildflowers."

I grab onto both of his wrists as he thrusts into me with blinding precision, rubbing his cock and thigh against my sensitive clit. My back hits the door from his vicious power, and I feel the inexplicable need to grab harder for balance. To feel all of him plowing into me, igniting the sharp tingles of pleasure inside me.

God. I think I'm broken.

I thought I wanted gentle, caring, and a lot of prep to be aroused, but it turns out, I need rough, filthy, and completely unapologetic sex.

The fact that Kane takes what he wants without asking for permission makes me dizzy.

Hell, it makes me wetter.

"Lower your hands," he orders in a rough voice.

I release his wrists and hold on to his waist beneath the jacket instead.

And pause.

Because I'm touching the definition of rock.

Was he this muscular before? Despite his lean waist, he's so toned.

"Dahlia..." The warning rolls off my skin as if he's licked me. "Don't touch me."

"You're touching me, too." I dig my nails into his skin, refusing to let him go.

His movements slow down, and I nearly scream in frustration. "Stop touching me or I'll leave your wet cunt unsatisfied."

My libido wins and I let my hands drop from his waist and press them to the door so I won't instinctively grab onto him. He doesn't seem to be a fan, despite the fact that he's all over me.

Hell, he's holding my face hostage. But I suppose there's a difference between his and my touch.

Mine is softer, seeking some form of connection. His is all about power, control, and absolute dominance.

He rubs his dick up and down my wet cunt, his movements long and steady, never turning frenzied or unrestrained.

His breathing is deeper, his touch is stronger, but he seems to be in complete command.

I, on the other hand? My pants fill the space, and holding in the small noises that rip out of me is beyond my reach.

"You're soaking wet for someone who swore to never

want to be fucked by me." His gruff voice fills my ears and penetrates my skin.

"Physical reaction." I try to sound normal, but my voice is hoarse and ends in a moan as the rhythm intensifies.

"Physical reaction?"

A tinge of fury rolls off him and seeps beneath my skin.

There's a long and deep retreat before he rams me into the door.

I think I'll come then and there.

But I don't, so I provoke him. "Yeah, anyone could do it."

"Anyone, huh?"

I think I see a muscle jump in his jaw, but it immediately disappears when he glides his cock so fiercely, a swell builds, overtaking me.

My eyes close, mostly because his are so intrusive that I feel like I'm going to burst under their scrutiny.

"Do you ride just anyone, wildflower?"

My thighs clench and I realize I've been shamelessly rubbing myself against his leg, faster and harder, needing the release more than my next breath.

Part of me is horrified that I even want this. That Kane can arouse me like no other man has been able to.

The very idea of Kane stirs a part of me I didn't know existed. My panties are damp and the texture of his pants creates delicious friction against my sensitive skin.

My thighs quake and my legs part farther, as if I can invite him to thrust into me through the layers of clothes.

The wet rubbing sound saturates my senses, and I shudder as my pussy tightens and a surge swells and expands until I can't think straight.

"Open your eyes. Look at me when you come on my cock."

I slowly stare at him. This close, with his hands around my cheeks and his piercing eyes seeing into my soul, I lose the battle.

In fact, I don't even feel it rushing in.

The orgasm comes crashing in, heightening and flowing through my entire body.

My legs lock around his, and I wrap my arms around his waist as I ride the blinding pleasure, fractured moans slipping out of my lips.

The release goes on and on, and although it's not as intense as when he fucked me on the ground, it's a close second. Probably because there was no penetration.

Jesus Christ.

Why am I thinking about penetration?

"I told you not to touch me." He releases my face and steps back.

I'm forced to drop my hands from his waist, my mind still floating in a pleasure haze. "I didn't mean to."

"Is that so?" He places a hand on top of my head, stroking my hair, then shoves me down. "Such a beautiful liar."

My knees meet the carpet, and I choose to believe the thud in my chest is due to the orgasm and not because he called me beautiful.

The sound of a belt unbuckling reaches me before I stare up. My mouth dries and the tingling in my pussy heightens to a painful throbbing.

Kane releases his huge cock lined with angry veins and strokes himself in one rough movement.

I almost forgot how big he is.

Almost.

He grips his dick in front of my mouth as if it's a weapon and I swallow thickly. His left hand bunches in my hair, gathering it in a ponytail and using it to tilt my head back. "Did you paint these lips red for me?"

I shake my head once, somehow enchanted.

He taps the crown of his cock against my mouth. Once. Twice.

"Hmm. Then who's this red lipstick for?"

His precum paints my lips and trickles inside until I taste the saltiness on my tongue.

"Doesn't matter." He slaps my mouth with his cock. "I'll mess up and use these red lips anyway. Open."

My throat dries, and, as if hypnotized, I let my mouth part.

I tell myself that after what I overheard tonight, it's useless to get close to anyone else. He's clearly the strongest member of the team and probably on campus.

I can get close to him and use him through his libido.

But the truth is, I'm starving for a taste.

I've never been a fan of oral or blowjobs, but this feels different.

Surreal.

Almost as if I want to do everything with this enigma.

Whenever I've given a blowjob before, it was only because I felt like I had to. Because guys need their cocks sucked to get in the mood.

Not now.

Now, my thighs are rubbing together at the prospect.

Kane thrusts inside my mouth. "Wider. Stick your tongue out."

I do, trying to accommodate him, but he's big both in length and girth. My jaw hurts, and it's a task to keep my teeth out of the way, but I manage to fit a considerable amount one inch at a time.

"You're taking my cock so well. You'll let me fuck your face and come down that pretty throat, won't you, Dahlia?"

My ears buzz whenever he calls my name in that slightly husky tone.

My response is to lick him and grab the base with both hands, twisting and matching the rhythm with my tongue. Now and again, I pull him out to lick and suck on the head.

Just because I've never liked blowjobs doesn't mean I'm not good. I look up at Kane as I lick, twist, and jerk off his hardening cock.

The darkening look in his eyes makes me more enthusiastic. Hell, it turns me on.

And I know it turns him on, too, because he keeps thickening in my hand.

"Who taught you to suck cock like that?" he asks, his voice low and gravelly.

"Mmm," I speak against his flesh, then kiss the tip and suck on it. "You like it?"

He tugs on my hair until pain erupts on my scalp. "No. I'm about to fall asleep."

My heart falls.

He pushes my hands from his dick and grabs it. "Open your mouth."

I do and he thrusts all the way back, gagging me. Tears spring to my eyes, and I think he's done playing and will get rid of me now.

"That's it." I feel him growing thicker and harder. "This is the proper way to take my cock."

A ringing fills my ears, and I feel like I'm going to faint, but he pulls out. I splutter and choke on my saliva and his precum, but his firm grip on my hair doesn't allow me to move.

"Again. Open."

I pant, but I follow the command. I don't want to owe him for that orgasm, and I definitely don't want to seem like a quitter. I can offer him the same pleasure he gave me.

My lips open of their own volition as I hold on to his thighs.

Another deep thrust, and this time, the tears flow down my cheeks as he fucks my throat, my face, my mouth, making me gasp and gurgle. He uses my tongue for friction, driving into me with so much dominance, I'm dripping wet.

There's no reason I'd be so aroused when he's using me, but I think *that*'s the reason.

The fact that he's using me as a vessel for his pleasure ignites a strange sensation inside me.

"You look so fucking beautiful on your knees, wildflower." He thrusts in and out, forcing me to look up at him. "You're choking on my cock so well. Mmm. Good girl."

My heart surges and I think his words will make me orgasm or something equally ridiculous.

His rhythm picks up, his hoarse, deep groans echoing in the room, and I watch with utter fascination as he throws his head back, his eyes closed, like a sex god.

His cum shoots down my throat, thick and long.

"Swallow," he orders. "Every last drop."

I try my best, but I can feel streaks of cum trickling down either side of my mouth.

Kane pulls his cock out of my mouth, and to my horror, it's still half erect.

He hits me with it on the mouth. "Lick it clean."

I grab him at the base and lick the skin, swiping my tongue over his length and sucking the tip into my mouth while maintaining intense eye contact. I probably continue the show longer than necessary.

Kane watches me the entire time, his eyes darkening, his finger twitching on the back of my head.

Then, all of a sudden, he pulls his dick from my grip, tucks himself in, and buttons his pants.

The motion takes me by surprise, so I just sit there and watch, my ears still filled with a dizzying buzz and my head floating somewhere else.

Kane lowers himself on his haunches in front of me, and I stare at him, panting. He seizes my chin and before I can think of what he's doing, he leans in and swipes his tongue from the corner of my mouth to my left eye.

Then he does it again on the right side, his tongue leaving tingles and goosebumps behind.

Is he…licking my tears?

What the…?

He stands up, shoving his hands in his pockets. "Don't cry. It makes me hard."

CHAPTER 12
Kane

THE DRIVE TO MY PARENTS' HOUSE IS QUICK AND NEARLY mindless.

I push my Porsche 911 Turbo S to its limits up the Hill, but I have full control over the vehicle. Which can't be said about the rest of the fucking night.

My fingers tap against the steering wheel as the house looms like a shadow at the top of Ravenswood Hill—an isolated fortress hidden deep within the trees.

The long, winding driveway is flanked by towering oaks, their branches stretching overhead like skeletal fingers. The car's tires crunch against the gravel as I approach my old asylum, the sound muted under the oppressive weight of the night. The air is thick with the scent of damp earth and pine, mingled with a faint metallic tang that always lingers in the forest.

I kill the engine and step out of the car. Cold bites into my skin, the crisp night air sharp against my face. My breath forms clouds in front of me as I walk toward the house, the soft thud of my shoes on the stone path the only sound breaking the silence. I've made this walk countless times, but it still feels like willingly getting trapped in a cave.

As soon as I got into college, I bought a penthouse in the

town center just to distance myself from this hellhole, but one can't escape his last name.

Or the fuckery that comes with it.

The Davenport compound is an expansive mansion made of dark stone, ivy crawling up its weathered exterior like veins. Its windows are black voids, reflecting nothing. The front door is heavy, creaking slightly as I push it open. Inside, the air is cooler and restrictive. The scent of aged wood and leather fills my nostrils, familiar yet suffocating.

Every stone of this house has witnessed generations of power-hungry, duty-bound, and control-freak Davenports. Their portraits line the long hallway I'm walking through, a reminder of the generational wealth and souls sold to the Devil.

The dim orange lighting casts eerie shadows along the walls, the weight of my ancestors' hollow gazes pressing down on me with each step.

I pause by a tall window that overlooks the dark expanse of the Japanese garden below and the forest in the distance. The rustle of leaves and the occasional hoot of an owl drift into the hall. My reflection stares back at me, expressionless and distorted in the glass, like the perfect machine I've been shaped into.

No emotions.

No fucking attachment.

No other human being is allowed to have a hold on me.

No. One.

"Kane?"

I slide my left hand into my pocket and slowly rotate to face the woman who gave birth to me.

She's dressed in a white silk gown and a matching robe, her ghost-like appearance fitting the house.

Helena Davenport was a striking beauty in her youth but now carries the weariness of a life spent in quiet suffering. Her once-lustrous dark hair has thinned and gradually turned silver at the scalp. It's swept into a simple but elegant bun, a remnant of her former sophistication. Her almond-shaped eyes, icy blue like mine, rarely show emotion, as though the weight of her depression has drained her ability to feel.

She walks silently toward me, her posture always slightly hunched as if burdened by invisible chains. Helena is slender but frail, as though a gust of wind could shatter her. Unless she's forced to by social obligations, she seldom engages with the world outside her private quarters, where she often remains hidden, staring at the same old book she never finishes or talking to the koi fish in the garden pond.

"Hello, Mother." I paint a smile on my face and bend down so she can hug me.

Her bony hand taps my back with no emotion. When she speaks, it's slow, as if every word is a hassle. "It's been a long time since I last saw you. You grew up and became so handsome."

"Thank you, Mother."

"Call me Mom like when you were young."

"It'd be better not to."

Her shoulders droop, but she doesn't fight it or even insist on it.

Though her beauty has faded, there's still a delicate grace to her movements, a hollow reflection of what she used to be. My mother's chronic depression has rendered her emotionally absent, her once-kind spirit dulled by years of belonging to the system.

I used to think Helena was different. She loved me and showered me with the affection her husband was incapable of, but then she retreated into her shell and left me for the sharks.

At the age of six.

After that, I stopped calling her Mom or thinking of her as a mother.

She's just another pawn in their game.

"Honey." She places her hand on my arm and it's like being touched by a ghost. "Mom is sorry."

"I know."

"I couldn't do anything about it."

"I know."

"Do you blame me?"

"No."

"Are you just saying that to placate me?"

"Of course not."

Her gaze grows blank, shadows settling within. "You speak just like your father. I don't like it."

I pat her head like she did when I was six—after I was waterboarded in Father's dungeon to near death—and say the same sentence she said to me then, word for word. "You'll get used to it."

A sob tears from her throat as I walk past her.

If I were the same Kane from fifteen years ago, I would've stopped and consoled her. I would've taken her to the garden to watch the koi fish or brought her flowers.

But my ability to excuse her for not being able to protect me or to feel sympathy for her plight has long been stripped from me.

My mother is just an unfortunate woman who got caught in the jaws of power.

She gave birth to a weakling—me—and my father made sure to fix it.

I knock on a dark mahogany door and then push it open.

A drink in hand, my father's tall figure is standing by the floor-to-ceiling window. He's dressed in a tailored gray suit, his back straight and his posture upright, unlike the wife he broke.

He tilts his head in my direction, and it's stunning how much I look like him. Same hair, same eye shape, same bone structure. The only difference between us, other than his grim gray eyes, is the creases of age in his face and his thin lips, which are always in a disapproving line.

Grant Davenport has always been my warden, not my father.

"Kane. You're here."

"You called."

He walks to the liquor cabinet and pours me a drink, the amber color glistening under the study's yellow lights.

My father offers me the malt whiskey, then takes a seat on the brown leather sofa and motions at the chair across from him.

I sit down, my legs far apart, projecting the commanding, relaxed posture he engrained in me through years of torture.

"Is there a reason behind my presence here, Father?"

"I can't ask to see my son?"

"You can, but you don't usually. If there's a purpose, I'd appreciate it if we could reach it."

A slight smile tilts his lips. "You're a true Davenport."

I hold my glass up. "I'll drink to that."

The alcohol tastes like fucking urine down my throat, but I keep up the façade he made sure I'd wear like a second skin.

"I'll cut to the chase." Grant leans forward in his seat

and swirls the alcohol in his glass. "The Osborns are making a move."

I raise a brow.

This town was founded by four families: Davenport, Armstrong, Callahan, and Osborn.

For centuries, we held a monopoly on the town, its politics, and people. Not only that, but we made sure to extend our influence to the rest of society.

It's why Vencor exists. Once you're backed by the extended wealth and connections the organization offers, your and your offspring's future is set.

This is why we attract many businessmen, politicians, and the scum of humanity.

However, what the outsiders don't know is that there has always been an internal rivalry between the four founding families. Each of them wants to rule, to cripple the other families and take hold of the reins.

Reputation is important, so one family has often publicized the other families' scandals to ruin their social standing within the town and encourage/incite a member vote to restrict their influence.

When we were the target of such an attack less than a year ago because of my uncle who was caught on camera fucking a man, my dad banished him from the family and the state.

Homophobia runs deep in this town, and no gay members are allowed in. Doesn't matter in what day and age we live. If you're not straight, you're not respectable.

Cheating like a champ is okay, though. Grant dipped his dick in all the pussy available and is considered a 'real man'.

Fucking morons.

At any rate. My uncle's sexcapades, though they were dealt with mercilessly by my father, still hurt the Davenport standing. Because he didn't kill him.

I kid you not, my uncle was expected to die for preferring dick over pussy. Talk about the Middle Ages.

My father didn't spare his life out of brotherly love. He doesn't have that emotion. It was more because he's categorically against spilling Davenport blood. It's a bad omen.

Also, my uncle controls the strongest arms of the Davenport trade operation to this day.

And he has the protection of his boyfriend's mafia connections, so even the other families need to tread carefully before they lay a hand on him.

I take a sip of my whiskey. "What do the childless Osborns intend to do?"

"Bring back their bastard."

"Marcus?"

"Correct."

"I thought illegitimate children were a no-no."

"They are. Unless it threatens their line. Their children are either dead or dying. Marcus Osborn is the only healthy male heir."

"So they're completely eliminating Serena Osborn, the literal reason they still exist, just because she's…a woman?"

"Yes." My father's lips lift in a snarl. "Women have no place in leadership roles anyway."

Says the man who was threatened by some female members of the Davenport clan after my uncle's banishment, so he had them expelled from the country.

I swirl my glass as I lean back. "Marcus grew up like a

thug in Stantonville, and I'm pretty sure he won't accept the Osborns' extended hand after they threw him and his mom out on the street."

"They'll find a way to rope him back in."

"And you'll allow it?"

"Not if I can help it. However, if there's a general vote, we can't deny their rights to bring back a male heir. It's imperative we make a move before that happens."

"What do you suggest?"

"He's the captain of the Stanton Wolves, no? Make sure he doesn't entertain the idea. Captain to captain."

"He's not on my level."

"Then use someone to do the job for you. Jude or Preston or that Drayton girl who wants to marry you. Women are only objects to be used and an accessory to wear."

Fucking moron. "Noted."

"The Osborns can't get back their standing. Not after the Armstrongs crushed and diminished their power recently. Everyone else is meant to be beneath us." He stands up and pats my shoulder, his fingers sinking into the flesh. "Remember, Kane. No distractions."

Images of soft skin, blushed cheeks, and smudged lipstick replay through my mind like an old-grained movie. I can still feel her bright-red lips around my cock and see the mess I made of that lipstick once I was done with her. Her jasmine scent—delicate, haunting—lingers in my senses.

A renewed craving floods over me, and a hunger like I've never experienced gnaws through me.

I shouldn't have touched her again.

I shouldn't have lost control over a nobody.

And she is a fucking *nobody*.

But the way she looked at me, those hazel eyes filled with

a mixture of curiosity and defiance, provoked a primal part of me that I can barely repress.

But I'm done now.

I'm back in control.

"What do you think I am? An amateur?" I tell Grant with an expression that mirrors his.

He nods in approval, assuming we're on the same side.

We stopped being on the same side the day he stopped being my father.

Every man for himself.

After I become a Founder, I'll bring this man down.

One more year.

Just one more.

I've survived twenty-one years. One more is nothing.

So I truly mean it.

Dahlia Thorne will not be a distraction.

The next morning, I show up at psychology class.

That Dahlia also happens to take.

And no, I didn't find that out because she's a distraction. I'm just observant by nature and perceive a lot of things about a lot of people, even when they're ignorant of the fact.

For instance, Pres here is hiding something, and while I'm not sure what it is yet, I know it's big enough that he's slipping.

By slipping, I mean both Jude and I have been tightening our observation of his behavior. And that says something since Jude isn't in any better shape himself.

Preston and I are sitting near the back of the lecture hall as the rest of the students buzz around, their chatter whirling like insects.

"What are you even doing here?" he asks from my right,

twirling a black pen and winking at the brunette sitting in front of us.

I flip through the textbook as if I give any fucks. "I signed up for the class at the beginning of the semester."

"But you never attend."

"I am now."

"Why now of all times?"

"It's as good a time as any."

"Yeah, yeah. I bet your entirely *rational* decision has nothing to do with your irrational actions last night."

I pause, then slowly flip the page. Preston sent a string of texts to our group chat yesterday, gloating and being a general pain in the ass.

Which I ignored, naturally. And Jude entertained.

"There was nothing irrational." I skim through the words on the page. "It's all part of a plan."

Preston grins, his face transforming from docile to demonic in a heartbeat. "So you wouldn't mind if I become part of the plan and make my move?"

I lean back against the chair, and even though I appear relaxed, the chatter of the students dissipates and so do the girls' attempts to catch our attention and flirt.

"You made a move and she shut you down, Pres. Take a hint."

"That wasn't a move. That was a suggestion. You haven't even witnessed my real move." His grin widens. "Speak of the devil."

My attention zeroes in on Dahlia, who's walking into class with a few books in her hand and a tote bag slung over her shoulder. It has an image of a cat wearing sunglasses, and right underneath it, a few words are written in a playful font, "Fluff you, you fluffin' fluff."

What is this? Middle school?

And yet my gaze studies her, taking her all in as if she's a drug I'm inhaling deep into my lungs.

And I don't even do drugs.

Dahlia is dressed in jeans, a white T-shirt, a beat-up leather jacket, and her usual white sneakers. Her hair is loose, falling to her shoulders in soft waves, framing the infuriatingly determined expression on her face.

I hate that look.

I hate that she always has it, no matter what she goes through.

It's what makes me want to break her to pieces.

Smash her.

Ruin her so thoroughly, she'll never be able to stand up again.

See if she'll dare to ever look at me.

"You're drooling," Preston whispers, then waves. "Thorne! Over here, saved you a seat."

The entire hall stares at her.

It's unusual for any of the girls to get to sit with us. Isabella and her minions made sure of it. So they only approach if one of us calls them over.

Dahlia lifts her head and pauses, her forefinger tracing cryptic messages on her thumb.

Like a witch.

Wouldn't be surprised if she's capable of making potions of some sort.

Her eyes meet mine and she holds my gaze for one second.

Two…

Three…

On the fourth, she slides her attention to Preston and offers a rehearsed smile as she walks up.

Her steps are unhurried and confident despite the whispers and unwanted attention directed at her. She stops beside us, and instead of walking straight ahead and coming to the vacant seat by my side, she does a whole detour and goes to Preston's side.

My index finger twitches, but I focus back on the textbook and start to read gibberish about politics.

"Hi," she whispers, and I feel her gaze on me.

"Over here, lovely." Preston points at himself like a gigolo. "I'm the one who saved you the seat."

"Thanks."

"My pleasure. Anything for a beautiful lady."

I calmly turn the page, even though I didn't read a single word.

Preston can't die.

Dahlia is just a pawn.

"Listen," he continues. "Heard Kane is giving you a hard time. Forget about him. He's too rigid and aloof and doesn't know how to treat women. How about you come to me? You can join me and the team next Friday after the game as my personal guest. It's a super-exclusive party for the close circle."

I can feel her gaze on me again.

As if she's waiting for a sign, a word, or anything to help with her decision.

I offer nothing.

Let's see how desperate she really is.

"Stop looking at him. He wouldn't mind. Right, Kane?"

"I wouldn't." I lift my head and smile. "In fact, you should bring some of your old friends from Stanton River College. It would be so much more…interesting."

Preston pauses and stares for a few beats. "You went to SRC?"

She nods. "Yeah. I only came to GU this year."

"Not only did she go to SRC, but she also dated your favorite hockey player, Pres. Who was it again?" It's my turn to grin. "Right. Osborn. You should invite him to our get-together, Dahlia."

"I didn't really date Marcus," she blurts out. "We went out, like, twice and then figured we didn't click."

"But you kind of dated," I say. "That's all that matters. Right, Pres?"

Since our first game against the Wolves, Preston has despised Marcus's guts. Probably because Marcus checks him any chance he gets and doesn't care about being penalized. Something Preston does care about and, therefore, isn't as aggressive in his plays.

It also happens that, other than me, Osborn is the only hockey player in the entire league who's not ruffled by Preston's provocations that are delivered with a smile. Something that infuriates my friend to no end.

So what does he do? He tries to exploit as many of Osborn's weaknesses as possible just to bring him down. Doesn't matter what the score is between the Vipers and the Wolves, Preston and Marcus always seem to have their game inside the game. And it'll probably remain that way until Preston gets the clear upper hand.

He truly, thoroughly, and categorically refuses to walk away from a situation that doesn't go as he wishes. He might seem agreeable, but he's an insufferable son of a bitch when pursuing a goal.

And because of his distaste for the 'charity team,' as he calls the Stanton Wolves, he's beyond disgusted with Osborn's entourage.

It doesn't help that Marcus once stole Preston's girlfriend. Or sort-of girlfriend.

Since then, the moment Preston finds out a girl has slept with his rival, he immediately loses interest. Which is rich coming from Preston, who fucks any girl available.

So that makes Dahlia off-limits.

Permanently.

Dad was right. I'll use Preston against Marcus and Marcus against Preston.

A win-win.

"Is that so?" he asks with a smile, but his eyes are muted. "Why didn't you guys click?"

A frown appears between her brows. "He's kind of an asshole."

I narrow my eyes. Osborn did something to her.

What? I don't know, but I'll find out.

"So is Davenport." Preston grins. "But you already know that."

The professor comes in as Dahlia looks at me, opens her mouth, then closes it and stares at her notebook.

Preston pulls out his phone and focuses on it instead of class.

Me?

I keep watching the girl I swore would never be a distraction.

The girl who shouldn't be in this town in the first place.

My phone beeps and I retrieve it.

Dahlia: Why are you suddenly attending this class?
Kane: Do I need a reason to attend a class I'm enrolled in?
Dahlia: A class you've never attended.
Kane: I'm doing so now.
Dahlia: Are you stalking me?
Kane: Do you want to be stalked? Because I'm game.

A tinge of red covers her cheeks, and she shoots me a piercing glare. Too bad there's no red lipstick today, but any red will do.

Dahlia: I thought you wanted me out of your sight?
Kane: I changed my mind. Seems I have to watch you closely after all, my wildflower.

CHAPTER 13
Dahlia

THE DNA SAMPLES DON'T MATCH.

This applies to the three guys whose DNA I stole at the party.

Price's, Novak's, and Kane's.

So after he fucked my face and came down my throat three days ago, I kept some of his cum in my mouth and then bagged it.

I'd like to think that's the only reason I let him use me like a rag doll, but the throbbing between my legs at the time and long after I got home testify against that theory.

At any rate, the fact that his DNA wasn't present under my sister's fingernails was a relief I didn't know I needed until I stagger against the laboratory counter.

Damn it.

Is his innocence that important to me?

Why?

Because I burn for his touch? Because his mere presence unsettles me to the point of losing control?

That doesn't matter, though. I've had sex before. Sex is physical and doesn't mean anything.

So why the hell…?

I stare at the DNA result sheet and then tuck it into my

lab coat. The last thing I need is to lose this scholarship for performing illegal DNA tests. *And* targeting the town's hockey gods.

Everyone here seems obsessed with the team. Even Mrs. Hales was asking if I could get Preston's autograph since we go to the same college. Apparently, he's the most popular and effortlessly attracts everyone.

Kane is second because he's just so well-mannered and *dreamy*—Mrs. Hales's words, not mine.

Dreamy, my ass. He just wears the mask so well. Even I was fooled by him in the beginning.

Jude, on the other hand, is a dark horse on and off the rink. There's a brutality in him that only attracts a certain category of people. He also doesn't make an effort to wear a smile like Preston or a mask like Kane.

What you see is basically what you get.

Since he and the rest of the team are my next targets for the DNA hunt, I need to get closer to the team.

After that, I'll figure out a way to influence Kane to make me an active Vencor member. Thus far, he's shot down any of my attempts to be active in the organization.

When I tried to befriend Preston, Kane somehow managed to say the right words to make his friend lose complete interest in my company.

I knew that asshole Marcus was trouble. I should've never gone out with him in the first place. At the time, his last name didn't really mean much to me, and I didn't want to believe the rumors floating around about him and his dark past.

Little did I know that he's, in fact, a major psycho.

I'm not sure how Kane got that information about my dating life, and it's made me more paranoid.

Just how much does he know about me?

How long can I fool him?

Hell, can I even *fool* him?

With his unreadable personality and unpredictable actions, he's the one who fools people, not the other way around.

Still, the only way to get close to the team and him is to make him trust me.

At any cost.

He did defend me the other day at Drayton's party, so it's not like he doesn't care at all. It's a good start.

Though I believe he cares more about degradation through sex. Which I can *tolerate*.

Liar.

My thighs clench at the thought of it. And I'm truly struggling to come to terms with the fact that I enjoy something so sick.

A loud vibrating sound echoes on the empty laboratory table and I flinch out of my thoughts.

My posture straightens when I see the text. Why does the mere sight of his name make me hyperaware?

> Kane: You signed up for the motorcycle club.
> Me: Yes, and? Is this another announcement of your stalkerish tendencies?
> Kane: There's no stalking involved. I'm openly watching you. And you won't be going to the club.
> Me: Why not?
> Kane: Because you're only there for Jude, and I can see your little tricks from a mile away. Cut it out.
> Me: And if I don't?
> Kane: Then I'll have to act on my warnings.

I lean my back against the counter. Something must've hit me in the head since that initiation because I type:

Me: And how will you act on them?
Kane: Ask your sore cunt and bruised jaw. They know exactly how I react to disobedience.
Me: I forgot. Perhaps you didn't make that much of an impression.
Kane: Or perhaps if I were to come there and touch you, I'd find you dripping wet at the thought of being used by me, Dahlia. You're burning for it. I can see it in your eyes when you look at me.

He's right, but he doesn't need to know that.

Me: You're not that special. Trust me, I've had better dick.
Kane: Nice try. These little games don't work on me.
Me: No games. Just facts ;)
Kane: The only fact I know is that if I were to touch you, you'd melt in my arms. You're a slut for my cock, wildflower.
Me: And you're a simp for my pussy, but you don't see me stating the obvious.
Kane: You're just a hole I use. Nothing more.

My lips purse and I hate the slight thud behind my rib cage.

Me: No real holes were used during the making of this movie. At least, not in the past…couple of weeks. No wonder you're not that special.

Kane: Dahlia.
Me: Yeah?
Kane: I told you not to tempt me.
Me: I'm just having a civil conversation.
Kane: You're only civil when you're silent. Which happens when you're choking on my cock.
Me: You're such a pervert.
Kane: I know. I spent the last couple of days imagining your cunt strangling my cock as you screamed and cried. I want to see your tears again.

My hand trembles around the phone. This...sick asshole.

Me: Hard pass. I don't like pain.
Kane: Questionable. Anyway, come watch the game tomorrow. I'll send you a ticket.
Me: Why would I go?
Kane: I thought you were my fan, no?
Me: Maybe I changed my mind.
Kane: It's adorable to think you can.
Me: People change their minds all the time.
Kane: Be there.

Then he attaches a ticket for a seat at the very front. I've never sat at the front at any game, let alone for an extremely sought-after team like the Vipers.

Not that I will follow his order and go there just because he told me to.

So I came anyway.

Doesn't matter how much I despise Kane's attitude on

a personal level. I still need him to trust me and allow me to get closer.

I even bought his jersey from the merch store outside and gave myself a major eye roll.

Tonight's game is against the Blackhawks, one of the fiercest teams in the league and Michigan's reigning champion.

Vipers Arena is packed full of people gaping at witnessing two titans going at each other. They buzz with uncontained excitement every time there's contact.

The rink pulses with life, the roar of the crowd vibrating in the air like an electric hum, which slips into my bones.

The cold air bites at my skin, even through layers of clothes. Like everyone else, my attention is glued to the game. The sharp staccato of skates slicing the ice, the thud of bodies crashing together—it all melds into a chaotic symphony of power and violence.

However, the game isn't really on my radar.

I'm more focused on the man who commands the ice like a warrior.

Kane.

And I realize the way he plays is an accurate representation of his personality. He moves like a predator, calculating every motion with deadly precision. His tall frame cuts through the opposing players, his ice-blue eyes never leaving the puck.

There's something about the way he plays, his presence magnetic, impossible to ignore. His skates scraping against the ice is like a knife through my senses. The cold sharpness of his movements slices through the air, making my pulse quicken.

The puck glides across the ice, and Kane seizes it. His

stick connects with the puck in a single, fluid motion that makes the crowd go wild. Even I find myself leaning forward in my seat. Every muscle in his body seems attuned to the game, the way he owns the ice, the control he wields—it's intoxicating.

No. Terrifying.

There's a calmness to him, an authoritativeness that contrasts with the chaos of the game. Every time he moves, subtle power peeks from beneath the surface. He finally shoots, and it's a perfect strike, the puck slamming into the net with a sharp crack that sends the crowd into a frenzy.

Kane doesn't react. His face remains unreadable, cold, as he skates back to center ice, not acknowledging the cheers.

I think I see him glancing in my direction, but it's fleeting and probably a figment of my imagination.

"We meet again, Dahlia."

The low, disturbingly malicious voice sets my nerves on edge. I've been so focused on Kane, I didn't pay attention to my surroundings, so I didn't notice when a demon personified approached me.

"What are you doing here, Marcus?" I speak over the crowd's chaos.

He sits beside me when I swear the seat was occupied by an older lady not ten minutes ago. I consider moving to another seat, but the arena is packed full of people.

"Is that any way to greet me, sweetheart?"

"I'm not your sweetheart," I grit out from between clenched teeth.

He smiles, but it's predatory at best.

Marcus Osborn is an unsettling presence, a force of chaotic energy barely contained within his tall, lean frame. His angular face is sharp, with high cheekbones and a jawline that could cut glass, but it's his eyes that reveal the depth of his brutality. His dark, nearly black eyes are cold and hollow, yet there's a flicker of wildness within them, like a storm that's constantly brewing.

A thin scar slices across his right eyebrow, a constant reminder of the violence he both endures and inflicts. His lips, often set in a cruel smirk, hint at his enjoyment of the pain he causes and the thrill he gets from pushing others to their limits.

Like he once did to me.

"Is that why you're wearing Davenport's shirt? You sure know how to climb the ranks."

"What I do with my life is none of your business."

"I know. I'm just disappointed in your life choices."

"Better than the life choices you had in mind for me."

He smiles but says nothing.

I notice angry purple bruises on his knuckles. Though not as bulky as Jude, Marcus has a wiry, muscular build, and he's no stranger to physical confrontations, his preferred method of communication often being fists—or worse.

He's just bad news all around.

I trace circles on my thumb. "What are you doing here?"

"Watching the game. Like you."

"Is that all?"

"Yes. The Vipers and the Blackhawks are our rivals, remember? Or did you forget where you came from once you fraternized with the posh rich boys?"

I open my mouth to say something when the boards in front of me rattle with a violent impact. My eyes widen as they clash with Kane's. He just shoved a Blackhawks player so harshly, I'm surprised the boards didn't splinter to pieces.

He holds my gaze for a brief moment. Chilly,

expressionless—but something flickers there, something dark and intense that renders me motionless.

The referee doesn't call a penalty, and the Vipers snatch the puck back. Kane skates to the offense, resuming the fast-paced game.

"Hmm." Marcus scratches his chin as he watches me. "Interesting."

"What do you mean?"

"Davenport doesn't check violently. He's usually extremely sharp and intervenes in a clean way. I must say, I prefer this version of him."

I frown, but before I can consider Marcus's words, he waves at the rink and mouths something I'm not able to read in time.

When I follow his field of vision, I spot Preston glaring back for a fraction of a second before he skates with the puck.

Preston is a shadow on the ice. He doesn't crash or shove, but his presence is still felt. There's a smoothness to his movements, an effortless grace as he navigates the rink, weaving through players with ease. He's not loud or aggressive, but his style is lethal in its precision. Every pass and every play is strategic, as if he's thinking five steps ahead of everyone else.

While Jude crashes into the opposing players with a force that sends bodies flying into the boards, Preston avoids that at all costs.

"Hey, Marcus?"

"Hmm?" he says without taking his calculative gaze from the game.

"Do you know Preston?"

He tilts his head in my direction with a faint pull at the edge of his lips. "Why? He said he knows me?"

"No. But he kind of dislikes me since he found out we were together at some point."

A slow, malicious grin stretches his mouth. "Is that so?"

"Yeah. What have you done?"

"*Moi*? Nothing."

"You want me to believe he dislikes you for no reason?"

"Oh, there's a reason. He can't beat or ruffle me, no matter what tactic he uses. It pisses him off. And I happen to enjoy seeing the little prince out of his depth."

"Are you sure that's all?"

"What else would there be? People like us don't run in the same circles as them, sweetheart." All his humor disappears. "You'll figure that out in your own time."

After that, he grows silent, more focused on the rink.

I'm distracted as well when the game turns into a literal war. A brutal clash of power and strategy.

Through it all, it's Kane who holds me hostage. Even in the chaos, his control is absolute, and the way he commands the ice is mesmerizing. Every time he moves, it's like a pulse through my body, reminding me of how dangerously close I plan to get to someone who should terrify me.

And yet the more I watch him, the stronger my sense of trepidation becomes.

What type of upbringing did Kane have that caused him to turn into a literal ice machine? Is it even possible for someone to be so technically perfect? I'm not sure if it's because I only recently got into hockey, but I haven't seen him make any mistakes.

After the game ends in the Vipers' favor—barely—the players skate to the bench area and then to the locker room.

Kane follows with a hand on Preston's neck as he speaks close to his ear, but he doesn't acknowledge me.

At the beginning of the game, the first place he looked as soon as he got on the ice was at me. I even think I saw an expression of satisfaction.

But now, he leaves the rink without a look behind.

My heart sinks.

Why the hell did he ask me to come watch him if he was going to give me the cold shoulder? Is this another tactic?

As the arena starts to empty out, the crowd talking animatedly, Marcus and I don't move.

He doesn't seem to be in a hurry, but the last thing I want is to stay near the asshole. The only reason I stay is because I want to milk him for information.

I face him. "Hey, Marcus."

"Yeah?"

"You're a center like Kane, but how come you two play differently?"

He spears both hands behind his head and leans back against the seat. "So now you're an expert in hockey? I swear you didn't even know how many players were on a team a few months ago."

"People learn. So tell me, what's the difference between the two of you?"

"What did you notice that's different?"

"Kane's movements are smoother."

"He's boringly technical. Just like Armstrong. They learned hockey from expensive coaches and camps that could only be afforded by their generational wealth. They feel violence is beneath them, so they steer clear of it, no matter what. They should play tennis instead of hockey."

"But Jude is violent."

"He's different. He has inborn talent that couldn't be killed by expensive coaches. He's the only one worthy of respect out of the three. Probably the one who dragged them into the game as well."

"Am I right to think acquiring such technical skills means rigorous training and a strict routine?"

"Yes. Heard they spent their childhood in an all-boys boarding school, where they were taught…severe *discipline*."

My scalp tingles with unease "How were they taught?"

"Ask him." He smirks. "If you dare."

Before I can probe some more, he stands up and walks out.

Some of the girls notice him and follow after him like moths to flames. I mean, I know Marcus is strikingly handsome with his whole *je ne sais quoi* attitude, but there should be some sense of loyalty to our college. Marcus is like our team's archnemesis.

I mean the Vipers'.

It's not *our* team.

After sticking around for some time until the arena empties, I'm asked to leave by security.

On my way out, I check my texts, and my mood sours when I find nothing from Kane.

I should've spent my precious time by Violet's side instead of catering to his stupid whims.

My steps are lethargic as I head to the parking lot where I left my bike. It's empty now except for a couple of cars. The light is dimmer here, and the silence lingers like a layer of smog.

I quicken my pace toward the bike parking area and pause.

The bike isn't there.

Someone stole it?

It's not even that great. I kick the pole, then groan in pain.

Goddamn it. My bike is my only mode of transportation. I don't have the money to buy another one.

A car stops beside me and I look up, my brow furrowing.

A golden Rolls-Royce's back window rolls down to reveal Isabella Drayton.

Her hair is gathered in a ponytail and she looks down on me as if I'm the dirt beneath her car's tires. "What's up, Charity? Can't find a ride home?"

"My name is Dahlia and my business is none of yours."

"I was going to offer you a ride. As charity, Charity."

"No, thanks." I search my surroundings just in case the bike was moved.

"You don't get to refuse me. When I order, you only comply, bitch."

I swing around toward her, about to give her a piece of my mind, but a shadow appears from behind me.

Before I can figure out who it is, something pricks my arm.

I reach for the scalpel I always keep in my tote bag, but it falls to the ground.

"You—" My tongue stops moving and my vision blurs.

The last thing I see is Isabella's vicious smile as the world goes black.

CHAPTER 14
Dahlia

HUSH NOW, MY DARLING, THE MOON'S IN THE SKY,
The waves on the shore sing a soft lullaby.
The stars in the heavens will watch while you sleep,
And carry your dreams to the ocean so deep.

Mama's soft voice echoes in my ears as my lids fall closed, flickering in that dreamy place between wakefulness and sleep.

"Mommy?" I whisper, but I'm not sure if any sound comes out.

My head's heavy and my limbs are gripped by paralysis, as if I'm shackled to the rugged bed beneath me. Mom's gentle features appear blurry behind my reddening eyelids, but her soothing voice carries on in the darkness.

Rest now, my sweet one, the night's gentle song,
Will cradle you close as the tides move along.
The sea whispers softly, the wind hums a tune,
And soon you'll be dancing beneath the soft moon.

"Are you here to get me, Mom?"

A calloused hand lands on mine and she stops singing. "Do you want me to get you, dear?"

"Hmm. I'm so tired, Mommy. It's exhausting."

"Then come join us."

"Dahl!" a familiar voice calls, panicked urgency lacing its usual softness.

"Vi?"

"Don't leave me, Dahl. We promised to be each other's family. Dahlia! Dahlia, please! I only have you."

The sea whispers softly, the wind hums a tune,
And soon you'll be dancing beneath the soft moon.

Mom's lullaby echoes around me mixed with Violet's screams, until my senses explode in maddening chaos.

My eyes pop open.

A white ceiling with a moldy spot at the corner greets me first.

I try to sit up, but my limbs are so heavy, my head crashes back down.

Hot.

I'm so hot, the back of my throat is dry and I feel as if my clothes are my worst enemy.

Where am I?

What happened?

I cast my eyes around. A small white room, completely sterile except for the metal bed I'm lying on.

The place is dim, bathed in a soft amber light that casts long, flickering shadows on the walls. Everything feels wrong. Hazy. The air around me is thick, pressing in, suffocating me with its weight.

Again, I try to get up, but it's as if my body is tethered with unseen bonds.

The world swims around me, blurring at the edges. Then my senses come back in sharp, jarring fragments. Unbearable warmth spreads over my skin, a fire igniting from the inside out. My heart pounds in my ears, each beat loud, pulsing through my veins.

Every brush of fabric sends shivers through me, amplifying the burning heat.

I breathe in, but my chest is tight, each breath shallow and ragged. The faint tang of sweat and something spicy hangs in the air and my throat every time I swallow.

The bed beneath me is soft, a contrast to the tension coiling in my muscles.

Something's wrong.

My body's too hot, my thoughts too sluggish. My skin prickles, every inch of me out of sync yet too aware of everything.

The air is like fingers ghosting over me, teasing, pulling at the heat that's building at an overwhelming pace.

I try to move again, but it's like I'm disconnected from my body, my limbs barely responding to my brain.

My mouth is dry, my mind racing, but everything is clouded in this thick haze of need I can't stop.

The pounding of my heart drowns out my thoughts and the faint hum in the air that throbs with the same rhythm as my pulse.

My legs lock together and that triggers the pressure. I can feel the wetness gushing from my pussy. My skin burns with an ache I've never felt before.

The door opens and I stare up as two men wearing the familiar silver masks walk in.

"Who...who are you?"

Oh God. Why does my voice sound so husky and needy?

They approach me and I slide back against the bed.

"No. Stay away..."

Doesn't matter what the hell Isabella and her minions injected me with, I won't let them touch me.

Not even if this is related to the organization.

"How about I start?" the taller one says to the other, his voice rancid and scratchy. "I wonder if she feels as good as she looks."

"No…" I try to kick him when he reaches for my leg, but he easily catches it and tugs on my jeans.

"Stop acting like a prude. We all know you let Kane use you like a slut." He undoes the buttons and pulls them down, exposing my bottom half. Only my panties and the oversized hockey jersey cover me.

"I will kill you if you don't let me go." I kick and flail, fighting sluggishly as my eyes fill with tears. "I swear I will."

Their cruel laughter echoes in the air, condensing over my head like a mocking cloud. "Good luck with that."

"Please…" I tug on my jersey, squeezing my legs together until my knees knock.

I hate that I have to resort to begging, but I'll do anything to leave this place in one piece.

Then I'll poison these two in their sleep.

The taller one grabs my thigh, his cooler hand a shock against my burning skin. A rush of pleasure rushes down my belly and I throw my head back with a groan.

Oh God. No.

Please no.

"See?" one of them sneers. "You can't wait to be fucked like a whore."

My mind is jumbled, and my body is desperate to alleviate the ache, but I still mumble, "No…"

"You wanted to be a Vencor member, didn't you? This is what members do, bitch. They open their legs whenever those higher than them ask."

"S-stop… R-red…" I whisper.

My safe word lands on deaf ears.

Right. That's only between me and Kane.

I don't think Kane is behind one of these masks.

At least, I hope he's not.

I'd never forgive him if he did this to me.

I'd kill him with my bare hands.

Part of the reason why I allowed the sex at the initiation and the party was because I trusted he'd stop if I said the safe word.

It's different if I'm being drugged and taken advantage of without the option to stop it.

Anguish rips through me, raw and consuming. I want to fight, to scream, to tear their hands from my skin, but the drug they injected me with wraps around me like a vise, pulling me deeper into suffocating heat.

"Outsiders like you should recognize their limit," one of them says as each pulls a leg to part them. "Consider this your warning. If you don't leave town within a week, you'll be fucked raw next time without the drug. Don't even think about asking Kane for help. We'll show him a video of you moaning for our dicks, and he'll lose interest. We'll also share it online so that you'll be known as the campus whore."

My racing heart slows down a notch.

It's *not* Kane.

Am I supposed to feel this relieved?

Happy, even?

"Ready for the night of your life?" the one on my right asks.

"Fuck...you," I mumble, but it ends in a muffled voice when he seizes my hair and yanks me up.

When Kane did this, I was turned on, even if slightly apprehensive. Now, I'm terrified to the core despite the artificial aphrodisiac.

The air thickens further, the scent of sweat and something sickly sweet clinging to my skin, smothering me. Everything is slipping away—my grip on reality, my control, my strength.

Vicious hands start to hook into my jersey, and I push with all of my might, but it barely touches them.

Get up. Fight.

You've always stood up for yourself. Fight.

Don't scream. Fight.

Don't cry. Fight.

Fight, Dahlia. Fight!

With painstaking effort, I pull my leg loose, aiming a desperate kick at the tallest guy's crotch.

I don't think it's that strong, but he wails in pain and lifts his hand.

Raising my arm, I place it in front of my face to protect myself.

"I wouldn't do that if I were you."

The whole room goes quiet at that voice.

The slap or punch doesn't come.

Letting my arm drop, I shift sideways with painstaking effort.

Jude.

He's standing by the door, his large frame blocking the exit. Leaning against the wall, he casually slides both hands in his pockets and crosses his feet at the ankles.

My heartbeat doesn't slow down, and no sense of safety overwhelms me upon seeing him.

What if he's in on it, too?

My blurry eyes sweep over the space behind him, looking, searching, scanning the door for someone else.

And I've never searched for someone to save me before.

I've done the saving.

For me and Vi.

"How…" The taller of the guys faces Jude as the other keeps me down. "No one knows about this place."

"That's what you think." Jude's voice is an effortlessly scary rumble without his having to do anything. "Since when do pawns like you think you have agency?"

"We're just acting on orders."

"Whose orders?"

Both guys remain silent.

"No matter who they are, they won't protect you from what will happen in exactly…" Jude checks his watch. "One minute."

The guys stare at each other, but the one who's grabbing my thigh, half leaning on the bed, doesn't release me.

I try to wiggle free, but I'm too weak. My heartbeat is so loud, I think I'll have an attack.

Through my blurry vision, I see the door slamming against the wall with so much force, I'm surprised it doesn't come off its hinges.

At first, I can't see correctly—my vision is slipping in and out of focus.

But I know it's him.

A sense of peace befalls me, and my heart slows down.

Kane.

He's here.

The quiet click of his footsteps echoes through the haze, steady and calm, but there's something dangerous lurking underneath.

There's a shift in the air, and the room contracts around him, bending to his presence. He doesn't rush, doesn't shout. He's too composed, too controlled, like the stillness before a storm.

"Less than a minute. Impressive." Jude's voice echoes around me, but he's far from being the center of my attention.

I blink, still trying to focus, to hold on to that anchor, but the drug drags me under again.

My body's fighting me, my thoughts drifting away like sand through my fingers. I barely register the cold ice-blue of his eyes landing on me. There's no warmth there, no softness.

Just a lethal edge that sends a shiver through the room.

My chest heaves, my mind muddling between the need to escape and the pull of his presence. His gaze flickers over me, taking in everything—the way I'm pinned down, the glazed look that must be in my eyes, and my helplessness seeping from every pore.

He shows no emotion as he tilts his head, focusing on the hands grabbing my legs.

I open my mouth, trying to say something—his name, maybe—but nothing comes out.

The men freeze, no doubt feeling the threat that simmers beneath Kane's calm exterior. A crackle of electricity lights up in the air as Kane's posture subtly shifts and he snatches one of the men's wrists, then twists it.

It doesn't look that forceful, but the man screams.

Kane's voice resonates with a rich, low timbre. "I already made it clear, didn't I? Which part of no one touches my fucking things do you not understand?"

"We didn't know... Fuck!" the shorter guy screams as a pop reverberates through the air.

He broke his arm—or wrist. The guy's howl bounces off the walls and rings in my ears.

The other guy dashes toward the exit, but Jude seizes him by the collar of his shirt with ease. "Not so fast."

The one with the broken wrist falls to the floor, still

screaming, but Kane stands behind him, grabs his left arm, and twists.

Pop.

His scream rings in the air, chilling, like something from a horror movie.

And it keeps intensifying as Kane kicks him in the nuts and crushes them with his shoe.

The man's mask falls, revealing someone I've never seen before. His face is red and his haphazard blond hair covers his forehead.

He curls up on the floor in a fetal position, wailing and crying.

Kane stands over him, his shadow still, his posture uptight. "Next time you touch what's mine, your whole body will be in a casket."

My eyes are barely open, but I see him walking to the guy Jude's holding. "Now, your turn."

He catches his arm. "Who gave you permission to touch what's mine?"

"I can't tell… I'll be kicked out—"

"You'll be kicked out anyway."

The pop echoes in the air. A gut-wrenching scream follows.

"Let's try again." Kane secures his other arm. "Who orchestrated this?"

"If I tell you, will you keep me on?"

"No. But whether you leave with your limbs intact or not depends on your next words."

"It was Preston—"

He hasn't even finished talking when Kane breaks his arm.

"You said you wouldn't hurt me!" the man screams.

"Changed my mind." He kicks him as Jude holds him upright.

I try to hold on to that sliver of the scene in front of me, but my body is slipping, falling into a fog. My vision blurs, dark spots dance in front of me, and my breath comes out in ragged, desperate gasps.

Finally, I let myself lose the fight to stay conscious.

As my world turns black, I come to a disturbing realization.

I trust a monster like Kane to keep me safe.

CHAPTER 15
Kane

MY VISION IS RED.

My vision is *never* red.

Ever since Jude called and told me he witnessed suspicious activity in the parking lot, my mood has taken a sharp dive.

After the game, I was already driving up the Hill for a meeting with Grant's closest directors in the company. I've mastered pretending to do my bidding in the business I'll inherit, but in reality, this is a way to build my connections and strip my father of his stronghold.

After Jude's call, I made a U-turn and barely offered excuses for my absence from the meeting I spent weeks arranging.

It doesn't matter that earlier tonight, I had this illogical need to strangle Dahlia because she was flirting with her fucking ex at my game.

While wearing my jersey.

With my name on her back.

That perplexing fire still burns my lungs, but it's drowned out by the rage that clouds my vision with a crimson haze.

I'm about to break every bone in the bodies of the motherfuckers who had the audacity to touch what's mine.

And I don't resort to violence. I don't even like violence.

In fact, I consider violent people—aside from Jude—weaklings with little to no brain capacity.

Yet the need to smash the two bastards' heads in beats beneath my skin like a need.

An urge.

This is beginning to feel too much like an impulse.

"I'll finish the job." Jude throws the wailing scum on the floor as if he were excess baggage, then motions behind me. "She's out."

My gaze flickers toward her, and for the first time tonight, the red slowly retreats as Dahlia comes into focus.

Her skin is flushed, her cheeks a shade too deep, heat radiating from her in waves, and I can feel it even from across the room.

The rise and fall of her chest produces shallow, uneven breaths.

She looks small—too small—crumpled in on herself, her tangled brown hair sticking to her damp skin.

There's a slight tremble in her fingers curling weakly on the bottom of the jersey, pulling it down to cover her upper thighs. It's the only movement she makes.

The rest of her…still.

A sickening unknown emotion bubbles up in my throat, but I swallow it down as I close the distance.

The heat in the room intensifies and that's when it hits me. Her skin burning, probably her body's reaction to what they injected into her. My left index finger twitches—the urge to destroy something, someone, barely held at bay.

I kneel by the bed, and my fingertips graze the bare skin of her arm.

Just like that, her warmth sears into me.

Hot. Too hot.

And it's not the right type of heat.

I clench my jaw as I slip my arms under her, lifting her effortlessly. Her head lolls against my chest and her body falls into me as if her place has always been here.

In my arms.

What a ridiculous thought.

And yet...

Her soft breaths land against my neck, shallow and too quiet.

Dahlia has never been quiet, so this is strange, to say the least.

The faint smell of jasmine rips through my nostrils, filling me with her scent. Her skin is damp, flushed, burning up beneath my touch. I hold her tighter, watching the way she folds into me, her weight fragile in my arms.

They tried to break her. To touch what's fucking mine.

The more her body curls into me, desperate for something solid, something safe, the hotter the fire inside me ignites.

Her fingers twitch against my chest, seeking an anchor. And the fact that she thinks of me as one—*me*—breaks through the fury muddying my head.

Dahlia is strong. Stronger than she knows. But at seeing her like this—broken, trembling, clinging to me for dear life—an unfamiliar feeling rushes through me.

An ache.

An urge to protect her in a way I've never protected anyone.

And that's dangerous.

No. It's *lethal*.

Because not only will it affect my plans, but it'll also knock her off the chessboard as a useless pawn.

I should be cold, pull away, and maintain that distance I've carefully crafted between us.

Maybe call someone. Let them be the one to offer help while I retreat to the shadows.

But I'm locked in place.

Unable to ignore her soft, quivering body pressed into me, her heat like a brand.

I grit my teeth as I hold her tighter, hardening my jaw at the feel of her frantic heartbeat fluttering against me.

I convince myself that the way my fingers are digging into her thighs and arms means nothing.

It's only to keep her from falling apart.

To later shove her back into the neat box I've created for her.

As I carry her out, Jude steps in front of me, his massive body blocking the door.

His face is set in hard lines, his eyes devoid of warmth.

It's no secret that he would rather not be here cleaning up after some lower-class Vencor members and wasting his time.

"You know what to do, Jude. Make them spit out what their plan was. I'll deal with Isabella afterward."

"I didn't even tell you it was her car I saw in the parking lot." He raises a brow. "How did you figure it out?"

"It's clear as day that she wasn't happy about my recent involvement with Dahlia. Since she can't touch me, she'd redirect her fury to the weaker party. A terrible miscalculation on her part."

"What do you plan to do to her?"

"Get her kicked out of Vencor. With your and Preston's votes, we can discharge a member. If she still insists on being a headache, I'll have her buried six feet under."

"Let's say I go with the vote, why would Pres?"

"He will once I tell him Isabella had her goons use his

name as the fall guy. You know he hates messy things if he's not the cause."

"I'll consider it." He stands taller, a flash of sadism sparkling in his eyes. "You owe me for today."

"I do."

"I expect an extra name in my inbox tonight."

I nod.

Of course Jude would cash in immediately. He greatly lacks the skill of gathering intel and saving it for later. Though by having those names, he's loosening himself further from my grip.

But it doesn't matter. For now.

Jude still needs me to reach his goal, and, therefore, I can still control him.

Instead of stepping away, he glares at Dahlia, sparks nearly flying from his eyes.

I fix him with a stony look. "Is there a problem?"

"Why the fuck is it her? Of *all* people?"

"She's just a pawn."

He bursts out laughing, the sound long and cruel. "The almighty Davenport lost his cool for a *pawn*? Try to fool a lesser person."

"Some pawns deserve extra care."

"Well, in that case, better take *extra care* that she doesn't mess with my fucking business."

"Noted." I motion at the door. "Will you move now?"

After one last ambiguous look at Dahlia, he steps aside and gathers the piece of fucking shit by his collar.

As I walk out, Jude's voice carries from behind my back. "I mean it, Davenport. She puts her nose where it doesn't belong and she'll see her maker sooner rather than later. All bets will be off."

I tilt my head in his direction and flash him a smile. "Won't be happening. As long as you keep your fucking stalkerish tendencies in check, we're all good."

By the time I arrived at my penthouse downtown, Dahlia was burning up.

I placed her on the sofa in the living room earlier. Since then, I've been standing cross-armed by the floor-to-ceiling window overlooking the town's luminous skyline.

What the fuck am I supposed to do?

I've never taken care of someone else before. Except for Preston when he goes off the rails, and even then, I usually let Jude handle him while I manage the fallout.

If Dahlia's fever doesn't come down, I'll take her to the ER.

I *suppose*.

A whimper rips from her lips and she thrashes, her movements making the leather sofa creak beneath her. She curls her fingers, stretching and pulling at the jersey. It rides up, revealing her white panties and stomach.

Even under the soft light, the contrast of the white jersey is striking against her tanned skin.

My dick twitches to life and I tear my gaze from her to look out the window.

Her throaty moans echo in the air, silky and fucking erotic.

Apparently, the concept of keeping myself in check escapes me when this girl is around, because I tilt my head in her direction again.

Dahlia has slipped her right hand into her panties, touching herself in a frantic, uncoordinated motion.

The scent of her wafts in the air as she releases a sound that's a mixture of a moan and a whine. Her left hand gropes and strokes her tits beneath the shirt.

Jesus fucking Christ.

I stride toward her and clutch her hand that's in her pussy and yank it out.

Big mistake. Because, now, not only does the room smell like her sweet pussy, but it's also the only thing I can breathe.

"Dahlia, wake up."

"Mmm."

"Dahlia, open your fucking eyes."

"P-please…please…"

God fucking damn it.

I adjust myself, but it does nothing to deflate the bulge in my pants.

My knuckles brush her warm cheek as I tap. "Begging will get you fucked, wildflower."

Her eyes blink open, slightly glazed over, the color more brown than green, sparkling as she studies my face.

"Kane…"

My name falls out of her mouth in a soft moan and I close my eyes.

Down.

Stay fucking *down*.

"Kane…" she moans again, softer, needier. "I'm warm."

I open my eyes and start to pull my hand away. "Do you want to take a shower?"

"No… It's uncomfortable. Mmm." She grabs my hand with both her smaller ones and presses it on her soaking wet panties. "Touch me. Make it go away."

Fucking hell.

Who knew that the ever-proud Dahlia Thorne, a literal thorn in my side, has this needy, seductive side to her?

"Want me to touch you here?" I lazily stroke her over the damp fabric and she throws her head back, her skin flushed, forehead sweaty.

"Yes, yes! *More*."

My fingers slip beneath her panties, and I circle her clit. Her thighs tremble and a shiver rips through her.

She's like a marionette in my hands, reacting to my merest touch.

Dahlia's moans turn deeper, more desperate. "Yes…there…right there."

"Here?" I slow down on purpose.

She grabs onto my wrist. "Faster…more…"

"Do you want me to fuck you, Dahlia? Want my cock to sink into that tiny cunt of yours and relieve the ache?"

"Yes…yes…it's warm…make it stop…"

"You'll take my cock so well, won't you? Even if it's big, you'll be gasping to take more."

"Yes…anything…yes."

"You'll be swallowing every inch like a very good girl and let me use you to get off?"

Her back arches as I thrust two of my fingers inside her.

Unintelligible noises of pleasure reverberate in the room, mounting and intensifying like a crescendo.

The air becomes stifled with her scent, dizzying and absolutely addictive.

No matter how much I've tried to deny it and how many times I've shoved myself back into that control box, ever since that first time, I've been fantasizing about fucking her again.

Owning her again.

Claiming her once and for all.

"You can barely fit my fingers, wildflower. How will you take my cock?"

"Mmm...I will. Promise."

"Beg me to fuck you. To use you however I see fit." I pump my hand forward and add another finger, thrusting into her at a steady rhythm.

Drawing every shudder and tremor and choked-up moan.

"P-please," she says through a gasp.

Her body jerks and I reach my left hand beneath the shirt, grab her tit underneath the bra, and then slap the hardened nipple. "Say the whole sentence properly."

She yelps, the sound coming out with a fractured moan. Her eyes are half open, dripping in yellow.

Gold.

"Please, Kane...please fuck me."

My rhythm increases, pounding her in deep as if my cock were inside her. As if I were claiming her again.

Her pussy stretches around me and I circle her clit with my thumb.

She soon clamps around me, her breath hitching as she throws her head back.

"That's it. Come for me, baby."

As she jerks, I release her breast, reach into my pants, and free my cock. My fingers fuck her cunt while my left hand jerks my own heavy cock.

Up and down in a rough, frenzied movement.

Precum glistens from the tip and the veins bulge with need.

This isn't about my pleasure. This is a punishment for losing control and wanting her.

Again.

"Say my name," I strain as I strangle my cock.

"Kane…" She glances down at where I'm twisting and jerking, her lips parting, and she swallows thickly. "Please fuck me."

"Jesus. Fuck." I pull my fingers from inside her, shove the jersey up, and then snap open her bra.

I groan as my cum decorates her tits, covering her hard nipples and dripping down to her belly button.

She watches me the entire time, her mouth open, her face red.

I gather my cum from her stomach and place my coated fingers in front of her mouth. "Suck them clean."

Dahlia slips my fingers inside and sucks on them, her wet tongue licking me softly.

While looking at me with those glittering yellow eyes.

Soon enough, her lids lower and she falls asleep with a soft sigh.

With my fingers in her mouth and my fucking sanity in her hands.

Every time I touch her, I lose all sense of reality and myself.

For a moment, just a moment in time, I forget who I am, what I exist for, and what I aim to do.

For just that moment, it's only her.

And I'm not sure if it can be fixed at this point.

Or whether or not I'm willing to do so.

CHAPTER 16
Dahlia

THE MORNING COMES WITH A STRANGE SENSE OF PEACE.

And a headache.

A sore throat, too.

I blink my eyes open a couple of times and a smooth ceiling with painted cherry blossoms materializes before me. The stunning 3D details are so well illustrated, I feel as if I've been transported into a fairy tale.

Slowly, the rest of the room comes into view and I sit up in the massive bed, holding the black sheet to my chest.

The first thing that hits me is the cold.

Not the icy kind that seeps into my bones, but the kind that creeps into the air, that wraps around me even under the covers. It's everywhere—spreading from the walls, the floor, and the very space around me.

Kane's space.

It smells like him. Woodsmoke and leather.

The room is massive, but it feels suffocating. Aside from the cherry blossom ceiling, everything else is devoid of warmth. Dark gray walls swallow the light whole.

Clean lines, minimalistic, with everything perfectly in place. There are no personal touches, no photos, and only a few hockey trophies opposite me.

There's nothing that says someone lives or breathes here. It's more like a carefully constructed illusion of control.

I drag my gaze over to the desk in the corner. Stark. Empty. Just like the man who owns it. There's no clutter, no evidence of life. It's pristine, as if everything in this room is a testament to how he keeps his world—perfectly ordered.

The only thing that stands out is the window—floor-to-ceiling, overlooking the town that seems to stretch on beyond the horizon. The morning light filters in, but it's muted, dull, as if even the sun can't warm this space. Outside, the town buzzes with life, but inside, everything is unnervingly still.

I shift under the sheets, my body aching, my mind trying to piece together how I got here.

The memories filter in like an old grainy movie.

The drugging. The kidnapping. The masked men.

And then...

Kane.

"Oh God." I cup my mouth, my eyes widening.

Please tell me I didn't beg Kane to touch me.

Fuck me.

And he *didn't*.

He only fingered me and came all over me, but he didn't fuck me.

Why the hell am I disappointed?

I wish the earth could swallow me alive and spare me the embarrassment.

My eyes land on a change of clothes on the foot of the bed, and I assume that means I can use his shower.

After a few seconds of internally kicking myself, I walk into the sleek bathroom.

I remove the jersey and my underwear, then pause at the

view of his dried cum on my stomach. He really loves leaving his mark all over me like an animal.

I should feel mad or something, but I'm more enraged by how *I* acted.

The elegant shower has so many settings, it takes me a few minutes to figure it out.

After I finish, I towel-dry my hair and put on his Vipers hoodie and sweatpants. I have to roll the waistband a couple of times and tie the drawstring so they'll remain in place.

The rich smell of food tickles my nostrils as I walk out of the bedroom and down the hallway full of impressionist artwork, then finally reach the living room I mildly recognize from last night.

This place is massive.

And frighteningly expensive.

I move carefully, self-conscious about touching or, worse, knocking over and breaking something. I bet I couldn't pay for it even if I sold myself on the black market.

My bare feet falter at the doorway of the kitchen, the sight of Kane hitting me like a punch to the gut.

He stands at the stove with his back to me, his broad, muscular frame covered in nothing but a pair of gray sweatpants that hang low on his hips.

The morning light filters through the window, casting a faint glow on the sharp planes of his body, highlighting the lines of his muscles.

But that's not what steals my breath.

It's the ink and scars.

As he turns to the side, I see a serpent coiling around his left shoulder, black and detailed, the scales gleaming in the light. Its head rests near his collarbone, mouth open as if ready to strike.

I can't look away.

My eyes take in every detail of the tattoo. It's all things Kane—cold, dangerous, poised.

Just beneath the serpent lie jagged, uneven scars, crisscrossing his skin like a roadmap of pain.

While I have no clue who or what put them on him, I know it must've been brutal.

My stomach churns at the sight as if I've seen a kicked puppy shivering by the side of the road. Only, in this case, I can't pick him up and carry him to a shelter.

And Kane is by no means a *puppy*.

How is it possible that someone hurt him enough to cause those scars? He always seems invincible. Untouchable. He's a hockey god and a monarch both on campus and in town. No one would dare come near him.

But they did.

And he's been hurt to the point of being permanently marked.

More ink wraps around his other arm, intricate lines that form a raven with its wings spread wide across his shoulder, its eyes hollow and dark. Beneath the bird, a small Latin phrase I can't quite make out curves around his ribs, disappearing into the shadows of his skin.

Everything about him is a warning.

The tattoos, the scars, the way his body moves with silent power like he's always ready to pounce.

However, right now, he's just a man standing in a kitchen, scrambling eggs like it's the most natural thing in the world.

"You're up." The low timbre of his voice carries through the room like a cool breeze.

"Yeah." I draw a circle on my thumb.

"Sit down. Breakfast is ready." He turns off the stove

and empties the pan's contents onto a plate with unnerving precision.

No mess in sight.

"Thanks, but I can figure out something to eat on my way home."

He lifts his gaze, looking at me for the first time this morning.

His icy eyes linger on my baggy clothes, heavy, as if he can see beneath them. It doesn't help that his woodsmoke scent clings to my skin, wrapping around me like invisible hands.

He walks over to the dining area with two plates and places them on the table. I catch glimpses of the raven's wing stretching to his chest before he retrieves a plain white T-shirt from the back of a chair and slips it over his head.

Killing my view.

He motions at the chair opposite his. "Sit down, Dahlia."

"Really, I can…"

"The food is already made. Don't rebel just for the sake of it, and sit down."

"I wasn't rebelling." I'm just not used to someone cooking for me aside from Vi.

My stomach growls.

Kane lifts a brow. "You were saying?"

I rub my nape, then slowly sit.

The table is absurdly full, and the aroma nearly makes me drool.

Plates are arranged with precision—eggs scrambled to a soft yellow, slices of toast perfectly golden, and a side of fresh fruit that seems to have been cut by a machine. A coffee pot, two high-quality porcelain cups, orange juice, and a milk jug.

There's jelly and butter, crisp and glistening bacon, and pancakes stacked high, steam still rising off them like some kind of picture-perfect domestic fantasy.

The fact that someone like Kane can make something as normal as breakfast while being fully capable of breaking people's arms with his bare hands is both astonishing and disturbing.

"Go on, don't just watch in amazement. Eat." He speaks as he cuts into his toast and eggs.

I don't need to be told twice. I dig into the eggs and shamelessly finish most of my plate in no time. This is so good. Honestly. And I'm a bit embarrassed to admit it, but I've never had this type of full breakfast before. I've been lucky to have coffee and some boiled eggs or something from a convenience store on my way to work or school.

A knife digs into the top of my toast. "Slow down or you'll suffer from indigestion at best or choke at worst."

I swallow the contents of my mouth. "Sorry."

"About what?"

"My table manners. I'm a bit hungry."

I think a slight smile twitches his lips, but it disappears as he continues eating. "Chew properly and take your time."

It takes effort not to devour everything in sight and make myself look like a cavewoman.

Kane watching me like some strict parent isn't helping.

He takes a sip of his juice, his eyes rolling over me like a sensual caress.

Like last night.

Don't think about it. Just *don't*.

"Is it a habit?" he asks.

"What?"

"Eating fast."

"I guess. I never really have time for food between school and my part-time job."

"And snooping around. And putting your nose where it doesn't belong. And being so fucking oblivious about your own safety."

I let the jelly spoon hang midway to my mouth and glare at him.

"Did I miss something?" he says with an unnerving smile. "Oh, and chatting with ex-boyfriends at my fucking game."

"I didn't invite Marcus. He came on his own, and he's not my ex."

"Didn't stop you from hanging on to his every word like all the puck bunnies vying for his attention. Miss him already?"

"That is *not* true. Marcus is an asshole, and I wouldn't look twice in his direction in this lifetime. He was just being antagonistic as usual and probably taking notes about your team play before the upcoming game." I release a breath. "I don't even know why I'm telling you this. We're nothing to each other."

"You came on my cock and fingers three times; I think we're something."

My mouth hangs open and my stomach contracts because of something other than hunger.

He narrows his eyes. "Surely you didn't think you could beg me to fuck you and then walk away as if nothing happened?"

"I was drugged. It doesn't count."

He takes a sip of his coffee. "It does for me."

"So…what are we?"

"What do you want us to be?"

"A partnership?"

"We're not a business."

I frown and nibble on my pancake. "Then what? Fuck buddies?"

"If that's what you want, all you had to do was ask."

"I don't *want* that. You're the one who seemed to lead me toward that conclusion."

"You have any objections?"

"Too many to count. Most importantly, I don't even know you."

"You will with time. For instance, I don't appreciate you flirting with other men at my game."

"I wasn't *flirting*."

"I have my doubts."

"I still know next to nothing about you."

"There's no need for a résumé if we're fucking."

I release a long sigh and drop the pancake to the plate. "Why would you want that type of relationship with me?"

"I don't want it per se, but it seems that staking a claim is the only way to ensure that no one will dare to touch my things."

"I'm not a *thing*."

"Not *a* thing. *My* thing."

"Well, your staking a claim or not didn't stop what happened last night."

His jaw clenches. "It won't happen again."

"Let's say I agree. And then what? You'd ditch me once you're bored?"

"Possibly."

"Wow. And they say romance is dead."

"I don't intend to romance you, Dahlia. I don't do that. So if you're looking for soft love confessions, a box of chocolates, and a bouquet of flowers, walk out right now. But if you prefer rough games and primal impact play, we might be able to work something out."

My throat dries up and a loud voice inside me tells me to run.

As fast as possible.

But I remain rooted in place.

This is the only way to get close to Kane. Though I'd be a liar if I said some part of me doesn't come alive at his words.

"Will you hurt me?" I whisper.

"Yes." The word is like a whip to my sensitive core.

I clench my legs. "How much?"

"To your limits. And I don't mean the limits you believe exist in your head, but beyond that."

"Will you give me a heads-up?"

"No." A slight smirk lifts the corner of his lips. "Where's the fun in that?"

I gulp, both deep fear and morbid expectation coursing through me. "Can I still use 'red' to stop it?"

"Yes."

"Okay, then."

"Red is the only word that can stop me. *No*, *stop it*, and *I don't want this* will only turn me on. Your fight turns me on."

"Sick asshole," I mutter under my breath.

"I heard that. And if I'm sick, what does that make you? Because you've been rubbing your legs together the entire time I've been painting a picture in your head."

"I have *not*."

He smiles like a predator who's locked in on his prey. "Now, shouldn't you thank me for saving you? I'll retrieve your bike and drop it off at your dorm. I'll also get Isabella off your back. Permanently."

"After you let her and who knows how many other people watch you fuck me, I don't see the point."

"Watch me fuck you?"

My fingers clench in my lap. "At the initiation. There was a camera, no? Isabella implied that she watched the entire thing."

"And you believed her?"

"What was I supposed to do?"

"Isabella is not a Senior member and wasn't even there. The only members present were me, Preston, Jude, and three others who aren't on the hockey team."

"Wow, thanks. At least now I know Isabella didn't see the video, but the others did."

"They did not."

"But...the camera?"

"Disabled."

"How did she and her brother know, then?"

"Probably Preston spreading rumors in his free time."

Oh.

A part of me is still skeptical, but when I stare into Kane's cool eyes, I believe him.

Which I probably shouldn't, considering the circumstances.

He watches me with intrusive intent.

"What?"

"I'm still waiting for you to thank me for last night."

"Do you usually save people to be thanked?"

"I don't usually save people, but in your case, yes, I want to be thanked properly."

"Thanks," I say around a bite of pancake.

"That didn't sound sincere."

"Well, you should've provided clearer instructions. You said to thank you, not to make it sound sincere."

He narrows his eyes. "That mouth of yours needs to learn some discipline."

"Or you need to listen to other opinions aside from your own."

"Not interested. Either things go my way or they crash and burn. No in-between."

The warning is clear.

I shouldn't mess with his system.

But something tells me that behind all that control, behind the walls and the cold, there's chaos.

And somehow, someway, I've been pulled into it.

Now, whether I get consumed by it or use it to my advantage depends on how I handle this new situation.

We finish breakfast in relative silence. Kane doesn't seem to want to talk much, and my attempts to start a conversation are met with monosyllabic replies.

It's the ice fortress that surrounds him, completely camouflaging him from the outside world.

And me.

As we stand to get ready for school, the doorbell rings.

Kane goes to the screen that shows who's outside. I trudge behind him and lean sideways to see.

A woman who looks to be in her mid-to-late forties stands there with a weary expression, her cheeks sunken and her icy eyes a replica of Kane's.

His mother?

I expect him to open the door, but he just clicks on the phone button, his voice completely detached. "Mother. What can I do for you?"

"Honey." She lifts a box in front of the camera. "I made you your favorite cookies."

"I don't eat those anymore."

Her expression sinks and she shifts her eyes to the side, awkwardly inspecting her surroundings.

"If there isn't anything else." He reaches for the hang-up button, but I press the unlock key first.

"Please come in, Mrs. Davenport," I say before the click of the door sounds in the distance.

Kane's head tilts in my direction, his eyes narrowing. "What do you think you're doing?"

"Inviting your mom in. Why would you talk to her through the intercom as if she's some sort of stranger?"

"You know, that's your problem, Dahlia." He barges into my space, his shoulders crowded with tension, and I step back. "You always meddle in shit that doesn't concern you."

My back hits the wall as his mother walks in. "Kane, hon."

He straightens and meets her halfway, hugging her ceremoniously, his posture rigid. "Hello, Mother."

I stand there observing the height and size difference between them. The fact that a frail woman like her gave birth to that beast of a son is fascinating.

Up close, her features look like she was a real beauty in her day. The lines on her face are a clue that's she's had a rough life.

"And this is…?" She looks at me with curiosity, her eyes much softer and kinder than her son's.

So it's not about the color.

"Dahlia," he says without looking at me.

"Your girlfriend?"

"N—"

"Yes," he cuts me off with a glare.

Jeez. Talk about intense.

"Hi." I wipe my sweaty hand on my hoodie and then extend it to her. "Nice to meet you, Mrs. Davenport."

"Call me Helena." She smiles. "This is the first time I've met one of Kane's girlfriends."

I peek at Kane, but he has both hands in his pockets while standing erect like a statue.

She offers me the box. "If you'd like, you can have these homemade cookies. They used to be Kane's favorite. I'm not a good mother and didn't know he doesn't like them anymore."

I'm curious what she means by 'not a good mother,' but I obviously can't ask that, so I accept the box instead. "Thank you. I love cookies."

"Oh, I'm glad to hear it."

God, seeing mothers like her makes me miss my mom. She used to bake the most delicious cookies and even let me mess up the kitchen.

Small fragmented memories.

Lost memories.

Kane doesn't know he has what many of us wish for. A caring, loving mother.

Someone to fall back on when it feels rough.

"We're getting ready for school, Mother." Kane's flat, unfeeling tone cuts through the moment. "If there isn't anything else…"

"Oh, right. I'm sorry to have disturbed you," Helena blurts out, seeming as if she's walking on eggshells around her son.

He even calls her mother. That's super impersonal.

It's sad that people like me yearn for a mother that doesn't exist while Kane still has his mom but doesn't seem to care about her.

I suspect he cares about no one.

"I'll walk you out." I fall in step beside her, but Kane

disappears down the hallway as if he doesn't want to spend one more minute in her company.

Once we're at the door, I awkwardly say, "I'm sorry about Kane. I don't know what's gotten into him."

"Don't be." She smiles softly and pats my hand. "I think you're a good person, Dahlia. So let me offer you a piece of advice."

"Yes?"

"Run away while you can. Once you're in, you'll never be able to leave."

CHAPTER 17

Dahlia

TWO DAYS LATER, KANE SENT ME AN INVITATION TO A party.

Not just any party.

A members-only party.

To say I wish I could high-five myself would be an understatement. I knew that patience would eventually get me here.

To Ravenswood Hill.

The Armstrongs are hosting this event in their extravagant mansion.

The security is tight around the gated community, and my invitation had to be scanned by some special infrared machine, and I was thoroughly searched for weapons.

Even though the invitation said to dress formal and wear the Vencor mask, I had to remove it for security reasons and then put it back on.

As for the formal part, I had to wear the dress I found in a box that came with the invitation.

The dress is pure sin, a deep, dark red that clings to every curve like blood-soaked silk. A slit slices up my leg, stopping just above my left knee, teasing with every step I take. The luxurious fabric hugs my waist, the neckline plunging just enough to toe the line between elegance and danger.

It fits me well. Too well, actually.

The fact that Kane knows my size is unnerving.

I tucked away the invitation card, but I couldn't hide the dress from Megan. She freaked out for half an hour about how stunning I looked and how gorgeous the dress was.

Oh, and there were black designer heels, which I'm struggling to walk in.

According to Megan, the dress and heels cost at least twenty grand. All I could think about was how that amount of money could help with my sister's medical care.

Though I'm uncomfortable with the gift and plan to return it as soon as the party is over, I couldn't come to my first Vencor party with an inappropriate outfit.

I'm also thankful for the mask. At least this way, anonymity protects me, in a sense.

My steps falter as I enter the main hall.

I've always heard stories about people living in a detached, different world, but I haven't fully understood the meaning until now.

The Armstrong mansion is a palace wrapped in shadows, opulence dripping from every corner. The massive crystal chandeliers cast fractured light across the black marble floors, the shimmer of gold and silver reflecting off the walls like a thousand stars trapped indoors.

Everything gleams—from the polished wood, extravagant sculptures, and the ancient art that shouldn't belong to this world.

I'm completely and utterly dazzled by a type of money I've never witnessed in my life. Not even in movies.

Suddenly, trepidation pulses through my every nerve, and I feel like a mouse trapped in cat land.

The ballroom is massive, too large for comfort, with

towering windows draped in rich velvet. The curtains fall heavy and dark, almost swallowing the light. Tables are scattered with fine crystal and gleaming silverware, the flicker of candlelight casting shadows that dance across the masked faces.

It's all too sparkling, too extravagant, as if the wealth and power could drown me if I stayed or stared for too long.

Everything about this place feels dangerous. Beautiful. Like a trap that glitters just enough to make you forget there's no way out.

The air is thick with the scent of expensive cologne, champagne, and something darker. It clings to my skin, mixing with the low hum of whispered conversations and faint laughter that echoes off the walls.

The members move like ghosts in the flickering light, their silver and black masks hiding their faces, but not the depravity in their eyes. Every movement feels calculated, every glance loaded with silent power.

This is on a completely different level than the Drayton party. That one feels like entry-level compared to this.

Which makes me abandon any ideas about collecting DNA samples or even snooping around. I glimpse numerous cameras blinking in every corner, and the feeling of being trapped and constantly watched coils in my stomach like a disease.

It's better to be careful this time, keep a low profile, and observe. Since it's my first invitation, it could be a test.

I grab a flute of champagne from a waiter and nestle in a corner. Even the staff is wearing silver half masks, and they're groomed to perfection.

My eyes keep flitting over the members with black masks and rings. Their number exceeds those who were present during my initiation. I spot at least twenty in total, but many of them have older voices, so perhaps they're politicians and public figures and, therefore, the mask is a perfect camouflage. Also, their rings don't have distinctive symbols like the ones on Kane's, Jude's, and Preston's.

I keep craning my head, looking for Kane, but come up empty. It's impossible to single him out among so many people.

I spot three silver-masked men by a table and inch closer so that I'm around the corner from them. Out of sight but close enough to hear their conversation.

"...And you're okay with your sister being kicked out, Gav?"

Ryder Price. That's his voice.

The one he's talking to is Gavin Drayton.

The latter loosens his bow tie and sips from his glass beneath the mask. "There's nothing I can do. If three Seniors vote her out, she's out."

"She did mess with Davenport's latest toy when he warned her to back off. She had it coming." The third one—a player because I heard his voice before, but I can't place him.

Gavin slams his glass on the table. "Well, my father is locking her up and taking her privileges for a couple of weeks. I think she's suffered enough blows to call it quits. No need to rub it in."

"Hey, don't get so worked up." Ryder wraps an arm around Gavin's shoulders. "At least you're still in, so silver linings. We can still make it to Senior members after graduation if we keep in line."

"Is something wrong, boys?" A woman wearing a stunning green dress and a black-and-red mask saunters to the middle of the trio.

Black and red.

A Founder?

A woman who's part of the upper echelon. I lean in against the wall.

"Nothing at all," Ryder says with a grin. "You look amazing, Serena. As usual."

Serena… Serena…

Where have I heard that name?

Oh.

An article I read a while ago comes to mind. "Serena Osborn Says Fundamental Change Is the Only Change Needed in the Industry."

The current CEO of Osborn Enterprises?

She strokes Ryder's mask. "You're a darling. Did any of you see Julian?"

"I don't think so," Gavin says. "We saw his brother, Jude, with Preston earlier."

Jude's brother, Julian. I remember reading about him, too. If I remember correctly, Julian Callahan's name was brought up as the country's top innovator in the pharmaceutical sector.

"I see." Serena pats Ryder's mask again and he freezes as if he doesn't dare to breathe.

It's amazing how an average-height woman can make three men who are double and triple her size stand so still in reverence.

"Have fun, boys." She pauses and then tilts her head to the side. "Don't give my brother a hard time in the upcoming game."

"Yes, ma'am." They all but salute.

Her throaty laughter carries in the air as she walks with purpose to the next group. All full of people in black-and-red masks.

I thought there were only four members who had those masks—meaning the heads of the founding families—but in that group alone, there are six. Serena is number seven.

"Don't give her brother a hard time?" Gav scoffs, his voice low. "I'm surprised she hasn't already put a target on Marcus's back, considering he's rumored to be absorbed back in so he can take her place in the family."

"Who says she hasn't?" the third person I can't name says even lower. "Marcus is just a cat with nine lives."

Right. Marcus.

I forgot that while I was observing. Marcus Osborn is Serena's half-brother.

But hold on. Absorbed back in?

Do they even *know* Marcus? He looks down on everything this world represents. I bet he'd rather be beaten to death than be part of the 'pretentious snobs,' as he calls them.

Ryder rubs his hair. "This internal power struggle is making me anxious. Dad says we need to pick a side sooner rather than later."

"The whole four-families thing is absurd in the first place," the third player says. "No matter how much they collaborate, they'll end up stepping on each other's toes sooner or later. Plus, the generation that preceded us, whether it's Julian Callahan, Serena Osborn, Atlas Armstrong, or the currently banished Kayden Davenport, only knows how to go at each other's throats."

"Our generation is different, though," Gavin says. "Kane, Jude, and Pres are tightly knit."

"For now." Player three stares into the distance. "After Kayden's banishment, Grant Davenport's business decisions suffered greatly, and it's starting to impact their standing. It's just a matter of time before either Serena, Julian, or

Atlas uses that opening and crushes them. That will signal a war."

"Fuck this," Ryder grumbles. "I don't like the unknown in this entire thing. I'd rather they send us to kill people instead of picking sides. Better yet, I just want to play hockey and hook up with beautiful women. Is that too much to ask?"

Gavin throws a hand on his shoulder. "We'll survive. In the game of predators, small flies like us only need to know our place."

As they walk away, I keep thinking about what they said.

Gavin Drayton, the son of the mayor, who lives in the biggest and most beautiful house I've ever seen, just called himself a fly. Also Ryder. Whose family literally owns a chain of shopping malls.

If they're flies, what the hell am I?

The sound of metal clinking on glass echoes in the air, silencing everyone.

The crowd's attention turns to the top of the marble stairs covered in a red carpet, where five people stand.

The man who's holding the champagne glass is wearing a black-and-red mask. The woman to his right is donning a black mask, and the man to his left has a black-and-red mask. Another man stands a step down wearing a black mask while holding the hand of a little girl who's wearing a pink, fluffy half mask.

I assume the man who commanded everyone's attention is Lawrence Armstrong, a tycoon who owns an international energy resources company. The woman is probably his wife, and the third man is Atlas Armstrong, his younger brother.

The guy holding the girl's hand is Preston, and the little girl must be his sister.

Lawrence raises his glass, then his voice echoes around

the hall. "I'm honored to host you at my humble estate. Tonight is about forming connections between the members. Please don't hesitate to ask our ingenious butler for your specific needs. No matter what they are." He motions at a man who's wearing a black half mask and he bows courteously. "With that, ladies and gentlemen, please enjoy your evening. In the shadows…"

"We rule!" everyone echoes at once, the hall vibrating with their voices.

The party continues with soft piano music playing in the background. I spot some Members, mostly in silver masks, being approached by the staff and then following them out.

I crane my head, searching for the best corner where I can hide and carry on my observation.

"You look lonely."

I startle at the sudden voice. Jeez, I didn't even notice him approaching. Dark eyes stare—or glare?—at me through the openings in the black mask, and his massive physique blocks my vision.

"Jude?" I ask, unsure if I heard his voice correctly.

He reaches a hand out, and I step aside, feeling a destructive energy directed at me, but he just grabs a silver fork from the table behind me and twirls it. "Have you ever heard of being at the wrong place at the wrong time?"

"Yes. Why?"

"You're in that situation right now."

"I was invited by Kane."

"And you trust him to keep you safe?"

My mouth opens and then closes.

I…do.

In a deep part of me I don't recognize, I feel like he'd keep me safe. Perhaps it's because he's shielded me twice—at

Drayton's party and after I was drugged. And though he can be intense with me, I don't believe he'd expose me to danger.

At least, not intentionally.

I *hope*.

"You do," Jude says when I remain silent. "You're a lot more stupid than I thought."

"Don't insult me."

"Then don't put yourself in situations where you're bound to be insulted." He glares at me and I'm lost for words.

Why would Jude have this much hostility toward me? It's almost as if he hates me. Though I noticed he treats everyone with the same energy, so perhaps it's not only me, and he hates everyone.

A man wearing a black mask and a tailored suit wraps his arm around Jude. "Big man. Why are you wasting your time here? The show's about to start."

Preston.

"What show?" I ask.

He barely casts a glance in my direction. "None of your concern, Delilah."

"It's Dahlia."

"Whatever it is, illegitimate Osborns and anyone related to them are not welcome here." I can hear the permanent smirk in his voice.

"I'm not related to Marcus just because I went out with him for, like, two weeks. I'm a member, which is why I'm here."

"On trial," Jude says. "I wouldn't hold my breath if I were you."

"Here's a secret." Preston lowers his voice. "Ninety-five percent of Trial members get banished, and the five percent who get in are of our social standing."

I swallow, staring between them as if they're demons rearing their ugly heads.

"Aw." Preston feigns sympathy. "You didn't honestly think we pick up strays off the street, did you? We might indulge in some charity to feed you, provide a roof over your head, and keep you alive so you can oil the machine, but that's *all*. The likes of you and that fucking thug Osborn are merely disposables. Your whole purpose is to serve as pawns on the chessboard that we can ditch at *any* point."

I tighten my grip on the champagne flute. Though I knew what people like them thought of people like us, it still fills me with rage to hear it.

"Fuck off while you can," Jude says in a hard voice. "I mean it."

"I thought I couldn't leave once I'm in."

"I can ask my father for an exception," Jude says. "Armstrong will help, right?"

"Gladly," Preston says. "I don't want you around."

"Kane does," I say, lifting my chin. "And to my understanding, he's the only one who has a say in my acceptance."

Preston strokes the chin of his mask, and I can almost see the evil slipping into his eyes. "He won't after his father learns of his illogical actions."

"You'd sell out your friend to get rid of me?"

"I'm doing him a favor. I'm sure Kane wouldn't appreciate a spy in our midst."

"A spy? For whom?"

"That thug boyfriend of yours."

"He was *never* my boyfriend, and why would I spy for him?"

"I don't know yet, but I'll figure it out. Soon."

Jude is about to say something when a member of

the staff who's wearing a half mask approaches us. "Ms. Thorne."

"Yes?"

"Please follow me."

I stare at Jude and Preston to try to make out if they're behind this, but they're already walking away.

My hand trembles around the flute of champagne. Is this part of the test? Are those two messing with me?

Considering their hostility just now, I doubt they'll make it easy.

"Ms. Thorne?" the staff member says again, his voice cold but professional.

I carefully abandon my flute of champagne on the table. "Where are we going?"

"Follow me," he repeats, completely ignoring my question.

My steps are heavy and my heels dig into my skin with every move. Pretty sure I have a blister, and it throbs with an unrelenting pulse. The discomfort mixes with apprehension, and I draw circles on my thumb as I study the long hall adorned with dark-green wallpaper and muted wall lamps.

There are no people nor is there any indication of our destination. The noise from the party slowly fades until it disappears, leaving space for the man's hushed footsteps and my louder ones.

"Where are you taking me?" My carefully voiced question pierces the silence.

"We'll arrive soon."

He doesn't even acknowledge me as he speaks.

Images from that hellish initiation play in my head on a loop, and I tense up in anticipation of whatever they have planned for me.

At the end of the hall, the man takes a few complicated turns that I can't keep up with and then unlocks a door and pulls it open. "Please proceed."

I hesitate, but upon seeing what appears to be a garden, I relax a little and step out.

The door clicks shut behind me, but I pause when I find out that I wasn't led to a garden, but more like a structure of strategically cut trees and hedges.

I walk for a bit, taking note of the trunks and memorizing the shapes. It's dark, though, with only a line of light tucked deep between the clouds, so it's difficult to see.

The cold air clings to my skin, sharp and biting, and I wrap my arms around myself for some semblance of warmth. The night is thick and heavy, pressing in on me from all sides, and the faint rustle of leaves is the only sound in this endless stretch of unsettling silence.

My heels sink into the damp grass with every step, the soft squish beneath me unnerving. The hedges loom tall, twisting and turning, swallowing the path in front of me.

Wait.

Didn't I just pass by that tree?

I look behind me and freeze.

This isn't just a quirky garden.

It's a maze.

I can barely see two feet in front of me. The shadows move as if they're alive, the moon slipping through the clouds doing little to pierce through the blanket of black that wraps around everything.

My breath fogs the air, mixing with the cold that's already sinking into my bones. Each step feels heavier than the last, my legs aching, the sharp pinch of my heels digging into my feet and worsening the blisters.

A rustle sounds behind me, but before I can turn, a large body envelops my back.

A cold blade presses against my throat.

My breath freezes and my body jerks, but a strong arm wraps around my waist, pulling me back. I stumble, the grass slick beneath my heels as I'm yanked into something solid—*someone* solid.

The air turns thick with danger, and the warmth of his breath skates across the back of my neck until goosebumps erupt on the flesh.

I'm pinned against him, the knife a whisper away from my skin. A strangled cry forms at the back of my throat but refuses to break free as I catch a glimpse of the horrifying black mask with heinous serpentine details.

My pulse thrums, my entire body awakening in response.

His breath is steady, barely a ripple in the air. Each exhale is slow, deliberate, brushing against my skin as if it's his hand.

It's warm despite the coldness of everything else around us but also feels like a warning—too quiet, too composed—as if he's holding back something darker beneath the surface.

"Kane?" I whisper.

"Shh…" He tightens his grip on my hip. "It's time to test if you truly want this, Dahlia."

"How…?"

"Run," he growls, the word sliding like silk over my skin, low and dangerous.

He releases me and I stumble forward, my heels slipping on the grass.

I turn around and can barely discern his shadow in the darkness, tall and cloaked by the night.

"Three." His voice is sharp, landing on my skin like a whip.

I take a step back, my heart hammering in my ears.

This is crazy.

"Two."

I turn forward and my vision blurs as adrenaline kicks in.

Why do I want this?

"One."

A yelp rips out of me as I lift my dress, kick off my heels, and do what he commanded.

I run.

CHAPTER 18
Dahlia

MY BREATH COMES IN SHORT GASPS.

The cold earth shocks my feet.

The air asphyxiates my burning lungs.

But I don't stop.

I *can't*.

The wet grass slicks beneath my feet, and every time my skin brushes against the damp ground, a shiver ignites in my bones. But I pick up speed, my heart hammering against my ribs. The maze looms over me, its towering walls of hedges swallowing me whole as I plunge deeper into the darkness.

The thick night air wraps around me in a suffocating noose. My shallow inhales scrape my throat as some of the branches claw at my arms, snagging on the fabric of my dress.

I hear the rustle of leaves behind me. My spine tingles with a sharp chill.

He's close.

I can feel him along with the beat in my chest.

Hear him amidst the buzz in my ears.

That quiet, steady presence hunts me through the dark. Sometimes clear, sometimes faint, as if he's playing with me.

Actually. He *is* playing with me.

He clearly said I'm his *toy*.

Now, if my insides wouldn't liquefy at the prospect of being chased, that would be great.

I try to focus on the path ahead, but the sound of his calm, controlled footsteps keep pulling me back. The thrill of knowing he's there, always just a step behind, twists with the fear in my chest. My mind tells me to run, but there's something else, too.

Something darker.

A part of me that wants to slow down.

That sick, twisted part wants him to catch me.

The ground beneath me shifts, wet grass slipping under my bare feet. I stumble, my body pitching forward, and my knees hit the hard earth.

A sting of pain shoots through my legs. I'm pretty sure I scraped my knees, but that's the least of my worries.

Thundering footsteps echo in the air and I push myself up and take off again. Despite my blurring vision. Despite the sharp metallic taste on my tongue.

It's survival.

I've always been good at survival.

Then I see a sliver of light in the hedge, barely wide enough to fit through. In a snap decision, I dart toward it, then break a branch and throw it in the opposite direction as far as I can aim.

Hopefully, that will distract him.

I slip into the narrow space, pressing my back against the rough leaves, and hug my knees to my chest.

The branches dig into my skin, but I ignore the discomfort. My chest rises and falls, my ears pound, and sweat coats my temples and trickles down my back.

The footsteps stop.

Thick, oppressive silence swallows me whole, and I bite

down on my lip, trying to steady my breathing. But my heart's frantic beat threatens to give my position away.

Not to mention that the air is so cold, I'm afraid I'll crumble.

For a moment, the only sound is the whisper of the wind through the hedges.

But I know better.

He's there.

Somewhere in the dark, stalking and watching like a predator.

The electric tension in the air makes the hair on the back of my neck prickle.

He's close. *Too* close.

Then I hear his footsteps carrying him in the opposite direction.

Oh. Thank God.

For a moment, just one moment, I think I've lost him.

But before I can release a breath of relief, a rough hand wraps around my ankle.

A sharp scream rips from my throat as I'm yanked out, my body sliding across the damp ground, my fingers scrambling for a branch or anything to hold on to.

My nails dig into the earth, dirt gathering beneath them as I claw at the grass, but it slips through my hands like water.

I twist, kicking my legs with all my might.

For a moment, I truly believe I'm in danger and fight, aiming for maximum damage.

However, his grip is effortlessly strong, and it fires me up even more.

The world spins as I'm hauled back, the ground rough beneath me, the grass scraping against my legs.

The cold, unforgiving wind slaps my face, but all I can

hear is his steady breathing as his deep voice rumbles in a hushed whisper, "Caught you."

A rush of crippling terror and morbid thrill courses through me, and I lift my trembling hands in the dark. "Kane...hold on...let's talk about this."

"Don't say my name. I'm nobody to you." His voice sounds lower, closer, each word wrapping around me like a simmering earthquake.

He flips me over with horrifying ease.

All I can see is the looming shadow of his body in the darkness—big, broad, and utterly intimidating. A strange flutter awakens in the pit of my belly.

Is it excitement?

Need?

Both?

More?

An animalistic, primal emotion rips through me like thunder, and an exhilarating tension coils at my core.

Kane slaps my knees apart and kneels between them. The last thing I see is the glint of the knife before he bunches my dress and slashes it open right down the middle.

A dress so expensive I was scared to wear it.

He brutally rips it off as if it cost pennies.

My gasp echoes in the air, and I shove at his chest. "Stop it!"

He firmly pushes my hand away and cuts through my strapless bra like it's butter.

My breasts spring free, the nipples hardening even further as he roughly squeezes one in his big hand. "Such a dirty little slut. Your body is made to be used by me. You'll swallow my cock and beg for my cum, won't you?"

"Don't touch me!" I kick his chest with everything I have.

He grabs my foot and slashes through my panties, then thrusts the handle of the knife inside me.

God. I'm wet.

I'm so wet by his manhandling, it should be embarrassing.

"You think you can fight me?" He thrusts again, pumping the handle with wicked expertise. "You think you can escape me?"

My back arches on the wet grass, but I still try to resist the blinding pleasure building inside me.

It feels like a need.

A sick, depraved *need*.

"You're so wet at the prospect of being used. So primed and ready. You're choking the knife as if it's my cock, aren't you?"

"You disgust me, you fucking asshole. Let me go!" I lift my right hand and slap him on the hideous mask.

He backhands me with his free hand. So hard, my vision blurs, and I think I come a little.

Oh no.

No.

No.

This is just a show, a test, and playing his game to get what I want.

I'm not supposed to enjoy it so much.

I'm not supposed to come.

"Think twice before you run your mouth." He reaches beneath me and presses a finger against my back hole and I tense. "I could and would fuck your ass bareback. Mmm. This feels virgin."

I buck and try to escape him, keeping my legs spread so I don't cut my thigh on the knife, my heart surging loudly.

"Let's test it."

The moment he slips the knife out of me, I kick him and turn over, crawling on all fours, panting like an injured animal.

I'm entirely naked, and the cold bites into my warm skin, but that doesn't matter.

It feels like I'm running for my life.

As if I'm in real danger.

But the truth is, I want to provoke him further, unleash the beast, and make him show his true self.

If only once.

Just for me.

A hand wraps around my hair and I scream as I'm yanked back so that I'm on my knees. My back presses against Kane's taut chest, his harsh breaths filling my ears.

For the first time, he's not calm. Not steady.

He's far from controlled.

He's *unhinged*.

"Where the fuck do you think you're going?"

"Away from you." I tilt my head back in spite of the pain and spit on his mask as I lie through my teeth. "Your touch repulses me."

"Is that so?" While he's still immobilizing my hair, I feel his right hand moving behind me and I hear the unbuckling of a belt, its sound echoing in the frightening silence.

"Yeah. You're a sick fucking bastard I wouldn't touch twice." My voice trembles despite my attempts to provoke him.

He said my fight turns him on, and I feel it.

I feel the bulge pressing against my ass, hard and heavy.

"If I'm a sick bastard..." He slaps my ass a few times and forces his cock between my thighs, sliding its length against my soaking wet pussy, then speaks against my mouth, his mask touching my lips with every rough word. "You're a dirty little slut."

Then he thrusts into me with a force that steals my breath.

Oh God.

Oh fuck.

It doesn't matter that I'm wet or on the verge of coming—Kane is huge. And he feels bigger than ever before as his cock pounds into me as if he hates me.

And I clench around him as if I hate him, too.

Still wriggling, fighting like I truly don't want this, even if my entire body comes to life.

Even if a surge of overwhelming pleasure pools in the pit of my stomach.

It doesn't help when he keeps whispering sinful words in my ears, like a mantra, an aphrodisiac.

Words that drag me to the edge of my sanity.

"Mmm. Your cunt is strangling me so fucking well."

"That's it, stretch for me. Good girl."

"Your body is made to be used and owned by me."

"You're taking all of me. So deep. So good."

"You're a fast learner. Roll those hips for me so I can fuck your tight cunt."

My head hums with a low, constant buzz, and my body resurrects.

From the ashes.

From the dead.

Kane is the only one who's ever managed to provoke this bizarre side of me.

Maybe it's due to his unorthodox methods.

Maybe because he fucks me hard and fast, confiscating all of my control whether I like it or not.

Maybe because I can't think straight.

Or maybe, just maybe, I'm sick in the head and only enjoy this rough play.

I love how with every touch, pleasure mixes with pain until the two are indistinguishable.

Every thrust goes deeper, harder, electrifying every fiber of my body. My moans and whimpers and veiled curses echo in the air, piercing the silence, fusing with the obscene sound of his in-and-out.

But he doesn't stop.

Doesn't slow down.

His breaths grow ragged and rough. "You're made for me. Only *me*."

I can't stay upright and grab onto him. My nails dig into the collar of his shirt—or jacket—but it's not enough. I loll forward with his powerful thrusts and nearly fall, but he wraps a strong hand around my hip and circles his fingers along my stimulated clit.

"Come for me. Show me how much you want this."

It's impossible to last.

I can't.

The moment he touches me, I'm a goner.

My body jerks and I tremble all over as I fall apart on his cock. I hold on to him for balance as wave upon wave washes over me, consuming my every nerve.

I press my eyes closed, feeling every inch of him as he fucks me, never slowing down or becoming gentle.

A part of me likes this. The part that never really liked gentle.

Kane releases my hair and squeezes a hand around my throat. "You're ruining everything. *Everything*."

I didn't think it was possible, but his rhythm intensifies,

becoming harder, his thrusts longer and deeper, hitting a sensitive spot inside me.

"Everything," he growls, his words sharp and raw.

There's no trace of the controlled Kane.

The one who hid in a fortress with no key.

He's entirely himself. Undiluted.

"You shouldn't have come into my life." *Thrust.* "Into my world." *Thrust.* "Into my fucking system." *Thrust.* "I'm going to break you to fucking pieces for daring to come close."

I can feel the remnants of the orgasm transforming into something more powerful.

I can barely breathe due to his fingers smothering the sides of my throat.

The pleasure intensifies the more he squeezes, mounting, heightening, until I think I'll pass out.

Still, I lift a shaking hand to his mask and push it up. My movements are stumbly at best, considering my lack of strength.

As soon as I reveal his mouth, I close the small distance and seal my trembling lips to his.

I suspect Kane doesn't kiss. He's never tried to before and he also doesn't like me to touch him.

But I need this.

In the midst of violence and degradation, I need some form of connection. I also need to own a part of him no one has dared to possess before. I need to turn his world upside down just like he did to mine.

He goes still for a moment, his massive body freezing as if he's been shot. His lips are cold and unmoving.

But it's only a moment.

Just one suspended moment in time.

A growl rips from deep inside him as he kisses me with a ruthless vigor that steals my thoughts.

It's not a kiss—it's a possession. His lips move against mine with a rough intensity, leaving no room for breath or softness.

Just Kane.

His fingers tighten around my throat, angling my face up so he can devour me.

The kiss is a clash, a war of heat and anger as he grazes his teeth over my bottom lip and plunges his tongue in and consumes mine. The taste of him is fire, scorching every thought from my mind. His breath is harsh against my mouth, his lips relentless, like he's trying to swallow me up, break me.

There's no finesse in the way he kisses. It's neither controlled nor refined. It's not even disciplined like the way he fucks. It's as if he's never kissed before and I get to witness every second of every bit of his brutal, heated, explosive power.

I crave it.

I *love* it.

I fall apart at the thought that he only shows me this side of him.

Without the restraints. Without the repression.

Just Kane.

His kiss is furious. It's dangerous.

It's *everything*.

Then he fucks me as he kisses me with a blinding passion. His hips jerk with the same rhythm as his tongue.

This time, I don't get a warning as I shatter on his cock.

I come so hard, I think I'll faint.

But I don't.

Still holding on to that unrestrained part of him, needing more and everything.

I'm so sensitive, so sore, moaning in his mouth as he continues to kiss me. Thrusting into me like he's punishing and owning me at the same time.

Though he probably doesn't know that I'm also owning a part of him as well.

A part no one else has seen.

"Fuck!" He wrenches his lips from mine and releases my throat as he pushes me down on all fours on the grass.

"Jesus fucking Christ." He grabs my hips, pulling my ass up as he drives into me with unveiled anger.

I love it when he loses control because of me.

He's cursing, shedding his outer layers one at a time.

Because of *me*.

So even though I'm fully spent, I lean my head on my hands, latch onto the earth, and let him fuck me like a beast.

Every delicious, punishable stroke nearly sends me over the edge, and I can't believe my drained insides are thinking of another orgasm.

I must really, *really* like it rough.

Kane's chest covers my back, his hand wraps around my hair, and I feel his teeth and lips, sucking and biting along my shoulders, my spine—marking me everywhere.

It hurts so good.

"You're a fucking nightmare," he snaps near my ear, his lips grazing the shell.

"Kane…"

"Don't fucking moan my name, Dahlia."

"Kane…Kane…" I moan louder, throatier, as the orgasm rips through me. "Come with me…please…"

"Fucking fuck!"

"I'm on birth control...come inside me."

"Jesus fuck." Kane pulls out and I feel his cum coating my ass and back, the sting of the hot liquid against the handprints he left on my ass cheeks pales in comparison to the sinking feeling in the bottom of my stomach.

Why am I disappointed he didn't come inside me?

Kane collapses on top of me, crushing me against the ground. "I fucking hate you."

"I hate you, too, asshole." I mutter, losing all my fight.

I think he'll kill me with his weight.

What a way to die.

Being crushed to death after the best sex of my life.

Kane shifts and I think he'll release me, but he pulls me in one swift movement so that I'm lying on top of him, my back to his chest, my head on his shoulder. My legs are trapped between his, his half-erect cock nudging against my ass.

I'm a mess, covered in cum, sweat, and even tears from the intensity that is Kane Davenport. I don't even want to think about the state of my makeup.

But Kane still wraps one arm around my breasts and the other across my hip and pussy.

I'm so sensitive, I jerk at the merest contact. My nipples poke against his hand and I don't like this whole scene.

It's vulnerable and I don't do vulnerable.

Which is laughable, really. I can handle being chased and dicked down in the middle of nowhere, but being held raises my alarms as if I've been doused in icy water.

I wiggle and try to turn around.

"Stop moving." His rough voice filters into my ears like a curse.

"I'm uncomfortable."

"I don't give a fuck. Stop trying to turn around. Stop messing everything the fuck up. Just stop."

I turn my face away. "I hate you, asshole."

His hand wraps around my throat and he angles my head up so that he speaks against my lips. "I fucking hate you, too, Dahlia."

And then he kisses me senseless.

He kisses me until I think I'll pass out.

He kisses me until I think he'll never stop kissing me.

CHAPTER 19
Kane

BREATHE.

Inhale.

Exhale.

Relax.

Lean into the pain.

My wrists burn where the chains cut into them, my arms stretched tight above me, my own weight pulling at my shoulders.

With every involuntary tremor that runs through my body, iron digs into my flesh.

The basement I'm hanging in swallows me whole, the cold biting into my skin. The stone walls are damp, reeking of mildew and the heavy smell of rusted metal.

As for the reason why I'm here—again—it's simple.

Tonight, we lost our away game.

The Vipers lost a clean winning streak. Against the Stanton fucking Wolves.

To say the team's morale is in the absolute gutter would be an understatement.

This was due to a culmination of unfortunate facts.

One, I wasn't focused, and while my body existed on the rink, my mental presence suffered greatly.

The immaculate discipline I've spent over fifteen years honing to perfection has chipped at the edges, small cracks appearing on the foundation.

Two, perhaps it was the lack of my assertive leadership, but the rest of the team also spiraled, struggling to hold the Wolves—especially their captain—at bay.

Osborn toyed with the team spirit and paid extra attention to Preston, checking and even falling on top of him until our left wing could barely breathe. Like a man possessed, Osborn made Preston a target and kept relentlessly going at him as if my friend was the only Vipers player on the rink. And that, in retrospect, made Jude pick more fights than usual—he's been notoriously protective of Preston since we were kids.

Three, Preston's usual cold-bloodedness was nowhere to be seen. He held out for the first period but eventually fell for the skirmishes and whatever Osborn whispered to him every time he knocked him down. In the third period, Preston cracked and sent Osborn flying against the boards, which shattered to pieces.

Osborn's only reaction was an evil laugh.

That was the first time Preston deliberately resorted to violence during a game. While he's fine with murder, he believes hockey violence is beneath him and those who rely on their muscles are peasants.

Even in real life, Preston often delegates tasks to his family's extensive network of private security guards, vehemently refusing to dirty his hands if the task is not interesting enough.

But he made a rookie mistake that landed him five minutes in the penalty box, which is a great part of the reason why we lost.

Those five minutes of power play were brutal, and Osborn made sure to wave at Preston every single time he scored. The Stanton Wolves crowd went wild for Osborn, cheering and chanting as if he were their god.

Even after Preston was released from the penalty box, he was practically useless. Osborn had already gotten into his head, so it was game over.

Jude and I held down the fort, which is why we didn't completely get our asses kicked, but it was still a loss.

I don't do well with losses.

I don't *lose*. End of.

My entire upbringing was customized to teach me that people like us don't lose. We're always on the winning side.

Every fucking time.

So naturally, my father was displeased, and as an expression of his fury, he locked me up in my own hell.

A dark room in the basement of our house, because, yes, Grant Davenport has a chamber of torture where he can teach his kid discipline.

It started right here before the boarding school picked up the legacy. After I graduated, this place returned to being my prison cell.

My eyes are closed as I hang from the ceiling by my wrists, only wearing my jeans as my toes barely touch the cold, damp floor.

Now and again, the ceiling above me opens and I'm drenched with icy water so I don't fall asleep.

A couple of years ago, I went into hypothermia, but Grant's doctor saved me. Sometimes, when he's truly disappointed in me, he'll electrocute me enough to hurt but not kill me.

I used to be apprehensive about the punishments. I used

to stiffen my muscles and lash out. But that only prolonged the suffering, so I learned patience.

Discipline.

Hardening my mind has allowed me to let whatever he sends my way roll off my skin.

The elements, the dark, the strain on my muscles—it's all normal.

While time in this room is impossible to count, I usually spend the night here and am released in the morning before practice or open skate. Grant can't have the outside world miss out on his golden boy, especially after I became a hockey star.

He takes my wins for granted and my losses as a slight to his honor.

Usually, I use this time to think about the next steps I need to take to bring him down, ruin his legacy, and smash his lifelong achievements.

But my head has other plans and keeps wandering back to a few days ago when I fucked Dahlia like an animal and let my last shred of control shatter.

I meant to fuck her and humiliate her. To use and discard her like that first time.

It was supposed to be a show of power so she would understand who was in control.

But then she took everything I dished out and enjoyed it. She *moaned* for it. Her inner animal clashed with mine, fitting my most depraved desires like a glove.

Not even in my wildest dreams did I think I'd meet someone who shares the same fabric of my depraved soul.

That's why I never showed that side of me. Didn't even consider it.

But with Dahlia? It came out so naturally.

She had the audacity to *kiss* me. To sink her tiny claws into me and sear me to her. To demand it, even.

Like she had *every* right to.

That's when any semblance of rationality scattered into thin air. I lost my decade and a half of discipline in a fraction of a second.

And just like that, I succumbed to my instinctive primal side.

My lips twitch as if I can still taste her on my tongue.

It's fucking irritating how a tiny woman with dubious intentions has the power to chip away at my barriers and erode my walls by just existing.

No. Not irritating.

Dangerous.

And the worst part?

After that encounter, she ghosted me.

Well, not quite, but ever since I gave her my jacket to cover up and led her out of the Armstrong mansion, then drove her to the dorms, she's been ignoring me.

Her texts have been dry at best, and she always comes up with a way to avoid me.

The following day, I saw her limping her way to class and I, being a *gentleman*, checked on her.

Me: You're limping.

Okay, it wasn't entirely checking, but she got the gist. Or not. Because her reply was not what I was expecting. Not that I knew what I was expecting.

Dahlia: Thanks for the observation, Sherlock.
Me: You hurt yourself?

Dahlia: You hurt me, prick. I can barely walk.
Me: It was that good, huh?
Dahlia: It was THAT bad.
Me: You came three times, wildflower. I don't think it was THAT bad. Besides, you didn't use your safe word.

She left me on Read.

Normally, I wouldn't give a fuck, but I narrowed my eyes and left it alone. The following day, I started anew.

Me: Is the limping gone?
Dahlia: What if it's not? You'll kiss it better?
Me: I can try. Come to my place tonight.
Dahlia: No, thanks. I'm not in the mood to die.
Me: I won't fuck you. Don't worry.
Dahlia: Yeah, no. I'm not falling for that.
Me: Avoiding me is not the solution to whatever is going on in that head of yours.

Read. Again.

At this point, my eyebrows nearly shot to my hairline, but I gave her a couple of days to get over whatever got her panties in a twist.

It didn't seem to be anything new in her life.

I know because I had my eyes on her. She's always quite busy with classes, school projects, her part-time job, and the hospital at the end of the day. She also has this habit of staying at the lab for a long time.

Me: Is your tantrum over?
Dahlia: I wasn't throwing a tantrum, but if you want one, I'll gladly deliver.

Me: Deliver yourself to my place instead.

Dahlia: I'm busy.

Me: Don't make me show up at your dorm and terrorize your roommate.

Dahlia: It's not open to outsiders.

Me: It's cute you think there's somewhere in this town I don't have access to.

Dahlia: Just leave me alone, Kane. I have to work late tonight.

Me: Then quit the minimum-wage nonsense. I'll arrange it so that you're accepted as a paid intern on the medical team. We'll triple your pay. You can start in two days.

Dahlia: Typical rich people. Throwing money at problems and hoping it works.

Me: I don't hope. I expect. Besides, didn't you want to work with the team?

Dahlia: That was before I figured out I don't want to spend more time in your company.

Me: Very funny. I'll make arrangements so that you're in more of an observant and medical log role.

Dahlia: Why that role specifically?

Me: So you won't be touching other players. I'm making your wish come true, so you should thank me.

Dahlia: Thanks, my liege, but I refuse. I'd rather earn my money fair and square.

Me: I didn't suggest you steal it. Quit the nonsense about poor people's pride and being stubborn for the sake of it. If an opportunity presents itself, you don't turn your back on it. You take it. I thought you didn't want to be an outsider, but here you are choosing to be one.

Dahlia: You done lecturing?

Me: I swear to fuck, you're the most infuriating thing on the planet.

Dahlia: Thanks. You're not so bad yourself.

Me: Take the job, Dahlia. Your bank account will thank you.

She left me on Read. *Again*.

At that point, I was frowning so hard, Jude, who was changing beside me after practice, kicked my shin. "Something the matter?"

"What does it mean if you're constantly left on Read?"

He paused, then slowly slipped his hoodie on. "Lack of interest?"

"She used to text me first."

"Then loss of interest."

"It's not that." I slammed the locker shut and left.

It was pointless to ask Jude anyway. He's never had a relationship—doesn't believe in them—and is a brute with no appreciation for anything soft and delicate. Jude is the type who calls flowers grass and chocolate an unnecessary sugar fest.

Preston could've been more help, but he's also allergic to monogamy and that wasn't the right time since he was in the zone prior to the Wolves game. That he still fucked up epically despite all his continuous warnings to Jude and the rest of the team to be in their best form.

It's been two days and I still don't understand the reason behind her leaving me on Read. Which might or might not have affected my play tonight—or yesterday. It's probably early in the morning now.

A noise comes from above my head, scattering my thoughts.

Icy water slams into my skin like shards of glass, seeping through flesh and bone. I grind my teeth, my muscles locking against the onslaught, but it keeps coming, each wave colder than the last, trickling down my back, soaking my jeans until I'm nothing but freezing skin and rattling bones.

The floor beneath me is slick, the frosty bite crawling up from the ground, through my feet, and into my spine. The chains rattle above me, and my wrists scream from the strain.

Until I can't tell where the water ends and the pain begins.

All I can hear is the steady *drip, drip, drip* echoing in the dark.

As my hardened body absorbs the shock, thoughts of Dahlia dim to a mere strip of light in the darkness, quickly vanishing under the whips of conditioning.

However, in this moment, I make a promise to myself.

This is the final time I allow Grant's goons to kidnap and chain me to this place.

Next time, it'll be him dangling from the ceiling.

As expected, Grant releases me at five in the morning.

Not in person.

He made it clear last night.

"My son can't be a failure, understood?"

"Yes, sir," was all I said before he closed the door.

One of his aides unlocks my chains and leaves me stumbling.

As I ascend the stairs to the main house, I find Samuel waiting with a towel, his erect posture appearing ready to snap.

He's a wrinkly old bald-headed man who's been our butler for as long as I've been alive. He barely speaks, but he always comes in with a towel and prepares me a warm bath, tea, and a meal after my torture sessions.

He also always has a doctor on standby just in case.

Grant certainly doesn't want his son and only heir to expire. Not after my uncle is now out of the picture, probably living his best life with that young boyfriend of his.

Sometimes, I think being banished isn't a bad idea.

But then I remember that I can't let Grant have it all.

I'm not as magnanimous as my uncle.

I thank Samuel as I step into the bath. Heat flows through me, melting away the chill, but my muscles still contract. So I submerge fully for a couple of minutes before I surface again.

"Sir. Your phone." Samuel stands by the side of the tub and hands it over.

But he doesn't leave.

I wrap my blue-tinted fingers around the device. "What is it?"

"Your mother wants to see you."

"No. Keep her away. I'll leave in half an hour."

"Noted."

He exits the bathroom, the huge ornate door closing behind him.

I lean back against the bathtub and open my phone.

Countless notifications pop onto the screen, and I'm about to delete them all when I notice a few texts.

I straighten up, the water sloshing around me.

Dahlia: I know you lost for the first time this season, but you did your best.
Dahlia: You're kind of a control freak, so you're probably taking this personally, but you shouldn't. If anything, Preston needs to feel bad and ask for

forgiveness on his knees. God, he was such a joke, especially in the third period. What a useless piece of shit.

Dahlia: Anyway, you're the reason the Vipers didn't get wiped out. Silver linings, right?

I throw my head back and laugh.

Jesus fucking Christ.

Without thinking, I stand up, dry myself, and get dressed.

Then I drive all the way to the town center and to Graystone General Hospital, where she spends most of her nights.

The head nurse and the staff bow upon seeing me, but I pay them no attention as I take the elevator up and walk to the room at the end of the hall.

Sure enough, Dahlia's sleeping in a chair, her head awkwardly lolling on the bed next to a pale-faced comatose woman. Her laptop is open and a few textbooks are scattered chaotically on either side of her.

The steady *beep, beep, beep* of the machines is the only sound that echoes in the room.

I walk to her as if she's ensnaring me with an invisible rope.

As I approach, I cast a look at the laptop screen.

A school project, countless research-related tabs...

What do we have here?

A tab with an article about tonight's game is minimized at the bottom of the screen. I click on it and enlarge it.

"The Vipers Are Crushed by the Wolves in a Sensational Night."

I scroll to find that she has an account and her username is—I kid you not—ColdAsKane. And this alter ego has already posted numerous comments.

"Oh, fuck off. Crushed. You sound like a fucking child who's yapping for attention and clicks. There was no crushing, and the Vipers would've held out just fine if it weren't for that bitch Armstrong."

"Sensational? More like pathetic. The Wolves couldn't 'crush' anything if they didn't have the refs in their pockets."

"Bitch, please. One game doesn't define a season. Get your facts straight, morons."

"Funny how a one-off win has Wolves fans foaming at the mouth. Desperate looks good on you."

"The Wolves got lucky, but luck runs out. Vipers never do, motherfuckers."

And when Wolves fans engaged, she was so passive-aggressive, calling them all sorts of names and trolling the hell out of them.

Jesus Christ.

She's like the most toxic little hellion online, channeling the fans' illogical feelings about games. I don't think I've ever heard her curse this way in real life, but she's proficient online.

It puts a smile on my face. At least she's moved on from the Wolves and their bastard captain.

The thought that Osborn has had his hands on her before me makes me murderous.

I close the laptop and stroke a strand of hair that's fallen on her face behind her ear.

She moans softly and leans into my palm, nuzzling her cheek as if she's a dog.

This woman will be the death of me.

Her eyes blink open and she stares at me for a few seconds under the delicate early-morning light. The hazel slowly transforms into the clearest, most enchanting green.

She's so fucking beautiful, it's hard to look at her without feeling a burn.

As if waking from a daze, Dahlia springs up and stares between me and the patient, her posture stiffening.

Seeing her transform into protective mode in the blink of an eye is fascinating.

"What are you doing here?" she asks in a clear, hard voice.

Well, fuck. I came without a second thought, so I didn't properly think of an excuse.

"An early-morning checkup before practice."

"Don't you have private doctors?"

"I do, but I needed to undergo tissue testing with a machine that's only available here."

She narrows her eyes. "How did you know I was in this room?"

"Jude."

"Jude?"

Sorry, big man. I owe you one.

I motion behind me to the other inert patient in the room. "That's his personal guard."

"Oh." She frowns. "I've never seen Jude visit him."

"Not when you're here since he doesn't like company. If you don't believe me, you can ask him."

She hikes a hand on her hip. "Then *you* ask him. Call him and put it on speaker."

"It sounds like you don't believe me."

"I don't. Go on."

Fuck.

I pull out my phone and call, but Jude doesn't answer.

Good save.

"Probably still asleep," I say as I hang up and then shoot him a quick message, pretending to frown at my phone.

Me: At the hospital. You better be on your way.

Dahlia's wide eyes are still narrowed, but she releases a sigh and tidies up her space. "You can go now. My sister is wary of strangers."

"Pretty sure she can't tell if she's in a coma."

She glares at me.

"Too soon?"

"Just go away."

I sit on her chair and throw a fleeting glance at the slumbering patient.

"Half-sister?"

She sits on the bed, blocking my view. "Why do you think that?"

"You don't look alike."

"Foster sister." Her voice softens as she takes her sister's hand in hers. "She's the only family I have."

"What happened?" I feign interest.

"We don't really know, but she was attacked and dropped off at a hospital in Stantonville. She's been in a coma since."

"I'm sorry."

Her eyes meet mine, glittery, with an unnatural shine. "Thanks, but she'll come back. I know it."

I want to tell her not to hold on to false hope and to hit her upside the head with hard facts that comatose patients don't just come back and she should give up, but I can't bring myself to.

Usually, I don't give a fuck about people's feelings.

Dahlia is proving to be an exception in ways I fail to recognize.

But I still say, "If you want to handle her medical bills, isn't it a smart idea to take the offer I gave you?"

"The foundation pays for her bills."

"Then you can have an internship with reasonable hours, higher pay, and with enough prestige to add to your résumé. It's the smartest thing to do."

She releases her sister's hand and whisper-yells, "You sure it's not so you can have access to me at all times for your sick games?"

I pull her by the arm until she crashes against my chest, her face a breath away from mine. "*Our* sick games, and I can have access to you whether or not you're on the team."

Her breathing escapes in long, choppy sounds, her eyes flickering between dark green and furious brown.

I see it then. The reason she's been avoiding me.

"You're scared, aren't you?" I murmur in hot words against her skin.

"I'm not scared." She pushes my chest.

"You're trembling, frightened that you love it so much. You're appalled that if I hunt and chase and fuck you so brutally, you'll fall apart all over again. Admit it, wildflower, your inner animal was made for mine."

"You made me do it. I'm not as sick as you."

"Then say 'red'."

She purses her lips.

I let my mouth curve in a smile. "You didn't even think about that word, did you? You were enjoying it too much to consider stopping it. Bet you touched your tight little cunt to the memory."

"Shut up."

"As you wish."

I lean closer, my attention on her mouth. Her fractured breathing skims over my skin.

I don't even like kissing, but ever since she kissed me, I've been fantasizing about biting her lips, sinking my teeth into them and devouring her through them.

"Get a room and stop disturbing the patients," Jude grunts, walking in with an ugly expression.

Dahlia stumbles back, her face paling and all traces of heat disappearing from her delicate features.

Fucking Jude will get his ass kicked in practice today.

We watch as he places a basket of fruit on his guard's side table.

Dahlia stands upright, moving slowly to the other bed as if she can protect the patient. "You really know Mario?"

"What's it to you?" He faces her fully and we exchange a look. "Besides, shouldn't you be gone around this time so I can visit in peace?"

Dahlia frowns but says nothing.

I stand and offer her my hand. "Let me take you to get breakfast."

She ignores me and kisses her sister on the forehead. "See you tonight, Vi."

When she straightens, she glances at my hand and pauses, then takes it like a very good girl.

Not my hand, though.

Dahlia wraps both her palms around my wrist and pushes the sleeve of my pullover up, revealing the purple marks from the chain. Her eyes widen and I curse internally.

I was so hasty to come here, I forgot to wrap bandages around them.

"What happened?" Her voice is soft, but the alarmed look on her face stabs me worse than her words.

I don't like pity in general, but I especially loathe it from Dahlia.

"Nothing you need to worry about." I subtly tug my hand free and pull down the sleeve.

She opens her mouth to say something, but I cut her off, "Let's get out of here."

I catch a glimpse of Jude, who shakes his head.

Dahlia doesn't resist as I guide her out of the room.

When I look back, Violet's hand twitches on the sheet.

CHAPTER 20
Dahlia

I CAN'T STOP LOOKING AT KANE'S RIGHT HAND.

The images of those deep-purple bruises and cuts on his wrist still play in my mind in haunting, disturbing strokes.

Especially since I already know he has multiple old scars slashing across his back.

Ever since I saw those bruises in the hospital, I've been watching him closely. I noticed his complexion is paler today, his lips slightly blue, and his eyes are colder.

What happened to him between last night's game and this morning?

And why the hell am I so invested when I spent days trying to put a healthy amount of distance between us?

Kane's ordeals should be none of my concern.

I lean back against Kane's car, the metal cool against my spine as the frigid air bites into my skin. Not sure if I should even be touching his expensive-looking car. But when I attempted to stand away from him, Kane dragged me back to his side.

Below us, Graystone Ridge stretches out like a map, the town still cloaked in the last traces of night, rooftops and streets softened by the dawn's dim light. The sun is just beginning to break through, casting a golden haze over the buildings, making everything seem almost peaceful.

As peaceful as this den of vipers could get.

The cool wind tugs at my hair, carrying the faint scent of pine from the woods behind us. And just for one suspended moment in time, it feels like we're the only two people awake in the world.

"You're staring." Kane doesn't look at me and, instead, eyes his convenience store sandwich as if it's spoiled goods.

"Sorry." I bite into my cheese and lettuce sandwich and follow with a long slurp of iced coffee.

"You better apologize for this travesty of food."

"Well, no other place was open this early."

"We could've gone to a proper restaurant."

"And have you miss open skate? Stop being picky and just eat."

He sniffs the bread before he takes a tentative bite.

"How is it?" I ask.

"Edible, but depressingly flavorless and not fresh."

I laugh and hit his shoulder. "You're such a snob."

"For wanting fresh food?"

"That's not a luxury all of us can afford."

"You can from now on."

My shoulders tense up. "I don't need your charity."

Funny because I didn't mind when Isabella or Preston called me a charity case. Hell, I'm keeping my sister alive solely through charity that Kane's family definitely pitches into.

But I don't want him to look at me like that.

Not now.

Is it a stupid sense of pride? Something else?

While I can't exactly put a name to it, I just don't like it.

Kane must feel my aggression, because he shifts, his weapon of a body straightening as his eyes pin me in place.

"You need to stop this line of thinking, Dahlia. I don't consider it charity. I consider it taking care of you. All you have to do is accept it and quit getting your guard up."

"I don't know. Preston told me I'm just a charity case who will never make a full Vencor member, because only those of your standing are allowed in. So excuse me if I have my doubts."

He faces me, his head tilting to the side, his voice dangerously low. "You believe Preston over me?"

I swallow the coffee trapped in my mouth, the sound echoing in the silence and only interrupted by the rustling leaves. "He seemed convincing."

"Answer the question, Dahlia. Whose words are more important to you? Mine or Preston's?"

I bite my lower lip but remain silent.

"If I say you're not a charity case and Preston says you are, who do you believe?"

"You."

"Then why do you stiffen every time I do something for you?"

"I'm not used to it," I whisper, then lift my chin. "I've worked for everything I have, no matter how small it is. I don't like owing others."

"I'm not *others*." He wraps his large hand around my throat, not choking, but holding me in place. "You'll get used to what I give you and take it without objection."

My pulse throbs beneath his thumb and he watches it, his eyes darkening.

I feel as if I'm falling into his glittery trap again. After everything I did to convince myself I'm not as sick as he is. Even attempting to believe he forced me.

But one touch. One look. And I'm slipping again.

The feel of his skin on mine is electrifying and my body pulses to life, wanting more.

I'm apprehensive.

No. I'm terrified by how much more I want from a man like Kane.

So I focus on what keeps us apart, not what we have in common. "What about the rest of what Preston said? Am I wasting my time?"

Kane releases me with a sigh. "Those who get full membership are indeed of our social standing, and I can do nothing about that. I don't make the rules."

"Then why didn't you tell me?" My voice trembles. "Did you like toying with me?"

"I didn't think you actually believed you'd make full membership. Surely you're smart enough to understand how much vetting goes on in such organizations."

A weight drops in my chest as a wave of hopelessness washes over me.

Yes, I knew it was hard, but I didn't think it was impossible.

I take a large bite of my sandwich to keep from lashing out.

"Dahlia, be reasonable. That's not a place you want to be in."

I keep chewing and stare ahead. The sky is a soft gradient, pale blue bleeding into shades of pink and gold, and the first rays of sunlight cut across the horizon, igniting the edges of the town.

Kane raises a brow. "Is this the equivalent of leaving me on Read?"

Swallowing, I face him, my tone lethargic. "What else are you hiding from me?"

"Possibly as much as you're hiding from me."

I lift my chin. "I don't know what you're talking about."

"Sure thing, wildflower. If you say so. But at any rate, whatever we're hiding doesn't matter. We're only using each other's bodies because we share the same depraved fantasies." He smiles, his voice dropping an octave. "Correction. *I* am using your body because you love being used."

"You—" I stop myself from calling him names.

It'll just backfire. And it's not like he's wrong. I ghosted him because I was terrified about how much I loved the sex in the maze.

I was horrified about how much I was turned on.

I contemplated therapy for real and spent days reading articles upon articles about rape fantasies and primal play and only came up more confused about how much I wanted it.

How much I *still* want it.

And the only person who knows my sick tendencies is the equally sick man standing beside me.

He smiles with unmasked cruelty, showing me the side of him that got off on hunting me down. "I'm what? A pervert? An asshole you hate but still fantasize about his cock?"

"Oh please. It wasn't that impressive. I've had better in my day." *Lie, lie, and more lies.*

"Dahlia…" The warning spreads across my skin in a sheen of goosebumps. "Don't make me bend you over the car and use that cunt. We'll see if any of the other dicks *you've had* are impressive when you bounce on my cock."

I step back.

Jesus. I was only trying to provoke him.

A smirk touches the corner of his lips. "Don't worry, I won't fuck you. When I do, you won't see it coming."

Damn Kane Davenport.

He has a way of keeping me on my toes. And why the hell am I overrun with both excitement and dread?

He leans back against the car, his gaze fixed on the town below. There's a calmness in him, a dangerous sort of ease, and the air between us feels charged, the small space separating us almost nonexistent.

I'm being pulled into his orbit, I realize.

Another star that's drawing too close to the sun.

But this star will crash before I let him consume me.

So what if Vencor's membership is off-limits? I still have the hockey team that he insisted I join.

And most importantly, I have *him*.

I'll use him fully to get my sister justice, even if my chest starts to tighten at the thought.

After I'm introduced to the team, I fill out the paperwork and speak with the medical staff about my new intern position. The team doctor tasks me with paperwork and with watching the players and detecting any possible injuries.

Kane doesn't like the last part.

Honestly, he doesn't seem to like any particular part.

I wouldn't say I'm accepted with open arms. I can see the doubt and even downright hostility from Gavin, Jude, and some other players who are also part of Vencor. The rest are mostly unaffected or don't even notice me.

I'm sure they're resistant to an outsider in their midst. Someone like me who doesn't belong to their high and mighty social standing.

The only reason the hostile ones don't give me a piece of their mind is due to Kane's presence. It's evident that no one on the team talks back to him. The players respect him immensely—which is easily seen from the focused and reverent way they look at him. Even the coach speaks to him like an equal.

Despite my motives, I'm serious about my job.

So I spend most of the open skate talking to the team doctor about ways to improve the players' agility and minimize injury. I also speak to the head physical therapist about the areas of potential muscle strain of each player.

He and the rest of the team check them regularly and often give them sports massages to help loosen their tense muscles. I'm fascinated by the amazing equipment and machines they have access to. But then again, the team is almost on a pro level and is the reigning champion of the college league, so the program makes sure they reach their full potential.

Doesn't hurt that many players are sickeningly rich, so their families pour endless amounts of money into the team.

Who would've thought that the field I chose, medicine with a focus on physical therapy to help with Violet's constant back pain and bad shoulder, would now be used to benefit the entitled assholes?

One of whom could have attempted to kill her.

By the end of open skate, I've got the gist of areas with potential improvement chances. So I head back to the bench area after the managing team leaves.

The players head to the showers, smacking each other, and talking loudly. It's a chaos of overwhelming testosterone.

There are a few female staff, the most important being the team administrative manager, but they're mostly in their offices.

As most of the team filters out, Kane skates toward me and stops at the barrier, then removes his helmet and runs a hand through his damp hair. It randomly falls to his forehead, partly camouflaging the iciness in his eyes. Though they're clearer now, less frozen and more…familiar.

He looks absolutely stunning in his hockey gear with his hair wet, fresh out of open skate. I'm sure I'm not supposed to find him hot or beautiful, but he's both of those and more.

I blame his depraved sexual tastes.

Because whenever I see him, my mind keeps replaying images from that maze.

Hot, electrifying, and erotic scenes that drive me insane.

Kane leans both his arms on the railing so they're hanging right in front of me.

"That looked fun." I clear my husky voice. "The team's spirit is back, right?"

"Partially."

"Why only partially?"

He pauses and stares at the gloves in his hand. "Preston ditched open skate."

"He's probably ashamed about his poor performance from last night. He'll come back."

"He never ditches open skate. Besides, he lacks the ability to feel shame."

I frown.

Honestly, Preston can choke, but I don't like that his absence causes strain on the team and Kane. That slimy bastard is one of the Vipers' indispensable pillars and has constantly been in impressive form.

Except for yesterday.

But, also, I seemed to have underestimated the bond between Kane and Preston.

Possibly Jude as well.

"Have you checked in on him?" I ask.

"I will." He watches me, his gaze heavy and imploring. "Enough about the team. Tell me, how was your first day?"

"It was fine. I have a lot to work on."

"Don't work too much."

"I'm confused. Didn't you push me to accept this position so I can work?"

"Not really. It's so I can keep an eye on you."

"So I'm here for your *entertainment*?"

His lips pull in a smile. "If you want to call it that, suit yourself."

"Wow. You're not even going to offer excuses?"

"I believe we're at the point in our relationship where we don't need to offer those, don't you think?"

I release an exasperated breath, trying not to think about the part where he said 'our' relationship. There's *no* relationship.

We're only using each other.

That's it.

I'll make sure that's *all*.

"See you tonight at my place." The vibration of Kane's low voice drags me from my thoughts.

I draw a circle on my thumb. "Why?"

"Be there, Dahlia."

"And if I don't want to?"

"I wasn't asking."

"You need to stop doing that, Kane."

"I'll send you the code. Let yourself in." He smiles, pats my hair as if I'm some sort of pet, and then joins his teammates.

What a prick.

Anyway, I pretend to clean up with the team and discretely gather DNA samples, mostly sweaty towels, especially from those I know are Vencor members—namely Jude.

I manage to steal his glove that he changed earlier after it tore due to his inhuman strength.

It's unfortunate that Preston didn't make it to practice today, but I'll eventually add his DNA to my arsenal. Hopefully, I can find a clue within the team's Vencor members, because infiltrating the actual organization is proving to be next to impossible.

And, hopefully, I won't lose myself in this world.

And, more importantly, in Kane.

Just the thought of what he's planning tonight makes me tremble.

Fear and excitement mingle so homogeneously, I can't distinguish them.

I tell myself I'll ignore him.

Even as I walk into his trap with my own two feet.

CHAPTER 21
Kane

I WAIT IN THE SHADOWS.

I'm *used* to the shadows.

The shadows have been my friends since the systematic destruction of my childhood.

It's what made me who I am.

That's probably also the reason I have deviant tastes and a thirst for sexual violence.

Which is why I've kept it under wraps.

Being celibate for months on end was easier than indulging in mind-numbing, soul-crushing vanilla fucking.

Trying to restrain myself was a painstaking task I preferred not to undergo. What the girls meant by 'harder' misaligned with my understanding of the word.

They meant deeper in a way that heightened their pleasure but didn't hurt them.

While for me, my flavor of sexual deviance was complete fucking control with a touch of pain.

A dash of sadism.

A sprinkle of tears.

It truly turns me on to see the woman I'm fucking enjoying the pain as much as the pleasure.

Dahlia is the only girl who takes my raw, depraved sexual dominance. And the best part? She gets off on it.

She comes harder when the pain and pleasure blend together until she can't breathe.

The only hiccup is that she's also terrified of it. I saw it in her eyes earlier today when I invited her over.

There was fear.

But there was also a tinge of anticipation—I'm counting on that part to bring her to my door.

The room is draped in thick, still silence as I lean against the wall. The town's lowlights slice through the darkness in jagged lines, catching the edge of the glass but never reaching me.

My pulse is steady, but underneath it, there's something darker, coiled tight, ready to snap. My index finger twitches and I force it back to stillness.

I've never been eager.

Never coveted something enough to break my rules for it.

I've even erased any semblance of emotion.

And yet I can't control the flexing of my muscles or the blood rushing to my groin.

I'm hard just thinking about what I'll do to her.

How I'll trap her.

Consume her.

Leave her no way out.

Deep inside, I know I shouldn't get involved any further with Dahlia Thorne, but fuck if my dick can understand logic. He's been restrained for months on end, and now that I've stumbled onto his favorite flavor, there's no stopping him.

The door clicks open.

I stand to my full height but don't change position.

She came.

A part of me thought she'd ghost me and shun this unorthodox agreement. But I should've known.

Dahlia's animal is a mirror of mine.

I can smell her before seeing her. The softest scent of jasmine carries in the air and seeps into my nostrils.

"Hello?"

I remain one with the shadows, my breathing muted and my presence concealed, but my attention is zoned in on the merest stutter in her breath, the pause in her steps, and each rustle of her clothes.

"Kane?" Her voice is slightly spooked, on edge, and has a faint tremor she's trying hard to conceal. "This isn't funny."

I smile to myself.

That's it. Come closer, my little prey.

"Where the hell are the lights in this place?" she grumbles, her shoes shuffling on the floor.

Concealed.

They usually go on automatically, but I disabled that option, so unless I turn them back on, we're bathed in my natural habitat.

Darkness.

The city lights flash outside, but it's all static—meaningless. The real storm is sharpening and coiling inside me.

Dahlia's feet come to a halt a short distance away as if she can feel my presence.

"Kane?" Her low whisper is heightened by the brutal silence.

"I'll count to three and then I'll chase you," I speak in a deep voice.

"What happened to hello?" she asks in a bravado tone, but she's already shuffling backward. "Can't you do normal for once, asshole?"

"You don't like normal, wildflower. It bores you to tears. *One.*"

A swallow—or, more accurately, a gulp—echoes in the air as she searches the darkness. When she speaks, there's a tense energy in her voice, caught between dread and anticipation. "What will you do when you catch me?"

"I'll fuck you so hard, you won't be able to walk. I'll own every inch of you, and your cunt will remember my cock for days. Two."

"Oh God." A few more frantic steps. "Wait. Let me mentally prepare myself. Count to ten—"

"Your time is up. Three."

She shrieks as I pounce from my hiding space. Her eyes widen for the briefest second, the light from outside breaking and highlighting those hazel gates of my nightmarish chaos.

It's only a moment in time, but she's smart enough to realize being immobile is the surest way to end up beneath my claws. Dahlia sprints in the opposite direction, mindlessly hitting the edge of the sofa and cursing.

That doesn't stop her, though. She's a fighter, my wildflower, and a cunning survivor, and soon picks up her speed.

My pace is steady and slow as I toy with her, reveling in her every frenzied move, every agitated breath expelling from her lungs.

The scent of her smothers me. The sound of her fear-laced gasps makes my cock twitch and tent against my pants.

She rushes to the kitchen area, her shadow large and magnified on the opposite wall.

Then all movements disappear.

Even her breaths slow to low muffles.

Hmm. She must be blocking her mouth with her hands.

I've always loved how her brain works under pressure. She has A+ survival instinct.

Unfortunately for her, I also have the most acute inborn predatory sense.

The fridge door opens, its light illuminating the space in a soft hue as a few kitchen stools get rummaged around.

"Given up already?" I round the kitchen counter and make my way to the fridge. "Didn't take you for a quitter."

Her breaths slow down further and her presence dwindles until it's almost nonexistent.

Almost.

I stop by the island. "I can smell you, Dahlia."

Instead of going to the fridge area, where she placed the perfect decoy, I tilt my head down to where she crammed her body between the stools and right beneath the island.

Both her hands cover her mouth and nose, and she's so still, someone would mistake her for a statue.

I let my lips pull in a sadistic grin. "Found you."

Her yelp reverberates in the air as she scrambles, knocking the stools over on her way out.

But my prey is trapped between my claws already. She just doesn't know it yet.

Dahlia doesn't make it three steps before I grab her by the ponytail and pull her back so hard, her shriek pierces my ears.

With one swipe, I knock away the counter's contents, pans and glass cluttering and crashing on the floor, then shove her against it. With her chest on the marble and her ass in the air, she looks like my favorite prey.

I lean over so my mouth hovers close to her ear. "You can scream all you want. No one will hear you and it'll only turn me on."

"Fuck you!"

"Patience. I'll get to that in a bit." With a groan, I roll my hips and thrust my pelvis against her round, full ass.

The urge to own this hole that no one has touched before me lurks in my bones and overflows my nerves.

A growl spills from deep in her throat and she bucks against me, trying to twist, so I unbutton her jeans, then grab the waistband and pull them down in one go.

She's about to fight, but I slap her pussy. Her bare fucking wet pussy.

Because Dahlia isn't wearing any underwear.

"If I'm disgusting, what does that make you?" I sink my fingers into her inviting folds. "Not only did you come prepared to be fucked, but you're also soaking wet for me. Can't wait to be used as my cumhole?"

I slap her ass a few consecutive times, reveling in the way it reddens.

She cries out, going still, so I do it again and again, until my handprints mark her tanned skin.

Then I part her ass and she stiffens.

"What are you doing—"

Her words end in a gasp when I thrust two of my fingers inside her mouth. "Suck. Make them nice and wet."

Dahlia's hot tongue wraps around my fingers and she lathers them with saliva. I stand with my legs shoulder width apart, my hardening cock brushing against her bruised ass.

Each of her licks make the tent in my pants grow bigger and thicker. The sounds of her licking mix with the fridge's *beep, beep, beep*.

With a grunt, I pull my fingers from her mouth and slide them between her ass cheeks, probing her back hole.

"Kane, no! Not there."

"Shh. I'm not asking for permission."

"No...fuck..." Her cheek lies flat on the island as I thrust my finger inside her tight hole.

"Mmm. This will be mine soon. You'll let me use this ass as I see fit, won't you?"

"No...stop...that hurts—"

I tighten my grip on her nape and whisper near her ear as I thrust inside her tight channel, "You know how to stop it, but you won't, you know why? Because you enjoy the pain as much as the pleasure like a dirty little whore."

"Fuck you..." The words spill out of her in a huff.

"As you wish." I stand up and force a second finger in and she shrieks, but her walls stretch around me, trying to accommodate me. "That's it. You need to fit my fingers so you can take my cock."

Her broken breaths echo in the air as I pump my hand in, enjoying the view of my handprints on her ass and the way she writhes, trying to take me in as much as possible. Her pelvis slams against the edge of the island with each back-and-forth.

She's trying to get off.

Not so soon.

I release her hair and pull my fingers from inside her.

Dahlia faces me, her cheeks crimson red and her lips trembling. Then this beautiful fucked-up hellion glares at me and slaps me across the face. "Don't touch me, you disgusting prick."

I laugh, the sound echoing around us like a dark tune.

She knows I'll slap her back. She does, and she still did it anyway.

I lift a hand and she tightens her body, ready for the hit, but I imprison her jaw, studying her expression under the fridge's soft light.

She tries to shove me away, and I rub my clothed cock against her thighs, making sure not to offer her any form of friction. "Fight me, wildflower. You know it makes me fucking hard."

Guttural sounds leave her lungs as she steps on my foot and punches me in the stomach. As hard as she can, packing all her strength into it, only to be met by my tightening muscles.

"Such a vicious little minx." I leisurely unbutton my jeans and free my hard cock. "You seem mad, but I don't feel it."

"I'm going to fucking kill you!" She punches, bites, and even pulls my hair, pouring all her energy into trying to hurt me.

She sinks her tiny claws beneath my shirt and scratches my skin.

Dahlia doesn't stop even as I grab her hips and lift her off the floor, her feet kicking in the air and her arms flailing around. I set her on the counter and yank off her jeans, her sneakers flying away in the process.

"Is that all you got?" I fist her hair and strain her face up, smiling. "I thought you hated me more than this."

She opens her mouth and I spit right inside it.

Dahlia freezes, a red hue covering her cheeks, but she swallows.

Her fingers sink into my hair as she bites my lower lip. The skin stretches and breaks beneath her teeth, but the sting barely registers as she thrusts her tongue against mine.

A cord snaps within me.

I devour her, biting down on her lip, blending our blood in a symphony of violent desire.

"Fuck me like you hate me," she murmurs, panting against my mouth.

"Careful," I whisper back. "You might not be able to walk for a week."

My little wildflower licks my bottom lip, then sucks it between hers before releasing it. "Promises, promises."

"I'm going to use you like a filthy little slut." My fingers tighten on her hip as I thrust into her with so much power, she bucks off the counter.

Her moan echoes in the air, and she holds on to the sides of my shirt for dear life.

With her head thrown back, her slick neck shines with sweat beneath the dim lighting. So I lower my head and bite her pulse point.

Her taste explodes on my tongue like my favorite meal, and I sink my teeth in, sucking deep, matching the power of my fucking.

"Oh God, yes...yes..." She opens her legs wide, giving me more access as her hand slips beneath my shirt, clawing at my back.

Clawing is fine.

I can handle her kitten-like scratches.

As long as she's not stroking or doing any of the disgusting sentimental shit she attempted the other time.

"You like being fucked like an animal, don't you?" I pull all the way back, then thrust in again. "You like being used to get me off?"

She screams, her body shaking around mine. "Shut up... just go harder..."

"Such a greedy whore."

I rise to my full height and push her back against the counter, then pull her shirt and slide the bra up, exposing her perky breasts.

At this angle, I plunge deeper, sinking into her with raw strength.

Dahlia tries to meet my thrusts, but she can't, so she

scratches me anywhere she can reach—my arms, my back, my stomach.

Her moans are raspy and throaty, her cunt stretching and swallowing my cock like it was made for me.

Dahlia was made for *me*.

Her body is mine.

Her moans are mine.

Even her violence is fucking *mine*.

I clench her shirt and it tears under my grip, so I wrap my hand around her throat and feel her swallows, the vibration of her vocal cords with each moan.

"You love choking." I incrementally tighten my grip. "Your pussy is strangling me."

She glares at me as she scratches me, definitely breaking skin, and I laugh. "You're going to come, aren't you?"

"Fuck you..." Her words echo in a muffled moan.

"You act so tough, but you're such a whore for my cock, wildflower." I pull back and ram against her sensitive spot.

Her eyes roll back, and all words seem to flee her.

So I do it again.

"Come for me." I release her hip and circle her clit. "Show me who owns you."

Dahlia's limbs jerk and I have to remember that I'm only using her for sex.

I have to remind myself that this isn't going against my rules and losing control, this is only to fulfill a basic urge—sex.

But fuck if I can ignore how damn stunning she looks when she comes apart on my cock.

Her moans are throatier, her skin blushed and slick with sweat, and her cunt smothers my cock, milking me for an orgasm I'm always on the verge of having when around her.

And the worst part?

She's now caressing me.

Her claws have retracted and she's gliding her fingers along my back, my sides, stroking all the scars no one should get close to.

Fuck *that*.

Fuck Dahlia Thorne and her disturbing touch.

I release her clit and pull her arms from my waist, holding both her wrists in one hand as I pump into her.

Rage coils inside me until what's left is a bestial, primitive need for dominance.

Dahlia's eyes widen, her hands flexing in my grip.

I don't know whether she's turned on or terrified or both, but I don't care.

She should've kept scratching me instead of touching me like we're anything but this fucked-up coexistence.

I tighten my grip on her throat until her pussy clenches.

"Kane…" she strains. "Come…inside…me…"

"Fuck!"

I pull out at the last second and come all over her stomach and tits, my cum creating a sheen on her skin.

Fucking hell.

If she hadn't said that, I would've filled her cunt with my cum and feasted on it.

I would've betrayed my second rule.

The first was no sex without a condom, which went down the drain the first time I fucked this infuriating woman.

And since then, I haven't been able to stomach the idea of not feeling her walls stretching and contracting against my cock. So I promised myself that there would be no coming inside her.

Ever.

But just now, I almost did.

If anything, I was looking forward to pumping her full of my cum.

Dahlia is a fucking thorn in my side and the one plot hole in my life I can't seem to find a solution to.

I release her and step back, breathing harshly.

"Why…" She swallows, looking so fucking mine while lying on the counter naked with my cum covering her. "Why won't you come inside me?"

"Shut the fuck up."

"Why do you not like it when I touch you?"

"I said shut the fuck up, Dahlia."

"Well, I'm sorry. I didn't think being fuck buddies meant a lack of conversation. Give better instructions next time."

I can't kill her.

Grinding my teeth, I pull up my jeans and tuck myself in, then walk to the fridge that gave up on beeping and grab a water bottle, throwing it near her.

She doesn't stir, but her droopy eyes follow my every move.

I retrieve my phone and enable the lights, then go to the guest bathroom, and draw a hot bath.

As the sound of the water fills the space, I check my phone.

I find a few unread texts in 'The Vipers' Den' group chat. Obviously named by Preston.

> Jude: The fuck you've been doing, Pres? Heard you fucked your stepmom's friend?
> Preston: Heard you picked up stalking as a side gig.
> Jude: Fuck is wrong with you?
> Preston: I thought we were highlighting what we're doing lately?

Jude: Is this because you couldn't handle Osborn yesterday?

Preston: Say that name in my presence again and I'll stab you :)

Jude: Seriously? You missed open skate and started a small riot in the Armstrong household just because of last night? @Kane Davenport. We need to restrain the motherfucker before this escalates.

Preston: I have it under control. May rip you a new one if I see you, though, big man. Be on the lookout.

Jude: Me?

Preston: Next time, don't start punching just because I got hit.

Jude: I ALWAYS do that. The fuck?

Me: It's because Osborn said Preston is a dainty prince who can't even defend himself. Made him look weak. It's probably why he lost his mind and went for his throat.

Preston: *Kane added to the death list*

Jude: The provocateur is being provoked?

Preston left the group chat

I shake my head, slide my phone in my pocket, and place a bathrobe on the rack.

As I step into the hallway, my senses fill with Dahlia's scent, and my dick twitches back to life.

Fuck. This is a problem.

"You can take a bath, then leave," I say from the hallway.

No response.

I walk back to the kitchen. "You need help getting up…?"

My movements halt when I find her sleeping. On the counter. In the exact same position I left her.

Her chest rises and falls, and she releases soft snores.

I can't help but stroke some damp strands from her forehead, revealing a serene face.

Fuck.

She's beautiful.

And all mine.

As I carry her in my arms, I have a disturbing feeling that she'll mess up my life in more ways than one.

That is, if that's not already happening.

CHAPTER 22
Dahlia

I'M COMING UP EMPTY.

Despite my attempts to dig into the Vipers' medical records and find any suspicious absences close to the date of Vi's attack, they're so neat and tidy, it's impossible to find any discrepancies.

In the span of the week since I started this job, I've managed to gather DNA evidence from most players, including Preston, and they all came out negative.

I'm back to square one again.

I thought maybe I could gather some clues about Vi's attack, but it's proving impossible.

Even if I get invited to Vencor's parties, what am I supposed to do under so much surveillance?

Out myself and possibly get killed before I discover anything, that's what.

As I sit in my small office in Vipers Arena, I flip through the backlog files in a last attempt to find anything out of the ordinary.

My ass hurts and I shift in my chair. A groan slips out of me as my muscles scream in pain.

That asshole Kane really meant it about my inability to walk. I can't even sit without feeling every inch of him inside me.

Since that time he ambushed me in his apartment, he's been asking me to meet him every single day. Sometimes, at his place, and other times, in secluded forests.

And let me tell you, that man is a fucking animal. I don't know where he gets the stamina or how he comes up with new ways to make me scream.

It's like a rollercoaster ride with no ending in sight.

He always chases me first, and when he catches me, he fucks me on all sorts of surfaces—the floor, the stairs, against a tree, in the bathtub.

Everywhere.

Every time I think I've figured out his pattern and come up with a plan to escape or hide, he always finds me. No exceptions.

It's a thrill. A high I think I'll never come down from.

I'm an addict who can't quit.

It's impossible to even think about abandoning the hit he injects in my veins with every encounter.

Whenever he sets up a meeting, I get a tingly feeling in my spine. A need for more.

More.

So much more.

Hell, I believe I've been conditioned so deeply, I wouldn't consider any other form of sex enjoyable anymore.

I'm surprised I even opened my legs for mediocre experiences in the past.

Kane is right. Normal sex bored me to tears. Before him, I thought it was expected not to completely enjoy sex, and those mind-numbing orgasms were the stuff of novels.

I never thought that being hate-fucked to within an inch of my life was the answer.

With a groan, I hit my head on the table. I'm so sick.

And so is he.

But somehow, it works.

I love sex again. I dream of him fucking me and wake up with my hand in my wet pussy.

The violence, the chase, the aggression, and even the name-calling turns me on.

His whole presence turns me on.

Pretty sure I've become a sex addict, even if my body barely keeps up with our brutal, bruise-inducing toxic-as-fuck sex.

The *whole* thing is toxic, really.

Kane is adamant about the 'using each other' part and refuses to budge. That man doesn't have a gentle bone in his body. Whenever I try to stroke his skin or hug him, he stiffens as if I plunged my hand into his chest and ripped out his heart or something.

He also always gets mad and shuts down, so I've stopped doing it.

I hate the lack of connection, but it's better than having him snap or completely withdraw behind his high walls.

At least when I pretend to be fine with the relationship as it is, he drives me back to his place and offers me baths. He even cooks me food and sends me so many clothes that Megan is getting suspicious.

So I had to tell her it's a sex-only relationship and that the rich love flaunting their money.

But this thing with Kane is highly dysfunctional outside of the sex. My imaginary therapist would point out that even the sex is dysfunctional as fuck, but we both enjoy that, so it doesn't count.

I tried being gradual in forming a connection. But he shuts me out so fast, it's a struggle to talk to him.

If I so much as ask about his life, try to get closer, or touch him softly, he completely abandons me.

The way he switches from cordial to an absolute asshole is starting to mess with my head.

I know I'm losing myself to this toxic cycle, but I'm actually scared of seeing his back.

I *hate* his back.

I hate how easily he could turn around and walk away as if I don't exist.

But then again, we're not in a relationship, and he made it clear that what we have revolves around sex only, and I agreed, so I shouldn't feel this way.

Besides, Megan was right. I shouldn't hope for anything more from a Davenport. He's using me? Well, I'm also using him to have access to the secret world he comes from.

If he's not much help, it doesn't matter. Because his mom invited me for tea three days ago when she dropped some pastries off at his apartment—that he refused to accept—so I'll make sure to go.

My fingers pause on a handwritten log that was kept by a previous medical assistant who used to watch the players' diets.

It's not because of the notes per se, but the date. September 20.

That's when Violet was attacked.

I read the notes, but they're normal, about the players' diets, the injuries, and the prescribed supplements.

Then my eyes widen when I find a small note at the bottom of the page.

Note: Hunter Maddox, Gavin Drayton, and Ryder Price missed practice for unknown injuries.

Unknown injuries.

My mind races as I flip to the following days. The three players aren't mentioned again until September 23 when they resume practice. No injuries are logged, and they get back to it with no rehabilitation programs or dietary changes.

This isn't a coincidence, right?

Gavin and Ryder's DNA came out as a negative match. Hunter's is the only one I haven't had the opportunity to gather. Probably because he's a neat freak and always wipes all his equipment down before and after use. He also tucks all his belongings in his locker and is particular about who touches his things.

Gavin is the goalie. Ryder and Hunter are defensemen. They usually hang out together, and their parents are influential in the town.

My mind pieces together the details from the event at Preston's house. The three masked Vencor members I listened to that night were Gavin and Ryder. The third was definitely Hunter.

Maybe I'm onto something.

My skin tingles with anticipation. Finally, a breakthrough.

Though it's not as good as finding the mastermind behind my sister's attack, this is a start.

My priority is to try accessing the team doctor's files from September 20.

Gather a sample of Hunter's DNA.

Maybe get closer to the three of them? Gavin kind of hates me after the fiasco at his place that time. And if the rumors about his sister's banishment and social suicide are true, I don't suspect he'll ever warm up to me. I don't think I've seen Isabella on campus since the day she sent people to drug me.

The other two pretend I don't exist.

Actually, most players do the same except for Preston, who loves to harass me every time he sees me, and Jude, who glares at me for no reason. I'm starting to think that's his default mood.

Twirling my pen, I'm considering ways to acquire Hunter's DNA sample when my phone vibrates.

I startle, kicking my thighs against the table, and I drop my pen.

Kane: See you tonight at my place.

I narrow my eyes. Maybe it's because I'm sick and tired of his entitlement, but I type:

Me: No, thanks.
Kane: ?
Me: ???
Kane: Are you being sarcastic?
Me: Idk, will you try to communicate better?
Kane: What does 'No, thanks' mean, Dahlia?
Me: It means no and thanks. Have you lost the ability to read?
Kane: What the fuck are you playing at now?
Me: I'm not playing. I just need time off. You know, so I can recover properly and mentally prepare myself for your asshole behavior after you blow your load.
Kane: Since when do you care how I treat you after?
Me: Since now. It's one thing to degrade and humiliate me during sex, but afterward is different. I don't like the cold shoulder and the clipped communication. I'm not your booty call.

Kane: That's exactly what you are. And I won't give you the cold shoulder when you know your place and stop being nosy.

I bite my lower lip. He's right. Kane never promised me anything but sex. I don't even know why I'm being this butthurt about it.

He means nothing.

In reality, I hate him and where the hell he came from.

Me: You're just another dick who's fairly decent at fucking, so I'm glad we're on the same page.
Kane: Decent? Is that what it's called when you shatter on my cock multiple times a night?
Me: I said what I said. Anyway, I still don't want to see your face for, like, three days. It's tiresome.
Kane: Don't make me act uncivil.
Me: Isn't that your default setting?
Kane: Be there tonight.
Me: Only if you won't fuck me and we watch a movie or something like normal people.
Kane: We're not normal people.

I leave him on Read.

Kane: Don't you dare fucking leave me on Read.

Read.

Kane: Dahlia…

Read.

He's not the only one who can play the detached game. I don't even like the asshole.

Not one bit.

As I'm leaving the office, the players are filtering out of the locker room.

Hunter and Gavin are clad in Vipers hoodies, with duffel bags slung across their bodies, and speaking in a hushed tone. I try to get closer to overhear what they're talking about.

A large body blocks my path. "Look who we have here. Daisy."

Preston smiles down at me, his eyes a bright green.

Great.

I swear he only does this for pure entertainment.

"It's Dahlia. Seriously, how many *D* names will you say except for my actual one?"

"As many as it takes." He stands closer, trapping me against the wall.

"As many as it takes for what?"

"Don't you worry about that. Tell me, what did you say to Kane that provoked his teenage girl moment that ended with slamming the locker shut? While everyone was having a good time joking around? Instant mood killer. You're such a drag. Anyone ever tell you that?"

I narrow my eyes.

Preston is really hard to read.

Sometimes, he's threatening and calling names, and other times, he's joking around. I'm not sure whether or not he's diagnosed, but he gives off major ASPD vibes. He gets off on humiliating others and he often does it in a very backhanded way.

He's the master at ruffling his opponent's feathers and always gets out of it unscathed. Except with Marcus. Now, that bastard is definitely diagnosed.

One thing I've learned is that being weak or lying down and taking it—or worse, avoiding conflict—feeds their sadistic energy.

And I'm also in the mood to pick a fight.

So I grin. "Aren't *you* the drag? You know, because your uselessness caused the Vipers to lose for the first time this season."

His smile remains the same, but the glint slowly dims. "Is that so?"

"Uh-huh. Everyone watched as Marcus wrapped you around his pinkie finger and dragged you through the rink like deadweight." I match his smile. "As I said, *useless*."

I realize I've overdone it when it's too late.

Preston reaches an open hand out and wraps it entirely around my face, his fingers digging into my skull as if he'll break it.

Fear locks my limbs and I don't dare breathe.

"You need to learn how to shut the fuck up." His voice is creepily cold, completely different from his usual devil-may-care attitude. "You and that dirtbag Osborn are nothing more than bugs. You might buzz a little, might even sting and be a general nuisance, but make no mistake, I can *squash* you whenever I wish. I *will* end your miserable, annoying lives as I see fit."

Pressure grows in my head and I think he'll make good on his promise.

He'll kill me.

I feel it in my bones—he'll snap my neck and walk away as if nothing happened.

Then he'll get away with it because he was born into the right family and I'm a nobody.

His hand disappears.

My lips part and I blink away the moisture that's gathered in my eyes as Kane appears in front of me.

He's tall. Taller than usual. As he partially obstructs my view, I only see his back, broad and wide, blocking Preston's face.

And for the first time, I don't loathe the view of his back.

"Walk away," he says calmly.

"I was in the middle of something, Davenport. How about *you* walk away?"

I sink my fingers into the side of Kane's hoodie. I don't know what the hell just happened, but I was so sure Preston was going to kill me.

It's bloodlust, I realize. I felt the red haze in his touch and each of his words.

That's a man who's probably killed before and would do it again in a heartbeat.

"That something is over," Kane says without paying attention to my hand. "Go."

"I don't take orders from you. Step away."

My hand trembles. What if Kane lets him do whatever he wants to teach me a lesson?

What the hell did I get myself into?

"Touch her again, and you lose that hand, Armstrong."

Loud laughter spills from Preston. "Is that a threat?"

"A warning. Dahlia is mine and I made it clear that I don't like others touching what's mine."

There's a long, unbearable silence before Preston slams his shoulder against Kane's. Hard. Then he walks off.

I don't look at him, focusing on my trembling, chopped-off breaths.

What the hell is this feeling? A shot of adrenaline? The sensation of narrowly escaping death?

"Are you going to hold on to me forever?"

I release his hoodie and wince at the wrinkled mess I leave behind. "Sorry."

Kane faces me, his expression closed off, his eyes dark. "Is that all you have to say?"

"Thanks."

"Instead of thanking me, learn how to read the room and pick your fucking battles." His tone is biting, his angry words cutting into me like knives.

I've never seen Kane this enraged. Hell, I didn't think he was capable of this type of rage.

And the part that twists my stomach? It's the feeling that he's mad *for* me.

For *my* safety.

I swallow. "I…didn't know."

"But you must've felt it." He releases a long sigh. "Stay the fuck away from Preston and Jude. You don't have the slightest clue about what they're capable of."

"What about you?" I whisper. "I don't know what you're capable of either."

He strokes my cheek, his voice low and gravelly. "It's too late to stay away from me. You should've taken the chance when I first offered it."

CHAPTER 23
Dahlia

I HAVEN'T GONE TO KANE'S PLACE FOR THREE DAYS.

That doesn't stop me from visiting his mom. She texted and invited me over for afternoon tea, and I couldn't say no.

I've been let into the extravagant mansion by a member of staff who merely bowed at me and told me to follow him.

My hand tightens around the flowers I bought on my way here.

The Davenport mansion rivals the Armstrongs' in grandiosity and sheer opulence. They're both huge, shining, and smell of old money.

They both reek of death as well.

My chest has been tight since the moment I walked in.

The butler's steps echo on the checkered marble floor, a soft but steady rhythm that cuts through the dooming silence. He moves with precision, his posture straight and his bald scalp catching the dim light as we pass towering walls of dark wood and art whose creatures feel like they'll pop out and devour me.

The air is heavy, laced with something old that presses against my skin like a warning.

So…this is where Kane grew up.

How could he breathe amid this repressive energy?

My pulse beats in my throat as I study my surroundings,

the walls seeming to close in more the farther we walk. Every corner of this mansion feels untouched, frozen in time, like it exists outside of reality.

And yet…

Every inch of it is Kane. The controlled edges, the cold perfection, all laced with something darker beneath the surface.

No wonder he transformed into a fortress with no access. He was born into one.

"Does Kane visit often?" I ask the butler.

He says nothing, just glides ahead with his stiff posture, leading me deeper into the belly of this house, past heavy doors and windows draped in velvet.

Suddenly, he stops and gestures to the glass door framed in dark wood up ahead. Beyond it, I can see the faint outline of the garden.

He slides the door open without a word, and the crisp, sharp scents of earth and water hit me.

The garden is alive in a way the mansion isn't—soft camellia trees drifting in the breeze, the quiet trickle of a stream somewhere in the distance.

The stones beneath my feet feel solid, but each step I take pulls me further into images of what it must've felt like.

Kane grew up here. He was made somewhere between the house's cold walls and the tranquility of this garden.

I make out Helena's silhouette standing by a large pond.

She's wearing a soft beige dress with a shawl draped around her shoulders as she feeds fat koi fish.

I'm mesmerized by the view of the fish gliding effortlessly through the water and opening their mouths.

"Dahlia." She pauses upon seeing me, a faint smile painting her lips.

"Hi." I offer her the bouquet of flowers I spent a fortune to buy. "I hope you like this small gift."

"Aw, that's so thoughtful, thank you." She hugs the flowers to her chest and strokes the colorful petals. "I don't remember the last time I received flowers."

She motions in the direction of the glass door, and a staff member walks out with purpose and takes the bouquet.

"Put it in my room," Helena says, then faces me. "I need to feed these little ones before I can sit down. I hope you don't mind."

"Not at all. They're so beautiful."

"They are." A glaze covers her eyes as she stares at the pond. "What most people don't know is that beneath that beauty lies the most formidable resilience and strength. They can survive in harsh weather and swim against currents. They give me hope."

I study her profile. She seems half alive, and her voice sounds a bit tired. Lifeless, even.

My heart aches for her.

Helena must've been so beautiful in her youth, but now, her cheeks have sunken, and she's skin and bones.

I try to cheer her up. "Do you have favorites?"

"Sora." She motions at the largest red koi fish, who keeps beating the others to the food. "I got him when I first found out I was pregnant with Kane. All his siblings passed away, but he's going strong, nearing twenty-three years old."

"What does Sora mean?"

"Sky in Japanese. The wide, unrestrained, and all-encompassing sky." Her eyes soften as if she were looking at Kane.

Now, she's breaking my heart.

And I'm really disliking Kane. Would it hurt him to show some affection to his lonely mom?

Some of us would kill to have a mom.

"Would you like to feed them?" She offers me the ceramic bowl.

"Can I?"

"Absolutely."

I grab the bowl and start throwing out some pellets. The prick Sora eats it all, leaving the rest with open mouths and no food.

He shares Kane's all-or-nothing personality for sure.

It's his way or the highway.

After that encounter where I was nearly murdered by *his* friend, that asshole Kane has ghosted me for three days.

No kidding. There have been no texts, and he hasn't talked to me in the arena.

Just because I said I didn't want to see his face for three days. I was actually being vengeful because he refused to get together if sex wasn't involved, but I didn't think he'd take it literally.

So I sent him a text this morning.

Dahlia: Wow. Talk about petty.

He left me on Read.

Not gonna lie, I don't like it when my tactics are used against me.

But, anyway, Kane who?

The guy I can't stop being curious about and, therefore, dropped by his parents' house, that's who.

With an internal groan, I focus back on Helena. "Is Sora always this greedy?"

She laughs, the sound airy. "I suppose. He's the oldest and believes in hierarchy."

"Just like Kane."

Her smile disappears. "No. Kane believes in control. Just like his father."

My fingers pause and Helena throws some food, her gaze lost in the depths of the dark pond.

"I don't want to be nosy, and you don't have to tell me if you don't feel comfortable, but I've been curious…" I swallow. "Why is your relationship with Kane so strained?"

"Have you seen the scars on his back?" she asks, not looking at me.

"Yes, and I also noticed bruises on his wrists not too long ago."

She stiffens, her face becoming so pale, I think she's getting sick. But when she speaks, her voice is strained, as though she's barely holding it together. "He's been trained or, more accurately, *tortured* by his father ever since he was six years old. He's had to go through physical, mental, and even poison training since he was a kid. And while he's more independent now, if he doesn't meet Grant's expectations, he's punished severely. I didn't protect him and he hates me. Rightfully so."

My lips part and the bowl nearly falls from my hand. "You mean to tell me those hideous scars were caused by his *father*? What type of father hurts his son that badly?"

"The type who's raising an heir and that heir needs to be a machine." A shine appears in her sunken eyes. "Before all of this, Kane was the sweetest boy. He was kind and happy. He felt bad for others and helped them. He played with the staff's children and gave them his favorite toys. He used to read me bedtime stories, not the other way around, and loved plucking flowers from the garden and giving them to me."

As she speaks, her smile widens, but then it disappears as the wind ruffles her hair. "But those beautiful personality traits were seen as weaknesses in Grant's eyes. He told me that his son would not grow up into a useless philanthropist, and there was nothing I could do to stop it. If I wanted to leave, so be it. But I didn't, and I had to stand helpless as Grant set out to destroy Kane's soul and purge all those pure emotions until he was as bleak and soulless as himself. And he succeeded. With flying colors."

A fierce surge of rage floods through me.

I don't even know who I'm angry at. Kane's dad or the damn world he was born into. I'm even mad at Helena for not stopping the abuse.

But at the same time, I want to hug her.

I feel like she's also a victim in a different sense. While she didn't leave, she also didn't help.

"I apologize for oversharing." Helena takes the bowl of food and places it on a shelf under the gazebo. "I don't know why I feel comfortable talking to you. Maybe it's because I lost my son, so I'm trying to get close to his girlfriend. If you don't mind keeping an old woman some company, that is."

I'm not his girlfriend. At least, not in that sense.

"You're not old," I say instead. "And I would love to. You have a lovely place."

"It's not mine. It's Grant's. Everything is Grant's. I'm merely an accessory in his shiny empire."

She guides me to a table under a heated, covered gazebo where some staff are pouring tea. There's a towering assortment of hors d'oeuvres and pastries.

"I didn't know what you like, so I had the chef prepare a little bit of everything."

A little bit is an understatement. She basically brought the whole kitchen to the table; it's pure European-style afternoon tea.

Which I've only seen in extravagant movies.

"This looks amazing, thank you." I sit down and try not to devour everything in sight.

Manners, Dahlia. Manners. Don't go showing your unpolished side in front of rich people.

I struggle with the numerous forks and knives, but Helena says not to worry about it and to eat however I wish.

She tells me about the happiest years of her life—since Kane was born—and the saddest—after he was conditioned by his father.

Helena also talks about how the house has felt lifeless since Kane permanently moved out a couple of years ago. Even though he ignored her or treated her coldly before, he still came home and she saw him every day. Now that he's gone and refuses to keep in touch, her depression has gotten worse.

I notice that she barely eats and the butler brings her medication. He hides the label, but she doesn't seem to care too much.

Prozac.

If she's taking antidepressants and still looks so damn sad, it's serious.

It feels like I'm using her by probing, but her son is a blank slate who won't tell me anything, no matter what I do.

After I swallow the most delicious muffins I've ever tasted, I say, "Can I ask you something?"

"Sure. Anything."

"That day when we first met, you said I should run away while I can. What did you mean by that?"

She lifts the colorful teacup to her mouth, then pauses. "I suppose I didn't want you to end up like me. I have no way out, and even if I managed to escape Grant's sphere of influence, I'd have to abandon my son and live in hiding for the rest of my life. But I realize I was wrong in suggesting that."

"Why is that?"

"Kane doesn't look at you the same way Grant looks at me. I was always a pawn for him. The daughter of a supreme court justice that he needed to further his endeavors, and he was the man I wanted to marry for status. Grant never loved me and I never loved him. Ours was a political union through and through. It's different for you and Kane. He cares."

I nearly choke on my tea and cover it up with a laugh. "*Cares*? Pretty sure he doesn't know the meaning of that word."

"Maybe not consciously, but he does." She juts her chin to the side. "Otherwise, he wouldn't have rushed here."

When I follow her field of vision, my lips part.

Kane is striding toward the glass doors, his silhouette swallowing up the horizon. He looks so dashing in jeans, a white shirt, and a leather jacket.

"You told him?" I ask.

"Samuel probably did. That's the butler who brought you in earlier. If Kane didn't care, would he come over, worried about the prospect of you meeting Grant?" she asks in a soft voice. "Though he knows that Grant only comes back home late on the weekdays, Kane is always cautious."

A few moments later, he stops by the table and says like a robotic soldier, "Mother."

"Hi, darling." She smiles and nods at an empty seat. "Join us for tea?"

"We're leaving." He grabs my elbow.

I release myself and tug on his sleeve, painting a smile. "Of course we're not. Kane would love to join, right?"

He glares down at me.

I glare back.

"You don't have to force yourself, darling," she says awkwardly. "If you have things to do…"

"He doesn't." I half stand and whisper in his ear, "If you don't sit down and join us, there will be no sex for a whole week."

"Then I'll find a substitute," he murmurs back in a dark tone. "Someone with less drama."

"In that case, you can forget about fucking me altogether. Oh, I'll also send you pictures of the latest dick I'll be riding."

"*Watch* it," he growls into my ear.

"You know I'm stubborn as hell, so either you give in to a harmless afternoon tea or risk an all-out war."

His brows pull together and I think he'll drag me out, judging by how his hand flexes, but then he reluctantly sits down.

Helena watches us and a genuine soft smile paints her lips. She falls over herself asking the staff to prepare some dishes and to bring more of this and that.

"There's no need," Kane says in the same dispassionate tone. "We're not staying for long."

"We are." I sling my arm through his and stroke it as I smile innocently. "The *whole* afternoon."

His icy eyes bore into me, filled with disdain, but he says nothing.

He also doesn't throw away my arm—probably because we're in front of his mom—so I take advantage of the situation and continue caressing him.

Maybe I'm kind of obsessed with how muscular his bicep is, or I probably missed him.

Though he'd never hear me say that.

Helena smiles as she pours him some tea that he barely touches. I can tell he's stiff, judging from his tightened muscles. He also doesn't talk much.

So I fill the gap, trying to not leave his mom hanging—something he has no problem doing.

Including him in the conversation is an uphill battle, but at least Helena seems less sad and her smiles are more natural.

She asks about school and training, which Kane responds to mechanically, but I add more punch to my replies.

"Oh, I didn't know you were on a scholarship," she says with awe. "That's impressive, Dahlia. It must've been a lot of work. And here I am taking from your precious time and asking you to entertain me."

"If you know that, don't invite her again," Kane says point-blank.

I elbow him hard and smile at his mom. "It's my pleasure. This peaceful garden is a nice change from the town's hustle and bustle. I'm truly grateful. Don't listen to Kane. His delivery sucks ninety percent of the time."

"Does it?" He smiles as he wraps a palm around my nape, tightening his grip.

"Duh. You can be so boring." I brush his hand away. "Anyway, we can totally meet whenever you wish."

Helena smiles and shakes her head.

Soon after, Kane has had enough of playing house and insists on leaving. His mom hugs him, but he pats her back in a detached manner. So when it's my turn, I give her the warmest hug, promising we'll meet again soon.

And I'm not even a hugger.

As Kane escorts me out of the garden and into the house with a hand on the small of my back, I stare up at him. "Maybe you should be kinder to your mom."

"Maybe you need to be less nosy." He halts in the middle of the long hallway and faces me, his shoulders tightening. "Why the fuck can't you stop making things difficult for one fucking day?"

"If you want easy, go search for easy."

"Dahlia…" He wraps a hand around my throat, his voice echoing in a low, dark timbre. "You need to learn how to stay the fuck out of my business."

I sink my fingers into his hair and pull, then get on my tiptoes and whisper against his mouth, "How about no?"

His hot, heavy breaths skim over my lips. God. Why do I want to kiss him? We're not even having sex, so I shouldn't need a connection.

This is confusing and illogical.

Kane's exhales turn harsher, his grip tighter, and his nostrils flare.

He's containing himself.

Shoving himself behind that wall I hate so much.

"I can handle you, Kane," I say in a whisper, stroking his hair instead of pulling it.

"You *think* you can."

"I *know* I can." I wet my lips, and his darkened eyes zero in on the motion, turning molten.

"You know *nothing*," he grinds out even as he watches my mouth. "You're just a fuck, Dahlia. Stay where you belong."

"And yet you want to kiss me." I lick his lower lip, leaving a shiny trail of my saliva on his soft skin.

His grip tenses up on my throat. "Stop *that*."

"Show me how I'm just a fuck." I roll my body against the taut ridges of his muscles. "Kiss me, Kane."

"You're a fucking nuisance."

"Kiss me."

"I hate you."

"I hate you, too. Kiss me."

"I'll fucking ruin you."

"Prove it. Kiss me—"

My words are stolen when he kills the distance and seals his lips to mine with a groan.

There's something different about this kiss.

It's deep and unhinged like the rest of him, but it's also slower, not as frenzied, not accompanied by his brutal fucking or his constant need to claim and possess me.

His hand tightens on the sides of my throat, his index finger tilting my jaw to the side as he devours my mouth, sensually sucking on my tongue.

There's anger, too, but it pales in comparison to the way he owns me.

I kiss him back, reveling in how he loses control.

How he shows me his true self.

Only *me*.

I pull on his hair, then stroke it.

I moan in his mouth and let him manhandle me any way he pleases.

I've come to the realization that I can let this man do whatever he wants to me as long as I have him all to myself.

It's selfishness, I realize. For the first time in my life, I'm coveting something I can't have.

It's terrifying, but I can't stop.

"Who's this?"

Kane goes still, but he calmly pulls away.

I see it then, in a fraction of a second when his eyes meet mine.

Anger.

No…fear?

He stands to his full height, slightly blocking me behind him, but I still see the man who just spoke.

An older version of Kane, with a hard expression and a tailored suit.

Grant Davenport.

It must be him.

The man who broke Kane and left scars all over his body.

He smiles, but it doesn't reach his eyes. "I didn't know you were bringing guests over, son. Introduce us."

"She's no one important," Kane says in a detached tone, but he's half hiding me now.

"Oh? If she's no one important, why is she at my house?"

"Won't happen again."

"Introduce us, son," Grant repeats in the same monotone voice.

I can feel Kane's entire back going rigid, and I don't like it.

A protective urge I've only felt for Violet washes over me, and I step from Kane's shadow and force a smile as I offer Grant my hand. "Dahlia Thorne. Nice to meet you, sir."

He shakes my hand. Hard. And I do the same, hoping to break the fucking hand that he put on Kane.

We finally release each other.

"I've never heard of the Thorne family."

"That's because they're not important."

"Not important," he repeats in a deadpan tone, then looks at Kane. "If you're done here, follow me."

Grant walks down the hallway without another look in my direction.

As he disappears around the corner, Kane faces me, his shoulders still tense but his expression neutral. All the passion and the glimmer of heat from earlier have disappeared.

His walls are back in place, and he looks like a shell of himself. "You go first. Samuel will drive you to your dorm."

I grab his wrist, an awful premonition tightening my stomach. "Why don't you drive me? I'll go to your place."

"Not tonight." He calmly starts to remove my hand.

I dig my nails in deeper. "Don't follow him. He's going to hurt you like that night against the Wolves. I know he's the reason you have those bruises."

Kane clenches his jaw but soon releases a breath. "I see my mother has been sharing things she shouldn't."

"She's worried about you." And I'm worried about him, too—*what the hell?*

"I'll be fine. It's nothing."

"Abuse is *not* nothing," I whisper-yell.

"Go home, Dahlia." He strokes my hair and then pats my cheek, the motion cold and lacking any of the warmth from earlier. "If you pity me again, I'll cut you the fuck out of my life."

And then he walks down the hall and into the lion's den.

My heart clenches so hard, I'm sure I'll be sick.

CHAPTER 24
Kane

AFTER THE MEETING WITH MY FATHER, I'M THIRSTY FOR A venting outlet.

Grant explicitly said that if Dahlia—the not-important member of the equally not-important Thorne family—proves to be a weakness, he'll personally eliminate her.

I'm already a freak accident of my mother's weak genes that he spent so much effort into molding into a true Davenport, and he will not allow any 'gold-digging trailer trash' to mess with his progress.

Progress.

I suppose that could also be another word for his fucked-up methods.

Regardless of Grant's threats and unpleasant methods, this has only solidified the idea I've been shoving into the back of my mind for a while now.

I need to stay the fuck away from Dahlia.

She's already proving to be a nuisance, digging her tiny claws where they don't belong and burying her nose so far up in my business, it's hard to maintain the mask I've been wearing almost all my life.

She knows the right words that push my buttons and

always has her fucking hands all over me as if she has every right to. As if my clear rejections mean nothing.

This is my chance to categorically cut her off.

For her sake.

And mine.

She's sent me several texts since Samuel had to drag her out of the house earlier this evening. And there was dragging, because I've seen security footage of that fucking girl trying to follow me. When Samuel stopped her, she screamed, "Either let me go or you check on him! Don't just stand there and do nothing. Why does no one do anything?"

Since Samuel shares the same emotions as a wall, he carried her out and managed to drop her off at her dorm. He later told me she called him and Grant names the entire ride.

Afterward, she proceeded to bombard my phone.

Dahlia: Are you okay?
Dahlia: Please tell me you're not hurt.
Dahlia: You're wrong about what you said earlier. I don't pity you. I'm scared, okay?
Dahlia: I know you think it's nothing, and I can't begin to imagine what it was like to have been exposed to that form of abuse since you were a child. But some of my foster parents beat me and, while it wasn't systematic and usually happened because I rebelled, I know shit like that messes with your head, Kane. Childhood trauma changes the fabric of your soul. It sucks out the positive energy and replaces it with fragments of darkness. I know because it affected me. Losing my parents and knowing it was my fault made me think I deserved every hellish thing I went through afterward. It wasn't until Violet came along

> and told me the accident wasn't my fault and that blaming myself and spiraling wouldn't make my parents happy in the least that I realized I was wrong. I still have my issues, and I'm by no means claiming to be perfect, but I don't sweep my trauma under the rug. You shouldn't either.
>
> Dahlia: I hope that didn't sound patronizing or wasn't too much information. I'm not used to opening up to people, so I'm kind of new to this whole thing. I just…want to help, I guess.
>
> Dahlia: Talk to me, Kane. We can listen to each other even if we come from different worlds.

As I said. I'm cutting her off.

She's getting too close for comfort, and it's reshuffling my priorities, hindering my goals, and clouding my judgment.

Liar. She's been clouding your judgment since the first time you saw her.

"Ready for some fun?" Preston's voice echoes around me, pulling me from my deep thoughts.

He's standing at my left, draped head to toe in black, including the gloves. Even his blond hair takes on a shadowy hue in the night as he draws his turtleneck sweater up to his chin and toys with a knife.

"You can have all the fun you want, but his life is mine," Jude says from my right as he twirls his hockey stick.

Like Preston and me, he's dressed in black, but he's also wearing a raincoat. Since he loves getting up close and personal with his victims—meaning smashing their skulls in—it's a good idea to protect oneself from all the blood splashes.

When Jude sent the text to invite us to his latest 'hunt,' I agreed.

Usually, I don't come along, leaving him and Preston to their own devices.

I don't revel in bloodlust. Don't consider killing and violence a viable purging method like Jude does.

When I'm assigned to kill someone, I do it with a gun and a silencer. Other times, I pay people to slip poison into their drink.

Because that's how I deal with things—in a clean-cut way and under complete control.

I don't like messes.

And I certainly loathe the cleanup.

Preston isn't violent on the ice or in public, but in the darkness or when it's only the three of us, he unleashes his unhinged side. Truth is, he's a bloodthirsty motherfucker who revels in seeing the life leaving people's eyes.

"No weapon?" Preston asks me.

I slip my phone into my pocket and push my jacket aside to reveal the gun.

"Man, you're so boring." Jude shakes his head. "I bet it comes with a silencer, too."

"Naturally. Can't leave evidence behind."

"This is literally my family's forest and we have the cleanup team on standby." Preston walks up to Jude and wraps an arm around his shoulders. "Just say you hate life, unlike me and the big man."

Jude slams his stick against Preston's shoulder. "Don't kill him. He's all mine."

"Finders keepers," Preston sings in a manic tone, then jumps off the porch.

"Motherfucker." Jude rushes behind him, and soon, they both disappear between the tall trees in a blur of movements.

I remain still for a few seconds, then take the stairs one at a time.

Jude released his target for the night about fifteen minutes ago, and we all watched the sleazy middle-aged man go north.

There's no need to rush.

Tall trees loom above me, their branches reaching out like skeletal hands against the dark sky. The moon slips in and out of view, its pale light flickering through the thick clouds, casting silver slashes across the forest floor.

As I walk, the dirt beneath my shoes crunches, the sound swallowed immediately by the weight of the night.

I stop, my breath steady as I study the ground and turn on my flashlight.

There they are.

Hectic, heavy nonconformist footsteps in the mud.

I ignore the other footsteps that barely leave any trace. They're Preston's. Jude's are heavier, but not as irregular and they certainly don't stink of terror.

The air smells of damp earth and pine, sharp and fresh, but it also reeks of decay. Old leaves rot in the underbrush, the scent mingling with the cold bite of the wind as it snakes through the trees. Although amidst it, there's the tangible smell of sweat, fear, and a hopeless ending.

But it barely touches me or breaches the surface.

Ah.

I'm bored.

I find no pleasure whatsoever in this sort of chase.

No excitement.

No fucking emotions.

I'd rather be chasing my wildflower as she comes up with all her clever ways to hide. Just the thought of being hot on her trail makes me hard.

Hell, my cock twitches at the memory of the last time I hunted her down at my place and fucked her on the stairs like a caveman.

Stop thinking about her.

This whole thing is meant to help me disassociate from her.

Somewhere in the distance, an owl hoots, its sound echoing through the trees. Small creatures rustle in the shadows before they vanish into the undergrowth.

A larger shadow breezes past me. Jude.

He's a blur, running at full speed between the tall, leaning trees.

I realize why.

On my other side, Preston is running, too, his lighter weight giving him leverage as he cuts the distance.

The prey skitters, its movements frantic.

I forge ahead without picking up my pace, observing the branches weaving together above like a cage. In a sense, this world has been our cage since birth. I used to wonder where the three of us would've ended up if we were born into normal families.

Jude wouldn't need to be so violent.

Preston wouldn't have lost his mind.

I wouldn't have to be this. Whatever *this* is.

But I learned to just accept it. Make the most of it, I suppose.

My steps are steady on the uneven ground that's slick with moss and damp leaves, making each move a potential hazard, but I know this forest like the back of my hand. The man we're hunting doesn't.

The moon flickers again, slipping behind a thick wall of clouds, plunging the forest into near-total darkness. A thud sounds in the distance and a muffled noise follows.

I stop.

The air shifts, colder now, brushing against my face as I advance deeper into the woods. My pulse is steady and calm, every muscle in my body coiled.

An outsider is here.

Aside from the target of the day, there are now four of us on the property.

Who the fuck dares to trespass on *our* private property? The Armstrongs own this forest, and we're the only ones allowed in it. We had our first tests of courage here. We were abandoned in that 'haunted' cottage for two days when we were kids and were forced to separate, every man for himself.

Not even regular Vencor members have access to this forest.

I reach into my waistband and retrieve my gun.

The trees close in tighter, the branches scraping against each other, and the owl calls again, but this time it's closer.

The wind picks up, carrying a faint familiar scent.

A scream echoes in the silence, followed by a *thud, thud, thud*.

The scream slowly fades until there's only the loud sound of the thuds.

Jude's stick.

He and Preston must've gotten the man and killed him.

But that doesn't matter now. There's an intruder who needs to be dealt with.

I push the low branches out of my way with the gun, my other hand holding the flashlight on top of my weapon.

A rustle comes from behind me and I spin around, my finger resting on the trigger.

A mouse scurries away, blinded by the light.

The sound of running reaches me, and I sprint ahead, then stop.

While I don't find the outsider, I spot Jude standing by the bloodied corpse of his latest victim.

The man's face is unrecognizable. Half of it has turned to mush as he slumps against a tree, his head lolled against his belly.

Jude's stick is dripping with blood, and his raincoat is smeared with dark stains.

He tilts his head in my direction, his face splashed, his eyes blank. "Not enough. He died too soon. Give me another name, Kane."

It's a high.

An obsession.

The feeling of never having enough of something, no matter how much you consume it.

It's why I steer clear of anything prone to muddying my logic.

I don't do fixations or attachments.

Obsessions or addictions. Until Dahlia fucking Thorne.

She's the addiction I can't shake off.

Even during the hunt I only joined to forget her.

My right hand still grasping my gun, I squeeze Jude's shoulder with the other. "Don't spiral."

"Fuck that." He shakes my hand off and steps back, pointing his bloody stick at me. "What do I have to do for you to give me the entire list?"

"Not possible."

"What if I kidnap your new little toy?"

"That would be both foolish and unproductive. You lay your hands on her and I'll burn that list to the ground."

He snarls.

I stare back.

Fuck.

I can't believe I'm threatening my friends and throwing away my bargaining chips for that fucking woman.

She's nothing.

Correction. She *should* be nothing.

"Preston is right." He slaps me across the face with the bloodied stick. "You've fucking lost it for pussy. That girl would betray you to get what she wants. She'd abandon you and not look back."

"I'm abandoning her first, but that doesn't mean any of you gets to touch her." I push his stick, sending it flying to the ground. "Where's Armstrong?"

"Fuck if I know. He stabbed the sorry fuck a few times, not enough to kill him, but then he disappeared altogether."

"Right before you found the target?"

"Yeah."

Preston would never—and I mean *never*—miss a 'death ceremony,' as he likes to call it. That's his favorite part of the hunt, whether he gets to kill the prey himself or watch Jude do it.

He loathes my swift killing methods and rarely lingers around for that, but he knew Jude would get this one and still disappeared.

Jude grabs his stick. "You think the uninvited guest is behind his disappearance?"

"You felt it, too?"

"Yeah. We have an outsider."

We share a look, Jude's frown mirroring mine.

An outsider. And Preston vanished. This is not good.

I motion north. "I'll cover you."

He runs and I sprint behind him, going down the paths

we learned through our childhood training. We know this forest inside out.

Preston does, too.

I'm usually concerned about that lunatic as is, but this is even worse.

Thwack.

Thwack.

Thwack.

The sound grows stronger as we get closer. Jude and I come to a halt at a small opening with intertwined branches.

A large figure is on top of Preston, punching him to smithereens.

And Preston is laughing like a fucking maniac.

Upon sensing our presence, the man shoves Preston against a tree trunk and scurries off. I catch a glimpse of a solid-white mask as he pulls his hoodie over his head and runs.

I aim my gun at him, but Preston, who was happy with being beat to a pulp not two seconds ago, jumps up and stands in my way.

"What the fuck are you doing?" I bypass him, but the intruder has already disappeared through the trees.

"I'll chase." Jude starts in the direction he disappeared in.

Preston places a hand on his chest and pushes him. "He's my prey. Back off."

His mouth is bruised, blood gushing from the corners of his lips and trickling to his neck. His shirt is ripped at the collar, and there's a knife slash on his arm, blood soaking his shirt and gluing it to his skin.

I raise a brow. "I haven't seen you this injured in a long time. You sure he's the prey?"

"Of course he is," he says maniacally and laughs loud, throwing his head back.

"He's lost his mind again." Jude sighs.

"Who is he, Preston?"

He smiles, all his teeth showing creepily. "He dared to hunt me in my own goddamn place. Love that!"

"You should've let us catch him, dumbass." Jude hits him upside the head.

Preston doesn't even retaliate, still laughing, still lost in a high. "No, I'm going to hunt him, too, before I chop him into tiny little pieces. Oh my, I'm getting hard thinking about it. I'm so fucking hard."

"Focus, man," Jude says.

"You fuck off, both of you. I'll arrange the cleanup and watch some security footage."

"Find out how he managed to trespass on this place, Pres," I say.

"Not important." He laughs as he walks away. "Not fucking important."

"Get your dick sucked," Jude shouts. "Don't go fucking crazy."

Preston only laughs again as he staggers between the trees, the sounds echoing like a symphony of chaos.

No one can handle him when he's in this mode. He hardly ever goes crazy, but when he does, it's a fucking drag.

"He's going to do something stupid and probably get himself killed," Jude says. "We should stop him."

I run up behind Preston and then hit his nape with the gun.

He falls to his knees and the annoying sound of his laughter disappears.

"Well, that definitely stopped him," Jude says. "He'll fuck you up when he wakes up. You know he hates being knocked out."

"Then he should've controlled his animal side better. I won't clean up his messes."

"You have a point." Jude surveys the forest with a critical gaze. "Who do you think that was?"

"I don't know, but we need to find and eliminate him." I sheath my gun and grab Preston's arm. "Help me carry him back."

"What a nuisance," Jude grumbles. "Always a damn fucking baby."

Even as he says that, he rips his shirt and wraps it around Preston's wound, then carefully slings the injured arm over his shoulder.

When we were children, Preston was slim and bony with baby features and often got bullied for looking like a girl. And while he made their lives hell afterward, mostly through some form of manipulation, he was physically weak and unable to defend himself. Somehow, Jude became his shield and proceeded to knock those boarding school kids' teeth out.

Unfortunately, it didn't stop at bullying.

Once, Preston was missing during a late-evening dorm activity, and Jude and I ditched the thing and went to search for him.

We found him in a cellar with a teacher, who was spreading Preston's naked legs and on the verge of sexually assaulting him.

Jude got a candelabra and hit him on the head over and over again while I immobilized him.

Preston's face was bruised, his bony body covered in semen, and he had a dead look in his eyes.

Until Jude gave him a knife and told him to finish him.

He only smiled when that sleazy teacher's eyes rolled to the back of his head and he spit out his last disgusting breath.

That was our first murder. At ten years old.

Naturally, our parents covered up the incident as a freak accident. But they didn't pull us out of the school.

In fact, Jude and I were punished for the mess. Preston was sent to a therapist, who, instead of helping him, diagnosed him with early signs of antisocial personality disorder.

Preston never talks about it, but Jude and I suspect that wasn't the first time something like that happened to him.

Until he was a teenager, people said he looked so beautiful with girly features, especially when he had his hair long. That, plus the fact that he's a provocateur who loves to insult everyone attracted the wrong crowd in a boys-only school full of sick freaks.

Which is why Jude and I have always been wary about any creepy fucks coming near him. It's also why Jude pummels anyone who dares to slam into Preston during games.

Jude is a protective mama bear of sorts, even though Preston became fully capable of defending himself a long time ago.

However, the scene from now is concerning. He just lay down and took the beating, which he never does. I'm wondering if he was triggered in some way.

"You think it's one of those motherfuckers?" Jude asks in a low voice as we balance Preston between us and walk through the dense forest.

"No. They wouldn't dare touch him as he is now."

"He went crazy, Kane." There's an edge to his words. "He rarely ever lets himself slip that far now that he's had himself under control for so long. What if they're targeting him again?"

"Simple. We'll maim every last one of them and let him bathe in their blood."

"Every last one of them." Jude smirks. "We might need a list. Your favorite."

I smile.

At least there's something to keep me distracted from the chaos in my mind.

Even temporarily.

"You haven't answered my texts."

That's the first thing I hear the next morning, coming from a tiny woman with an overflowing temper.

Dahlia blocks the arena's entrance with a hand on her hip. Her brown hair is pulled into a messy ponytail, her eyes are bloodshot, and she has dark circles that could be spotted from a mile away.

So much for keeping a distance.

"That should've been your clue," I say in a cold tone and start to bypass her.

She opens her arms wide, halting me in place. "All I wanted was a confirmation of whether or not you're okay."

"Since when is that any of your business? You're nothing to me, Dahlia."

"Liar." She lifts her chin. "You care about me."

I let out a mocking laugh that fills the space. "You fell for that? You're much more naïve than I thought, but then again, you've always been a bit slow to catch up to things."

Her lips tremble.

A gleam appears in her eyes.

I've never seen Dahlia cry outside of sex. And while I crave it when I'm fucking her, right now, I want to impale myself.

But I remain silent. She needs to fuck off out of my life.

I need the peace and quiet I used to experience before she came along, and not this constant state of being on the edge of something. What? I don't even know.

"Are you pushing me away?" she finally says, her voice low, almost weak.

Dahlia doesn't do weak. Not even when I fuck her like a damn inhumane monster.

My cold voice is completely detached from my thoughts. "See? You're slow, but you always get there."

"Why are you doing this? Because I care? Because I want to make sure you're okay?"

"Because you're starting to get emotionally involved. I told you that's off the table. You shouldn't have allowed me to crush you through those idealistic, gullible feelings."

She balls her fists even as her chin trembles. "So that's it?"

"That's it. You're officially banished from Vencor. I'm done with you now."

"Done with me? Liar. You're a fucking liar, Kane. You're not done with me. You're *running* away because you're a damn coward who can't handle your emotions for me. You can't handle how you let go when you're around me." She stabs my chest with a finger. "You can't fucking handle *me*!"

The spot she touches burns as if she's injecting poison into my veins.

I let the mask remain in place and speak in a calm tone. "You can stay on the team if you stop bothering me."

And then I bypass her.

"You'll regret this!" she shouts at my back. "I'll make sure you regret this, you fucking asshole."

I'm regretting it already.

But it's better I let her go of my own volition before she's violently snatched from me.

Dahlia Thorne is a mistake that should've never happened.

I was greedy for the first time in my life, and if there's something I know about greed, it's that you always pay.

In blood.

CHAPTER 25
Dahlia

KANE HAS MADE GOOD ON HIS PROMISE.

He hasn't looked at me since he ended things a little over a week ago.

Not even once.

Not even when I made sure I was in his field of vision during practice and the head doctor's checkups and briefings.

So I matched his energy.

Kane *who*? I don't even *like* the asshole.

If he's going to give me the cold shoulder and erase me as if I never existed, he'll receive the same treatment.

But I've been finding myself becoming irrationally angry lately, especially since Isabella came back into the picture.

I thought she'd spend the rest of the year hiding after Kane somehow made her disappear, but apparently, I was wrong.

Not only has she started showing up at the arena, using her brother as a pretext, but she also rubs herself all over Kane any chance she gets.

And he lets her.

So you know what? I'm going to make him regret it like I promised.

It's not even about him being my way in anymore. It's

about my pride. I won't allow that dick to walk all over me and get away with it.

I'm not someone he can simply use and then discard as if I lack any form of human emotion.

Besides, I've been following the Gavin, Ryder, and Hunter lead. And while I still haven't been able to obtain Hunter's DNA, I've gotten close to Ryder. Mainly because I helped him with a strain in his shoulder.

He now frequently stops to say good morning, oftentimes accompanied by a silent Hunter. Gavin is less welcoming and doesn't talk to me, but he doesn't glare at me the entire time either. Probably because everyone heard about my official banishment from their stupid organization.

In any case, I'm pretty sure I'll be invited to the next party that will be thrown at Hunter's place, if not by Hunter, then by Ryder, and that will be my chance to gather the DNA sample.

In the meantime, I pretended to need access to the team doctor's records for paperwork, and searched for the one from September 20, but it didn't mention anything about their 'unknown injury.'

So I tried talking to the doctor, but I'm pretty sure he's related to Vencor or, at least, pretty close, because when I asked about the 'unknown injury' entry, he said, "That's what we put sometimes when players miss practice due to a hangover. Don't overthink it."

Yeah, right.

I didn't push, though, because that would only make him suspicious.

But I'm still holding on to hope about Hunter's DNA. If it's a positive match, I can finally find out who hurt Violet.

In the meantime, I'm focusing on building a friendship with Ryder.

One of the perks of joking around with Ryder is him telling me about the coffee shops and bars the team members hang out in. He also invited me over once, but then withdrew it.

After a talk with Kane.

Fuck that asshole. It's not like I was dying to be in the same space as him.

Anyway, turns out Ryder was also getting close to me for a reason—Megan. He'd wanted my 'cute' friend's number ever since he saw us together at a coffee shop.

As I'm walking off campus, I call Megan and tell her about the news.

She screams in my ear for, like, a minute before saying, "Thank you, Jesus, for finally giving me what others have. I prefer Jude, but I'd ride Ryder any day. Or, like, he rides me? You know, like his name?"

"So that's a yes?" I ask.

"Heck yeah, baby."

"Shouldn't you think this through? I think he's associated with the people controlling the town."

"Doesn't matter. It's only sex."

"All right, but be careful, yeah?"

"I will! Do a girl a favor and don't make me look desperate."

"I got you. I'll say you don't know about it, and I'm doing him a favor. Act surprised when he texts."

"I'll be the queen of drama. Gosh, what am I wearing? I want to borrow that hot green dress of yours, but my ass won't fit. How about the stretchy pink one? Can I borrow it?"

"No. I told you I'm sending them back with the others."

"You already did and they were returned to you."

"I'll donate them to charity, then."

"Me!" she says, offended. "Donate them to me."

"I don't want to see them, Megan. If I give them to you, he'll think I kept them out of sentimental value."

"D, honey, this shit can bring you at least a hundred K if you sell them. You can keep the money for physical therapy once your sister wakes up. Quit with the stupid pride. Since that boy broke your heart, you get to keep all the shit he gave you. That's the rule."

"He did *not* break my heart."

"*Totally* believable with the way you've been acting this week."

"I've been acting just fine."

"You've been a grumpy mess and have been cursing Kane out of the blue as if you're possessed. That's a broken heart right there."

"Nope. I'm just planning my revenge."

"Another sign of a broken heart. I warned you to stay away from the Vipers."

"And yet you're excited about Ryder."

"I don't catch feelings for dick. I'm excited to fuck him, not date him. Anyway, want me to help with selling the clothes and shoes?"

"Do whatever you want."

"Including borrowing the pink dress?"

"You can keep it."

"OMG. Love you. I'll consider it my commission. Got to go." There's a sound of shuffling on the other end. "Make me seem like the hottest girl ever when you talk about me to Ryder."

"He's already smitten. You don't need it."

"We always need a bit of a morale boost. Laters!"

I shake my head as I hang up.

A body slams into mine and I pause as pink pumps stop in front of me.

"Watch where you're going, Charity."

I inhale deeply as I raise my head and smile sweetly at Isabella. "Me? Seems you're the one who has no sense of direction."

One of her minions is about to say something, but she holds up a hand. "Don't waste your breath on a nobody who was dropped so fast, no one remembers her name."

My hand fists around my phone, but I remain silent, my smile still in place.

I refuse to give her the satisfaction of seeing me fall.

"If you're done wasting my time." I start to walk past her.

"Don't take it personally," she speaks close to my face. "People like you come and go all the time. You could've never competed with me. Kane has always been mine."

"Funny because I swear you disappeared from his side for weeks after you tried to drug me and he got you kicked out of the organization. He either threatened or hurt you, I'm not sure which, but what I am sure about is that your feelings aren't reciprocated."

"And yours are?"

"Probably not. But I'm not delusional."

"Maybe, but you sure are jealous. You're always glaring at me—it gives me the creeps." She smiles. "Got to go and get ready for meeting *my* Kane later. Try not to commission a voodoo doll and curse me, *Charity*."

I won't punch her in the face.

I will not stoop that low for some asshole.

As she walks away with a sway to her hips and mocking laughter, however, I bring out my phone.

Isabella and Kane can go to hell for all I care, then have tiny babies blessed by Satan himself.

But I meant it about him regretting this.

Two can play his sick game.

And, yes, I'm petty.

Me: Hi.
Ryder: Thorne! You got me the number?
Me: Maybe. If you tell me where you guys are hanging out tonight.
Ryder: Man. Captain will kill me for this. He made it clear that you're not to be invited anywhere he's at.

I draw a circle on my thumb and try not to be affected. Thinking it is one thing, but actually knowing the truth feels as if I've been stabbed.

Is it supposed to hurt this much?

No, this isn't pain. It's anger.

It *has* to be anger.

Me: I'm not asking you to invite me. Just tell me the place. No one will know.
Ryder: You're so lucky you have a hot friend. Here's the address.

He sends me a location and I reply with Megan's number.

Ryder: Sweet!
Ryder: Also, don't let Captain know I sent the address. He's already a pain in the ass these days. Don't want to get on his bad side.
Me: Don't worry.

I exit the chat with Ryder and open a new one with the contact titled, "Two Week Mistake."

Me: Are you in the mood for some drama?
Two Week Mistake: Always.

Later that night, I arrive at the club with my arm wrapped around Marcus's.

It was his choice to come here, knowing it's full of the Vipers, but if there's one thing I'm sure about when it comes to Marcus, it's that he doesn't give a fuck about anyone.

Me included.

He's only here to stir up chaos like he does wherever he goes.

The club pulses with life, a low hum of music vibrating through the walls and under my skin. The air is thick with an overpowering mixture of alcohol and perfume.

Neon lights flash above, cutting through the smoke that hangs in the air and casting the room in shades of green and red. It's crowded, packed with bodies swaying to the bass-heavy beat that thumps from the speakers, loud enough to rattle the glass bottles lined up behind the bar.

I step through the door, the click of my heels drowned out by the music, and I can feel eyes eating my skin.

Megan managed to turn me into a swan again. Thick eyeliner, smoky shadow, and red lips. She also insisted I wear the green dress she couldn't fit into. It clings to my body, the silky fabric sliding over my skin with every step. It's bold, with a plunging neckline, an open back, and a slit that teases more than it reveals.

It's meant to be noticed.

It's also meant to be a message—I'm wearing the dress he bought me while I'm with another man.

And not just any man.

Marcus Osborn is the archnemesis of the entire Vipers team and a reminder of their recent humiliation.

His presence is solid beside me, but it's all for show. His hand rests possessively at my waist, and I let it. His body heat presses against mine as he leans in to whisper, "Is it just me or do you now make more effort to look so fucking hot."

"Should've kept me when you had me instead of trying to share me with your friends."

He laughs, the sound drowned out by the thrumming music as we stop by the bar. It's dim, mostly lit by a purple neon glow, and animated by people shouting over the music.

"You're still mad about that, Dahlia? I told you I don't do relationships. They're a fucking drag, and I let you go, didn't I? But maybe I'll try to seduce you again tonight."

"That train has left the station."

"I can see that. Davenport is such a boring choice, though. You could've gone for someone more interesting."

"What's your idea of interesting?"

"The prince." He grins as he raises his glass to the second floor. "On second thought, *anyone* but the prince."

My ears prickle and I can feel heavy eyes stripping me naked and clawing at my skin.

When I follow Marcus's field of vision, I see almost the entire Vipers team in the VIP area above. Some are dancing, but many of them are standing by the glass barrier, all scowling at Marcus.

All except for Preston, who looks bored as he sips from his drink. And Ryder, who winces at me.

But the one who's glaring the most? The one who seems to be on the verge of exploding?

Kane.

He looks so cutthroat and domineering in black pants and a white polo shirt with his hair slicked back. He watches me with cold intensity, his fingers tightening around his glass.

And Isabella is standing by his side, running her claws all over his collar.

But his entire attention is on me.

Eyes burning.

Lips slightly snarling.

I can almost feel his hand wrapping around my throat, squeezing as he whispers hot, angry words in my ear.

And I smile.

This is me making him regret what he said. What he's done.

If he doesn't care about me like he said that day, why would he look like he's on the verge of decapitating my date medieval style?

"Whoa." Marcus laughs. "I can feel the hostility. Oh my. They hate me that much, huh?"

"In their defense, you're the hate-inducing type." I look at him and pretend to smile at what he's saying.

"I am, right?" He grins. "So why isn't *he* hating?"

"Who's he?"

Abandoning his drink, Marcus grabs my arm. "Let's give them the show we're here for."

He drags me to the dance floor, wraps his arms around either side of my waist, and crushes me to his chest as we sway to the music.

I push him back a little. "This is only an act. Don't get carried away."

"Shh…" He lifts my hand and places it on his chest. "I thought you wanted revenge, so show him how much he's missing."

You know what? He's right. The entire point of this little plan is to mess with Kane as much as he's messed with me.

I sway to the trendy song, then turn around and rub my ass all over Marcus.

The music thrums, a deep bass line that resonates in my chest as I glide my fingers into my hair and give it my all.

Marcus's hands wrap around my hips, flowing in sync with me.

When I look back, he's smiling with a manic edge. "One."

"What are you counting?"

He spins me around and palms my cheek. "Two."

"What are you doing?"

"Three."

He leans down.

I step back and whisper-yell, "Don't kiss me."

His breaths dance along my skin. "Four."

"Marcus!"

"Five—"

He barely finishes saying the word when an arm slashes through the air, coils around his throat, and yanks him back with raw power.

Preston is the one who did that, immobilizing him. But the one who's grabbing his arm and twisting it in the air is Kane.

Cold lines stretch across his face and his nostrils flare.

"My, oh my." Marcus laughs and doesn't attempt to fight. "I'm honored by the warm welcome."

Kane twists harder.

"Don't," I say once I recover. "Let him go."

"You defend him again and I'll break his arm." Kane doesn't look at me. "Just say one more fucking word, Dahlia, and I swear he'll never play another game in his life."

I purse my lips.

"I'm *so* scared." Marcus looks back at Preston, grinning. "Save me?"

"You better shut the fuck up if you know what's best for you," Preston says in a deadpan voice.

"My heart is pounding...from absolute boredom. Hey, sweetheart." Marcus licks his lips. "I think we should get out of here. You said you couldn't wait to ride my cock."

Preston strangles him harder at the same time that Kane twists his arm.

Goddamn it. That asshole Marcus doesn't seem to care about his life.

I'm not sure whether Preston will choke him to death or Kane will break his arm first.

I certainly don't want to be the reason Marcus loses his career, especially since I was the one who invited him to the vipers' den.

There's nothing I can do about Preston, but Kane...

I release a dramatic sigh. "This is such a hassle. I'm going to find someone else."

And with that, I walk out as Marcus's laughter echoes around me. I'm not sure if Kane follows, but I keep my head high as I push through the crowd.

A few seconds later, a strong hand grabs my wrist, and Kane swings me around in one swift motion.

His face hovers so close to mine as he growls out, "You truly fucked up, Dahlia."

I yelp as he throws me over his shoulder and walks out of the club.

CHAPTER 26
Dahlia

WARMTH BLOOMS ACROSS MY FACE.

Both because of the blood rushing to my head and the embarrassment of being carried out of the club like a sack of potatoes.

People watch us, their whispers penetrating my ears and drowning out the music, but they part for Kane without being prompted. No one dares to get in his way as he strides with determined ease.

My stomach is draped over his broad, taut shoulder, and his big arm is wrapped tightly around my ass, restricting my movements.

"Let me go!" I scream over the loud music.

Either he doesn't hear me or he doesn't care.

I wiggle and lift my head, but it's no use.

I think I see Preston dragging a laughing Marcus into the shadows while still having him in a chokehold, but the scene disappears as Kane walks out of the club.

Icy air envelops me and goosebumps erupt on my skin, mingling with the bubbling anger coursing through me. I ball my hands into fists and bang on his muscled back, his waist—anywhere I can reach.

"Put me down—"

My words end in a gasp when he smacks my ass. Hard. So hard, my pussy throbs.

So hard, I'm scared that if I brush against him one more time, I might embarrass myself.

Apparently, my body didn't catch the memo that we're closed for business.

I punch his back again, needing to escape this humiliation. "I said put me down!"

Smack.

I jolt against his shoulder and my nipples harden against his back due to something entirely different from the cold.

"Run your mouth again and I'll fuck you here and now, Dahlia."

"Let me go, you fucking asshole!"

My world tilts off its axis as he maneuvers and slams me against the hood of a car.

His car.

"If you wanted to be fucked, all you had to do was beg for it."

My back is glued to the cool metal, my hands pressed at my sides, and I'm spread-eagled, my dress riding up to expose the lace thong Megan said I needed with this type of dress.

The parking lot's lights flicker, forming shadows on Kane's stoic face. His chest that's usually so calm and controlled is now rising and falling in an unprecedented rhythm.

The more his darkened gaze sweeps over me, the harder it is to breathe.

He leans down, blocking the horizon, and thrusts his knee between my parted legs. A tremor ripples through me as his hand skims over my skin before he grabs the dress's fallen strap and twists it between his lean fingers.

"You had the fucking audacity to come to my territory,

wearing the dress I fucking bought you, while wrapped all over another man."

There's a deceptive calm to his words, but his voice is rough, unrefined, edged with a barely contained fury. He's also cursing, so he's not as much in control as he pretends to be.

I support myself on my elbows and lift my chin, acting like his presence is meaningless and not—in fact—messing with my head. "Why would you care? We're done, aren't we? I'm *nothing*, aren't I?"

"You *are* nothing. You're so below nothing, you don't even exist on the map."

Rage ignites deep in my belly, but I force a smile. "And yet here you are. Acting unlike yourself for a *nothing*."

His shoulders bunch tightly, coiled with tension, and his authoritative tone wraps around every word. "I'm only warning you that while you're working for the team, you can't flaunt yourself around with our rival."

"What I do on my own time is none of your business. Whether I flaunt myself with your rival or let him fuck me or ride his cock all night isn't something you should worry about." I push at his chest. "Now, if you'll excuse me, I have a date to finish with Marcus."

One minute, I'm sitting, the next, Kane's hand wraps around my throat and he shoves me back against the car, his grip not choking, but tight enough to render me motionless.

A breeze sweeps through his hair as he hovers over me like a monster, and his words come out clipped. "You seem to have been deluded into thinking you can allow another cock to claim you, Dahlia. The thing is, you don't have that liberty. You can't belong to anyone else when you're fucking mine."

He lowers his head, his lips hovering over my mouth, so close, I can taste the violent passion. So close, his hot breaths mingle with mine.

And for a moment, I want to give in. To let him consume me again.

Own me.

Show me that what we share is only ours.

I don't know what fabric people are made of, but his and mine are identical. We revel in the hate and violence, and I'd be lying if I said I didn't miss his touch.

Or the liberty that comes with relinquishing my control to him.

But I didn't go through all of this shit just to get him back.

Things have to happen on my terms.

At the last second, I turn my face, looking at the silver car parked next to his.

Kane pauses, his grip loosening a little from around my throat as if he's been caught off guard.

I look at him again and, sure enough, a puzzled look takes refuge in his icy eyes and his brows dip. He can't imagine me refusing a kiss, especially since I was always the one who initiated them.

Craved them.

Demanded them.

Not now, though.

My fingers wrap around his hand that's on my throat. "Tell me you care about me first."

"What?"

"You heard me."

"I know I did, but I'm not sure whether or not you're joking."

"I'm not. I want to hear you say you care, and that, from now on, you'll allow me to get close. I want a true relationship, not a sex-buddies situation. You'll take me on dates and tell me about yourself. You'll watch movies with me and let me just chill at your place, even if there's no sex involved."

He pauses.

I pause, too.

That's not what I had planned. I only wished for him to stop pushing me away, but maybe, deep down, that's exactly what I've wanted this whole time.

I really hate it when he emotionally abandons me as soon as the sex is over.

It didn't bother me in the beginning, but then it started to make me feel anxious.

"You're out of your mind," he says in a bewildered tone.

But he still has his hand on my throat.

He still hasn't left, his fingers burning metaphorical holes in my skin.

"For wanting normal?" I ask.

"We're not fucking *normal*, Dahlia."

"I know, but sex isn't all we have either, no matter how much you try to convince yourself that's the case."

His fingers tighten around my neck. I can see the conflict in his eyes—that part of him that fits perfectly with mine—wavering, flickering, but there's also his annoying control-freak part, the one that always drags him back behind his defenses.

The part I've never managed to win against.

"The answer is no." He releases my neck with a shove.

My heart falls and a piercing pain rips through my rib cage.

"I can fuck you if you need that, but there will be no relationship."

I press my trembling lips together. "A relationship or no fucking."

He shrugs.

"Fine." I plaster a smile. "Step aside. I have a date to go back to."

A muscle jumps in his cheek. "Don't make me go back in there and choke him to death."

"Be my guest. I'll find others."

"I'll slice each and every one of their throats. Go ahead. Fucking test me."

"You won't possibly know them all."

"*Try* me."

"It'll be a hassle to clean up."

"I have enough money to take care of the problem." He squeezes my chin with his fingers. "You let another man put his hands on you and it'll be the last time they touch anything."

"You'd rather go through all that damn trouble than be in a relationship with me?" I shout, shoving at his chest. "What the hell is wrong with you?"

"You!" he shouts back, the veins in his neck nearly popping. "You're everything that's fucking wrong with me. You're ruining my goddamn life."

"You're destroying mine!"

"Then walk the fuck away, Dahlia."

"Let me go, then!"

"I already did!"

"No, you didn't. It's not considered letting go if you threaten to kill my possible prospects, Kane."

"You have no other prospects but *me*." He yanks my dress to my waist, exposing my panties.

A shiver rushes through me. I've been soaking wet since

he carried me out, but it became worse with his touch and the back-and-forth.

I'm burning for him in ways I've never felt toward anyone else.

In ways I can't truly control.

It will feel good when he touches me. I know it will, but I simply can't tolerate what happens afterward anymore.

I slap his hand away. "Don't touch me unless you're ready to fully commit. And this is not a 'don't touch me that means you can use me.' This is a 'red,' Kane."

He freezes, his index finger twitching, then he steps back and runs his hand through his hair. "Fuck!"

I've never used the safe word, not even when I thought it could get to be a bit too much. I loved it when it hurt, when he fucked me so hard I couldn't walk for a while.

But I'm using it now. This is the red line I didn't know I had.

I refuse to have his body without his heart—and soul, if need be.

I refuse to be another stop on his journey. And even if I end up being that, I want to be the unforgettable stop he can't purge out of his mind.

The one episode in his past that he can't stop thinking about.

"Fuck!" he roars louder, but this time, he clutches my jaw again. "You don't know what the fuck you're asking for, Dahlia."

"I don't care."

"You'll regret this."

"I won't."

"If this happens, you can never back off."

"That's okay." I stroke his face, mirroring his ruthlessness with my gentle touch. "Kiss m—"

The last word isn't even out of my mouth before he slams his lips to mine, kissing me with so much fervor, my head spins.

Maybe it's because I haven't touched him for a long time, but everything is electrifying. The brush of his lips against mine, the pads of his fingers tilting my jaw back so he can deepen the kiss, his hand fisting in my hair, his jeans brushing against my thighs.

Everything.

This kiss is claiming but also surrendering.

He *wants* me. So much so, he can't hold back.

I'd like to think he needs me enough that he doesn't want to let go.

And I need him, too. He's the only man I've ever craved with every fiber of my being.

My hand slides over his lean waist, his back, touching, stroking. I've been so deprived of him, I've experienced withdrawal symptoms.

This kiss is my long-awaited hit.

Still kissing me, he releases my jaw and I pause, thinking he'll push my hands away as usual, but he reaches between us and the sound of a buckle echoes in the air.

"Kane..." I whisper, half excited, half horrified. "We're in a public place."

"You should've thought about that before you provoked me. All bets are off, wildflower."

I moan as he rubs his hard cock against my panties, over my clit. Pleasure pools at the base of my belly as he repeats the motion agonizingly slowly.

"You're so fucking wet." He slides the flimsy fabric aside and glides the length of his cock against my slit. "You've been dying for my cock, huh?"

"Oh God." I wrap my arms around his neck.

"Or is this because you planned to fuck Osborn, hmm?" He aligns the crown with my opening.

I clench, so ready to suck him inside me, but he only thrusts the tip in slow, shallow movements.

"Kane…" I groan in frustration.

"Tell me, Dahlia. Did you doll up and turn into a fucking goddess for Osborn tonight?"

"It was for you, asshole." I wiggle against the car.

"For me, huh?"

"Yeah." I pant as if I've just finished a marathon. "I knew you'd be jealous."

"Hmm, so it was to make me jealous?" He thrusts his entire massive cock in one go.

Jesus.

This man is a beast. It's been some time, so it hurts, but it's a good pain.

The pain I've been missing.

Kane doesn't move for a few seconds, his cock throbbing inside me as I get accustomed to the size.

Both his arms slam on either side of my face as his molten gaze sinks into mine, a dark glint growing in his light eyes.

"What else did you want to accomplish tonight, Dahlia?"

"Prove you can't let me go." I scratch at his neck and grin. "I was right."

He retreats and then thrusts back in. I scream, my back arching against the metal.

Oh fuck. I almost forgot how brutal he can get. And how much I love it.

A grin paints my lips. "You're crazy."

"Because of you." He drives into me again, his rhythm picking up.

"I'm crazy too, you know." I bite the lobe of his ear and

whisper, "If I see another woman's claws on you again, I'll invite you to watch my next orgy."

He grabs my hair and shoves me back so that he's staring down at me. "You need to stop bringing up other men when you're being railed by my cock."

"Does that mean I can bring them up at another time—" I moan when he thrusts against that pleasure spot, my lips forming in an O.

"What was that?" His mouth pulls in an evil grin.

Why is this man so damn hot?

"I said I can bring them—oh fuck!" He rams into me in quick succession, so I have no choice but to cling to him, my words turning into intelligible moans.

He fucks me deep and hard, just the way I like it.

He fucks me like he hates me.

But he doesn't. Not in the least.

He lets me hold on to him and hugs my back.

"You need to shut that fucking mouth, Dahlia. This cunt is mine. *You* are fucking mine." He slaps my ass cheek. "Do you understand?"

Tears gush from my eyes, but they're pleasure tears. The tears only this man can provoke.

My nails dig into his neck, and I bite on the lobe of his ear, then moan. "I'm not sure I do."

"Watch it." He sinks his teeth into my bottom lip and pulls. "You're provoking me."

"Is it working?" I moan as he hits that spot again.

"Jesus fucking Christ." He pushes me into the car and lifts my legs up so that they're resting on his shoulders.

The new angle gives him deeper access and Kane uses it to his advantage. He thrusts into me harder, faster, the car rocking beneath our weight.

"Want me to ruin you, Dahlia? Want me to fucking claim you so if anyone comes out and sees us, they know who the fuck you belong to?"

My ears ring and I'm barely listening as the wave grows near.

"That's it." He circles my clit. "Come for me."

I do.

Deeply.

Fiercely.

Uncontrollably.

Kane claims my bruised lips, eating up my scream.

I roll my hips, riding the wave, kissing him back, getting so lost, I forget where we are.

As his movements turn more frantic, more urgent, I grab his face with both hands and pull away. A trail of saliva connects us as I whisper, "Come with me, please."

"Mine," he growls, his mouth devouring mine, and then I feel it.

The warmth.

The deep warmth that fills my insides.

He comes for a long time, his cum filling me up and gushing out, on the car, the dress—everywhere.

"Such a fucking mess," he grunts against my lips.

"Your mess." I kiss the tip of his nose, feeling so damn light and happy.

I thought happiness was snuggling up with Vi at the end of a long day and watching a true crime documentary or trash TV while eating popcorn.

Happiness used to be having a roof over our heads and sorting out the month's bills.

Happiness was a scholarship, a small door of opportunity, or a stranger handing us their used clothes.

But right now, as Kane mutters a curse and carries me in his arms, I realize there's a different type.

Happiness I didn't know I needed.

Happiness that scares the living hell out of me, but I still want it anyway.

CHAPTER 27
Kane

I MADE A MISCALCULATION.

To be blunt, I fucked up. Big time.

I sit on the edge of the bed, where Dahlia sleeps soundly, her face relaxed and peaceful, except for the mascara smears around her eyes.

Soft mumbles leave her parted mouth, and I can't resist stroking her lips, her jaw, and her cheek. No matter how much I touch her, it barely scratches the surface of my deviant fixation.

I could swallow her the fuck up and it'd still be a far cry from enough.

Dahlia leans into my touch, stroking her cheek against my palm as a moan leaves her lips and lodges itself deep in my chest.

Something is wrong with the fucker—my chest—because it's *moving*. I probably need to consult with my doctor and have him check what the fuck is wrong with my head while he's at it.

Because I truly and undeniably fucked the hell up.

It's been a couple of hours since I drove her back to my place. She fell asleep in the car and didn't stir when I carried her in my arms and tucked her in bed.

Usually, Dahlia sleeps in a fetal position, making herself

as small as possible, but right now, her arms are thrown out on either side of her, taking up most of the bed. Almost like a child who's exhausted after a busy day out.

Is it because she feels safe?

Because she's tired?

Whatever the reason, I appreciate the view. And I like her here. In my bed. My space. My life, even.

I like it more than I believed would be possible.

Which is also part of the reason *why* I fucked up.

Last week, I thought I could cut things off without looking back.

I thought if I chopped off the branches, it'd all be over, but I failed to realize that she left her roots somewhere I didn't know existed.

I thought I could threaten my teammates to stay the fuck away from her *while* ignoring her. They all know not to touch, flirt, or even *talk* to her outside of work-related issues.

Just because I let her go didn't mean she was a free pass for them.

However, Dahlia had other plans and forced my hand.

She knew the one spot to hit with all her might—my illogical possessiveness toward her. And she didn't pick just any guy to flaunt in my face.

No.

She went straight for the jugular and brought the one guy I already *knew* she'd dated. The one guy I saw her flirting with at my fucking game.

And she did that while looking mouthwatering in a dress I bought her, intending to rip it off her body.

When Osborn tilted her head back, his lips hovering an inch away from hers, I forgot about all the reasons why I should stay away from her.

I forgot that my father would kill her just to teach me a lesson.

I forgot all the mantras I kept repeating to myself about a greater purpose and higher fucking goals.

At that moment, all I wanted was to claim her and kill Osborn—which I would've done if Preston hadn't interfered.

I couldn't even wait to get her somewhere out of view. I had to own her then and there.

Make her mine again.

Only mine.

But now that the possessive edge has lessened, reality hits me, and I can't ignore it anymore.

Dahlia Thorne has become a weakness.

One my father can use to dismantle me.

One that's able to destroy all my plans.

But letting her go and allowing other fucks to touch her is out of the question, so I need to devise a plan to protect her.

I stand up and fetch my phone. After closing the bedroom door as softly as possible, I head to the living room and dial a number I thought I wouldn't need this soon.

The town's bright lights fill the distance as I stop by the floor-to-ceiling window, listening to it ringing.

He finally picks up, a sound of shuffles echoing on his end as he lets out a groan and speaks in a husky tone, "Ever heard of a thing called sleeping time?"

"Nice to hear from you, too, Uncle. I'm glad you missed me."

"I'd miss you more during reasonable hours." He lets out a sigh. "What do you want?"

"Your help."

The sound of steps padding across the floor stops, and a long silence stretches between us.

"Since when do you ask for help?" he asks slowly, all sleep gone from his voice.

"Since I made a miscalculation."

"Explain."

I tell him about the Dahlia thing, and how the very fucking fact of her existence is ruining all the strategies I devised to bring Grant down.

So now that I've decided to keep her, I'm unsure whether or not I can proceed with my agenda. Uncle Kayden knows I've already won over half of the board members and that I'm working on the other half.

It was supposed to be a matter of months before I snatched the reins of power and brought back Uncle Kayden and all the other family members—mostly women—that my father kicked out.

Once I graduate and become a Founder member, I'd turn the tables on Grant, facilitate his being voted out by his own people, and then take over. Little by little, I plan to undo all his decisions and rebuild the Davenport name the way I see fit.

Truly, it's Grant's fault for having me be so involved in the company. He wanted to train me properly, but I've been using that chance to corner him.

My uncle listens without interrupting. While Kayden is Grant's younger brother, they couldn't be any more different. They also never really liked each other.

Since Uncle Kayden caused quite a stir last year and got banished from the organization and the state, he's lucky to be alive.

But then again, his much younger menace of a boyfriend, Gareth, wouldn't allow it and provided him the protection of the Russian mafia.

Also, even though Kayden got banished from Vencor, he still owns half of the Davenport empire. He has considerable influence over directors and would take my side when it's time to bring Grant down.

"You know the precise solution to this clusterfuck," he says after I finish talking.

"I'm not letting her go."

"I was going to suggest neutralizing her."

My fingers tighten around the phone, wishing I could reach the other end and punch him. "That won't be happening."

"She's a weakness that will cause your downfall."

"Just like Gareth was."

"That's different. Gareth is self-sufficient and comes from a strong family that would start a war to protect him. She's a nobody. Grant knows that and will eliminate or use her to cage you further under his thumb."

"You're underestimating her." Dahlia might not have Russian mafia ties and come from an empire like Gareth Carson, but she's the strongest person I know.

She's been through so much shit, but she's always, without fail, bounced back up, ready for another fight.

"You're *over*estimating her." Kayden's deep voice carries in the silence like a knife. "You're also presenting your weakness to Grant on a silver platter. Take my advice and eliminate her before it backfires. If you can't kill her, send her to a different coast or, better yet, country. If you care about her, surely you know she won't survive in that world. Do you wish to create another version of your mother? An aimless ghost who survives on pills and talks to fish?"

"She's not Helena."

"Right now, she's not. Do you think Helena was always like that? She used to be cheerful and antidepressant-free. She used to have a soul, but it was crushed into the dust of time. Just like everyone else's."

"That won't happen to Dahlia," I insist in a clear voice, even though his words stab me in the chest. "If you're done being a pessimist, I have a plan I need your help with."

"Which is?"

"I'm going to throw Grant a bone, give up some influence in the upcoming business deal I've been planning in secret in exchange for him staying away from Dahlia. I want you to approve it."

"Fucking fool." His voice vibrates with disapproval. "If Grant knows you have a card up your sleeve and you're willingly giving it up for her, you'll prove that she's not only a weakness but also someone he can use to manipulate you."

"By that time, I'll be out of his control."

"Highly improbable. If anything, once you reveal a card, he'll be extremely wary of you."

"Doesn't matter. I know how to deal with him. Just tell me, will you help?"

"Suit yourself." There's movement on the other end.

A low male voice carries from my uncle's side, and I assume it's Gareth. "Who are you talking to this early?"

"Nephew," Kayden says in a softer voice, and I can almost see his smile.

My uncle doesn't smile, not much anyway, but he seems to be always in a good mood if Gareth is around.

"Go back to sleep, baby," he says in a low, gentle tone.

"Mmm. Not alone." Gareth's husky, sleepy voice sounds closer. "Hey, Kane. How are you? Still kicking ass in hockey?"

"Yeah, as usual, Gaz," I say with a smile. I like him, mostly because he makes my uncle happy, despite all the shit they went through.

"His name is Gareth," Uncle grumbles in my ear.

I had a bit of a whiplash when I met them for dinner one time. My uncle—who people compare to a stoic, emotionless robot—nearly chased me away because his man was talking to me longer than he liked.

Which was five minutes tops.

I hear a rustle from his side and a small hum before he says, "We'll talk again at a reasonable hour. In the meantime, think carefully about the clusterfuck you're getting yourself into because of a girl you've only just met. Is she worth it?"

After my uncle hangs up, I stare at the town for what seems like hours, contemplating his last question.

Logically, Dahlia is not worth it. She's a hassle and brings nothing to the table.

She's not even part of Graystone's elite, like Isabella or any of the other girls vying for my attention, who I could use in my power play.

But fuck if I can use logic when it comes to her. I tried that before and it only backfired.

My phone lights up with notifications from the group chat.

Jude: Pres? What did you do to Osborn?
Jude: @Kane Davenport, why the fuck did you leave him to his own devices? I'm absent for two fucking hours and all hell breaks loose?

Why did I leave him again? Right. I lost access to my logic and forgot the simple fact that Preston has been volatile as fuck lately, specifically since the forest hunt.

Preston: Reporting live from the latest crime scene, bitches.

Jude: JFC, what the fuck did you do now?

Preston: I only do genius things.

Jude: Pres, don't make me come there and strangle you.

Preston: Chill. It's nothing serious. Unfortunately.

Jude: You didn't do something stupid to Osborn?

Preston: Stupid is your middle name, not mine.

Jude: I swear to fuck I'm going to beat you to a pulp.

Preston: Scared to my nonexistent core. Brb, calling my mommy as we speak. Wait. I don't have one.

Jude: Be serious for three fucking seconds. You know we're not allowed to hurt Osborn. At least, not yet.

Preston: Yikes. Must've missed the memo.

Jude: Don't tell me you killed him?

Preston: He's still polluting the earth with his existence. For now. More importantly, you have a hunt coming up, big man? I could use a purge.

Jude: @Kane Davenport?

Preston: Probably too lost in pussy to see straight.

Me: Not yet. Save that energy for the next game.

Preston: Boo, everyone join me in calling Kane a fucking killjoy.

Me: *thumbs-up emoji*

They're both typing when slender arms wrap around my waist and the scent of jasmine fills my nostrils.

Dahlia's breasts press against my back as she rests her cheek against my shoulder.

I let the phone hang in my hand as her presence invades my senses until she's the only thing in my surroundings.

Her soft breaths, her warmth, and her gentle curves mold to me so naturally, as if she always belonged here.

With me.

"Couldn't sleep?" she asks in a groggy voice.

"I'll be fine. Go back to bed."

As I face her, she stumbles, her movements sluggish, and I grab her by the waist.

She wraps her arms around my neck, and then this fucking woman who could barely stand jumps and encircles my waist with her legs, and I have to support her back so she doesn't fall off.

Dahlia smiles, looking like a fucking goddess even with the messed-up mascara and ruined makeup. "Come to bed with me."

I raise a brow. "Is that an invitation?"

"We can have sex later. Now, I just want to hug you."

Fucking hell.

What can I even say to shit like that?

Instead of speaking, I walk her to the bedroom and start to lower her to the bed, but she doesn't let me go.

So I lie down on my side and Dahlia buries her face in my neck.

"You're awfully clingy today," I say against her hair.

"Nope, this is the right amount in a relationship." Her lips brush against my throat with each word. "I think."

"So you're not sure?"

"I'm a beginner, but I think so are you?"

"Yeah, I don't do relationships."

"Awesome. That way, you'll consider this the standard. Just so you know, I'm going to annoy the hell out of you."

I chuckle. "More than what you're already doing?"

She lifts her head and studies my face with wide eyes, the green killing all other colors.

"What's wrong?" I ask.

"Nothing. It's just too rare to see you laugh genuinely." She grins. "It makes me happy."

"My laugh makes you happy?"

"Mmm. Because I'm the reason." She strokes the back of my head. "I'm glad you didn't let me go."

"You forced my hand into a relationship. Is that really what you want?"

"It is." A delicate frown creases her forehead. "If you discard me again, I'm walking away. For good. If another woman touches you, I'm also out."

"You're the one who had your fucking arm around Osborn, Dahlia."

"And Isabella had her claws all over you." She narrows her eyes. "Did you fuck her?"

"You think there's another woman who can handle me?"

A smug look covers her features. "Well, you better remember that."

I fist her hair and jerk her back. "And you better remember you're fucking mine."

"Okay, caveman."

"And if this is an attempt to weasel your way into Vencor again, that's out of the question."

Her throat works up and down and I release her hair.

"I understand."

Silence beats like a presence as she shifts. "Kane?"

"Hmm?"

"Why don't you ask me about my real reason for wanting to get in? You must've figured out it's not for some vain purpose like status or power."

"If I ask, will you tell me?"

"Maybe one day."

I nod.

She doesn't need to tell me. Not really.

Because it doesn't matter. Now that she's mine, nothing and no one will change it.

"I just want you to know I didn't mean to use you." She swallows. "Maybe that was true initially, but I just want to make this thing between us work right now."

"Me, too, Dahlia." I stroke her back. "Me, too."

She smiles, her eyes so bright, I want to fucking engrave them in me. "Tell me something I don't know about you."

"What's with this all of a sudden?"

"I want to get to know you better. I'll go first. When I was younger, I wanted to be a rich lawyer who used my money to do as many pro bono cases as possible. I wanted to focus on those who were failed by the system."

"But you chose medicine. Why?"

"Because Violet has always had poor health. I wanted to take care of her." A sheen of sadness flickers in her eyes, turning them a turbulent yellow. "Not that it matters much right now."

"How did you come to care about a non-blood-related person this much?"

"Vi is my world. You don't need blood to care. If anything, some blood relations are like a curse."

"Touché."

"I didn't mean to—"

"It's fine. You wanted to know something about me? My father considers me a machine instead of a son." The words carry in the silence, loud and heavy. "I'm not allowed to lose, mess up, or humiliate the Davenport name. If I do, he'll make sure I remember it, preferably with a physical or psychological scar."

Dahlia shifts until her face is close to mine. "Can't you cut off your relationship with him?"

"No."

"Why? Are power and money more important than your well-being?"

"It's not about power and money. What I have in mind is more valuable."

She palms my cheek. "There's nothing more valuable than yourself, Kane. Why can't you see that?"

I take her hand and slowly lower it. Partly because I'm not entirely used to her touch and it's burning my skin.

"I have it under control."

She makes a face. "I hate that word. I also hate that you're so closed off sometimes."

"You hate so many things about me and yet you still want a relationship with me?"

"I know, right? I'm thinking about changing my mind."

"Too late. You're not going anywhere." I lift her chin and kiss her. Slowly. I take my time, not feeling the imminent urge to fuck her just because I'm touching her.

I'm only staking a claim.

Proving that this girl is mine.

To answer Uncle's question, she's, without any shadow of a doubt, worth it.

Even if it destroys me.

CHAPTER 28
Dahlia

"HONEY?"

"Wake up. It's time to go, Dahl."

Mom...?

Vi?

They're both standing in a blindingly white distance, their shadows spilling on the ground, but not touching my feet.

Blood gushes from Mom's forehead, slides down her arm, and slithers onto her hand that's holding Vi's.

My dad appears on Vi's right and takes her other hand in his disfigured, bloodied one.

I step forward, but I'm jolted in place by invisible chains, unable to move.

They walk in the distance, their tall, distorted shadows retreating until I can only see their backs and the blood trails left behind.

Drip.

Drip.

Drip.

"Where are you going?" I scream, tears cascading down my cheeks. "Come back. Don't leave me alone. You promised, Vi!"

They come to a halt and Vi looks back, her face pale, eyes sunk in, her hair having lost its shine. She looks like a ghost of herself with crimson blood dripping from her delicate fingers.

A version of Vi I don't recognize.

Broken-down.

Decimated.

"Goodbye, Dahlia."

"No...no..."

"Wake up now, Dahl."

"Vi, no, don't go."

"It's okay. You'll be okay."

"Nooo!"

"Dahlia!"

"Dahlia."

"Dahlia, wake up!"

My eyes fly open, my breath coming in ragged gasps as hot tears cling to my lashes.

"It's okay. You're okay. It was just a nightmare."

I look up as Kane sits in bed, gliding my damp hair back, his fingers stroking my face gently.

He reaches to the bedside table and offers me a bottle of water.

I sit up and gulp most of it while still panting. Images of Vi leaving with my parents play so vividly in my head, a taste of nausea crawls up my throat and I feel like throwing up.

"You feel better?" Kane's deep voice sounds soothing. Consoling, even.

Which is a rare version of him.

He takes the water from my fingers and watches me closely as if he can peek into my brain.

I wrap my arms around my knees and rock back and

forth. "I had a nightmare that Vi went with my parents. That she...she died and left me all alone. She said I'd be okay. She said her goodbyes."

"That was only a nightmare."

"What if it becomes real?" *Back. Forth.* "I...I'm barely over my parents' deaths and only because I have Vi. If she... if she...leaves as well, I don't know how I'll go on."

A big hand wraps around mine and gently pulls it, stopping the rocking. I stare at Kane and his handsome, composed face calms my breathing.

There's a firm yet soothing authoritativeness in his expression, like I can fall and he'll catch me. No questions asked.

"Violet is still alive, but most importantly, you are alive, too. Besides, you're not all alone. You have me." His mouth twitches in a small smile. "Didn't you promise to annoy the hell out of me? Let's see whether or not you succeed."

My lips part.

A warm feeling I've never experienced spreads inside me like a hug.

You have me.

Kane said I have *him*.

God. Who would've thought the guy I approached to avenge my sister would be the one consoling me about her?

A part of me feels guilty for ever using him. For lumping him in with the rest of the unfeeling psychos.

Kane is different.

Entirely different.

He's not the green flag I mistook him for, but he's not entirely red either. He's a mixture of colors, and I'm growing attached to all of them.

The red, the green, the black. All.

I open my arms and engulf him in a hug, burying my face in his chest, right on top of his steady heartbeat.

He feels warm.

So warm.

Kane awkwardly pats my back, his body a bit stiff, probably not used to this amount of clinginess, but it doesn't matter.

I'm not used to it either, but it's okay with Kane.

I feel like I can let go and he won't use it against me.

At least, I hope he won't.

Having raw feelings for someone who's way out of my social standing is scary, but I'm willing to take the leap.

But at the same time, I feel like I'm losing focus of why I got entangled in this world in the first place, and I can't seem to find my way back in.

Slowly, my breaths even out and I think I fall asleep in his arms, because the next thing I know, I'm being laid back on the bed.

I blink the sleep from my eyes as Kane stands up and removes his shirt.

My heart burns at the view of the scars, visible even under the early-morning light slipping through the window.

But I also can't help but admire the sheer strength in his build, each muscle etched and honed as if he's been carved from marble. Every ridge, every line is sharp and precise, just like Kane himself—disciplined, formidable, almost impossibly defined.

The way he moves with effortless confidence is a natural, unforced power that's as magnetic as it is unsettling. There's something in the way he holds himself, like he owns the space around him without needing to declare it. It's that quiet, commanding presence that makes looking away feel impossible.

He walks into his closet and emerges a few minutes later dressed in sweatpants and a Vipers hoodie.

His eyes meet mine and they darken a little.

I pull the sheet to my chin. "Morning."

"Go back to sleep. It's still four thirty."

"Where are you going? Isn't it early for practice?"

"Jude and Pres are here. At the front door, I mean. They won't leave unless I let them in."

"Is something wrong?"

"They often do this when they're drunk."

"So if we hadn't come back, you would've gotten drunk with them?"

"Probably not."

"Why not?"

"Let's just say Jude and Pres feed off each other's destructive energy. I put a leash on mine." He ruffles my hair and smiles. "Adorable bed hair."

"Hey!" I push his hand away. "Don't make it worse."

"I don't think that's possible." He walks out of the room, the soft click echoing in the space.

For some reason, it feels massive without him here.

I try to go back to sleep or pretend to, anyway. I'm more curious about Jude's and Preston's drunken state and whether they can offer me any clues…

I really should stop thinking about using Kane or his close friends. It doesn't align with the new start we've established, so it's better to focus on Hunter and the DNA testing.

After some futile twisting and turning, I get up and go to the bathroom to freshen up. The first thing I notice is my half-torn dress and my hideous face.

Oh my God. Mascara and makeup have run down my face and turned me into a zombie movie extra.

Jeez.

No wonder Kane said it can't get worse. How the hell did he even look at me?

Can the earth open up and swallow me?

I take a quick shower and wince with every move. Kane definitely fucked my brains out last night. I can feel him inside me with every step.

It takes me more time than needed to shower, but at least I manage to wash my face clean. I put on one of his hoodies that swallows me and almost reaches my knees, and I have to roll up the sleeves to free my hands. The whole time, I'm surrounded by Kane's scent, and it feels like a hug.

Or maybe I need to seriously stop being so into the man.

My feet gently pad on the wood as I head to the living room.

"Do it gently, you brute!" Preston shouts.

I lean sideways, grabbing the wall with both hands.

Kane is by the stove, cooking something that smells divine.

Preston sits on the kitchen stool opposite him as Jude stands beside him and holds an ice pack to his cheek.

"This gentle?" Jude asks as he presses harder.

"Ow, give it to me. I'll do it myself." Preston snatches the ice pack.

Jude rummages through Kane's cabinets as if he's in his own place, produces a few pills, and then throws them at Preston's head. "Take those."

Preston groans. "You're using this to fucking torture me."

Jude lifts a shoulder. "Shouldn't have gotten into a fight when I wasn't there."

"Fuck off. I can handle my fights."

"Since when do you even fight?" Kane glances at him sideways.

"Since someone needed to be put in their fucking place." Preston grins in that manic way.

"Sure it wasn't the other way around?"

"You should see his face." Preston laughs. "I turned it into an impressionist art painting."

"I don't know about that." Jude hits him on the back of his head.

"Fucking bitch!" Preston kicks him, but Jude dodges and it barely grazes his leg.

"Enough." Kane slides a bowl of what looks like soup in front of Preston and another one in front of Jude. "I told you to keep your voices down or I'm kicking you out."

"Yeah, yeah, Mr. Pussy-Whipped." Preston mocks as he grabs a spoon.

Is Kane cooking for them? This early?

"Man, this shit's amazing." Preston gives up on the spoon and drinks straight from the bowl.

"It's hot, take it easy." Jude pulls the bowl away and passes him a napkin. "Wipe your mouth."

"I made a lot and pizza is on the way." Kane pours Preston another bowl and places a water bottle by the pills. "Don't eat fast."

I frown.

Why are they...treating Preston like that?

I've never noticed this before, not even in practice. If anything, I thought Jude and Preston barely get along and always fight, but right now, when it's only the three of them and Preston has a bruise the size of Texas, they're...*fawning* over him?

I don't know if that's the right word, but they're definitely treating him differently.

Especially Jude.

He keeps watching Preston as if looking for something. What, I don't know.

"Did you at least sleep before or after your nocturnal activities?" Jude asks.

"Nope." Preston grins. "I found something better than sleep."

"Catch some in the guest room," Kane says.

"Nah. I'll sleep after practice."

"Can you even survive practice in your state?" Jude says.

"We'll know once I kick your ass today, big man."

Jude smiles, but it's menacing. "Nice dreams to have."

The scene looks weirdly intimate. I feel like I'm trespassing on their bond or something.

While I think Kane has a way better personality than both Jude and especially Preston, I'm starting to think the three of them share something a lot deeper than Vencor or even hockey.

Standing here seems like I'm intruding, so I clear my throat and walk in.

Three pairs of eyes zoom in on me, but only Kane watches me with that edge. The one I feel would consume me on the spot if given the chance.

His eyes size me up, stopping and narrowing at where his hoodie stops at my thighs.

"Look who we have here." Preston whistles. "Deborah. The Wolves' spy."

"It's Dahlia, and I'm not a spy."

"Looked like it when you were rubbing yourself all over their captain a few hours ago."

I bite my lower lip. "I did that to make Kane jealous. There was no spying whatsoever."

"I vote a spy." Preston raises his hand. "A la guillotine."

Kane knocks his hand down. "Behave yourself, asshole."

"Pfft, you just don't want guillotine action. Jude, let's all boo him again."

Jude says nothing and focuses on eating.

Weird. I would've sworn he'd jump at the idea of dragging me through the mud with Preston.

Actually, Jude hasn't been antagonizing toward me at all lately and even pulls Preston away when he starts.

Kane rounds the island and comes to my side, wrapping a possessive arm around my waist, then whispers in my ear, "What are you wearing?"

"Your hoodie," I whisper back.

"It barely covers *anything*."

"Are you kidding? It covers *everything*."

"I don't like the idea of other men imagining you naked, Dahlia."

"You're being ridiculous. Pretty sure Preston would rather chop my head off instead."

"Touché, Dakota!" Preston claps his hands and points a finger at me. "Are you interested in testing my experimental new execution device?"

"No, thanks?"

"Aw, and here I thought we could be friends." He wraps an arm around Jude's shoulders. "What about you, big man?"

Jude throws his hand off him. "Hard pass."

"Ouch, you pierced me right where I don't give a fuck."

Kane drags me to the stools and helps me hop on one. "I'll pour you some soup. I also ordered some pizza so the drunks can have something to eat before practice, but you can have some, too."

"Ew." Preston makes a face. "I'm getting diabetes."

"Fuck off, then." Kane goes to the other side and pours me a bowl.

"And miss seeing you be a domesticated dog?" Preston grins. "Here, little doggie. Who's a good boy? Is this the part where we give you a treat—"

Kane whacks him with a dish towel. "Shut your mouth."

"Juuude!" Preston whines. "Did you see that?"

Jude smacks him upside the head. "Take your medicine."

"You fucking—" He takes a deep breath, then smiles at me. "See how they can't live without me?"

"I don't know. Looks like you're a troublemaker." I take a sip of the soup and it tastes better than it smells. As expected of Kane.

"Me? Ha. Have you seen Jude on the rink? He's the troublemaker whose ass we all have to clean up after."

I lift a shoulder. "Doesn't look the same off the rink."

"Even she can tell," Kane says. "You're like a bad investment that keeps haunting the rest of the portfolio."

"Bitch, please. Your lives would be boring without me."

"I'd take that chance," Jude says.

"The betrayal is sending me." Preston smiles again at me, but it's fake at best and menacing at worst. "Never mind them. Tell me, Daniella. You're not by any chance fucking both Kane and the Wolves' dog at the same time, are you?"

"Preston…" Kane warns.

"Shut it. I'm doing this for your sake."

"Not that I have to explain myself to you, but I'm not."

"Good. Because if you do betray my man, I might truly chop your head off."

I swallow as that cloud of bloodlust hits me again. Preston remains still, but his eyes are cold, and the purple bruise makes him look monstrous.

For a moment, I think he'll reach out and crush my face like the other time, but Kane grabs him by the hair and jerks his head back.

He glares down at Preston. "Threaten her again and we'll have serious problems. Don't ever think about hurting her."

"Oh, I will, but only if she betrays you. Now, let me go. That hurts."

Kane releases him with a shove and comes to sit beside me. "Ignore him."

I try to.

But even as I swallow, the soup gets stuck in my throat.

I'm not betraying Kane in a sexual or romantic sense, but is previously using him—or attempting to—considered betrayal?

While Preston is scary, it's Kane who frightens me.

He might be calm and collected, but I know, I just know that if I fuck up, he'll cast me out of his life as if I never existed.

And that leaves me shaking with anxiety.

Is it truly a new beginning if I have too many skeletons hidden in the closet?

CHAPTER 29
Dahlia

THINGS HAVE...CHANGED.

Since the first time I slept in Kane's arms over three weeks ago, he's been different.

We spent Christmas and New Year's together, mostly with Preston and Jude. I don't really like the holiday season, but this one felt different. Because I had Kane, but also I felt the need to celebrate for Vi.

She always took them seriously, insisting we celebrate like a 'normal' family and put up this small Christmas tree she goes overboard with decorating. It felt empty this year without her, but at least I had Kane.

He's been changing over the past few weeks.

It's been subtle and gradual, but it's heart-flutteringly noticeable. He still doesn't like it when I touch him for too long, but he's not so quick about removing my hands.

We spend entire nights talking about everything and nothing. I told him about my whole childhood and all the shit I went through so Vi and I could survive—but I also told him about the good things as well.

Part of the reason why I opened up was in the hopes that he'd also talk about his own childhood in depth, but he rarely does, and when it happens, it's usually without any emotion.

Kane might have let me in, but his walls still stand tall. Completely and utterly indestructible.

But I'm not complaining.

This whole time, I've only felt Kane lose control—momentarily—during sex. But lately, I can see glimpses of him doing so even if he's not fucking me.

He's one meticulous bastard and hates it when I leave things lying around. He also has these strange quirks like cooking in silence and not listening to any music. He also does the same in his home gym when working out—no speakers or headphones. When I asked about it, he said he uses that time to think, and he doesn't really listen to music or anything audible, because it interferes with his thoughts.

Kane also wakes up early and is always the first player who arrives at practice.

But he doesn't drag me along and often tells me to sleep some more, especially if I visited Vi the previous night.

I'm starting to feel guilty because I can't spend the whole night by her bedside anymore. I try to stay for a couple of hours and give her updates—mostly related to Kane—but I feel like it's not enough.

My days are busy with work and school, and the nights... well, if I'm not being chased and dicked down by Kane in the sickest, most perverse ways, we're either going out with his teammates or snuggling up for a movie or cooking the most random shit I find on the internet.

Or he cooks and I just stand around like the most useless assistant.

And on the weekends, I insist that we spend time with his mom—something he dislikes, so he grumbles and acts like a general asshole. However, when we went to his parents' house yesterday, he was mostly silent as he watched with a cryptic expression while Helena and I fed and talked to the koi fish.

Then he left us to have a meeting with his dad. I'm not sure what was said, but afterward, Kane had a defeated but relieved smile. Grant merely narrowed his eyes on me as he stormed out of the house.

Since last night, Kane has been more relaxed. He fucked me so hard that I was screaming, and I woke up this morning with his head between my legs. Best morning ever.

He also said I should move my stuff into his apartment, to which I was left speechless.

To be honest, I've only dropped by the dorm lately to check on Megan and grab some clothes. Basically, we've already been living together, but making it official is different.

I'm not sure I'm ready for that.

What if things don't work out and he kicks me out? That's my worst nightmare.

"Go Price!!"

My attention is drawn back to the present as Megan shouts Ryder's last name, then erupts in loud cheers when he checks an opponent, snatches the puck, and scores. Then he raises his stick in our direction.

"OMG!" She shakes my shoulders and then hugs me. "Did you see that?"

"Everyone did." I smile as I hug her back.

"He's amazing!" She lowers her voice. "Aside from fucking like a porn star."

I hit her shoulder jokingly. Let's just say Megan hasn't been in the dorm much either and is now attending a hockey game of her own volition.

We have the best seats in Vipers Arena, thanks to Kane and Ryder, and ever since we got here, my friend has been hyping up the entire crowd. This is coming from Megan, who used to claim that the Stanton Wolves were the strongest team in the league.

"Who let the trash in?" Isabella says loud enough for us to hear.

The worst part about having the best seats, which are usually reserved for family and friends, is being forced to share space with Isabella and her goons.

She's sitting behind us with her friends and has been talking shit throughout the game.

Megan ignores her, sometimes even going quiet, until Ryder touches the puck again.

I was going to ignore her, too, but I need to put assholes in their place. So I turn and smile at her. She glares.

"Do you mind shutting up?" I shout over the cheers. "I can hear your bitterness."

Her face contorts, and I blow her a kiss, grinning wide.

As I'm about to focus back on the game, I catch the gaze of an older man, probably in his late twenties to early thirties. He's standing at the farthest, highest part of the seating area, both hands in his pockets, as if he wants to have a full view of the rink.

His dark gray suit stands out against the fan gear and hockey jerseys most people are wearing. And he's staring. No, glaring?

What the hell?

There's an impassiveness to him. An unsettling presence that makes my blood run cold.

It feels like I've seen him before. But where?

I run my gaze over his frosty features and then pause. It's the eyes. They look distinctively familiar.

"Why are you staring?" Megan pulls on my jersey. "Don't go asking for trouble, D."

"Who's that?" I ask. "Is he related to Jude?"

"Yeah. That's Julian. His older brother."

Oh. So that's the Julian who Serena Osborn was searching for at that Vencor event. He's definitely one of the hotshots in the organization.

But why was he glaring at me?

Have I perhaps seen him somewhere before?

"How do you know him?" I ask Megan.

"Everyone does. He's the face of the Callahans' multibillion-dollar pharmaceutical sector monopoly." She surveys our surroundings and then whispers in my ear, "Some people are saying he's forcing his dad into early retirement and there's an internal Callahan power struggle."

I steal another look behind me and see Julian walking out with none other than Grant.

My heart squeezes and I develop an irrational hatred for Julian. Anyone who's friends with fucking Grant Davenport is on my shit list.

The crowd's cheers bring me back to the game. Megan takes my hand in hers and jumps up and down as Preston scores after some impressive team play.

My entire attention is on Kane. He looks his best when he's on the rink—free, in a sense. He still plays with immaculate control, but he lets go on the ice and glides within the defense's lines with infinite technical prowess.

I love seeing him in his element.

I love how he subtly but firmly directs the team.

How quickly he realizes when one of his teammates is off and offers silent support.

Kane never blames the others for a loss, even during practice, even when Preston had that awful game against the Wolves. When I asked him why he didn't make it clear to Preston that he fucked up, he simply said, "Our bond is stronger than a mere game."

So I've tried not to talk a lot of shit about Preston online. What? He's still an antagonistic bastard and I'm part of his hate club.

He's definitely a hockey prince, though. I can't deny that, especially since I started working for the team.

Anyone can tell that Kane, Jude, and Preston are an unstoppable trio. They effortlessly make passes between themselves without prior communication to the point that the other players struggle to keep up with them.

Helena said the three of them grew up together, so it makes sense that they're so aware of each other.

However, I still wince at Jude's aggressive nature. Sometimes, even Kane finds it hard to control him.

He also gets sent to the penalty box the most. Like now. He looks like a caged animal who'll get the penalty again if given the chance.

The Vipers hold out during the other team's power play, mainly due to Kane and Preston. Soon after Jude returns, a buzzer sound indicates the end of the game.

Megan and I jump and holler as the crowd erupts in maddening cheers.

As the team celebrates the win, Kane's eyes meet mine.

I give him two thumbs-up, then turn around to show him the jersey I'm wearing. Davenport. 19.

When I look back again, he's smiling.

God. I love his smile.

I love that it comes out more often lately.

He motions at the bench area and mouths, "Come down."

Megan squeals. "Oh my God, oh my God. He has the game puck! Go!"

My legs shake as I rush past the lively crowd and head down, then I take a detour and rush to the players' bench area. I nearly fall when I hurry toward Kane, but he slides in just in time and catches me.

I wrap my arms around his neck and my legs around his waist. He carries me with infinite ease, and it baffles me how easily I'm getting used to this.

I'm getting used to being vulnerable with him. To letting him see parts of me no one else can.

And it scares me. So much.

But I can't stay away. Even if I can't use him to get my revenge. I want to believe that I can have both.

Him.

And revenge.

He's removed his helmet, his brown strands sticking to his face. I stroke his hair back, completely forgetting that we're surrounded by the entire world.

"You were amazing!" I say.

"Does that mean you'll sing my praises online, ColdAsKane?"

"Oh my God. How do you know about my alter ego?"

"Coincidence?"

"Now, I have to kill you."

He laughs, the sound rushing past my rib cage and piercing my heart. I hug him tighter, drowning in his scent and feeling every rush in his breaths.

It's moments like these where I think I can *feel* the real Kane. Not the image he wears so well or the control he allows to rule his life.

Don't get me wrong. He's definitely a sadist who gets off

on hurting me during sex. But then again, I love that. We're compatible in that sense.

I just don't like the emotional sadism, and lately, I feel like we're making progress. He doesn't hurt me—at least, not intentionally—and he listens when I say I don't like something.

The other day, I said I didn't like it when he fucks me clothed and he's never done it again.

Kane wipes the puck on his glove and then offers it to me. "For you."

"Really? I can have it?"

"The captain says you can."

"Thank you!" I kiss his cheek, leaving a stain of red lipstick. His favorite.

"You can do better than that." Kane fists my hair and devours my lips.

In front of the whole campus, league, and crowd.

A blush creeps up my neck even as I let him kiss me. I always believed I didn't care what others thought, but as Kane stakes a claim in public, I feel exposed.

But also lost in a surreal world.

I can hear the players hooting and whistling. I can hear the crowd's cheers and whispers, but all I can focus on is Kane.

He's so dazzling, so godly, so irresistible, I can't help it.

I don't care that we come from different worlds. That I'm reaching for something I shouldn't touch.

Vi used to say an aimless star should never get close to the sun or it'll crash and burn.

But right now, none of those facts matter.

He's consuming me.

I'm letting him.

Even if I end up regretting it.

I finally managed to get Hunter's DNA.

Mainly because I stole his water bottle while he wasn't paying attention after the game and switched it with a similar one that I'd emptied to the same level.

And I only got away with it because of the frenzy and chaos after the win.

Since the team is having a party at one of the town's bars, I tell Kane that I need to finish a last-minute test at the lab, then leave.

Judging by his expression, he didn't like it, but I managed to slip away when he was surrounded by the others.

I spend a few hours on the extraction, then I save the sample and make a note for no one to touch it so I'll be able to proceed with the following step.

It's possible to continue now, but it's close to midnight, and Kane has called me twice in the past fifteen minutes.

He'll soon come to pick me up and I can't have him getting a whiff of what I'm doing.

Tomorrow, I'll finish the amplification and try to move to—

A creaking sound echoes in the silence.

I go still.

The white sterile lab feels larger and more oppressive. Who would come in this late?

"Kane?" I ask as I head to the door.

It automatically opens as two men walk in, clad in suits.

The same suits from earlier tonight.

Grant Davenport and Julian Callahan.

My blood freezes and the room seems to grow smaller with their presence.

Up close, Julian is more unsettling. He stands motionless

in a tailored gray suit, its sharp lines cutting against his lean frame. There's a ruthless edge in the set of his jaw, tempered by a polished, almost effortless sophistication. His dark-brown eyes—the same color as Jude's—hold the same predatory focus, scanning me with a quiet, calculating intensity that feels like a cold blade pressed against my skin.

"Hello, Dahlia," Grant says in his composed, unfeeling voice. It's what Kane sounds like when he's emotionless. When I can't reach him. But with Grant, it's more disturbing.

I wipe my hand on my lab coat and hold on to my cool. "What can I do for you? Though I'm not sure what you need in a lab at this hour."

"You do enough by spying on our team," Julian speaks in a cutting tone.

"Spy?" I ask, dumbfounded.

Julian motions at the lab. "Isn't that what all the DNA tests are for? Is there a pharmaceutical company that paid you enough to extract our players' DNA so they could dig into their genetics and possibly use that information to produce athletic supplements? Or perhaps target them? For your own safety, it better not be the latter."

My mouth hangs open.

How the hell did they know about the DNA tests? Have they known for some time but kept it under wraps to…what? Why are they confronting me about it at this stage?

"Now, Julian." Grant squeezes his shoulder. "Dahlia is not *that* sophisticated. Her DNA tests were only forensic in nature, so she's just being a little Sherlock, that's all."

I swallow.

The walls feel like they're trapping me, their white color resembling a blindfold.

They're going to hurt me.

I feel it. Deep down.

This is what happens when I get too close to the sun.

"In that case," Julian says. "What are you investigating?"

"I don't know what you're talking about." I speak in a voice that's so steady, I don't recognize it.

"Miss Thorne." Julian walks toward me with a leisurely pace, then stops a few steps away, his voice and eyes stabbing me in place. "My family dominates the pharmaceutical and medical industries, running large medical complexes and cutting-edge research labs. We are key players in drug development, healthcare innovation, and medical technology. We hold patents that affect the treatment and health of countless individuals. I know of every single piece of research, test, and even accidental findings that happen in our labs. Including this one. Especially when my brother's DNA is involved. So you know exactly what I'm talking about, and you will tell me the reason if you wish to leave in one piece."

Goosebumps prickle over my skin, and the only thought in my mind is to run.

Get as far as possible from here.

God. Talk about some fucked-up genes.

Julian might not be physically aggressive like his brother, but he's equally hostile.

I feel like he'll bring out a gun and shoot me between the eyes.

"Tell him, Dahlia," Grant says while leaning against the wall. "It's forensic, no? Possibly related to your foster sister's recent case? Violet Winters, if I remember correctly. What did Detective Collins say? Right, they found traces of human skin under her fingernails, but they couldn't identify it. With that, the only evidence that could be used to locate her assailant is useless. You're just trying to do what the police couldn't accomplish."

The room spins.

My head aches.

And I feel as if the ceiling will break and crush me.

He knows. *Everything.*

He's in direct contact with the detective. I wouldn't be surprised if he's in Grant's pocket.

"Why?" the word spills out in a whisper.

"Why what?" Grant asks.

"Why did you wait until now? You...obviously knew what I was doing."

"Julian wanted you dead after the first DNA test you did, but since you didn't communicate with any rival companies and merely seemed to be comparing them to another DNA sample, I asked him to wait and see where this was going. Especially since you seemed interesting enough for my son to insist on protecting you." Grant strides toward me and stands beside Julian. "In hindsight, I should've eliminated you before you grew into a pesky problem."

"I'll leave it to you," Julian tells Grant. "I want her banned from all Callahan property. Including the hospital."

"My sister is in the hospital!"

"Not anymore," he says, then walks out.

"What do you mean?" I shout, all my cool disappearing. "What did you do to my sister?"

"Nothing," Grant says. "For now."

"If you hurt my sister, I will—"

"Do fuck all," Grant interrupts me with a smile. "I could kill your sister a thousand times over and you wouldn't be able to lay a finger on me. People like you shouldn't even *look* up at people like me, let alone try to touch us."

I bite the inside of my cheek so hard, a metallic tang explodes on my tongue. If there's anything I've learned from dealing with Kane, it's that emotions and tantrums don't faze him.

So I take a deep breath. "You want something, right?"

"I do."

"What is it?"

"I want you to break up with Kane and make him believe it's real. I'll tell him about how you DNA-tested him and his teammates. I'll also tell him that you only approached him to use his power and influence for your little investigation. When he confronts you, don't offer excuses. You have to say that you never cared for him. That his only worth was the power his last name provides. I want you to sever any bond or idealistic feelings he has for you. I want you to break his emotions so that he hates relationships and foolish love."

A whole-body tremor overtakes me, and tears of anger gather in my eyes. "Why are you doing this to him? Haven't you hurt him enough?"

"Hurt him?" He tilts his head to the side. "I never *hurt* him. I built him from the ashes of his weak emotions. My son used to be the perfect heir to the Davenport empire. He's even been planning a coup d'état against me. For two years, he's been patient and methodical, converting the directors and spreading his sphere of influence in the company. He's been so subtle and smart, even I didn't notice. Kane has been waiting for the end of the year when he becomes a Founder member to pull the trigger on his plan, but do you know what that fool did? He offered to abandon his ambition if I leave you alone."

I take a step back, my ears ringing. Kane...gave up the takeover of his father's empire for me?

No, that can't be true. Kane isn't the type who would do that…

My thoughts trail off at the reminder of the recent subtle changes.

The look in his eyes.

The way he seemed after meeting his dad the last time.

The relief.

Oh God.

"You turned my perfect son into a fucking weakling." Grant's voice hardens. "You ruined all my years of hard work by just existing."

"Hard work? You abused him, you sick monster!"

"You have a day to do what I've instructed," he says with calm. "If he finds out about my involvement, your sister dies. You complete the mission successfully, and I'll arrange for your disappearance from the East Coast and a reunion with your sister. I might even tell you what truly happened to her. Be smart."

As he leaves the lab, a sob spills from my lips.

The world splinters into pieces around me.

Vi.

Kane.

They're both slipping from between my fingers like sand.

Everything I ever cared about is vanishing, and I can't stop it.

I fall to the floor and scream.

CHAPTER 30
Kane

I'VE BEEN ON EDGE EVER SINCE DAHLIA DISAPPEARED from my side.

A lingering discomfort has been wrapped around my throat like a noose, tightening further the more she doesn't answer my calls.

Or texts.

I drive to the lab, breaking all the speed limits.

The place feels abandoned by the time I get there. The icy wind blows away the naked branches from the closest tree.

My steps are careful as I study my surroundings as if expecting a sneak attack.

It's been a long time since I've had this feeling—the unsettling reality closing in on me. The invisible eyes lurking, watching, planning to set me on fucking fire.

I stand in the middle of the empty parking lot, but I can see the shadows spilling, stalking, and multiplying.

Over the past few years, I've stopped having this sense of dread. Of the unknown. Of the next mission. Of whether or not we'll find Preston dead in a ditch somewhere.

Because I took control of my life. I had a plan to topple Grant, take over, and mold Vencor according to my preferences. *My* way.

I was close. So fucking *close*.

One more year.

No, just months at this point, not even an entire year.

The notion of a countdown made me lose all sense of fear. It didn't matter what Grant did, because I had my backup plans. He could torture me all he wanted, but I'd become numb to his methods. No matter what he did, I knew it'd end with his downfall.

I knew I had the upper hand in the form of a bulletproof plan.

The future was mine.

Until it wasn't.

My uncle was right. I'm back to being a cog in the machine.

I've reduced my role from a chess master to a mere pawn on Grant's board.

Yes, I can and will rise again, but it'll take more time and effort. Now that Grant knows what I'm capable of, he'll be waiting for me at every turn.

Over the past week, I've been thinking about what I could've done differently to avoid this unceremonious downfall.

But I keep coming to the same conclusion. Short of not meeting Dahlia, nothing could've been changed.

And if that reckless part of me that my uncle called a fool could go back in time, he'd still insist on meeting her.

I walk into the lab, my steps heavy, but it's not because of what I've lost or what I could become at the end of the season.

Not really.

It's that uneasiness that's been lurking behind my rib cage ever since she announced the sudden project she needed to finish.

After I claimed her for the world to see following tonight's game, I felt her eagerness to take what we have a step further.

Go deeper.

Bury the past.

Forget the past.

Crush the past to fucking pieces so she never sees its blood-soaked fragments again.

But right now, something's off.

The bright white lights flicker as I stride into the work area. The sharp smell of antiseptic and chemicals lingers in the cold, sterile air.

Fluorescent lights buzz faintly above, casting a harsh glow on everything. I've often arrived early to pick up Dahlia from here and remained in the shadows for some time, just enjoying the view of seeing her in her element.

She said she only chose to study medicine for her sister, but Dahlia's a fucking genius at what she does. A hard worker and somewhat of a nerd. She gets excited about the most niche, unknown, and completely unheard-of scientific research and can talk about how important it is for hours.

Right now, however, there's no trace of her moving around while humming some obscure band's song.

I'm about to call her for the thousandth time, but my fingers pause on the phone.

Dahlia's curled in on herself in the corner, small and fragile in contrast to the harsh, large surfaces surrounding her.

Her arms are wrapped tightly around her knees, her face buried, hiding from the world.

A slight tremor runs through her, barely noticeable. It cuts through the stillness of the room, the sound of her shaky breaths louder than the quiet hum of the machines.

Her hair spills forward, a tangled mess hiding her face, but I recognize this state.

It's how she protects herself when distressed or experiencing a nightmare.

I carefully move toward her, the sharp echo of my footsteps bouncing off the sterile walls.

I hate how the tension in her body tightens at the sound, but she doesn't look up, as if she's waiting for the darkness to swallow her whole.

"Dahlia…?"

No response.

I crouch before her and grab her wrist, then slowly release it. She doesn't resist, as if the fight in her is gone.

My fingers tense when I lift her face.

Her eyes are filled with moisture, and all the mischief is gone. They're a muted brown, colorless.

No. Lifeless.

Tears streak down her red cheeks, clinging to her chin, then slipping to her jersey beneath the lab coat, wetting the blue to a darker color.

While her tears during sex turn me on, these make me murderous.

I don't like it when she cries. Mainly because she rarely does.

"What happened?" I stroke her cheek, wiping away the moisture. "Who did this?"

Her lips tremble and fresh tears gush out, soaking my fingers.

I grab her face with both of my hands. "Tell me who the fuck did this so I can end them."

"Kane…" Her voice is low, weak, barely audible.

This is *not* like her. Who the fuck managed to mess with her?

I wipe her tears again. "I'm here. Talk to me."

"I…" Her voice breaks with a sniffle.

"What is it?"

She smiles through the tears and shakes her head. Dahlia always said I have high walls, but hers are equally high. She only recently started to act without putting her guard up around me.

But right now, I sense those walls building, growing thicker, and pushing me out.

She stands up and forces me to lower my hands.

Dahlia wipes her face with her sleeves. "It's stupid, really. I just thought of Vi."

I get up as well and watch her closely, but her face stays impassive, keeping her thoughts locked away.

She walks out to where she keeps her stuff, her shoulders hunched and her back crowded with tension.

I follow, my temper barely tucked away. "Out of the blue?"

"It's not really out of the blue." She opens her locker and starts throwing things into a tote bag. "I've known it for a long time, but I refused to face it. It's been over three months since the attack. Every day she spends in a coma lowers her chances of ever waking up again. Her mental activity is diminishing, and the doctor basically told me to give up hope and stop getting excited whenever her fingers twitch. It's involuntary. It's reflexive. It means nothing. I should lower my expectations. Just now, I had the very scary but realistic thought that I might never…have a conversation with my sister again."

I lean against the wall, my index finger twitching as tears gather in her eyes and she wipes them with the back of her hand.

This is the only time in my life I regret not having the ability to console others.

I doubt my and Jude's method of kicking and hitting Preston while offering him food and meds is considered consolation for normal people.

"Sorry for being all gloomy on your victory night." She smiles as she faces me. "I'll make it up to you by being a cheerleader online."

"That's not important. Do you want to go see your sister?"

She shakes her head.

"How about food? I can cook you something. Maybe your favorite pasta?"

Another shake.

Fuck. Food is the only soft thing I know how to do correctly.

"Then what do you want, Dahlia? Unless you tell me, I don't know."

She grabs my sides beneath my jacket, her nails sinking into my T-shirt. When she looks up at me, her features soften and a shine flashes through. "I want to have fish."

"Fish?"

"Uh-huh."

"I don't think we'll find any at this hour."

"Not here. In Maine."

"Maine?"

"Yup."

"Maine is more than a six-hour drive."

She sulks. "Is that a no?"

"It's a why Maine all of a sudden?"

"I want to see my hometown again. Can you come with me?"

There's only one answer to that question.

Especially when she's looking at me with a softness I've never seen before. Maybe there's also a smidge of fear, but I understand that.

She probably thought she'd never step foot in Maine again.

I've seen the footage of her parents' deaths. While she was watching it, I heard her murmur that she never wanted it to happen.

I know deep down that she blames herself for their deaths, which is probably why she never went back to Maine.

But right now, she wants to heal, and I'll be part of that trip.

My and Dahlia's understanding of road trips is entirely different.

For me, it's simply driving and reaching the destination.

For Dahlia, however?

It's a bizarre experience, to say the least.

She stuffed the car full of snacks, has blasted obnoxiously loud music, and has been singing her heart out—out of tune.

Oh, and apparently, we both need to power off our phones so that it's distraction-free. She proceeded to do that and lock the phones in the glove compartment so we don't have to 'worry about anything we left behind.'

"That was amazing! Phew." She grins as the song comes to an end. "Maybe the radio will repeat it."

"I hope not. It was painful to hear the first time around."

"Rude!" She hits my shoulder. "What's your favorite song? Let's see how you sound, Mr. Captain."

"I don't have one." I focus on the road, the early-morning light painting the sky a deep magenta.

"No way." She lowers the volume as the DJ speaks in

the background. "I know you said you don't listen to music much, but you must listen to something. Instrumental, maybe? Classical or jazz or, like, cool theme music?"

"Not really. It's distracting."

She sits sideways facing me as she stuffs her mouth full of gummies. "You're like an alien. Hold on. How about a favorite movie?"

"Maybe *The Game*?"

"I don't even know what that is. Mine is *Scream*."

I laugh. "What a cliché."

"At least you know what movie that is, unlike your pretentious choice."

"Pretentious?"

"Yup." She shoves a few gummies in my mouth. "You don't even eat candy. What a pretentious, posh boy."

I chew on the disgusting things, their extensive sweetness flooding my taste buds. "I'm an athlete. We should watch our diet, Ms. Medicine Major."

"It's okay once in a while. I bet you haven't had anything sweet since you were a kid."

"I'm not a fan of the taste."

"Then what are you a fan of?"

"Fucking, chasing, choking, pounding, biting. Rough sex in general."

A red blush covers Dahlia's face and she chokes on the piece of candy in her mouth.

I suppress a smile. "You all right there?"

"You did that on purpose, asshole."

"I was only answering your question ever so innocently."

"There's nothing innocent about you." She nudges me with her foot, then rests it on my lap. "Have you always loved rough sex?"

"I suppose."

"So…how many victims did you have before me."

"Victims?"

"Women you chased."

"I didn't chase any woman before you."

"You…didn't?"

"Finding someone compatible with such a rough kink is harder than you think. Besides, I didn't feel the real urge until you bulldozed through my life."

"Wow. So it's my fault?"

"Yeah." I wrap my hand around her leg in my lap. "You'll take responsibility for the monster you provoked."

"Some would argue the monster has always been there. By some, I mean me."

"Maybe, but you're the one who broke the spell."

"I mean, you broke the spell for me, too, so I guess we're even."

"Me?"

"Yeah." She strokes my cheek. "I didn't know I loved that type of sex until you. It kind of made me suspect my morals and consider therapy, but I accept myself now."

I tighten my grip on her leg. "As you should."

"Oh my God, I love this song!" She hikes up the volume and starts singing again, shamelessly loud, and tries to feed me the sugary things from the bag she's holding.

Her cheerful mood, however, slowly withers when we arrive in Maine. It turns into terrible silence when I stop in front of her previous address in a small town by the coast.

The house sits quietly by the water, its silhouette framed against the early-morning light. It's small, nothing like the sprawling estates I'm used to, but it's well-kept. The white fence that borders the front yard is freshly painted, straight, and sturdy, though a bit weathered by the salt air and covered with a few layers of snow.

The ocean hums in the background, the faint sound of waves lapping at the shore just behind it. The air is cool, carrying the scent of saltwater and morning dew.

A couple steps out of the house, their soft laughter rising in the quiet as their kid bounces ahead of them, kicking the snow with his feet. The boy's giggles cut through the air as the parents half laugh and half scold him.

The scene feels out of place, like something from a different world. A world where everything is simple.

Dahlia's world.

That must've been her life before everything ended.

I watch her as she watches them, her eyes watery, her hands shaking around a bag of chips.

This time, I don't hesitate as I take her hand in mind. She shudders, and I think I feel her stiffen before she goes still.

"Does it make you sad?" I ask.

"On the contrary. I'm relieved that the house is well-loved and kept. Mom and Dad would be so happy if they saw this." She grins. "Hey, Kane?"

"Hmm?"

"Let's go by the ocean."

"When it's this freezing?"

"It's the best! I know people say coastal towns are depressing in the winter, but it's like a fairy tale. Believe me."

"I have my doubts."

She just laughs and drags me out of the car. We trek by a rocky path that she said she remembers, but it turns out, her memories failed her.

It's ridiculously icy weather to get lost in, but Dahlia just laughs and says it's perfect for exploration.

We end up hiking to the peak of a large snow-covered rock that overlooks the deep blue ocean. The colors here are cold—white, navy blue, and unforgiving gray.

Dahlia stares at the violent waves below, throws her hands wide apart, and screams at the top of her lungs, "Mom! Dad! I'm home!"

The echo of her voice is swallowed by the wind as her long brown hair flies behind her. She looks like a goddess.

"I'm sorry I didn't come back before! I'm doing amazing things. You'd be so proud of me! I have a sister now. Her name is Violet and she's the sweetest person ever. You would've loved her so much."

Her voice breaks, but she turns around and takes my hand, then pulls me to her side. "I brought someone. You would've loved him, too. Probably!"

"Probably?"

"Shh, it's a fifty-fifty chance," she whispers, then yells at the ocean again, "He's filthy rich, buys me ridiculously expensive clothes, and even cooks for me. He's not that bad sometimes."

"Sometimes?"

"Just stay silent. This isn't about you." She glares and then smiles at the ocean again. "You don't have to worry about me anymore. Your little girl is a grown-up now. Thank you for everything!"

Her hand shakes in mine, and I squeeze it tight.

"You think they heard me?"

I wrap my arms around her waist. "Hopefully not the part where you said I'm not bad sometimes."

She chuckles. "You're so petty."

"Only *sometimes*."

She laughs, the sound so light and endearing. "Thank you."

"What for?"

"Accompanying me on this bizarre trip."

I pull her against my chest, lift her chin with my index finger, and kiss her frozen lips. Warmth seeps between us and she hugs me while kissing me back.

Her body becomes one with mine, her nails digging into my jacket, and it feels like she desperately doesn't want to let go.

My lips leave hers and she smiles. "Want a poor people's town tour? I'll give you a discount."

"By all means."

Dahlia obviously forgot most of the town, and many places have changed. But she still gets excited whenever she sees a familiar shop or house.

We do have the fish she came all the way for.

We also buy a lot of fishermen's catch, and Dahlia donates them to the local restaurants. I suppose that's her way of honoring people who have her dad's profession.

She doesn't stay still for the whole day, going from one place to another like a busy bee. It's almost as if she doesn't want to stop and breathe.

By sunset, we're walking back to the car, her hand in mine, when she hesitantly stops by a small bridge.

"What? Is there somewhere else you want to visit?"

Her lips pull in a small smile. "I think I saw my dad's friend. I'll go and say hi."

"Fine, let's go."

"You just go bring the car. It won't take long. I'll be here."

"All right."

I'm about to leave, but she doesn't release my hand, her fingers digging into the back of it.

"Kane?"

"Yeah?"

"You know how I always say I hate you?"

"What about it?"

"I don't. Actually. I really like you." She grins. "Like a *lot*."

A drop of heat expands behind my rib cage, melting away all the years my father spent attempting to turn me into ice.

A few words from Dahlia and I'm touched by warmth.

A few words and it's like I'm transformed into a new person.

"I really like you, too. When I don't want to strangle you."

"What a romantic." She smiles, but it's sad. "I'll be waiting. Go ahead."

She hesitantly releases me, and it takes me about five minutes to reach the car.

After I get in, I open the glove compartment. I know I promised Dahlia no phones, but it's been a whole day without checking in on Preston's deteriorating state.

I pause when I don't see Dahlia's phone.

When did she take it?

With a frown, I power on my phone and pause at the bombardment of missed calls by Jude.

Fuck.

What happened to Preston now?

I'm about to call Jude, but then I see the texts.

Jude: Where the fuck are you, man? This is an emergency.

Jude: Violet has been kidnapped from the hospital under the guise of a medical transfer.

Jude: My brother and your father are behind this. I

> don't know what the fuck they want, but my brother's driver mentioned a trip to the lab. I'm guessing they're using Violet against Dahlia. I'll see what I can do from my end.
>
> Jude: Update: I still can't locate her.

My fist tightens against the steering wheel, and I hit the Start button. My body flattens against the leather as I speed to where I left Dahlia on the bridge.

The trip.

The strange behavior.

The way she was holding on to me the whole day.

Now, I see why it all felt so weird.

The moment I reach the bridge and find it empty, the realization hits me across the face.

This entire day, Dahlia has been saying goodbye.

CHAPTER 31
Dahlia

I SHOULD'VE KISSED HIM ONE FINAL TIME.

Hell, I should've fucked him.

I should've taken something of him with me. Maybe if I had, it wouldn't hurt this bad.

Maybe it wouldn't feel as if I'd ripped my heart out and left it in the palm of Kane's hand.

But I couldn't possibly think of anything during this entire trip. I wanted more time with him, even if it was a couple of hours.

Minutes.

Seconds.

That's why I came up with this stupid idea of visiting my old hometown.

I only wished to delay the inevitable, but I ended up with the best down-memory-lane trip of my life. Having Kane beside me, his hand wrapped possessively around my waist, has made it more enjoyable and less of a tearjerker.

Until now, that is.

I sit in an old, empty cathedral, hidden in the corner, staring numbly at the large crucifix on the altar and hoping my heart doesn't break to pieces and leave me hollow.

Wait. It's too late for that.

My fingers shake and my vision blurs.

"Hey." I talk to the crucifix, tears flowing down my face. "Can you make it stop? No? Why not? You took my parents away and Vi, too. Now, Kane? Is my life a joke to you? Am I not allowed any form of happiness? No matter what I would've done differently, it would've ended this way, wouldn't it? Why? Just tell me why!"

"Because you yearned for something you shouldn't have looked at in the first place." Authoritative footsteps echo in the air as Grant walks to the altar and then stands in front of it, his back to the relics.

He looks like a devil fresh out of hell. The tailored suit and groomed appearance don't hide the pure evil that lurks in that man's soul.

"You got greedy, Dahlia, and people like you aren't allowed to be greedy. If you looked up long enough, that neck would be broken."

I wipe my tears with the back of my hand. "Were you following us?"

"Your day is almost up and you didn't do what I asked."

"I'm not going to hurt Kane with my words. He's already experienced enough pain from you. If you...tell him about my motives, he'll stop looking for me and even despise me. So you get what you want either way." I lift my chin despite the breaking sound that reverberates in my chest. "Let me and my sister go, and we'll move to a different state and stay as far away as possible."

He tsks, the sound loud in the silence. "That wasn't the deal. I specifically asked you to be the one who hurts him. If it's me, that will only make him hate me and end up idolizing you more. He can be stubborn with his feelings. It took me a long time to stop him from seeking his mother like a fucking weakling. But if I have to break him again so he'll erase you and go back to being normal, so be it."

"Normal? That's not normal, that's a robot!" The urge to strangle this man beats beneath my skin like a need.

A fucking urge.

Maybe I can kill him and rid Kane of his evil. Maybe Kane and his mother can finally reconcile. I suspected it before, but now, I'm sure. Grant is the reason Kane keeps his distance from Helena.

Yes, Kane probably still holds her accountable for what's happened to him, but he also recognizes just how abusive his father is. He knows that the more he seeks his mom out or spends time with her, the more Grant will punish him, and probably take out his wrath on his wife.

Surely, if I kill Grant, the world will be a better place?

I reach a hand into my tote bag and feel for the scalpel I usually keep for self-defense.

"What I do with my family is none of your concern." Grant's gratingly condescending voice echoes in the air.

My fingers latch onto the scalpel case and I open it as I speak. "Have you ever felt sorry for the shit you've put him through since he was a kid? Have you ever wondered that maybe you stole his childhood and molded him into a gloomier version of what he could've been?"

"Sorry?" He says the word as if it's an insult. "Why would I feel sorry when I *saved* him? I made him into the perfect man who can rightfully inherit my empire. He had to be a wolf or he would've been eaten by one."

I scoff as I clutch the scalpel's handle in my shaky hand. "So you tortured him, left permanent scars on his body, and broke his soul for *his* sake?"

"Don't be ridiculous. It's for the empire's sake. He only

exists to fulfill a role. We *all* do. Yours is to stay in your lane."

"So it's narcissism. You only brought him into the world so you could use him." The pain stagnating inside me whirls and transcends the situation I got trapped in.

"He's a Davenport. That's his duty."

"He's not only a Davenport, he's just Kane," I murmur in a low voice he probably can't hear as I stand up, shoving my hand with the scalpel in my pocket.

I don't feel my legs, as if I'm floating on air.

My senses sharpen and a red mist covers my eyes.

This man needs to die.

For Vi.

For Kane.

For Helena.

For *me*.

My legs carry me with ease.

It's funny how I got entangled in this entire mess to seek revenge, but right now, I only want to stab him to death.

"What were you murmuring to yourself?" he asks when I stop in front of him.

From this angle, the crucified Jesus looks looming, tall, the blood surrounding the holes in his wrists matching my red haze.

"I said Kane is just Kane. He's not your plaything!" I shout as I pull out the scalpel and aim it at his throat.

Grant steps back at the last second and the scalpel only grazes his jaw. He grabs my hand and twists it so suddenly, a scream of pain bubbles out of me.

My grip loosens on the scalpel and it hits the ground with a clink as Grant kicks me in the stomach.

I fall to the harsh floor, coughing. A metallic taste fills my mouth and blood spills out of my lungs.

But I still crawl to the scalpel.

I'm going to kill him.

I'm going to kill him…

I'm going to kill him…

Just when I'm about to grab it, a shoe steps on my outstretched hand and I groan, then scream when he applies pressure.

Grant stands above me and motions somewhere behind me. He wipes the gushing blood from his jaw as he shakes his head.

"Looks like your time is up, Dahlia."

My scream comes to an abrupt halt as something sharp pricks the back of my neck.

The scalpel turns blurry and a tear slides down my cheek.

As the darkness swallows me, my thoughts are of deep failure.

I'm sorry, Vi.

I'm sorry, Kane.

My senses come back in pieces—disjointed, hazy, but sharp enough that I jolt awake.

No matter how much I widen and blink my eyes, I only see darkness.

The air is thick, suffocating, reeking of mildew and something else—damp, rotting wood, maybe. A drip echoes in the distance, slow and methodical. It plants a seed of fear at the bottom of my stomach.

I try to move, but pain slices through my shoulders. The ache burns so much that everything snaps into focus.

My wrists are bound above me, the rough chains digging into my skin, pulling tight every time I shift. My bare feet barely touch the ground, just enough to feel the slick, wet floor beneath them, but not enough to steady myself.

Where am I?

Panic floods my chest, drowning out every coherent thought.

The thick darkness presses in on all sides as if the room itself is swallowing me whole. I blink rapidly, trying to adjust my sight, trying to see something, *anything*.

But there's nothing.

Just the cold air clinging to my skin and the sound of my ragged breathing filling the space.

My mind scrambles, racing through fractured images. The last thing I remember is being injected with something and losing consciousness. After that…nothing.

My thoughts stutter and freeze like static cutting through my brain. My wrists burn from the strain, my muscles screaming, but it's the fear that twists my jumbled insides.

What if Grant is using me to get back at Kane?

What if I'm his downfall?

I need to get out of here. Wherever *here* is.

My fingers curl instinctively, grasping the chain and pulling myself up, but I fall back down. The sound of my breath is louder now, echoing in the small space, filling the silence with my rising panic.

The drip in the distance fades, replaced by a low grinding metallic sound.

My heart kicks into overdrive, panic swelling as I strain to figure out the source of the noise.

Something shifts above me, and before I can brace myself, a torrent of freezing water crashes down, drenching me.

It's cold.

Ice-cold.

Shockingly cold.

I stop breathing as the water slices through my skin like a thousand tiny needles.

It doesn't stop.

It keeps pouring, soaking through my clothes, clinging to my body like a second skin.

I gasp, choking on the air. The ache in my shoulders sharpens, and the weight of the water jerks me down harder.

My feet slip on the wet floor, barely grazing it as I try to find some footing.

Oh God. Am I going to freeze to death?

The water stops, but I remain shaking in place.

It hits me then.

This is one of Grant's torture methods. One he probably used on Kane countless times.

A fresh wave of terror rolls over me. The thought that a kid could have gone through this, that Grant subjected his son to this type of punishment churns my stomach.

The cold, the chains, the pain—how could Kane have hidden all this behind that calm, emotionless mask?

Water drips on the floor, each icy drop like a reminder, a piece of the puzzle that Kane never let me see.

How…how did he survive this all these years when I feel like I'll die?

My body shakes, trembling against the freezing weight of the water. This must be why he had bruises that one time and his complexion was pale.

He still lived through it, though.

The thought hits me like a blow, but it doesn't bring comfort. It just makes the darkness around me feel more suffocating.

Hopeless.

I don't know how long I've been here, but it's long enough that my shoulders are going numb while still screaming in pain.

A door creaks open and I close my eyes as strong light flickers above my head and bathes the room in bright white.

Grant walks in with two men dressed in black. One of them is bald with tattoos all over his head, and the other has a scar right beneath his eye.

I'm shaking uncontrollably as Grant walks to a table covered with black boxes off to the side. He opens one and then grabs a whip.

"Now." He smiles. "I'm sure Kane won't look your way again once we disfigure your face and body."

My chin trembles as I say, "He'll *never* forgive you."

"Good thing I don't care." He smiles, his lips curling slightly. "Shall we begin?"

CHAPTER 32
Kane

"ANY NEWS ABOUT VIOLET?"

I swerve the car in and out of traffic, driving as fast as I can without crashing the fucking thing.

I've been going like this for the past several hours, ever since I received the call from Samuel that made my worst nightmare come true.

"She's in the dungeon."

In the dungeon.

Dahlia.

In Grant's fucking dungeon.

A place no one should ever be in—especially not Dahlia.

Not after what I gave up to keep her out of Grant's claws.

That's when the dooming realization hits me.

Uncle Kayden was right. Revealing my cards might have given Dahlia immunity for some time, but Grant will never let her survive.

Not after she's proven to be my Achilles' heel.

He'll eliminate her just to maintain a hold on me.

He's hurt her just to teach me a lesson.

I considered asking Jude and Preston to save her for me, to get as many of their guards as they could and just march in, but they and their guards don't compare to the small army my father has on the estate. Besides, Grant would call their fathers and that would be the end of that.

The heavy breathing from the other end of the phone fills my car, and the shuffle of footsteps follows before Jude's rough voice filters through. "I couldn't locate Violet in any of our hospitals or safe houses. I'm done searching blindly, so I'm walking to my brother's office and won't leave until he gives me the information I need."

My hand tightens around the steering wheel. "Julian can't be threatened and you know that."

"Not him, no. But his wife? That's a different fucking story."

"He doesn't give a fuck about his wife."

"If he didn't, he wouldn't have made her live in a goddamn gilded cage."

"He got her expelled from the society, Jude."

"That's his idea of protection. I know because I'm having the same thoughts. Guess I'll have to test the theory."

"Don't. It's risky."

"I have to take my chances."

A mumble of voices follows, Jude ignoring his brother's assistant and then shouting, "Everyone out!"

The shuffle of feet, murmurs, and then Julian's clear voice. "You need to quit your punch-first-and-ask-questions-later habits. They're a disgrace to the Callahan name."

"I'm going to show you the actual disgrace, big bro."

"Jude, don't," I say in a tight voice. "I didn't mean it's risky as in it might not work. It's risky because it *could* work. Threatening Julian will only make him more antagonistic."

"I don't give a fuck," he spits out.

"Let me talk to him."

"I can handle this."

"No, you can't. Pass Julian the phone. Do us both a favor and let me do the talking."

There's a low curse before his voice sounds far away. "It's Kane. He wants to talk to you."

I tap my finger on the steering wheel as Julian's clear voice echoes in my car. "What can I do for you, Davenport?"

"The real question is, what else can you do to grow the Callahan empire?"

"Are we having a business talk?"

"Nothing that different from what you had with Grant."

"You're far behind, kid. Besides, I'm disappointed in you."

"Disappointed?"

"You brought a liability into our midst. A little girl with several tricks up her sleeve and shady motivations that could sabotage our ways. You either allowed her to perform DNA tests on you and your teammates, or you weren't aware, which is even worse."

My fingers tighten until I'm sure I'll break the steering wheel. I knew Julian was in the know about everything that goes on in the Callahan facilities, but I didn't think he'd care about a nameless campus lab.

"Grant is correct," Julian continues. "I had extremely high hopes for you, especially after watching your behind-the-scenes methodical modus operandi. However, you allowed a mere fucking girl to topple it all to the ground."

"Not all."

"Oh?"

"You think I'd hand Grant everything in my arsenal? That I'd remain defenseless? Me, of all people?"

"Good for you. However, I still have no interest in internal conflict. I have my own to take care of."

"Then stay out, completely, and I promise, whatever the outcome, you won't be a loser." I pause. "You know Grant's temper. You're well aware of his failing business decisions lately, due to which he had to cut funding for your new experimental drug."

"His failing business decisions don't compare to your massive loss of judgment."

"It's not a loss of judgment. It's part of a plan."

"What plan?"

"Let Violet go. And we might discuss this further."

"Good one. Unfortunately, however, Violet is a family issue now, as it affects my brother."

"Let's go outside," Jude says from the other end. "We'll fight it out."

"I have no intention of throwing fists. What an uncultured motherfucker. It's an embarrassment to call you my brother." Julian sighs, then tells me, "If I see a manifestation of your plan, I might consider backing off. But that's all I can offer. Now, if you'll excuse me, Jude is going to punch me and I need to break his arm."

Beep. Beep. Beep.

"Fuck!" I hit the steering wheel but take a deep breath.

It's useless to try to convince Julian with words anyway. If he wants action, then so be it.

An hour of reckless driving later, I arrive at my parents' house and nearly hit the entrance.

The late-night air is suffocating. To think I had the best time of my life not twenty-four hours ago, and now I'm back to this absolute shithole is fucking revolting.

As soon as I get out, I spot a slim silhouette walking back and forth by the massive front door. Upon seeing me, Helena charges toward me.

Her night robe clings to her frail body and her eyes are sunken, dark circles surrounding them like bottomless pits.

"Kane, honey, don't go in."

I stop and stare down at her bony hand clutching my arm. "Let go, Mother."

She adds another hand, digging her nude nails into my black jacket, shaking her head. "I heard Samuel call you. You shouldn't have come back. You...shouldn't be here."

"I shouldn't be here? Then where should I be? Hiding? Burying my head in the sand? Being you?"

"You don't understand. If you go in there, he'll torture you."

"Something I'm extremely familiar with, but she's not, Mother!"

She flinches, her cheeks losing all color.

This is the first time I've raised my voice at her. I might have kept my distance from my mother, but I've treated her cordially, with respect, as expected of me.

Now, though? I turn around and grab her by her shoulders and shake her. Hard.

"She defended you, Helena! Even after she knew you stood by and watched while the man you chose to have a kid with *tortured* that kid. She said you must've been *helpless*. You must've tried to stop it but couldn't. She said you're mentally fragile and couldn't handle this type of life, so you withdrew as a defense mechanism. She gave *you* the benefit of the doubt. She begged me to be kinder to you, to not forget and erase you. She asked if you and I could turn over a new leaf. I started seeing you from *her* perspective. Through *her* eyes. Because she lost her mother at a young age, she has these rosy concepts about mothers and affection, so I shouldn't have listened to her warped logic. But I still came by, didn't

I? I still conformed to the benefit of the doubt she gave you. And now you're asking me to let her be tortured and watch? I'm *not* you, Mother. Do you understand?"

Tears stream down her face as she trembles uncontrollably. "I just…I just want you to be safe. I hate for anything to happen to Dahlia either. She's been the only color in my life lately, and I begged Grant to let her go, but you know he never listens to me. I don't want her to be hurt, but I would hate losing you more."

"You already lost me fifteen years ago, *Mother*."

I let her go and push past her as I stride through the mansion, down the dim halls with the ugly dark-green wallpaper.

Throughout the years I've been walking these halls, I've only felt numbness and, lately, the consolation that this will soon come to an end.

But right now, my muscles are tense, my steps wide.

I've never rebelled against my father, and it wasn't because I couldn't. After I hit puberty, I became as big as he is and even more muscular. If I'd wanted to hit him, I would've.

But violence is not my style, and I refused to be molded into a copy of him.

So I connived behind closed doors. I gathered all the intel about his trusted executives and used it to turn those pigs against him. I actively sabotaged each of his new ventures, starting talks within the company and even Vencor.

I didn't want to physically harm Grant. That wouldn't have accomplished anything.

Seeing his empire crumble before his eyes, however? Witnessing the son he labeled a weakling take over?

That would break him.

Two of my father's men stand guard in front of the dungeon's metal door, buff, muscular, their gazes mean.

They're part of the crew my father uses to do his dirty work. Some thugs who specialize in intimidation and breaking bones.

The bald one extends an arm. "No one is allowed in."

"Step away. I won't repeat myself."

"Boss said no one—" I pull out my gun with the silencer and shoot him between the eyes.

His friend reaches for his weapon, but I shoot him in the face before he can act.

Blood splatters on my face, reddening my gaze.

They both fall to the ground with a thud, and I step over them as I sheath my gun.

The moment I open the door, everything comes to a halt. The place reeks of dampness and rot, the familiar stench of cold stone and blood curling into my nostrils.

But that isn't what makes the world stop.

It's Dahlia.

The white light casts a harsh shadow on her face as she hangs from the ceiling, her body limp, dripping wet clothes clinging to her discolored skin.

Water pools beneath her feet, reflecting the light like shattered glass. Her features are lifeless, devoid of the cheerful and defiant energy she wears like a badge of honor.

Her soaking hair is plastered to her skin. Blood gushes from where the chains dig into her flesh, deep-red rivers trickling down her arms, mixing with the water that drips from her clothes.

Her eyes are clamped shut and she's shaking.

Every breath she takes is a thin cloud of mist that barely escapes her lips before dissolving.

The sour tang of sweat and blood sharpens and fills my senses as I spot Grant standing in front of her, tall, erect, with that sadistic gleam in his eyes as he approaches Dahlia with a whip in hand. She flinches as he gets closer, a tremor quaking her entire body.

Something inside me snaps.

All the torture I've lived through pales compared to this. No matter how brutal they were, how painful it got, I was born into this. It's what was expected of me.

Dahlia is fucking different.

Grant's third lackey approaches me. "You're not supposed to be here—"

I shoot him in the head and bypass him.

My father finally turns in my direction. He has a bandage on his chin that, according to Samuel, is due to a cut he had when he came back, and he was cursing Dahlia for it.

That made me so fucking proud.

He might have kidnapped her, but my wildflower didn't leave without a fight.

My father looks at his dead man and narrows his eyes on me. "What the fuck do you think you're doing, Kane?"

I let the gun rest at my side. "You gave me your word. You said you wouldn't touch her."

"That was before I learned how much you actually gave up for this nameless bitch. She's a liability that needs to be taken care of."

Trembling uncontrollably, Dahlia flutters her eyes open. Their color flickers between brown and yellow as she shakes her head and mouths, "Go, Kane. Please."

That fucking girl thinks she can protect me, even though she's hanging from the fucking ceiling.

What the actual fuck?

I burst out laughing, holding the gun flat against my temple.

It hits me then. Seems that aside from the chains my father wrapped around my wrists, I subconsciously shackled myself, too.

I believed his hypocritical speech about 'the Davenport bond'. Somehow, even though I grew taller and much stronger than him, I never considered hurting him physically like he hurt me.

Because, at some point, I believed his words—that I was a defect he was fixing—and didn't consider his punishment wrong. When I was younger, I even blamed myself for being born a weakling and not meeting his expectations.

Jude and Preston didn't need to be locked up in their fathers' basements to be cold-blooded; why wasn't I the same?

Why wasn't I...*wrong*?

The answer is, I'm not the one built wrong. He is.

He's the one who twisted me the fuck up just to fit the mold that suits his vision.

And I still thought I couldn't hurt him, because he spawned me.

But now, the fog has lifted.

The metaphorical rusty chains that I've clasped around my own wrists since I was a kid break, and I laugh harder.

"Have you lost your goddamn mind?" Grant asks.

"On the contrary. I've never seen things so clearly." I let out a sigh. "You know, I figured out that becoming like you is the ultimate goal. I had to be so ruthless, so detached and cold, nothing would faze me. Not personal relationships, not people I spent my whole life with. Not even my own mother. Connections are only formed for mutual gain. Being emotionless was the true answer to any problem. Treating everyone like pawns would get me to the top faster and more efficiently."

"That is correct."

"Yes. But you see, Father, you're in my way."

He faces me, his shoulders bunching. "Me?"

"Yes. I want the Davenport throne, so I can do things the way I see fit and fix your fuckups. You're a hindrance, preventing my progress."

"The Davenport throne?" He scoffs. "Don't make me laugh. You gave it up for this nobody. Do you believe I'll ever let you ascend it in your state?"

"Let me?" I raise my hand, the gun steady, my finger relaxed. "I don't need you to *let* me."

"You'll kill me?" He snarls. "For *her*?"

"For *me*. Messing with her was only the last straw."

He curses and swings his hand in Dahlia's direction, to hit or kill her, I don't know.

It doesn't reach her anyway, because I pull the trigger.

The bullet hits the back of his head.

I don't see his face as he falls, his body hitting the ground.

Motionless.

Finally...silent.

I wait for the feelings of guilt. For the conflict. For the slightest hint of remorse.

Nothing.

Huh.

I guess he really brought me up well.

"Kane..." a small voice whispers in the midst of the blood-soaked silence.

So small and calming.

So small and...sad.

I look up and freeze. Dahlia looks at me with tears streaming down her cheeks, dripping to her collarbone.

Right. She saw me do that unsightly thing.

She must think I'm a true monster now.
Her chin trembles and she whispers, "I'm so sorry."
And then her head falls forward and she passes out.

CHAPTER 33
Dahlia

A DEEP VOICE SWIRLS AROUND MY HEAD.

A very familiar rough voice that only softens for me.

My eyes flutter open, adjusting to the dim light illuminating the room. My body's heavy, and everything aches against the soft sheets beneath me. They're cool against my skin, smelling faintly of cedarwood and fresh detergent.

Where is this place...?

Recent memories slash through my psyche.

The torture. Kane's father.

Kane's words.

Kane.

I startle into a sitting position.

Am I in his old room? It's surprisingly simple aside from the luxurious cream wallpaper. The furniture is sleek, minimalist—everything sharp edges and clean lines. No clutter, no personal touches, except for the faded scent of him lingering in the air, a mix of something dark and woodsy.

That's when I see him.

Kane's standing by the window, staring at the night staking its claim on the Japanese garden while talking on the phone in a low, hushed tone.

A breath spits out of my lungs.

And I breathe.

For the first time since I was cornered by his father, I inhale and exhale a large gulp of air, fill my lungs with it, completely flounder in it.

He's okay.

He looks like himself—vicious chaos contained in a thread of calm.

"You prepared the boat?" he asks, then listens, his index finger twitching against his thigh. "No crew members, correct." More listening, more staring out at the horizon. "I'll be there shortly."

I pull the soft black sheet to my chin.

The trembling returns.

The realization.

The doomsday feeling.

Kane killed his father. He shot him in the head in a cutthroat, emotionless way. He didn't hesitate, didn't think twice as he killed his own father.

For me.

No.

Because of me.

What have I done?

He tilts his head in my direction, his eyes sharp, his expression cold.

My jittery insides quiver, and I feel so small in the vast bed, my emotions jumping all over the place, flaring up and detonating like a box of matches.

"You're awake." He speaks slowly, with no emotion.

He's like that demon from the initiation. The unfeeling monster I couldn't reach inside of, no matter what I did.

My heartbeat quickens as he walks toward me at a deliberately slow pace, the sound of his footsteps echoing in my chest.

"You feel better?" His words are monotonous. Robotic, even.

I don't even pay attention to my bandaged wrists or the warm bathrobe covering me. The pain doesn't matter anymore. Not when he's looking at me as if I'm a stranger.

"Kane…"

"Yes?"

"I'm sorry about your father."

"I'm not. I would've eventually gotten rid of him, but this came earlier than calculated." He stops at the foot of the bed, both hands in his pockets.

He's towering over me.

Intimidating.

It makes me tremble, despite my attempts to rein it in, push it down. Put on the façade I wear so well.

But right now, I can't.

"I believe you ought to be sorry for something different, Dahlia."

I flinch, my fingers sinking into the sheets.

He knows.

Right. Grant promised to tell him everything.

"I…" No words follow. What am I supposed to say?

Am I even allowed to say anything?

"You're what?" He seems larger, taller, and nothing like the Kane who held my hand while I goofed around in my hometown.

There's no carefree energy, no soft looks, and certainly no rare smiles.

But there's only one thought that buzzes through me.

I don't want him to hate me.

I don't want to lose him.

"Hear me out?" My voice is low in the silence, broken.

Lightning brightens up the sky and spills into the room, casting a menacing shadow on Kane's face. Rain patters before it pours, its rivulets trickling down the window.

"I'm listening."

There's no encouragement, no softness. Only a depressing emotionless voice. But at least he's willing to give me a chance to explain myself.

"For over eight years, Vi's been the only person tethering me to life. She's my world and the reason I've survived thus far." My voice is still quiet and withdrawn. "So when she was attacked, I watched my world shatter before my eyes. I swore to exact revenge. I promised I'd make whoever was responsible pay, no matter what. And since my only connection to life was taken away, I felt invincible. Like I had nothing to lose."

"Nothing to lose," he repeats slowly.

"Yeah. So when I went through her journal and found an entry where she described being followed by suspicious men, and she drew pictures of the rings with unintelligible symbols they wore and mentioned the Vipers, I dug deeper and found out about Vencor. I remembered when I went out with Marcus that he was always rumored to come from a very influential family that belongs to a secret society, but I also knew he was never part of the family, so I didn't get close to him again, not to mention he even tried to share me with his friends—"

"He *shared* you?" His jaw tics, his finger twitching.

"No, he didn't get the chance. I left and broke up with him. I didn't sleep with him either. He's nothing in the great scheme of things, to be honest. But he did mention that most of the Vipers are rotten to the core and I heard rumors that many are in Vencor."

"So you got close to me to achieve your vengeance."

"No," I blurt, then wince. "I mean, yes. That was the goal at the start, but I soon realized you couldn't have possibly let something like Vi's attack happen. I admit that I wanted you to get me into Vencor so I could investigate and find clues, but you didn't allow that anyway. But really, I didn't suspect you. If anything, the more time I spent with you, the more the lines blurred, and I couldn't control my emotions."

"Did you stop suspecting me before or after you extracted my and the team's DNA?"

I gulp. He knows.

Of course he knows.

"I was only searching for Vi's murderer. I…didn't mean to harm anyone."

"But you did, Dahlia." A muscle jumps in his jaw. "Why the fuck would you leave my side in that town? Why the fuck wouldn't you let me know that Grant and Julian threatened you? That your sister was kidnapped? Why the fuck did you keep all of that to yourself?"

"Because I didn't want you to get hurt!" I shout, my vision blurry. "Because your father said he'd never let me see my sister again. Vi… Where is she?"

"She's somewhere safe, but this isn't about her." He rounds the bed and grabs my chin. His skin is both warm and cold. Gentle but commanding. "This is about your reckless fucking actions that nearly got you killed. Do you have a death wish?"

"Of course not. You think I wasn't scared? Because I was. I was so scared, I could barely breathe, but do you know what terrified me more? The fear of losing Vi or you."

"Then you should've never left my side." His cool is chipping, ripping at the seams, revealing his undiluted chaos beneath the calm.

"I didn't have a choice."

"You always have a fucking choice." His fingers dig into my jaw, the pads probably bruising the skin, but it doesn't matter.

Because I see it. Deep in his eyes.

Turbulent blue.

A color I've never seen in them before.

Worry mixed with fear.

I clutch his bare arm, my skin electrifying at the touch, but I still hold on to my courage as I let the blanket fall, then shift to my knees.

His grip loosens around my jaw, enough to allow me some movement, and I brush my lips against his, softly, tentatively.

They twitch. His jaw flexes, but he remains still, so still, I think he's a statue. "What the fuck are you doing?"

I grab on to that courage, my breath escaping in a fractured rhythm.

This is the first time I've wanted something with all my broken parts. The first time I'm willing to compromise.

To even let go of the one thing that's kept me going since Vi's attack.

My pride.

"When we separated at the bridge, I regretted not kissing you." My words are only interrupted by a flash of lightning and the pattering of rain. "I regretted not holding on to you one final time. I know you probably won't forgive me, and that's okay. You're angry, so take it out on me. If you want me to run, I'll run."

"Shut up, Dahlia."

"I'll make it harder to catch me, I promise. Just one more time—"

"I said." He pushes me back against the bed, the mattress

creaking under his weight as he straddles me, his hand gripping my bathrobe's belt. "Shut the fuck up."

My heart trembles. And so does my entire body.

I arch my back, my fingers reaching for his shirt, but he's already taken it off. It's somewhere on the floor now, and all I can focus on are the hard lines of his muscles.

The proportionate cut planes of his chest and stomach, the dark ink that slips from his side to his abs, the snake's head at his collarbone, the scars crisscrossing his chest.

He's a sight to behold. An enigma caught between morbid ruthlessness and authoritative composure.

I place a trembling hand on a scar as if I can erase it, as if I can cast a spell and make all the pain disappear.

A sharp inhale expands his chest, inflating it against my hand. But he doesn't remove it. Doesn't scold me for daring to touch the sun.

It still burns, but that's okay. I can handle him.

Kane undoes the belt of my robe in one ruthless movement, and it slips open, exposing my nakedness. My nipples are hard and perky; my breasts feel swollen.

All because of his gaze.

"Take it out on you," he repeats, his voice tense, his chest heaving as he unzips his jeans, lifts himself, then removes and throws them and his boxer briefs on the floor to join his shirt.

"Yeah." I lift my other hand to his face, but this time, he grabs it and slams it over my head on the pillow.

But he doesn't hold my injured wrist and, instead, flattens his palm against mine.

As he leans down, his chest grazes my nipples, and I let out a small moan of need.

Of something much deeper than need.

"There are a lot of things to take out on you, wildflower, so what should we start with?" He wraps his hand around my throat, angles my head to the side, and bites on my earlobe. "Your lies?"

My heart jolts, a flux of both fear and pleasure rushing inside me. Kane sinks his teeth into my jaw, the crook of my neck, my shoulder, my collarbone. My nipples.

Everywhere.

I scream, trying to grab onto him.

"Your betrayal?"

He sweeps his tongue against my tortured nipple and I wiggle, welcoming the pleasurable feeling, but then he bites again. "Your lack of confidence in me?"

I arch my back, my lower stomach rubbing against his hard cock.

A stickiness trickles between my thighs, and I clench them together in search of some friction.

But he releases my hand and slaps my thighs apart, settling his massive weight between them as he continues to suck and bite my nipple.

Every lick of his tongue is a zap of pleasure to my throbbing pussy, and every bite is a reminder that this isn't only about pleasure. It's not even part of our twisted games.

It's a punishment.

One I'm willing to take.

He bites a trail down to my stomach, nibbling and sucking on the soft skin until he reaches my pussy.

I throw my head back as his lips wrap around my clit, his tongue rolling and twisting, his teeth slightly nibbling.

Slick sweat covers my body as I writhe, and although the bathrobe is soft, it feels rough on my skin.

My fingers sink into his hair, pushing, clenching. His grip

on my throat increases with his rhythm, making me tighten and grow slicker.

More turned on than I thought would ever be possible.

I'm going to come.

I'm going to come all over his mouth.

Just when the wave is about to overtake me, Kane lifts his head, his lips still smeared with my arousal as he releases my throat. "So tell me, Dahlia. Where should I start?"

I bite my lower lip to keep from groaning in protest.

This isn't about me.

I shouldn't be mad.

And yet...

I'm panting, trying to ignore the pulsing in my pussy. The primal need to rub myself all over his face and come.

"We should start here, don't you think?" He sits on his haunches and his large palms cover my hips as he roughly slides me forward and maneuvers my legs onto his right shoulder until his cock is nudging at my pussy.

I nod, grabbing on to the sheets. A sting of pleasure goes through me as he shallowly thrusts in my opening. With every push, I go slack, expecting him to slam in as usual, but he doesn't.

My pussy's so wet, the third time he thrusts shallowly, I tighten and my eyes roll back on a groan.

The orgasm is sharp and powerful, making my legs shake on his shoulder. I love the contrast of my tan skin against his lighter tone, the way his shoulder flexes, providing support against my curled toes.

"You're coming already?" he tsks, slapping his cock against my sensitive clit. "Your cunt is that greedy for my cock, huh?"

I whimper as the remnants of the orgasm quake through

me, or maybe it's a brand-new one bleeding into the previous one.

"You know what I think?" He plunges his cock into my wet slit, eliciting electric jolts from the base of my belly. "I think I should fuck your virgin ass, Dahlia. I should stuff my cock into this tight hole and claim you as mine once and for all."

He slides my wetness to my back hole, spits on his hand, then slides it between my ass cheeks and plunges his middle finger into my tight channel.

I groan, my back arching as he adds another finger, thrusting, loosening me up.

Kane has often played with my ass when he's fucked me. The last time he did this—a few days ago—he fucked me with three fingers.

It was strange and hurt in the beginning, but it always made me come. But then again, I love the way Kane dominates me, no matter what he does.

I'm a bit apprehensive about anal. His cock is way bigger than his three fingers, but I can handle him.

I'm the *only* one who can handle him.

He angles me up so only my head and upper shoulders are on the mattress, spits on my back hole again, then rams a third finger in.

My gasp echoes in the air, my fractured breaths synching with the pattering of the rain.

"You're still so tight, no matter how much I play with you." He slaps my ass cheek. "How are you going to fit my cock here, Dahlia?"

I lather up his hard cock that's already covered with my juices. Precum covers my hands, and I use it to lube him up more.

"Mmm. That's it." He thrusts in my hand while he pumps his fingers inside me. "Make my cock nice and wet so I can fuck your ass."

My pussy throbs and I guide him to my back hole.

"So impatient." He pulls out his fingers. "Want me to fuck you when you're barely ready? It'll hurt."

"I like it when it hurts."

"You're trembling."

"It's okay. It's you."

"It's me," he growls the words. "If it's me, you'll let me do whatever the fuck I want with you, wildflower? You like it when I do whatever the fuck I please, don't you? Your cunt becomes so wet and compliant, and you turn into clay in my fucking hands. Because no one can give you what I can. No one but me can fucking own you."

My heart's beating fast because he's breathing harshly. Sweat shines on his toned muscles, and his eyes are so blue, his pupils so blown up, I can see my reflection in them.

"You're right." I smile as tears gather in my eyes. "No one but you can own me."

Because I've never loved anyone but him.

And I don't think I ever will.

The reason I want him so much isn't only because of the sex. It's because I feel the strongest connection when his body fuses with mine.

It's like I can touch his soul.

And I think I do, because a harsh breath expels out of him and he speaks in a rough tone. "Say it again."

"You're right?"

"No, the part that no one but me can own you."

"No one. I'm yours. Only yours."

"Only mine." His big hands wrap around my waist.

He wants to flip me on my stomach, I realize.

No. No, not now.

I clutch his arm, my palms trembling on his skin, and I shake my head, my eyes wide, my cheeks heated. "No."

"No?"

"I want to see your face."

He doesn't release me and I start to panic, but I whisper, "Please."

"Jesus fucking Christ," he mutters, then keeps one arm around my waist and parts my ass cheeks with the other hand, nudging his cock against my hole.

And then he enters.

It's slow. Agonizingly slow, and it feels full.

So damn full, I think I'll burst.

Oh fuck. I feel my ass stretching, accommodating, greedily sucking him in.

"Relax," he strains, his tone rough, his muscles taut. "I barely managed to get the tip in and you're tightening up. Do you want to break my cock?"

Oh fuck.

Oh shit.

That was only the tip?

I'm sweating profusely, my fingers clawing at his lean waist for leverage, but I don't think I can do it.

"Relax your ass for me." He kneads the cheek, then slaps it. "You've taken my cock in your cunt; you can take it here as well."

My pussy clenches and I moan, then go still.

"You like it when I spank your little ass?" *Slap*. "That's it. You're doing so well. Good girl."

My throat closes up and my heart swells at his words.

I'm so turned on, I barely feel him thrusting in a bit more.

It hurts. Yes, there's pressure and stretching and a sting of pain, but I like it.

The best sex has always been a mixture of pain and pleasure for me. A combination only Kane does this well. There's always enough of both to keep me on my toes. Enough to make me wet and expectant.

Thrilled.

Enamored.

So I relax for him, wiggling my hips and letting him slide farther in.

"Fuck." His biceps bulge, his fingers sinking into my stomach, grounding me in place. "You're taking my cock so well, wildflower. You're stretching to swallow me deeper and deeper."

I moan, stroking his sides, staring at him through my blurry vision.

Kane doesn't break eye contact as he starts moving inside me, his cock sliding gently in my tight channel. There's nothing of his usual brutality. No slamming. No fucking like he hates me.

And that makes me wetter, my wiggling more frantic, my heart soaring so high, I think I'll never come down. So I roll my hips and meet his every thrust with renewed frenzy.

"Slow down." He slaps my ass cheek again, the sting making me a puddle. "You'll hurt yourself on my cock."

"Fuck me like usual," I gasp on a moan, still wiggling against him.

"I won't fuck your ass like I fucked your cunt the first time." *Slap*. "Stop moving."

My limbs go still at the command, and I see it then.

The look in his lust-filled, enlarged pupils.

He doesn't want to hurt me. He didn't care the first time in that tunnel, but now, he does.

Now, he moves slowly, going deeper but unhurriedly.

He's keeping himself in check, under control, the veins in his neck throbbing with tension, his hair damp. A droplet of sweat falls on my nose and he grunts.

But he doesn't ram into me.

Doesn't slam harder.

Instead, he watches for my body's signals, and only when I relax, only when I accommodate him, he picks up his pace.

Gradually.

Slowly.

Treating me like a treasured flower instead of the wildflower he's always called me.

Damn it.

I think I'm falling in love with him harder than I ever thought possible.

A zap of pleasure slashes through me, and my head becomes foggy.

My hips roll, matching his rhythm, going gently, so gently, and tears slide down my cheeks.

Kane leans forward, darts his tongue out, and licks those tears, swallowing them, leaving a warm stickiness on my cheeks.

"Why are you crying?" he grunts. "Does it hurt?"

"No. It feels so good. It's the tears that turn you on."

He chuckles against my mouth, his teeth grazing the corner of my lips before he sucks them into his mouth.

Kane kisses me as deeply as he fucks me, but it's at a leisurely pace, taking his time to nibble on my lips, play with my tongue.

And when his hand that's around my waist reaches down to my clit, I'm a goner. I can't last long.

Not when he fucks me as if his body is telling me things. Things I don't understand but still fall for anyway.

Maybe it's also his form of goodbye.

Or maybe, just maybe, he's ruining me for other men.

Because no one can touch me like he does.

Kiss me like he does.

Make me feel safe like he does.

I moan in his mouth as the orgasm rips through me, lighting me on fire.

My arms wrap around his neck, my nails clawing at his back at those scars, wanting them gone, but also loving him more because of them.

Because he *survived* them.

This man killed two men before my eyes not too long ago. One of them his father.

And I still shatter in his arms like I never have with anyone.

Kane's rhythm picks up, thrusting at a commanding pace. Maybe it's because I'm still hazy from the orgasm, but it doesn't hurt.

Yes, I feel full.

So full, I think he'll burst out of my stomach, but it's the good kind of fullness.

I hold on to him tighter, hugging him to me as he buries his head in the crook of my neck, and then warmth fills my ass.

The world goes still for a moment.

Our harsh breaths echoing in the air, his body wrapped all over mine, his cock throbbing inside me.

My fingers stroke his rich brown strands, my eyes half open, my heart completely full.

I love you, I want to say.

But the words get stuck in my throat.

Though he said I'm only his, the fear that he'll never get over my betrayal paralyzes me.

So I'd rather not make a fool of myself.

My hand falls to my side and I close my eyes to commit him to memory.

His warmth, his breaths, his loudly beating heart, his scent. His everything.

"Don't sleep yet." His husky voice echoes in the air. "I'm not done with you."

My eyes blink open and Kane pulls out, his cum trickling out of me and onto the bed. I want to talk to him some more. I want to ask a lot of questions, but I want to bask in this moment for a while longer.

I want to just live in this moment.

He lifts me up in one smooth movement, and I squeal as I wrap my arms and legs around his neck and waist. He walks me to the shower with sure strides while I'm all over him.

"Kane?" I breathe, half exhausted, half thrilled.

"I'm going to fuck my cunt. This time, it'll be rough."

And then he does exactly as he promised.

And I wish this moment would never end.

I wish reality would never come.

CHAPTER 34
Dahlia

I MUST'VE FALLEN ASLEEP.

Because the next time I open my eyes, Kane's not in bed.

It's large and consuming and smells of him, but he's not here.

Morning light spills through the large window, but the room is empty and desolate.

My throat closes and bile rises up, choking my breaths.

I think I'm going to be sick.

The silence sounds violent, cruel. There isn't even the rain to distort it.

I look in the direction of the bathroom. "Kane?"

Even as I call his name, I know he's not there. His presence is gone and so are his kisses, his dirty and soft whispers.

"Go to sleep now, Dahlia."

Those were the last words he told me, after he dried my hair and held me to his chest. After I asked him about his tattoos and he said the crow represented freedom and the serpent was about control.

After he let me stroke his chest and mumble incoherent words against him. After he kissed my forehead and I felt like a little girl who was just too exhausted and needed sleep.

Because his arms were safe.

His voice was safe.

So I thought if I closed my eyes a little, he'd be here when I opened them again.

I thought because he lathered my body with soap, carried me in his arms, and dried me, he might forgive me.

I thought because I saw the concern and cryptic emotions in his eyes, he might keep me.

But maybe I thought wrong.

Because he's gone and I'm the only one in this vast bed.

Maybe he can't get over my betrayal after all.

My breathing comes in slow, chopped sounds, and I think I'm having a panic attack.

Breathe.

Just breathe.

Who the hell do you think you are, Dahlia? Keep you? A rat from the streets who shouldn't even look at him, let alone touch him?

His father was right.

Megan was right.

Preston and Jude were *so* right.

He's a Davenport.

No matter how hard I try to erase that last name, it defines him.

And now that his father is dead, it is *him*.

I pull my knees to my chest and a whiff of his cologne fills my nostrils. It makes me want to cry.

Why did he treat me that way if he was going to discard me?

If he were crueler, it probably wouldn't have hurt this much.

A phone that's plugged into a charger lights up on the nightstand.

It's mine, I realize.

My fingers shake as I grab it. There are a few worried texts from Megan because she hasn't heard from me in a while. I text back that I'm fine and it's a long story.

I should get up, locate my sister, and—

My heart nearly stops when I find texts from Kane.

A few of them are from when I disappeared in the village, but the ones that make me shake all over are the latest ones, from an hour ago.

> Kane: I need to take care of Grant's death fallout. Don't move. Call the kitchen from the room's intercom and they'll prepare whatever food you like. We'll talk once I get back.
>
> Kane: PS. I'll take you to visit your sister once I'm done.

My fingers shake around the phone. The only words I see go in and out of focus.

We'll talk once I get back.

We'll *talk*.

We. Will. Talk. Will I have to pay a price for what I've done? I don't regret any of it, but I know how Kane will perceive my actions.

Betrayal.

Or maybe it's something else?

Against my will, a flicker of hope spills in the dark corners of my chest.

A knock booms in the silence, and I think it's the doomsday feeling in my head, but it comes again. Louder this time.

"Dahlia?"

I scramble to my feet at the sound of Helena's soft voice and quickly throw on Kane's shirt that he left on the floor. It only reaches my thighs, but it's better than nothing.

"Just a sec," I call as I rush to the ornate golden door. I feel self-conscious for even touching it.

When I open it, I find Helena standing outside, barely filling out her straight white dress, her skin pasty against the color, but there's a flicker of life in her sunken eyes.

"Hi," I say awkwardly, pulling down on the shirt.

"Thank you for seeing me."

"Anytime. Um, sorry for how I look. I don't know where my clothes are."

"They're being cleaned. The staff will bring them as soon as possible."

"Thank you."

She takes my hands in hers. "I'm the one who should thank you. And apologize to you. I didn't want Kane to come and get hurt, but he reminded me of everything you did for us. He reminded me that he's a much better person than I'll ever be, and I want to apologize for ever asking him to turn his back on you."

"You were just scared for his life," I say in a low voice. "I should be the one to apologize. It's because of me that... uh...your husband...died."

"On the contrary, I'm grateful."

"Even if...Kane became a murderer?"

"It's not his first murder and won't be his last. But at least this time, he did it for himself. He finally got himself and me—though coincidentally—free of Grant's chains. So thank you, Dahlia." She squeezes my hand. "I'm glad you're in Kane's life."

No. I'm glad he's in mine.

A tall man in a butler's suit walks toward us carrying a basket. Samuel.

Helena releases me as she wipes her eyes. "There. Samuel brought your clothes."

"Julian Callahan is here," he announces as soon as I take the basket.

My hand tightens at the name. Helena merely frowns. "If he's here for Kane, then tell him he's not in."

"He wants a word with Miss Thorne. He's in the late Mr. Davenport's study."

My heartbeat skyrockets and I think I'm shaking, because Helena wraps an arm around my shoulders and strokes my arm.

"Tell him to return when Kane is here," she says to Samuel.

"Very well, madam."

"No, it's okay." I spit out a breath. "I'll change and be right back."

"You don't have to do this." Helena's frown deepens. "Julian is a snake no one likes for a reason. It's better if you wait for Kane."

"I'll be fine."

If Julian intends to press charges for the DNA tests and using his laboratory illegally, I don't want anyone, let alone Kane, to be there.

After I get into my clean, fresh-smelling jeans and T-shirt, Helena still tries to persuade me not to go, but I assure her that I'll be fine and follow Samuel.

As he opens the door and stands outside, I realize I'm lying big time.

Julian gives me the chills. I swear he's creepier than his brother. At least Jude is more up-front and doesn't have the macabre aura that hits me as soon as I step into a room.

The door closes and I regret not bringing Helena along.

Grant's study is as dark as his soul. The shelves and the desk are a dark brown, the sofas are black, and the wallpaper is a depressing green.

Julian stands by the shelves, leisurely flipping the pages of a hardcover. I catch *Diogenes of Sinope* on the spine before he tilts it down and stares at me, his gaze piercing, his body effortlessly upright.

"You wanted to see me?" I ask, keeping a safe distance away from him, and close to the door.

"Yes, I figured now would be the best time before Kane finishes making his father's murder look like a boating accident." He smiles. "I don't indulge in cannibalism, so you can relax. I won't eat you."

He flips another page even though he's looking at me, the act meticulous and somewhat menacing. Though maybe it's not the act itself, it's the dead look in his eyes.

So this is what a Vencor Founder looks like at all times.

It's suffocating.

"You see, Grant made a mistake." He flips a page, pauses, then flips another one. "He underestimated Kane's emotions. He never thought the son he molded into a copy of himself would take a page out of his book and simply remove him from the picture to achieve his goals. He also underestimated you and your capabilities to be the catalyst that pushed Kane to take that last step. He truly lost his touch at the end, especially after he was kind of forced to abandon his brother and some of his power. Sad, don't you think?"

"I'm only sad because Kane had to live as that asshole's son for twenty-one years."

"My, you're becoming his guard dog already." He grins, the gesture haunting. "This will be fun."

"This?"

"Miss Thorne, I suppose Grant never got the chance to tell you who tried to kill your sister, right?"

My muscles tighten and my fists clench.

"I'll take that as a no, especially since you're still here." He flips a page. "Other dogs bite their enemies. I bite my friends to save them."

"What?"

"Diogenes said that."

"Are we here to discuss philosophers?"

"Kane is a cynic ripped right from Diogenes's flesh. He'd hurt Jude and Preston if it meant that would keep them safe. He's better than Grant in that regard and a true pragmatist who weighs every option before taking action."

"And?"

"And do you believe you'll remain unscathed from the way his mind works?"

"That's none of your business."

"You see, that's where you're wrong. Story time. You might want to sit down for this."

"I'm good."

He lifts a shoulder as he skims through the pages as if that's where the story is. "A couple of years ago, a woman was stabbed to death, in broad daylight, twenty times. Do you know what being stabbed twenty times means, Miss Thorne? It means she must've felt the pain from the first stab the most, in her kidney. It must've been sharp and hurt a lot, and it was probably more painful than when she gave birth. She screamed, alerting everyone on the street to what was happening. The second stab was even worse. It went through her stomach. So did the third and the fourth. She collapsed afterward. Crawling, bleeding, her mouth gurgling with the metallic taste, and begging for help. Someone. Anyone. They didn't come. But the fifth stab came. This one went into her heart. She died then. She was bleeding out on the pavement, her empty eyes staring at the God she believed in, but he let her die like a dog. But it didn't end there. Her corpse was stabbed again and again—in the chest, the genitals, the stomach—until her intestines were hanging out; her face was hit on the pavement until her eyes bulged out—"

"Where are you going with this?" I snap, feeling sick to my stomach. But most of all, I don't like where this is leading.

"Just a description of the backstory. It's fascinating how you can't handle listening to it, but the people present watched and did nothing."

"What does this have to do with me?"

"You see, one of the people who was present and who turned the other way while that woman was murdered in cold blood is none other than your dear, innocent sister, Violet Winters."

I step backward, my hand flying to my mouth to cover my gasp.

"Surprised that your affectionate, angelic-faced sister who wouldn't hurt a fly stood by and watched a woman be killed?"

I shake my head. "She would never—"

A zap snaps in my head.

Memories of Vi coming home and throwing up, her face pale, her entire body trembling. She said she ate something bad and had a stomachache. She went to sleep early and left early the next day. She was off for over two weeks, withdrawn and completely out of it.

Whenever I asked, she said it was stress from work, school, and bills, and I believed her.

Because Vi never lied to me.

"She did. There's security footage to prove it. Or there was. I made sure to erase and get rid of it all."

"Are you related to the dead woman? Is that why…?"

"She was my stepmother. Jude's mother."

Oh God.

Oh God.

"You see, Jude really, *really* loved his mother. I liked her, too. She was different from mine. She was sweet and tried her best with me. She even attempted to protect me from my own father. Silly woman. Most importantly, she treated Jude like her treasure. So you can imagine his anger and need for vengeance. But I erased that footage from the records to stop his bloodlust haze. However, do you know who got a hold of some of the footage before I could delete it all? The one who bites his friends to help them?"

I'm shaking my head, back and forth. Back and forth.

"That's right. Kane. To comply with Jude's need for killing and revenge, he cut that footage into tiny clips and gathered a list with all the names of those who were present that day. He made files, too, full of information about them, their families, their weaknesses, what made them tick. Even their habits are there. Tucked neatly in his filing cabinet. Every once in a while, he gives Jude a name and helps him in making their lives complete hell. It's poetic, really. Jude wants every witness to hit rock bottom, to make them have to ask for help and not find it, just like his mother. Then, once they've had their fun, Preston, Jude, and Kane kidnap them, release them into the forest, and indulge in some old-fashioned hunting."

My legs fail me and I grab on to a nearby chair to remain standing.

This can't be real.

Julian is lying. He's lying—

"Needless to say, Kane knew about your existence long before you came here. He must've seen you, too, during one of his and Jude's stalking sessions. Now, I'm not sure whether or not he pulled the strings to bring you here, but knowing Kane, he probably did. Maybe he wanted to toy with you, too. Maybe you caught his attention, I'm not sure. He sure went through a lot of trouble to arrange a fake initiation."

"Fake?" My lips tremble around the word.

"You didn't possibly think it was real, did you? Oh my, you did. You see, this is why outsiders should remain on the outside. They're fickle and unable to discern dreams from reality. Our actual initiations alter the very fabric of your soul. If you had undergone the real deal, you wouldn't have survived. Kane has a soft spot for you, which is why he planned the whole watered-down charade and even asked his friends to participate. If it were real, you wouldn't have been accepted in the initial vetting process in the first place. Only those born into Vencor get to initiate, and occasionally, we invite those we deem worthy to be in our midst."

It wasn't real.

The whole psychological torture and brutal fucking was a charade?

No. How could that possibly be true? Julian must be trying to mess with my head.

"It's not him," I say so low, even I barely hear it.

"What was that?"

"Kane didn't hurt Violet. He couldn't have!" I shout, heaving. "He wouldn't...he wouldn't do that. He...wasn't a match on that DNA test."

"Oh, that. The DNA that was found under your sister's nails was actually swapped with a dead person's. Of course there will be no match." His lips pull in a smirk. "Who do you think swapped it?"

"No...no..."

"Kane."

"No!"

"I don't care if you don't believe me. You can stay here and murder him for all I care. Or wait long enough for him to get bored of his games and murder you. Doesn't make any difference. But there's something else you should know first."

I stare at him through my blurry vision.

"Your sister. She's awake."

"W-what?"

"Technically, her coma is induced."

"What the hell are you talking about? The doctors said she was in a coma."

"*My* doctors. *My* hospital. *My* system. I'm about to give you a lot of information, and I want you to be quiet and listen. I can assure you that your sister is awake and recovering well, and you can find out more about her location if you make the right choice. Violet actually woke up the same day she was admitted, and she wanted to run away from Jude at any cost, but she knew he'd find her, no matter where she went, so we struck a deal. She volunteers to test my experimental drug that would make her look as if she's in a coma and, in return, I arrange for your and her relocation where Jude can't find her once she wakes up. That way she'll be able to escape my brother's notorious hunts. But she woke up earlier than predicted because we couldn't keep administering the drug when he kidnapped her after I took her out of the hospital, and by the time I got her again, she was starting to wake up. As it happens, my brother was already getting suspicious because she's not showing the same signs as his actual comatose bodyguard. We reached the end of the trial anyway, and I'm satisfied with the results."

Jude kidnapped her? But if Julian found her again, then that means she's okay, right?

My mind reels as the pieces start falling into place.

Vi's bills being paid in full without any conditions.

Vi's doctor who refused to allow any other doctor to come near her.

Jude's comatose guard, Mario, right next to Violet.

Now that I think about it, the hooded guy who was looming over Vi's bed had a very similar build to Jude.

Oh my God.

"You have two choices." He lifts a finger. "One, you stay here, wait for Kane, and lose your sister." He lifts another finger. "Two. You disappear with your sister somewhere safe that I'll arrange. For good."

My lips tremble. "Why…are you doing this?"

"I don't like you or your sister. Outsiders should stay on the outside. This way, Jude and Kane will come back to their senses already. Cleaning up after them is a hassle."

I hang my head as tears gather in my eyes and drip onto my beat-up white sneakers.

Could Kane be the one behind everything?

Could he have manipulated me like a puppet on a string?

He wouldn't have made me feel bad for lying when he already knew everything.

Right?

Or have I finally been burned alive by the sun?

CHAPTER 35
Kane

AFTER I RETURN FROM FEEDING MY FATHER TO THE sharks, Dahlia's disappeared.

Again.

She's vanished right from my grasp.

Fucking *again*.

I came back to tell her the truth. To assure her that everything is forgiven. In fact, there's nothing to forgive.

After last night, after the way she slept peacefully in my arms, I figured it was time to start with a clean slate. I can't force Jude to like her, and he probably never will, but I can protect her from him.

She has nothing to do with his obsession anyway.

Her sister does, but her sister is practically dead.

It might hurt, but she'll eventually accept that reality.

She'll accept that I'm all she has.

The *only* one she can have.

But she's not here.

She even left her phone behind.

Julian goddamn Callahan came by and talked to her, and she left with him. That's what my mother and Samuel said.

That's what I watch on the house's security footage over and over again, on a damn loop. I can't stop looking at the way she trudges behind him, her movements lethargic, her eyes soulless.

Her fire completely extinguished.

She didn't even have that look when Grant had her chained up in his goddamn dungeon.

A dungeon I spent the last hour blazing through with a machete, as if that will extinguish the torturous memories or the image of Dahlia hanging from the chains while bleeding.

And now, Julian has taken her away.

Julian is interfering in my fucking business.

He definitely didn't learn a lesson from Grant's murder. If I can kill my own father, nothing and no one will stop me anymore.

Not Julian, not the rules.

Not even fucking Vencor.

My steps are wide as I walk to the secondary annex, where my father's lackeys reside, followed by Samuel. He already informed them about their new owner, and this new owner has his first mission for them.

As we're walking, I pull out my phone and text in the group chat.

> Me: @Jude Callahan, I'm informing you that your brother is getting in my way and I might or might not have him killed.
> Jude: Not before I do. He kidnapped Violet. Again.
> Me: Fuck. That must be why Dahlia went with him.
> Preston: Whoa. Messing with Julian, are we? Count me out. I'm just gonna stay here and get high.
> Me: Is Julian at the main house?
> Jude: At his wife's house.
> Me: Even better. Remember when I said threatening

him was risky? Forget about that. I'm bringing our men.

Preston: Hey…let's take a deep breath. Inhale. Exhale.

Jude: I'll bring the men I have access to.

Preston: Jesus fucking Christ. Slow down. You want to get killed?

Me: I am now the head of the Davenport family, and Julian came onto Davenport property and took what's mine. He needs to pay.

Jude: It's long overdue. He needs to stop his fucking meddling.

Preston: Sounds dangerous. I'm in.

A few hours later, we're all gathered in front of Julian's wife's house on the outskirts of town, far away from Ravenswood Hill, bordering where the poor people live in the neighboring town.

After Jude and I direct our men to surround the house, we take out the security in front and we head to the second floor, where the bedrooms are. It's almost midnight, so the motherfucker should be sleeping.

Despite the lack of light, Jude, Preston, and I move with ease. We've been plunged into the darkness our entire lives. This is child's play.

"So…" Preston walks backward in front of us so that he's facing us. "We're risking my precious life for pussy?"

"Shut it, Armstrong," Jude says without even looking at him.

"I'm just setting the record straight. I'd never do this for pussy. It's so fucking lame, I'm thinking about throwing you out of Preston's Privileged Close Circle Club."

"Consider me thrown out," I say, my muscles bulging with tension.

"I never wanted to be in it in the first place," Jude adds.

"Liars. You love me and can't survive without me. If I were a woman, you'd be fighting over my beautiful self."

"Fighting over who gets to chop your head off first," I say. "Which we're already doing."

"I'd be playing so hard to get, Dallas would have nothing on me." He grins, ignoring my words, then headlocks Jude. "I think I'll still pick big man, though. His dick is bigger."

Jude elbows him. "I'll stab your dick if you don't take this seriously."

"Not my precious dick. How the fuck am I supposed to unwind?" Preston lets go with a pout and continues to walk backward. "Besides, this whole thing is stupid, and Julian will probably light our asses on fire. You shouldn't even be this invested, Jude. Your brother would be doing you a favor if he kills that nobody."

Jude glares at him, his eyes nearly shooting daggers. "No one but me gets to kill my targets."

"Shh." I raise a hand to my mouth and pull out my gun at the sound of Julian's cool voice.

Jude motions at the door behind him, and then the three of us inch closer.

I kick the door open, gun in hand, but we freeze upon seeing Julian sitting in a chair, reading out loud from a book as his wife, Annalise, lies in bed, sleeping.

She startles at the loud kick and sits up, her eyes unfocused, her face pale.

Annalise Callahan is the greatest mystery in this town. She's barely seen, less than my mother, and rumor has it that Julian's using her as a subject for his latest experimental drug testing.

No one really cares, though.

"Julian…?" she asks, her voice low, almost scratchy.

He strokes her hair and smiles. Didn't know the motherfucker was capable of that.

"Go back to sleep. I'll be right back."

She grabs onto his shirt and shakes her head, but he releases her grip and looks at us, his smile dropping in a blink.

"Let's talk outside."

Preston jumps out first. "I was dragged here against my will. They did it!"

We all step out. Jude doesn't really want to hurt his sister-in-law, and he made it clear that threatening Julian with her life is fine, but she's not to be touched.

"Annalise is not to be harmed," were his exact words as soon as we arrived here.

The de facto leader of the Callahan clan casts one last glance at his wife, then closes the door and runs a hand through his hair. "Now, I have to maim you."

"Not me." Preston raises his hand. "Against my will, remember?"

I jam my gun against Julian's temple. "Where's Dahlia?"

He doesn't even flinch. "Somewhere far away from you."

"We have the house surrounded, Julian. If you don't tell me where she is right now, I'll blow your brains out."

"Be my guest. In the event of my death, my people will blow both Dahlia and Violet up."

I freeze.

Of course he'd have such a backup plan. It wouldn't be Julian if he didn't.

Jude grabs his brother by the collar of his shirt. "What the fuck are you doing?"

"Putting your heads back where they belong. On the game, on your roles. Without distractions."

Preston claps. "Thank you! That's what I've been saying."

"You think I won't find her?" I breathe close to his face. "I have all the resources to, and those promises of investment I made to you? Consider them canceled and divided between Serena and Atlas."

"Doesn't matter whether or not you find her. She knows everything about your involvement in her sister's attack and how she ended up in Graystone Ridge. Poor girl was shaken at the reality that you're the mastermind. She really tried to defend you as well. Until she couldn't deny the truth."

"You...told her?"

"Yes. How else would I get her to leave?"

I raise my hand and punch him in the face. "You had no right to tell her. That wasn't your conversation to have."

"It's up to me how I use the information at my disposal." He wipes his bloody nose. "As for business matters, you'll come to your logical senses. Neither Serena nor Atlas can help you maintain the Davenports' shaky foundation like I can."

"I don't need you for that. I have my uncle."

"Kayden can't come back so soon, even if Grant is dead, and you know it. You need to get stronger and enforce your own rules first."

"Julian," his brother growls. "Don't make me hurt you."

"You can try." Julian stares me down. "Here's the deal, Kane. If you manage to bring Dahlia back willingly, I won't touch her again, and you won't throw a tantrum regarding business matters."

My jaw clenches.

"Now, get off my property. If you barge into my house again, I'll kill you."

Then he turns and goes back into the bedroom, closing the door behind him.

"Night, Julian!" Preston says in a singsong voice. "Sorry for the late-night visit! Will send flowers in the morning!"

Jude strides toward the door, but Preston holds him back. "I'm not disposing of your corpses tonight."

"Forget it, Jude." I let my gun fall to my side. "I'll find them myself. Even if it's the last thing I do."

Preston snaps his fingers in my direction. "Now, that's the spirit. I still hate where this is going, but anyway. We're out of here."

He starts to drag us out, joking about how we escaped with our skin unscathed while Jude hits him upside the head.

When we're in the driveway, my phone vibrates and I pull it out, expecting Samuel.

Unknown number.

I pick up, and as soon as I hear harsh, fractured breaths from the other end, I go still, my fingers tightening on the phone.

"Dahlia?"

"Is it true?" Her voice is weak, hoarse, as if she's spent hours crying.

"Whatever Julian has told you is massively blown out of proportion. Where are you? I'll pick you up—"

"Just tell me. Did you know all along about Violet? About the connection to Jude's mother? About *me*?"

"It's not as it seems—"

"Yes or no." She speaks over me. Again.

My jaw tightens. "Yes."

She laughs then, the sound piercing my ears as sobs echo through it.

I can't help but remember the first time I saw her laugh.

That day, from the top of the roof.

"God, you should be proud of yourself. You played me so well, Kane. I hope I entertained you enough."

"You were never a subject of my entertainment," I snap, then rein it in and breathe calmly. "Let's meet. We need to talk."

"So you can finish the job with Violet?"

"I won't harm her."

"But Jude will. Like he did a few months ago."

"He didn't—"

"Stop lying to me!"

Fuck. If she talks over me one more time, I'm grabbing her throat through the goddamn phone.

Why the fuck isn't she letting me speak?

"Just so you know, if Jude comes near her, I'll kill him." All her sniffles disappear and she sounds stone cold, far away. "Don't let me see your face again or I'll kill you too."

The phone goes dead.

CHAPTER 36
Kane

Six months ago

"IS THIS THE PLACE?"

Jude's voice carries on the wind, doing nothing to interrupt the fucking chaos below.

"Unfortunately, yes," I say.

Most of the streetlight bulbs are burned out—only three work across the entire street. But as his dark eyes scan the area below, carefully observing the sketchy-as-fuck neighborhood, he looks like a grim reaper with a thirst for blood.

The place reeks of so much poverty, we had to leave Jude's motorcycle and my car at the gas station to avoid standing out and rented a Hyundai to reach this fuckery of human society.

The stench of piss, vomit, and rotting trash fills the air, thickening and swirling in the night's stale humidity.

From up here, we have a perfect view of the grimy streets, of the skittering shadows moving like ghosts beneath flickering streetlights.

Small-time dealers lean against the walls, barely hidden in the dark, slipping bags of powder or pills into greedy hands, their eyes darting around, their rancid breath polluting the air. The faint murmur of exchanges is punctuated by the occasional shout or cough from the alleyways or the paper-thin walls. Now and again, there's the dull clatter of a bottle rolling on the cracked pavement.

A couple of homeless people huddle in a corner, too far gone to care about the fights brewing around them. Their rags hang off them like dead skin, their hollowed-out faces lost in the shadow of a world that doesn't give a damn about them.

There's the breaking of glass bottles and a muttered quarrel rising between two small-time gangsters under the glow of a busted neon sign, their voices low but threatening, tension vibrating in the air.

"What a shithole." Jude grins. "Fitting, really. Rats do live in sewers after all."

"What are your plans for this one?"

"Big. As usual." He tilts his head in my direction. "Though it'll be a challenge to make her life more miserable than the literal hell she lives in."

"I doubt there's a worse hell than you."

"Won't argue with that—"

He purses his lips when a girl trudges down the street, her shoulders hunched. Her light hair is hidden in a hoodie as she quickens her steps, narrowly escaping the two fighting and throwing broken glass at each other.

It takes me a second to figure out she's our target.

Violet Winters.

"That's her," I say. "Back from her late-night shift at some other hellhole."

Jude says nothing.

His eyes narrow, and I think I catch a spark lighting up the dark brown before it flatlines to its usual deadliness.

"Another fucking one bites the dust," he mutters, and even though it's low, his voice is deeper.

His posture is straighter, his gaze more calculating than usual.

Violet stops by the sleeping homeless men no one notices, then she reaches into her plastic bag, pulls out two sandwiches, and puts them on their plates.

She rises to her full height, starts to walk, then halts, fishes a few bills from her pocket, sighs, and places them beneath the sandwiches, carefully hiding them from view.

Jude laughs, the sound low and sinister. "We have a fucking saint on our hands, Kane. The irony."

"Not really irony. That day, she was the only one to call 911. She's also the cleanest of the bunch. No matter how deep I dug, I couldn't find any dirt on her." I stare up at him. "Honestly, if you leave her to rot, her life will do the honors."

"Her disgusting innocence will kill her, huh?"

"Possibly."

"Too bad I don't believe in innocence. No one from that day is fucking innocent."

As she hurries toward the house where the landlord rents her and her sister the attic, Violet is swung back by her elbow.

By one of the swaying drunks. Oily haphazard hair, a beer belly, and slurring speech.

"Hi, beauuuutiful. Care for a ride?"

Her face goes red and she attempts to pull her arm away. "Please let me go, Dave."

Too soft.

Too pleading.

What a lamb.

I'm surprised she's lasted this long in this type of neighborhood.

"D-Dave, you're hurting me…please…" She pulls herself free, but she doesn't make it one step before he catches her from behind, his hands groping everywhere.

Jude takes a step forward.

"What the fuck are you doing?" I whisper. "We're only here to watch."

He takes another step when the door to her house blasts open.

A petite girl in a baggy T-shirt rushes outside, in fucking flip-flops, her dark hair gathered in a bandana. And she's holding a gun in her right hand.

"Let her go, Dave!" she shouts.

He immediately steps away, lifting both hands in the air. "Whoa. Fuuucking hell, you bitch."

"Fuck you, asshole!" Still pointing the gun at him, she pulls Violet to her side.

I'm standing now.

Even from here, I can see the way she holds herself—defiant, sharp, shoulders squared despite the filth that surrounds her.

Dahlia Thorne. Violet's foster sister and only form of family.

Her pictures don't do her justice.

She's much more of a firecracker in real life.

Her eyes, which I know are hazel, are blazing with fire, her grip on the gun steady.

She's shooing away the drunk despite his slurred curses. Her sister stands just behind her, wide-eyed and fragile, but Dahlia's firmly pushing the drunkard back.

She's been through this before.

Hmm. So she's the reason Violet hasn't ended up in a ditch somewhere.

The drunkard lurches toward her again, but she pushes harder, her voice clear and guttural. "Fuck off, Dave! Lay off the booze."

This time, he stumbles away into the night, lost in the gutter.

She keeps pointing the gun until he's out of view.

A fighter.

My index finger twitches and I roll my ring. A sudden urge I've never had before takes root in my head.

I want to break her, see beneath her skin and find out what makes her tick.

Dahlia wraps her arm around her sister as she guides her to the house. The contrast is clear even in the darkness. Violet is fairer, more demure, and a wallflower. Dahlia is tanner, louder, and has an energy that can be felt from a mile away.

"I've been waiting for you, Vi." She side-hugs her as they walk.

"Where did you get the gun?" her sister scolds.

"Mr. Song paid me to clean it. He wanted to give me ten bucks, but I negotiated my way to twenty. Isn't that awesome?"

"It's dangerous. Give it back to him."

"It's empty, but Dave is an idiot so—" She stops, then laughs awkwardly.

"Was that your stomach? You didn't eat all day, did you?" Violet asks and starts to push her away, but Dahlia hugs her tighter.

"You know I hate cooking. I was so busy with school, I forgot."

"What a child." Violet sighs and hands her the plastic bag. "Here, I bought you a sandwich. I'll cook you something for tomorrow."

"Ugh, I love you, Vi. I also got you something. Guess what?"

"What?"

"The magical patches for back pain! I also learned this new massage technique from Mrs. Liu next door. She swears it will relieve the discomfort."

Her sister pats her hair, and their voices mingle and end in an indistinguishable chatter as they go into the shack they call home.

I find myself leaning forward, trying to catch one last glimpse of her before she completely disappears.

Dahlia, not Violet.

We came here for Violet, but it's Dahlia's smile that's imprinted in my mind.

In a second, multiple scenarios flash in my brain.

All of them ending with her under my claws.

I face Jude, who's still watching the house, his eyes dead, his posture rigid. "Tell me your plan concerning Violet."

He grabs my shoulder, then pushes me sideways. "Stay out of it."

"Will do. On one condition."

"What the fuck is that?"

"Don't touch or implicate the sister."

Jude's eyebrows shoot up, but he has enough understanding not to antagonize me when I have control over his weakness.

All right, then.

Dahlia Thorne has just piqued my interest, and that might be the worst mistake of her life.

CHAPTER 37
Dahlia

I CRIED SO MUCH, MY HEAD HURTS.

I cried until I thought I'd never stop crying.

I cried for so long, I don't think I have any tears left.

And now, I'm just numb.

My eyes track the looming trees from the back seat of the car as it takes me to my sister.

Somewhere in Rhode Island.

I pull my knees to my chest and lay my head on the window, letting grief wash over me.

When Julian told me everything, a part of me chose not to believe him. That stupid in-love part that trembled at the tiniest hint of Kane's affection put its foot down and told me not to judge him.

Julian is not the good guy here. He threatened me with Grant the other day. Why would he be telling me this now?

So I asked the driver for a bathroom break and used one of those old pay phones.

I didn't care what Julian said. I mostly followed his orders just to see Vi.

So I had to talk to Kane.

I had to hear him say it was all a lie.

But it wasn't. A lie, I mean.

It was far from a lie and the closest thing to the truth that I've been searching for all these months.

The truth he clearly knew I was hunting for and still, he chose to toy with me.

Make me his entertainment.

Everything he said and did, from that first time in the arena to last night, was to keep me under control so I didn't harm his friend.

To see how far I'd go before he crushes me.

A fresh wave of tears blurs my vision.

And it's not only because I feel victimized or used. It's deep rage.

The need to hurt him as much as he's hurt me.

I want to punch his face and call him names. I want him to feel a sliver of the pain that's ripping me open from the inside.

But I'd have to give up my sister's safety if I were ever to consider seeing him again.

The sister he plotted to kill.

Kane and Jude.

They were the ones with the black rings my sister talked about in her journal.

The men who stalked her and made her life hell until she ended up in a coma.

I need to buy a gun. If I see them again, I'm shooting them between the eyes.

My dark thoughts disperse when the car comes to a halt in front of an old-looking house at the end of an empty suburban street.

The white fence is dirty and could use repainting, and the grass is tall and unkempt, as if no one has been at this place for months.

The partition between me and the driver lowers in a hush of mechanical movement before her voice echoes in the air. "We're here, miss."

I hear the click on the door unlocking and stare at the house, then the well-groomed driver, who I assume is also security detail, because I spotted her gun earlier. "Is my sister here?"

"Yes." She looks at me through the rearview mirror. "The key is in the armrest."

I open the compartment by my side and, sure enough, there's a key branded #121.

My clammy fingers wrap around the cool metal and I exit the car.

As soon as I do, it drives away.

My heart is in my throat as I walk to the scratched-up white door.

The key doesn't go in on the first try because of my sweaty hand.

On the second try, the door creaks open and I catch a glimpse of a baseball bat, then hear a furious battle cry.

My hand freezes on the knob.

The bat stops in midair.

The scream turns into a gasp.

Violet...?

For a moment, I think I'm in a dream. The light casts a shadow on her angelic features.

It's really Violet.

She stands there, awake, alive, and so *real*, it knocks the breath from my chest.

Her strawberry blond hair looks thicker and glossier than I remember as it falls in soft waves, framing a face that's no longer pale and hollow.

Her skin glows with health, flushed, alive, and her eyes—those deep, familiar blue eyes—are wide and filled with a spark I thought I'd never see again.

She looks…different. Still soft and demure, but there's a void in her gaze. As if her soul was broken and she hasn't exactly gathered all the pieces.

Still, I see my sister in those eyes.

Here.

Awake.

There's grace in the way she holds herself, the way she looks stunning even when wearing a simple gray sleep shirt.

The bat falls from her hand and clatters to the old wooden floor as she whispers, "Dahlia."

"Viiiii!" I jump her in a hug, wrapping my arms around her so tight, I'm surprised I don't crush her.

My tears flow again from both joy and anguish.

Pain and relief.

Vi's back.

Vi's here.

She sniffles and hugs me tighter, her fingers stroking my hair. "Don't cry."

"Am not."

"You so are."

"You're crying, too."

"Am not!"

We both chuckle as we face each other, tears streaming down our cheeks.

I take her hands in mine and study her closely. "You okay? Do you feel any pain anywhere?"

She smiles through the tears. "I'm fine."

"Is it true…? That you woke up a long time ago and made a deal with Julian to test his drug and be put in a coma?"

She hangs her head. "Yeah, I'm sorry."

"Why didn't you tell me?"

"I was scared. I still am." Her hands shake, her face turning pasty white. "I...didn't want to drag you into this, but I think I already have. I'm so sorry, Dahl. I really am. I'll pay you back for everything."

"Hey." I stroke the tears on her face. "Nothing I ever do will compensate for what you've done for me all these years. You don't have to be sorry. You're the victim here."

Her chin trembles and fresh tears form in her eyes, making them a darker denim blue. "I am not. The real victim is Susie Callahan, who was stabbed to death in front of me while I did nothing."

"That...wasn't your fault."

"It is! It was! I could've stopped it, but I was a coward. I can...I can still hear her calling for help in my nightmares. All the time." Vi falls to the floor, looking small and wounded.

I drop to my knees in front of her and hold her hands again. "You couldn't have stopped it. The guy had a knife. Her tragedy doesn't justify what Jude did to you."

She grows still. Her sniffles, her trembling.

It's like she's turned into a statue.

Her fingers twitch in mine, her face so pale, I think she's having a stroke.

"Vi?"

"He didn't do anything." Her voice is barely audible.

"What? Of course he did. He stalked and attempted to kill you."

"He wasn't behind what happened to me."

I frown. "Then who was it?"

My heart thunders so fast, I think it'll stop. It couldn't be...?

"Was it K-Kane?" I ask, barely hearing my voice over the buzzing in my ears.

She shakes her head.

I hate how relief sinks in my chest.

"Then who?"

"You don't need to worry about it." She clutches my shoulders. "I'm a moving target, Dahl. You're not. You should go. Maybe somewhere sunny on the West Coast. You're smart and such a tough cookie, I'm sure you'll be okay no matter where you go."

"No! I'm not going anywhere without you."

"Listen to me—"

"No, *you* listen to me. You never abandoned me, no matter how hard it got. If you think I'll ever turn my back on you, I've got a news flash for you. Won't be happening."

"These people don't compare to our sleazy landlords or touchy foster parents, Dahl." Her tone turns spooked. "They kill people and get away with it."

"I know. I've seen it with my own eyes."

"You…have? Oh, Dahl."

"It's okay, nothing happened to me. Kane did it to protect me—"

I bite my lower lip.

I need to gargle some bleach so I can stop thinking about him and saying his name.

"The guy you kissed on TV at the end of the last game?"

"Were you awake at that time?"

"Yeah, recovering."

"I didn't know back then. I'm sorry, Vi."

"What are you apologizing for?"

"Getting in bed with the enemy." *And falling in love with him.*

"Whose enemy?"

"Yours."

"Kane's not my enemy."

"He's the one who gave your name and information to Jude!"

She pales again. I noticed that whenever I say Jude's name, she flinches.

"He would've found me anyway." Her small voice is barely audible. "I'm the one who ran away when his mother was being killed."

"That still doesn't excuse what Kane did."

"You love him, Dahl. I can see it through the pain in your eyes. I saw it when you held on to him and kissed him like you couldn't live without him. If he treats you right, you should go back to him."

"No way in hell. He lied to me. He knew everything and didn't tell me. He played me like a chess piece. If I see him again, I'll kill him." I hug her once more. "Besides, I'll never leave you. Ever."

Violet's only response is a sad smile.

Vi and I have spent the last couple of days catching up. We go on walks in the nearby park, then buy all the snacks and stuff our faces full. Though they're now tasteless after that road trip with Kane.

Vi is Vi with her soft voice and little smiles, but she's also not the same person from three months ago.

She still refuses to tell me who was behind the attack and often closes in on herself.

Sometimes, I catch her watching the windows with wide, frightened eyes as if she's waiting for Satan himself to barge in.

She wakes up every night screaming. It's gotten so bad, she barely sleeps and has dark circles surrounding her eyes in the morning.

I stand by the kitchen doorway as she prepares lunch and listens to the radio. If I ask her to go out, she refuses and insists I should either go on my own or go back to school and not sacrifice my scholarship for her.

She always thinks about everyone but herself.

I hate it so much because I don't know how to make it better.

Or how to stop her from feeling like she's waiting for her doom in this unremarkable, miserable place.

I stare at her movements—lethargic, with no soul, and entirely different from Kane's purposeful strides when he's cooking.

Damn it.

Why does everything make me think of him?

Vi notices me sulking and forces a smile. "Don't just stand there. Come in."

"Want me to help?"

"You can't cook to save your life."

"Wow, rude." I pout. "I found a snow shovel in the garage. I'll shovel the driveway."

"All right. Be careful."

"Yes, ma'am." I salute and head back to the garage armed with a thick coat.

It's full of some DIY stuff, tools, an old lawn mower, and a sharp-looking axe.

I put on some gloves, then drag it outside and bend down to tie my shoes.

As I'm standing up from my kneeling position, the sun gets blocked by a large cloud.

Wait. It's not completely blocked.

I shield my eyes as I look up.

It's definitely not a cloud.

The sight of him is like an electric shot to my heart.

"I like the position, wildflower."

CHAPTER 38
Dahlia

I SPENT THE LAST COUPLE OF DAYS HATING, CURSING, and metaphorically stabbing a voodoo doll with Kane Davenport's face all over it.

It got so bad that I momentarily thought of going back and punching him in the face or doing something more drastic like breaking either his arm or his leg so he could kiss his beloved hockey career goodbye.

That urge was mounting when I got in touch with Megan on my new phone and she sent me pictures of the Vipers' latest win and said I missed an 'amazing' game.

He can still play amazing games, so maybe I should ruin his final college season.

Maybe I let him off the hook too easily and should have hurt him as badly as he tore me apart.

I should have burrowed so deep beneath his skin that he'd be tossing and turning in bed, unable to sleep, his head only full of thoughts of me. I should've made him so attached to me that life without my presence feels bland and tasteless.

Because that's how it's felt for me lately, no matter how tough I tried to act.

But now, I won't get the chance to act on my promises, because he's come here of his own volition.

Asking for it.

I jump up, storm back to the garage, and reach for the axe, my hand shaking around the chipped wooden handle as I rush back outside.

"Are you going to stab me with that?" he asks nonchalantly.

It pisses me off.

How could he still look absolutely gorgeous in a brown wool coat, dark denim jeans, and a beige cardigan? His hair is styled back, his face is covered with a light stubble, and those eyes...icy, cool, and downright provocative.

Why isn't *he* a mess?

How can he be *so* put together?

"I told you I'd kill you if I saw you again." I point the axe at him. "Don't blame me for your chopped-off arm."

He pulls his hands from his pockets and opens them wide. "Do it."

My hand freezes on the cool handle.

"Which one?" He stretches out his right hand. "My dominant arm for maximum damage? I'll give it to you."

"As if you'd let me hurt your precious arm."

"I would."

"What about hockey?"

"Irrelevant."

"You're bluffing."

"Try, then. If you attack me, I won't move." There's no hint of mockery in his voice. It's firm and grounded, and I know, I just know that if I do attack, he'll let me injure him.

I let the axe fall to the ground, its clang echoing in the silence. "You've...lost your mind."

"I don't, usually. I'm actually the calmest person I know and the voice of reason in the middle of a storm. But all those qualities seem to vanish when you're around."

His voice isn't as commanding as it normally is. There's a weariness to it, making it a bit huskier. Now that I look closer, faint dark circles surround his eyes.

"So it's my fault?" Emotions rip my chest open and my words come out too guttural. Too harsh.

"Yes. You ruined my life, and I need you to take responsibility."

I storm toward him and punch him in the chest. "You're the one who ruined *my* life!" *Punch*. "You *lied* to me." *Punch*. "*Used* me." *Punch*. "Made me trust you, then *betrayed* me!"

Kane doesn't move, doesn't attempt to stop or even console me. He lets me drive my fists into him, over and over, until my strength wanes and my eyes sting.

I'm *not* going to cry. I will *not* let this asshole see me cry.

I'm so mad at myself for not being able to stab him.

Hurt him as much as he hurt me.

But the very thought of his pain only brings *me* pain.

Just when the hell will these emotions disappear?

I need to get over him and go back to the life I knew before him, even if I don't clearly remember it.

"Are you done?" His words are smooth as silk. "Will you listen to me now?"

"There's nothing you could say that I'd want to listen to." I step away, my shoulders hunched, all my fight gone. "Just go away and don't show me your face again."

"Not going to happen. So either you listen to me, or I'll stay here until you will."

This motherfucker.

I glance back at the house and Vi, who'll probably have a panic attack if she sees him.

Worse, what if Jude is also here?

She becomes so weird when he's mentioned. I don't want to think about her reaction if she were to actually see him.

"Make it quick and leave," I say.

"I never used or betrayed you. Technically, I didn't lie to you either."

His words clash with the wind and slap me across the face.

I think I'm really going to stab him this time.

"So your knowing about Violet, about the reason why I even approached you, is not a lie? Toying with me while you knew everything was *not* using me?"

"It's not." He spills out a harsh breath, his chest straining against his cardigan. "I never toyed with you. Do you believe I'd be with someone as difficult as you if I were *toying* with you? Do you think I liked it when you were trying to figure me out? When you put your nose in my business and tried everything under the sun to make me lose control? I *hated* it. I hated it so much, it messed with my head. I tried to keep my distance and discard you, but we wouldn't be here if I'd succeeded. So no, Dahlia. There was no using or betrayal involved. I decided to keep you after that time I fucked you on the hood of my car. Nothing and no one will change that. Not even you."

Fire bubbles up my spine and a ticking time bomb launches a countdown in my head.

Tick.

Tick.

Every tick is shoving me closer to the edge.

"Are you even sorry about your lies? Your omission of the truth?" I bang a hand against my chest. "I *trusted* you. I fucking trusted you, and you stomped all over it."

"I didn't choose for Violet to be Jude's target."

"But you chose to give him her file! You chose to exchange the results of the DNA found under her nails."

"I didn't know her or you at the time. Besides, he would've found her whether or not I was involved."

Those are the exact words Vi said and I hate it. I hate that they're both pushing me into a corner.

I hate that everything I did over the past few months was for nothing.

But what I hate the most is giving my heart for the first time, and to this bastard of all people.

"Did you stalk her, then? Were you one of the people who made her life hell prior to the attack for your precious friend?"

"No on all accounts. I haven't been involved with Violet since the time I took Jude to your old neighborhood in Stantonville, and I have no knowledge of what transpired between them prior to what happened to her."

"And *what* exactly happened to her?"

"I take it that she didn't tell you herself. In that case, I won't either. It's not my story to tell."

I grind my teeth. The fact that he knows what the hell happened and I don't is driving me insane. No matter how much I beg Vi to tell me, she just shuts down.

I inhale deeply, my chest inflating with so many pent-up emotions. "Let's say you didn't know me when all this started. Then what about after? Hmm? Why did you talk to me that first time in the arena and give me hope that I could join Vencor? What about then?"

He runs a hand through his hair, tense, unlike his usual composed self. "You captured my interest."

"What?"

"That day, the first time I saw you in that unsightly

neighborhood, I wanted to see you again. I made myself think I wanted to protect you from Jude, which is why I made arrangements for you to be offered a scholarship into GU. It's why I put on the whole show about the initiation."

"A show where you showed me my worst nightmare and fucked me like a beast on the ground?"

"I won't make excuses for that. I didn't truly know you at the time and I had to make it convincing, and while I'd never psychologically torture you if I could get a redo, I still enjoyed the sex, as I know you did. I truly am sorry about digging up your childhood trauma, I don't want to hurt you and I feel bad about that, especially after seeing how much it affected you. Truth is, I'd wanted to own you since I first saw you, and I foolishly thought fucking you once would be enough. It wasn't. All that first time managed to do was unleash the animal lurking inside me. In reality, I wanted you in my space. Selfishly. Even if I had to make you think you'd possibly get into Vencor. It didn't matter as long as you didn't get close to anyone but me."

My lips tremble.

My whole body does.

Sweat covers my palms, and I swipe them against my jeans, hoping this whole thing will go away.

His confession still rings in my ears and churns my stomach.

Kane takes a step forward and I take one back.

He stops, hesitating.

Kane Davenport actually opens his mouth, then closes it again.

Something I never thought he'd be capable of.

His chest expands before he speaks again. "I won't deny my involvement in what happened to Violet or that I hid the truth from you. It might seem like an excuse, but I just wanted you, Dahlia. No matter the method. I realize that was wrong. I realize you hate me for it, and that's okay. I'll keep coming back and asking for your forgiveness until you offer it."

"You'll be wasting your time," I say over the stupid tears trying to escape. "I'll *never* forgive you. Not when you're aiding the man who's placed a target on my sister's back."

"Jude won't hurt her. You have my word."

I scoff. "Only if I agree to be with you. Is that it?"

"No. I won't use her against you. Not when I know how much she means to you. That's why Jude doesn't and won't know about my visit. I used everything at my disposal to locate you, but he doesn't have the same access to the resources I do, especially since Julian picked one of the unmapped safe houses. You guys are safe."

My lips part, but I seal them again. "I still won't forgive you."

Kane reaches a hand out, and before I can stop him, he wraps it around my waist, pulling me close to him.

His fingers burn through my clothes, and my heart jolts as if it's been shocked back to life.

God. I almost forgot how delicious he smells.

Calming, too.

A week ago, all I wanted was to bury my face in his chest and fall asleep.

Now, I'm so mad at him, I want to *hurt* him.

"I'll wait for you until you do."

I lift my chin. "You'll be waiting for a long time."

He drops a kiss on my nose. "As long as it takes to get back what's mine. And you *are* fucking mine, wildflower. Don't forget that."

"Ughh!"

My groan is loud as I flop onto the stool facing Vi.

She pours me a cup of coffee and slides a plate of scrambled eggs in front of me.

But I'm focused on the view through the kitchen window. Kane's standing by his car, his left hand in his pocket and his right hand scrolling through his phone.

As if sensing I'm there, he lifts his head and flashes me a smile, then waves.

I glare back.

He's there all the time.

Shoveling snow when I try to.

Doing our grocery shopping and buying us more shit than we need.

Following me if I go out at night for a walk.

Always.

There.

Like a damn parasite.

"Fucking asshole," I mutter and then angle my chair so I'm not facing him. "Why doesn't he just go away?"

"He's been there for two weeks, Dahl, missing three games in the process without batting an eye. He said he feigned an injury nonchalantly, but you know that's serious, not to mention school and practice." Vi smiles as she sits opposite me, a coffee in hand. "I don't think he'll be going away anytime soon."

"Well, I didn't force him to miss his games." I stab my fork into the eggs. "It's not my fault he's sabotaging himself and his team."

"Instead of this vicious cycle, maybe you can just turn the page?"

"Not even if he stands there his entire life." I narrow my eyes. "Why are you taking his side?"

"I'm on *your* side. You've clearly been suffering since you came here. You've been restless lately, taking apart the radio, the mixer, and other electronic devices and putting them back together again, often breaking them in the process."

I take a sip of the bitter coffee. "I said I'll buy a new mixer."

"It's not about that." Her eyes soften. "You're kind of destructive without a purpose, and you *really* hate that you're not in college or in the lab juggling a million projects at the same time, don't you? What about the scholarship you worked your ass off for? You're going to lose it just like that?"

My chest tightens, but I say, "Doesn't matter."

"It does to me." She pats my hand on the table. "Listen, I know it's hard, even impossible for you to trust people, and you never had friends."

"Not true. I have you. And Megan! She's really sweet. You'll love her..." I wince. "Not that you'll get to meet her since she's in *that* town."

"All right, but my point stands. Trusting people is foreign territory to you, so when Kane broke that trust, it hurt you badly. You don't want to be in pain again, which is why you're pushing him away. But ask yourself, Dahlia. What hurts more? Losing him or being with him?"

My fingers loosen around the fork and I glance sideways.

I flinch when I find Kane still staring at me.

Jeez.

I stab the egg again and glare at Vi.

"What?" she asks.

"What did he tell you that time I came back from the library and found you feeding him in the kitchen? Why are you this...*chill* about the whole thing?"

The only upside of Kane's presence is that Vi has kind

of relaxed, and she's not always watching the windows as if she'll be kidnapped by the boogeyman.

She still looks out the windows, but it's more of a habit now.

"He said it was unnecessary to tell you, but I disagree. Actually..."

"Actually?" I lean closer.

"Kane forced Jude to delete my name from his list. He offered him the entire list in return."

"No way. Julian implied that's the only way Kane can keep Jude under control."

"Well, he gave that up for you." Her shoulders drop. "I wish he'd stop his friend instead of enabling him, but I guess there's nothing we can do about that. The point is, he's serious about you, Dahl. It's up to you to decide whether or not you're serious about him."

My grip tightens around the cup. "So what if I am? What if I love him? Those feelings will eventually die, and I'll be stuck in a world where I'm always an outsider. Kane and I shouldn't have crossed paths in the first place."

"And you're okay with that? Not fighting? That's so unlike you."

"There's nothing to fight for."

"Pity. I would've loved to see you have someone you truly wanted."

"Won't be happening," I whisper and swallow a huge bite of food, nearly choking.

It's just...not happening.

I will never forgive him.

CHAPTER 39
Dahlia

THE FOLLOWING MORNING, KANE DISAPPEARED.

This happened after I couldn't sleep that night.

Tossing and turning, I kept thinking about what Vi said. It didn't help that when she brought me a glass of milk before bed, she offered to follow me to Graystone Ridge if I chose to go back.

She said that while trembling.

While looking like she was on the verge of a panic attack.

But she still insisted on facing her demons and hoped it would inspire me to face mine.

My soft, entirely innocent, and a bit of a scaredy-cat sister has been more courageous than I ever will be.

She also forgave Kane. She always took him snacks and told him good morning. She talked to him even when I tried to pull her away.

Though I'm not sure whether or not she was doing that genuinely or forcing it for my sake. There are a lot of strange things about Vi lately, and the worst part is that she barely tells me anything.

Anyway, when I woke up today with a headache and deep apprehension, I still showered, styled my hair, and put on a white knitted dress I got from the local Target. I even put on red lipstick.

Kill me.

Talk about trying too hard.

But when I walk into the kitchen and glance out the window, there's no one.

Not the flashy sports car that the neighborhood kids begged to take pictures with, and not Kane standing in front of it.

Just nothing.

My shoulders hunch as I tilt sideways to see if he's parked along the street. Though he never has before.

He only leaves for a few hours to shower and change clothes in a local hotel, then he comes back, often with groceries.

He also only sleeps a few hours per night in the hotel and is always there when I wake up. And for some reason, it made me feel safe to know he was out there.

But now, he isn't.

"He left early last night." Vi slides a coffee cup in front of me.

I clear my throat. "I don't care."

"You sure about that? You look like you're going to cry."

I wipe my eyes with the back of my hand, just in case. "I'm fine."

Even as I say the words, my rib cage closes around my heart, squeezing until I struggle to breathe.

Asshole.

Liar.

He said he'd wait for as long as it takes, but that's apparently only two weeks.

Though he did miss his hockey games.

But they don't have a game today.

"I'm sure he'll come back." Vi rounds the island and hugs me. "You look so pretty, it's his loss if he doesn't."

I grab my phone and pause when I notice a few texts from Megan and him.

I open Kane's text so fast, I'm surprised I don't drop the phone.

Kane: Something urgent has come up. I have to go back. I'll return tomorrow if I can.

I keep staring at the words with my fingers hovering over the keyboard.

For these past couple of weeks, he's often texted me. Sometimes about groceries or what I want to eat. Other times, it's to check on me.

His last text before this was 'I miss you, wildflower.' Which might have contributed to my sleepless night.

And because I planned on actually talking to him today, I type:

Me: Is everything okay?

I watch the screen for so long, I forget to blink. But there's no reply. He doesn't even read it.

I scroll back to Megan's texts that she sent early this morning and freeze.

Megan: OMG OMG OMG!!! You won't believe what happened last night!
Megan: Preston's car was thrown off a cliff AND blew up. Kane and Jude were also there.
Megan: Girl!!! Where are u!!!

The phone clatters to the counter, and I pick it up with shaky fingers.

My face heats and a wave of panic chokes my throat, my breaths coming in low, choppy sounds.

A morbid feeling I've only felt when I heard about Vi's attack explodes in my chest.

Fear.

All I keep thinking about is the last time I saw him. Yesterday morning.

When he smiled and waved.

And I glared at him, then ignored him.

I even ignored him for the rest of the day, staying cooped up in my room and reading a boring medical book because I couldn't stop thinking.

Because I was too caught up in my head to face him.

And now this?

I know I'm unlucky, but not to this extent. It just can't be.

I don't know how I type the text to Megan.

Me: Are they okay?

Megan: OMG FINALLY. Idk though. I know for sure that the trio were together before (or was it after?) the car was thrown off the cliff and blew up. The entire team is freaking the fuck out, as you'd expect, because they have no further info, and Ryder isn't answering my calls.

Me: There's no news from anyone?

Megan: No, probably because their families are blocking it. But rumor has it that the Wolves' captain was standing at a viewpoint, watching with popcorn. That bitch Marcus is gonna get it one of these days.

Marcus.

Of course it's fucking Marcus.

It's a known fact that his father never recognized him, and the only reason he has the family's last name is because the grandfather wanted some form of guarantee for the future.

I asked him once, "Do you hate them?"

Marcus merely smirked as he stared at the sky. "Hate? No. They're not worth such emotions. I'll still ruin each and every one of them until all their precious heirs are squashed beneath my feet. Just because I can."

I thought he was talking shit.

How could he, a nobody like me, even get close to the gods, let alone crush them?

But it's happening.

It's him.

He was lurking in the shadows for so long, but he's finally taking action.

I lift my head and stare at my sister. "Vi, I...I..."

"You need to go back. I know." She smiles gently even though her face pales. "I'll come with you."

A couple of hours later, I'm back in the town I thought I'd never step foot in again.

This time with Vi.

She stays back with Megan, who showers her with love and a thousand questions.

But to my dismay, my roommate still doesn't know much about what's going on except for the rumors—each one worse than the previous.

There's talk of retrieving bodies.

No injuries, just corpses.

I refuse to think about that and take a cab to the Davenport house. The driver can't go past Ravenswood Hill's security gates, but I can since I was whitelisted by Helena. I hope I still am.

So I hop out of the car and run the rest of the way.

My legs burn, and my heart is in my throat, but I keep calling Kane and getting an out-of-service reply.

With each failed call, my brain fogs up and I resist the urge to cry.

I'm panting when I reach the big gate. My dress sticks to my back and my new pair of white sneakers—one of the dozen pairs that Kane gifted me for Christmas—starts to give me blisters.

I bang on the hard metal, my hands stinging. "Is anyone there? Open the door!"

A golf cart appears in the distance, and the gate slowly creaks open.

Samuel.

He stops the cart in front of me. "If you'd called ahead, we would've arranged for a smoother pickup. Please get in, Miss Thorne."

As soon as I'm sitting beside him, I blurt out, "Where's Kane?"

"Unavailable."

"Unavailable how?"

"I'm not at liberty to say."

Samuel doesn't say another word, no matter how many times I ask him about Kane.

He merely drives me to a different entrance to the garden and stops. "You can wait here."

"Where's Helena?" I ask as I step out.

"Outside," he says, then drives away without a single word.

I trudge along the cobbled path, my chest feeling so heavy, I can barely stand.

Grabbing the bowl full of fish food, I crouch by the pond and toss some in.

Sora doesn't come over or fight the others, mostly swimming by himself at the edge.

"Hey, are you also mad at me?" My eyes burn and I throw a few nibbles his way. "I'm sorry I called you fat and an asshole. I take it back, okay? Come over."

The other koi fish eat the food, but he barely opens his mouth.

"Sora…please…"

A breeze blows my hair back and sends leaves from the camellia trees into the pond. I bend over to remove the nuisance, unsure if they could harm the fish.

I slip and the bowl falls over.

The fish and Sora go crazy over all the food, and I close my eyes, resigning myself to the fact that I'm going to fall into the water.

A large hand wraps around my waist and lifts me up at the last second.

My yelp ends in a gasp when I'm spun around, and my front is flattened against a hard, muscular chest.

"I must say, I don't like the sound of you begging someone else."

His deep, slightly rough voice invades my ears and sets my skin ablaze, and the earth shifts beneath my feet.

The wind ruffles his hair back, and he looks a bit worn-out.

But he's right here. His tall, imposing figure is a dark

silhouette against the soft glow of lantern lights and the gentle sway of the trees.

His jaw is clenched, the faintest tension creasing his brow, but his arm around my waist is firm, warm, grounding me as the world spins in disbelief.

The scent of damp earth fills the air, snowflakes drifting down around us like fragile confetti, but all I can focus on is the hard planes of his chest against me.

The heat of his body encompassing mine.

All of him. Here. Alive.

But it still feels unreal.

Maybe this is a figment of my imagination.

"K-Kane? You're here."

"I'm the one who's supposed to say that." He strokes my waist, his fingers gentle and possessive at the same time. "Not that I'm complaining."

"Megan said there was an accident with Preston, and you were there and…and…"

"And you were worried about me?" There's a small light in his eyes, a flash of careful hope, maybe.

"Of course I was!" I hit his chest, tears streaming down my cheeks. "I thought you jumped off the cliff to save Preston or something. I would've never forgiven you if you'd done that."

"Good thing I didn't, then." A light smirk tilts his lips. "I'd hate it if you didn't forgive me. My worst nightmare."

"Are you joking around right now?"

"I'm dead serious. I hate it when you give me the cold shoulder. I hate it when I can't touch you. But most of all—" His right hand strokes my cheek, wiping away the tears. "—I hate when you cry because of me."

"Says the man who gets hard at the sight of my tears."

"Different tears. The ones you release because you love it when I fuck you. These, however, I loathe."

"Then you shouldn't get into dangerous situations. For Preston or anyone else."

"I will try not to. For these beautiful eyes."

My nails sink into his shirt. "So you won't abandon it completely?"

"I can't. Preston and Jude are my family. They're the only family I've ever had. You can't ask me to abandon my family, just like I can't ask you to abandon Violet."

"Is that why you got Jude off her case? Even if it meant sacrificing your leverage over him?"

"Yes."

"Why? So she'd be on your side?"

"So *you*'d be on my side. Everything I did, I did for you, Dahlia. Not anyone else. Just *you*." He drops his forehead to mine, his hot breaths skimming my skin as he closes his eyes. "I can't live without you. I don't *want* to live without you or your warmth, your nosiness, or your spirit that overflows into mine. The few days where I couldn't find you were hell on earth. You were everywhere, but I couldn't see you. It turned me into a fucking madman."

"Kane…" The lump in my throat is so big, I can't properly form any words.

"It's okay if you can't forgive me now. I'll wait for months or years if that's what it'll take. Just let me be close by. Let me see you. Let me protect you. Let me breathe you in." His hand wraps around my jaw and he inhales me. "My obsession with you might have started as a form of limerence, a need to possess and dominate. An urge to prove that you're a phase and mean nothing in the grand scheme of things. But you have slithered between my heart and rib cage and I'm unable to breathe without you. You've conquered me, heart and soul, Dahlia. I don't know what love is and whether or not it's real, but if it exists, you're its definition for me."

He opens his eyes again and they're darker and the clearest I've ever seen. "Why are you crying again?"

"Because you're not supposed to say shit like that when I'm so jaded." I sink my fingers into his hair. "Asshole."

"I'm sorry," he whispers, dropping a kiss on the top of my nose.

"You're not! You're not sorry that you're the first man I've loved. The *only* man I've ever loved and probably the only man I'll ever love. You had me in the palm of your hand and refused to let me go. No matter how much I think about it, I just can't let you go either. No matter how much I tried to deny it, I'm miserable without you."

"Is that so?" His features ignite in a myriad of colors.

"Shut up. I swear if you hurt me again—"

His lips cover mine, and my words end in a groan, but he quickly pulls back.

"Won't be happening. You have my word."

"You better keep your word. You know I can ice you out."

"I'm well aware. You'll be my queen. Actually, you already are."

"Even if we're worlds apart?"

"You're my world. If anyone dares to touch you, I'll end their miserable life."

"You're awful."

"You love it, wildflower."

I smile and he kisses me again.

This time, deeper, slower, and for the first time in my life, I breathe properly.

Kane broke the unlucky chain.

He's my knight in shining armor in the most unconventional way.

I've always lived on the run, but I'm ready to stop now.

And just be with him.

EPILOGUE 1
Dahlia

Two weeks later

THE CROWD IS BUZZING WITH INFECTIOUS ENERGY, chanting the Vipers' names, getting drugged by the team's perfect play.

Led by Kane.

Today, he's an absolute star. He's scored the most, more than any offensive player, and has been the best defenseman as well, smoothly cutting off the opposing team's offenses, and forcing their players to commit penalties and get sent to the penalty box.

He's bringing his A game.

Absolutely smashing it.

Leading his team to new heights.

Making the crowd go wild whenever he touches the puck.

Even Megan, who's mainly here for Ryder, has been screaming her head off whenever Kane is gliding on the ice like an unstoppable gladiator.

I've been screaming, too. I brought my online energy to real life and have been cheering him on from start to finish.

But I still suffer from a minor heart attack whenever he points at me, usually after he scores.

Between periods, as the others head to the bench area, he skates toward me and taps the plexiglass with his stick while smiling wide.

If only we didn't have this barrier, I'd jump him and kiss him for the whole world to see.

When I first got back to town, I thought I'd stay a bit mad at him.

That I'd try to punish him a bit more. Even if out of pettiness.

But the thing about Kane? He truly knows how to treat me.

He's the only one who recognizes the right buttons to push and the way to my heart—my sister.

Not only did he arrange for Vi to attend college next semester, but he also paid for it. In full.

He also got her an apartment. I mean, it was for me, but Kane and I basically live together now, so it's hers.

I really didn't want to leave Vi alone, and I try to spend a couple of nights a week with her.

And even though I know he's not a fan, Kane doesn't complain, fully understanding my need to keep an eye on her in her current fragile state.

He says he gets it because he has to watch over Preston as well, especially after the car incident, and, to a lesser extent, Jude.

I swear those two will make his hair turn white one of these days.

In the midst of all of that chaos with his troublemaker friends and the mess he's had to deal with after his father's alleged 'accidental death,' Kane still looks out for me the most.

Vi's college tuition as well as the apartment are only

scratching the surface of what he's doing for me. He somehow managed to have me whitelisted at the Callahan labs and hospital so that I can pursue my career.

These reasons and more are why I just had to accept and go along with it, because Kane did it for me.

He helped Violet because she's my family.

Because he cares about my happiness, and Violet's well-being is my happiness.

Despite the relative peace, Violet still feels off and often zones out. She refuses to attend any of the hockey games with me, no matter how many times I try to convince her.

Hell, I have to watch my mouth and not talk about the team when she's around, which is hard as hell, considering I'm a shameless Kane fanatic now. The queen of trolling people online for the Vipers. I have a great following as well due to my trolling skills.

Anyway, I know part of the reason why Vi's like this; she's still scared of Jude despite Kane's guarantee that he won't hurt her.

And honestly, with Jude's nature, Kane can't control him. No one can.

Not even Julian Callahan, who I suspect is the Devil in a suit.

Kane scores again when the clock is ticking down toward the end. Megan and I hug each other as we jump up and down.

I love seeing Kane happy.

Smiling.

Don't get me wrong, it's still not often, but ever since his father died, he's been more relaxed.

As if the weight is slowly lifting off his shoulders.

And I'll do everything in my power until it's completely gone, just like he helped with everything concerning Violet.

Kane said that this is his last season. He never intended to go pro anyway, no matter how many offers are flowing his way.

So he intends to enjoy it to the fullest. To get the Vipers the national championship—even if he has to kill Marcus for it.

There have been a lot of threats to kill Marcus lately—especially from Preston. Pretty sure that one still hates me, though he's stopped threatening me.

Anyway, with Grant's death, both Kane and Helena are free.

On the other hand, his relationship with his mother is still not the best, but it's not the worst either. He has visited her twice these past two weeks, but only because I'm playing the role of mediator.

Now that Kane is the head of the Davenport family, he's easily fallen into his role and seems to be in complete control. But it's not the type of control where he suppresses himself and caters to others' expectations.

It's more about his natural ability to lead and effortless knack for solving crises. In a short time, he's been able to demand everyone's respect for his new role.

The other night, he was telling me about his plans to reform Vencor from the inside, and to do that, he needs to further strengthen his influence and then help Jude and Preston snatch power in their families so that the three of them can team up.

He has a lot of plans about bringing back banished family members, especially his uncle, as soon as his position is solidified enough to do so. He was so passionate, I was in awe.

But I also know that his plans might start a riot in the dangerous depths of an organization like Vencor.

The prospect of him having a target on his back scares me, but Kane said he'll be fine and only asked me to be by his side.

Which I agreed to. No matter what. He's stuck with me whether he likes it or not.

As the final buzzer sounds, our crowd goes wild, cheering, whistling, and clapping.

I cup my mouth and call Kane's name.

He turns my way, removing his helmet, as if he can single out my voice from the thousands of spectators.

As if I'm the only one in the crowd.

He looks mouthwateringly gorgeous with his damp hair sticking to his temples and his eyes reflecting the ice but somehow warm, soft.

For me.

Only me.

Preston headlocks him, and the other players drag him with them.

He laughs as they all gang up on him.

And I record that laughter in the depths of my soul. I'm totally saving the game video later and keeping it in my folder that's full of everything Kane.

As the players start trickling out of the rink, I also rush out and head to the tunnel that leads to the locker room.

I'm still the team's intern so I have an access badge. I'm also basically Kane's personal physical therapist.

Though that pervert starts out by asking for a massage, then ends up stripping me naked and fucking me in all possible positions.

Sitting on his lap, against the wall, on the island, in the bathtub.

And that's when he's not chasing me and taking me like an animal in heat.

I love our little games.

I love it when I arrive at the penthouse and the lights are off, and I don't know when he'll start to hunt me.

But I also love when he wakes me up with kisses or while eating me out.

When he fucks me slowly just to set my world ablaze.

I honestly thought I only liked rough sex and that gentle sex only gave me lukewarm orgasms. But that was before Kane.

Before that time he took my ass so slowly and with so much care. Since then, he's been alternating between a hunt and slow sex.

The unpredictable pattern and the inability to figure out what he has planned always keeps me on my toes.

When I arrive near the locker room, where many players are filtering in, their chatter and voices are so loud in the confined space. I crane my head to catch a glimpse of him to no avail.

After most of them disappear inside, his tall frame staggers out. He's still in his gear, minus the helmet and gloves.

Kane kills the distance between us in a few steps and wraps a hand around my waist, the other one above my head as he cages me against the wall.

Suddenly, my senses are filled with him, his woodsy scent, those sharp eyes, and the absolutely gorgeous mouth that's now set in a line.

"Hi," I breathe.

"What are you doing outside a room full of naked men, Dahlia?"

I reach my hands out and slip them in his hair, ruffling and running my fingers through it until it's messy but somehow more beautiful. "I'm only here for one naked man, though."

A groan falls from his lips as he wraps a hand around my throat, slightly squeezing. "Don't tempt me or I'll fuck you here and now, my wildflower."

My insides tighten, but I still whisper, "We're in public."

"Didn't stop me before. So go ahead. Tempt me."

I trap my lower lip between my teeth and it takes an effort to not actually tempt him.

It's impossible to keep any rational thoughts when I see those ice-blue eyes that look at me with so much heat. So much warmth and affection.

As if I'm his entire world.

He's also mine.

The man I never knew I needed by my side.

So I get on my tiptoes and seal my mouth to his, then suck on his bottom lip before releasing it. "You were amazing tonight. I just wanted to give you an after-the-game kiss."

His glistening lips pull in a slight smile. "I'm going to need a fuck as well."

"You're so greedy."

"When it comes to you, yes."

"Only me?"

"Only you."

"Maybe I'll come over after Violet goes to sleep tonight."

There's a frown between his brows, but it quickly disappears, and he says nothing.

"Come on." I palm his cheek. "I have to check up on her."

"I know."

"If it wasn't for that brute Jude trying to kill her…"

"I don't think he ever wanted to kill her, to be honest."

I pause. "What do you mean?"

"Forget it."

My phone vibrates and Kane steps away when I open the text from my sister.

> Violet: You forgot your umbrella, Dahl. It's raining. I'm in the arena's parking lot near Kane's car. Come pick it up.
> Me: Aw, thanks, Vi. You didn't have to.
> Violet: Of course I did. I don't want you to catch a cold.
> Me: On my way.

I look back at Kane. "Vi's brought me an umbrella. I'll wait for you by the parking lot?"

"You can go home with her if you like."

"And miss the victory party? No way in hell."

"You're getting a bit too addicted to those."

"I love seeing my man being the center of attention." I smooch his mouth. "See you in a bit."

Kane smacks my ass and I gasp in mock horror before I hurry outside, pulling the hoodie over my head. The parking lot is starting to empty out from all the spectators, and the rest are running to their cars to escape the pouring rain.

I can't find Vi in the midst of the chaos, so I try calling her, but she doesn't pick up. I go back to where Kane's car is parked. Not here. The area is practically deserted now except for some players who are heading to their cars, chatting amongst each other.

A flash of movement catches my attention from a corner near the building.

I inch toward it in case Vi chose a secluded place to hide. She doesn't really do well with crowds and always finds a corner.

My lips part at the scene unraveling before me.

A large, muscular body is flattening my much smaller sister

against the corner. His right arm is on the wall above her head while the other clutches her chin in what looks like a painful grip.

Jude.

When the hell did he even leave the locker room?

An open yellow umbrella lies on the ground and the rain pours down, drenching them both, rivulets forming on his leather jacket, her hair sticking to her pale face as she stares up at him. I'm not sure if it's rain or tears that stream down her cheeks. Or a mixture of both.

He leans down and whispers something in her ear. His muscles are tight, his posture stiffer than usual.

Vi's eyes widen as he speaks and I march forward, about to rip him a new one.

Slap.

I freeze.

Did Vi just…slap Jude? The Jude Callahan, whose name she trembles at the mere mention of?

What the hell did he even say to make my sister, who'd never hurt a fly, *slap* him?

Jude's lips pull in a smile as he strokes his cheek where she slapped him.

Jude smiling? I've never seen him do that. Like *never*.

I snap myself out of my daze.

Before he can retaliate, I rush over to my sister and pull her to my side. She's trembling all over, and something tells me it has nothing to do with the rain.

"Go away, Jude!" I hug her closer as I glare at him.

He glares back as if he wants to bash my head on the ground for daring to interrupt whatever the hell he was going to do.

But he casts one last dark, cryptic look at my sister, and she stares back. Vi rarely looks at people directly. She usually stares at her shoes or anywhere but the other person.

Jude finally walks away, and she releases a long exhale as if she forgot to breathe.

I grab the umbrella and hold it over our heads. "You okay, Vi? I swear I'm going to kill Jude one of these days."

"It's nothing."

"That didn't look like nothing." I study her. "Did he hurt you?"

"No. I'm all right." She forces a smile. "Now that I brought your umbrella, I'm leaving."

"Want me to come along?"

"Stop worrying so much, Dahl. I'll be fine." She motions behind me. "Your boyfriend is waiting."

As she walks away, her movements are stiff, and I frown.

A strong arm wraps around my waist before Kane's soothing voice rushes into my ear. "What's wrong?"

"Jude was cornering Vi. He whispered something I couldn't hear. She slapped him and he was…smiling. What's up with that?"

"Hmm," is all he says, his expression neutral.

"What type of response is that?"

"Just stay away from whatever foreplay they have going on."

"Foreplay? What the hell are you talking about?"

"Probably nothing." He presses me against his rock-hard chest. "More importantly, can I have your attention now?"

I grin. "You *always* have my attention."

"Damn straight." He lifts my chin. "I need that proper kiss now."

And then his lips devour mine.

Until I completely forget we're in public.

Until he's my entire world.

And I'm his.

EPILOGUE 2
Kane

A year later

MY HEARTBEAT IS STEADY AS I LURK IN THE SHADOWS OF my mother's extravagant garden.

No one is here.

In the garden.

Or the house.

I dismissed the entire staff and security team after my mother went on an international trip for the mental health charity she's now spending most of her time—and money—on.

Dahlia doesn't know that, though.

She thinks we're having a family dinner and is probably dolling herself up to look her best.

But I have a surprise in store.

The garden is cloaked in profound silence as I patiently wait.

Snow blankets the ground, the white layers softening the contours of the stone lanterns and bridges, turning the sharp pond edges into gentle mounds.

The bare branches of the cherry trees stretch toward the

dusky sky, their bony figures etched against hues of deepening indigo and violet.

Tires scrunch against the gravel in the distance before I hear her soft voice, low, barely audible in the wind as she probably thanks Samuel and interrogates him.

He hates when she interrogates him.

And she seems to enjoy egging him on.

The tires screech again, and Samuel disappears like the rest of the staff.

So it's only us.

I linger behind a towering black pine, its needles dusted with frost, offering just enough concealment. Each breath is a sharp inhale of icy clarity that fills my lungs, then escapes as a faint cloud.

The crunch of boots on snow reaches me before I make out her silhouette. Dahlia's wrapped in a beige winter coat and a furry hat covers her head, but her brown locks fall in a bouncy rhythm on either side of her shoulders.

Lanterns flicker to life along the winding path as she walks, their warm glow casting elongated shadows that dance across the snow. She stops by the koi pond that lies still, a thin veil of ice forming at the edges, and waves. "Hi, guys. Sora, did you miss me, you bad boy?"

Dahlia and her freaking recent habit of talking to fish. Mother's influence—and part of their bonding, apparently, because they're planning to go koi fish shopping in Asia soon.

The pale light catches in Dahlia's hair, a fleeting shimmer as she turns her head to take in her surroundings. Her breath forms delicate plumes that linger before fading away.

The subtle rustle of her clothing brushes against the silence. "Kane?"

She gets closer, like a magnet, as if knowing exactly where I am. The cold brings a faint flush to her cheeks, and the scent of jasmine reaches me—a rare warmth amidst the winter chill.

My gaze sharpens, tracking her movement between the slender trunks of bamboo that sway ever so slightly in the evening breeze.

I remain still, the rough bark of the pine pressing against my back, and anticipation coils tight within me.

Controlled tension.

But also lawless.

As she moves closer, the details sharpen—the way her eyelashes catch tiny crystals of snow, the almost imperceptible curve of a smile tugging at her lips.

My little wildflower is humming with excitement for when I'll ambush her.

Craving it.

Trembling for it, even.

This is why Dahlia is the only one for me.

She's able to embrace both my tame and unhinged sides. She's always along for the ride. Even *demanding* the ride when I think she could use some rest.

This woman was fucking made for me.

I don't care if we're worlds apart. If we weren't born in the same world or taught the same manners.

She's mine.

Always.

I step forward, breaking free from the shadows.

Dahlia freezes at the soft crunch beneath my boot, but she doesn't turn around.

No.

She knows better than that.

A low squeal escapes her as she runs, leaving her footsteps in the snow, deep and uncontrolled.

"I swear to God, Kane!" she screams as she darts between the trees. "It's freezing."

"And yet you're still running." I'm barely jogging behind her, letting her take the lead.

"All right, all right. I'm as crazy as you, but let's at least go inside."

I grab her by the waist, fully lifting her off the ground, and she yelps, then kicks her feet.

My prey knows how to fight me.

She kicks and screams.

She even bites me.

Not only is my Dahlia a fighter, but she also knows exactly how to turn me on. Rubbing her ass all over my cock and sliding her hands along my arms, my thighs.

Anywhere she can reach.

I carry her to the enclosed glass house overlooking the garden.

Warmth instantly hits us and dozens of dim lanterns automatically shine, bathing the large bed in a soft light.

Dahlia freezes for a second and I throw her on the bed and toss away my jacket, then my T-shirt. She watches me with hooded eyes as she gets rid of her coat, revealing a little white knitted dress that complements her tanned skin tone.

When I kick my boots off, she does the same, and then I'm removing her dress while she's unbuttoning my jeans.

"Don't touch me," she murmurs as she frees my cock and slides it in her mouth, her deep eyes, now the color of a forest, boring into mine.

She releases me with a pop, and I think I'll fucking come here and now.

I pull her to me using her bra. "What did you just say?"

"Don't touch me, asshole."

The bra rips and I pinch both of her nipples. A moan spills from her lungs and I push her back, slapping her bare pussy.

"Is that why you came ready to be fucked? Your cunt is soaking wet, so I think it wants me to touch you."

Her moans of pleasure echo in the air as I slide my cock against her slit.

Then I grab her by the hair, lift her up, and bring her down on my hard cock.

Dahlia's arms curl around my shoulders, and her face buries in the crook of my neck.

I thrust deep and she rolls her hips, meeting me stroke for stroke.

When I suck on her shoulder, she bites my neck, leaving her own mark and branding me for good.

"You're riding my cock so well, wildflower." I stroke her hair, whispering in her ear, "Your cunt was made for me."

"Show me." She sucks on my earlobe. "Harder."

"Fuck." I fist her hair, then wrench her head back and kiss her deep as I go harder.

Faster.

Until she's bouncing on my cock and speaking in unintelligible syllables.

I can be inside this woman every day, three times a day like a fucking meal, and I still can't get enough.

She trembles, holding on to me tighter, and I go deeper, knowing how much she loves it.

What I love, however, is hearing her scream my name as she shatters around my cock.

Her body trembling, her lips reaching mine, kissing and whispering my name.

I don't last long, thrusting into her warm cunt a few more times before I fill her up with my cum.

One day, I'll fill her up with my baby. Babies, plural. And she'll be mine forever.

Our family will be the break from the past for the both of us.

We'll never leave our kids in a cold world on their own, and we certainly won't be torturing emotions out of them.

"I love you," she whispers, panting as she looks at me with those eyes, a mixture of yellow and green. "I love you so much, Kane."

"I love you, too, Dahlia." Wrapping an arm around her back, I reach under the pillow and produce a red velvet box, then open it. "Be my wife. My Mrs. Davenport who'll join me in giving the world the middle finger."

Her eyes widen as she stares between my face and the blinding ring that matches her eye color. A perfectly imperfect mismatch of green, brown, and yellow.

A rare gemstone that was worth every cent.

"Oh my God. This is stunning."

"Is that a yes? Actually, you don't get to refuse."

"I won't. You're stuck with me." A shine glints in her eyes as she offers me her hand. "I'll have no other man but you, Kane. You have my heart, body, and soul."

"And you have mine."

As I slide the ring onto her finger, she kisses me while smiling.

And crying.

And I lick those tears.

Happy tears.

The only tears Dahlia will ever shed from now on.

Because she's my world. And I'll burn anyone who comes close to it.

THE END

What's Next?

Thank you so much for reading *Beautiful Venom*! If you liked it, please leave a review. Your support means the world to me.

If you're thirsty for more discussions with other readers of the series, you can join the Facebook group, *Rina Kent's Spoilers Room*.

The series continues with *Sweet Venom*, featuring Jude and Violet's story, and *Tempting Venom*, which follows Preston and Marcus.

About the Author

Rina Kent is a *New York Times*, *USA Today*, and #1 bestselling author of all things dark romance.

Better known for writing unapologetic anti-heroes and villains, Rina weaves tales of characters you shouldn't fall for but inevitably do. Her stories are laced with a touch of darkness, a splash of angst, and just the right amount of unhealthy intensity.

When she's not busy plotting mayhem for her ever-expanding *Rinaverse*, she leads a private life in London, travels, and pampers her cats in true Cat Lady fashion.

GOD OF MALICE

Look for the first book in Rina Kent's riveting Legacy of Gods series.

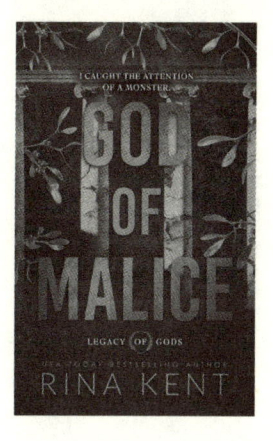

I caught the attention of a monster.
I didn't ask for it.
Didn't even see it coming.
But the moment I do, it's too late.
Killian Carson is a predator wrapped in sophisticated charm.
He's cold-blooded, manipulative, and savage.
The worst part is that no one sees his devil side.
I do.
And that will cost me everything.
I run, but the thing about monsters?
They always chase.

For more info about Sourcebooks's books
and authors, visit:
sourcebooks.com

GOD OF PAIN

Look for the second book in Rina Kent's riveting Legacy of Gods series.

I made a terrible mistake.
Being a mafia princess, I knew my fate was already decided.
But I went ahead and longed for the wrong one.
Creighton King is bad news with a gorgeous exterior.
He's silent, brooding, and obviously emotionally unavailable.
So I thought it was over.
Until he awakens a beast inside me.
My name is Annika Volkov, and I'm Creighton's worst enemy.
He won't stop until he breaks me.
Or I break him.

For more info about Sourcebooks's books
and authors, visit:
sourcebooks.com

GOD OF WRATH

Look for the third book in Rina Kent's riveting Legacy of Gods series.

I'm trapped by the devil.
What started as an innocent mistake turned into actual hell.
In my defense, I didn't mean to get involved with a mafia prince.
But he barged through my defenses anyway.
He stalked me from the shadows and
stole me from the life I know.
Jeremy Volkov might appear charm-
ing, but a true predator lurks inside.
He's out to possess, own, and keep me.
But I have no plans to stick around in his blood-soaked world.
Or so I think.

For more info about Sourcebooks's books
and authors, visit:
sourcebooks.com

GOD OF RUIN

Look for the fourth book in Rina Kent's riveting Legacy of Gods series.

I'm out for revenge.
After careful planning, I gave the man who messed
with my family a taste of his own medicine.
I thought it'd end there.
It didn't.
Landon King is a genius artist, a posh rich
boy, and my worst nightmare.
He's decided that I'm the new addition to his chess game.
Too bad for him, I'm no pawn.
If he hits, I hit back, twice as hard and with the same hostility.
He says he'll ruin me.
Little does he know that ruination goes both ways.

For more info about Sourcebooks's books
and authors, visit:
sourcebooks.com

GOD OF FURY

Look for the fifth book in Rina Kent's riveting Legacy of Gods series.

I'm not attracted to men.
Or so I thought before I slammed into Nikolai Sokolov.
A mafia heir, a notorious bastard, and a violent monster.
An ill-fated meeting puts me in his path.
And just like that, he has his sights set on me.
A quiet artist, a golden boy, and his enemy's twin brother.
He doesn't seem to care that the odds are stacked against us.
In fact, he sets out to break my steel-
like control and blur my limits.
I thought my biggest worry was being noticed by Nikolai.
I'm learning the hard way that being wanted by
this beautiful nightmare is much worse.

For more info about Sourcebooks's books
and authors, visit:
sourcebooks.com

GOD OF WAR

Look for the sixth book in Rina Kent's riveting Legacy of Gods series.

I fell for the villain.
It happened back when I was a clueless girl.
But he ruthlessly broke my heart and trapped it in a jar.
Since then, I've sworn to hate him to the end of my days.
Eli King might be a savage devil, but I'm
out of his way. And league.
That is until I wake up in a hospital and find him holding my hand.
He tells me the words that change my life forever.
"We got married two years ago, Mrs. King."
So I set out to investigate how I landed
myself into this marriage.
Turns out, my memories are darker than my present.
I thought I was ready for the hurricane.
I thought I could handle his soulless eyes and cold shoulder.
I thought wrong.

Nothing can stop my husband.
Not the secrets surrounding us.
Not the hatred between us.
Not even me.

For more info about Sourcebooks's books
and authors, visit:
sourcebooks.com